# Books by Hortense Calisher

# Tale for the Mirror

# HORTENSE CALISHER

---

# Tale for the Mirror
## *A Novella and Other Stories*

Little, Brown and Company · Boston · Toronto

"The Rehabilitation of Ginevra Leake," reprinted from *New
World Writing*; "So Many Rings to the Show," reprinted by permission of *The New Yorker*; "The Night Club in the Woods," reprinted from *Discovery #5*; "The Seacoast of Bohemia," reprinted
from *Charm*; "Time, Gentlemen!" reprinted from *Harper's Bazaar*;
"May-ry," reprinted from *The Reporter*; "Saturday Night," reprinted from *Discovery #1*; "What a Thing, to Keep a Wolf in a
Cage!" reprinted by permission of *Mademoiselle*; "The Hollow Boy,"
reprinted from *Harper's*; "Mrs. Fay Dines on Zebra," reprinted
from *Ladies' Home Journal*; "The Coreopsis Kid," reprinted from
*Charm*; "The Scream on Fifty-seventh Street," reprinted from
*Harper's Bazaar*. "Tale for the Mirror" appeared in *Harper's Bazaar* in abridged form.

45, 217
July, 1963

*Published simultaneously in Canada
by Little, Brown & Company (Canada) Limited*

PRINTED IN THE UNITED STATES OF AMERICA

*For*
*Bernice Cozzens*

# Contents

# The
# Rehabilitation
# of Ginevra
# Leake

EVER since our State Department published that address of Khrushchev's to the Twentieth Congress of the Communist Party, in which he noted the "posthumous rehabilitation" of a number of Russians who had been executed as enemies of the people, I've been nagged by the thought that I owe it to our bourgeois society to reveal what I know about the life of my friend Ginny Doll — or as she was known to her friends in the Party — Ginevra Leake. If you remember, Mr. Khrushchev's speech was dotted with anecdotes that all wound to the same tender conclusion:

> On February 4th Eihke was shot. It has been definitely established now that Eihke's case was fabricated; he has been posthumously rehabilitated . . . Sentence was passed on Rudzutak in twenty minutes and he was shot. (Indignation in the hall) . . . After careful examination of the case in 1955 it was established that the accusation against Rudzutak was false. He has been rehabilitated posthumously . . . Suffice it to say that from 1954 to the present time, the Military Collegium of the Supreme Court has rehabilitated 7,679 persons, many of whom were rehabilitated posthumously.

Being dead, Ginny Doll would certainly fall into the latter category if anyone chose to rehabilitate her, but since the manner of her death has elevated her, however erroneously, to martyrdom in the American branch of the Party, it's unlikely that any of her crowd will see the need of arousing indignation in the hall. The task therefore devolves on me, not only as a friend of her girlhood, but as her only non-Party friend — kept on because I represented the past, always so sacred to a Southerner, and therefore no more disposable than the rose-painted lamps, walnut commodes and feather-stitched samplers in the midst of which she pursued life on the New York barricades, right to the end. If to no one else, I owe to the rest of us Southrons the rehabilitation of Ginny Doll, even if, as is most likely, it's the last thing she'd want.

I first met Virginia Darley Leake, as she was christened, Ginny Doll as she was called by her mother and aunts, when she and I were about fifteen, both of us daughters of families who had recently emigrated from Virginia to New York, mine from Richmond, hers from the town that, until I grew up, I assumed was spelled "Lenchburg." My father disliked professional Southerners, and would never answer invitations to join their ancestral societies. However, on one summer evening when he was feeling his age and there was absolutely no prospect of anyone dropping in to hear about it, he succumbed to momentary sentiment and went downtown to a meeting of the Sons and Daughters of the Confederacy. He came back snorting that they were nothing but old maids of both sexes, just as he'd expected; he'd been trapped into seeing home a Mrs. Darley Lyon Leake who'd clung to him like a limpet when she'd found they both lived on Madison Avenue, and he warned my mother that he was afraid the woman would call — his actual phrase for Mrs. Leake being "one of those tiny, clinging ones you can't get off your hands —like peach fuzz."

Mrs. Leake — a tiny, coronet-braided woman with a dry, bodiless neatness — did call, but only, as she carefully explained to my mother, for the purpose of securing a Southern, presumably genteel playmate for her daughter. My mother was not Southern, but she shared her caller's opinion of the girls Ginny Doll and I brought home from school. The call was repaid once, by my mother with me in tow, after which it was understood that any *entente* was to be only between us girls; my parents and Mrs. Leake never saw each other again.

On that first call I had been relieved to find how much the Leake household, scantily composed of only three females — Mrs. Leake, Ginny Doll and Ida, the cook — still reminded me of our own crowded one, in its slow rhythm and antediluvian clutter. Three years spent trying to imitate the jumpy ways of my New York girl friends had made me ashamed of our peculiarities; it was comforting to be reminded that these were regional, and that at least there were two of us on Madison Avenue.

With the alchemic snobbery of her kind, Mrs. Leake had decreed that the intimacy must be all one way; Ginny Doll could not come to us. So it was always I who went there, at first I did not quite know why. For, like many of the children introduced to me by my parents, and as quickly shed, Ginny Doll was a lame duck. It would be unfair to suggest that she and her mother were types indigenous only to the South; nevertheless, anybody down there would have recognized them at once — the small woman whose specious femininity is really one of size and affectation, whose imperious ego always has a socially proper outlet (Mrs. Leake wore her heart trouble on her sleeve), and whose single daughter is always a great lumpy girl with a clayey complexion. At fifteen, Ginny Doll was already extremely tall, stooped, and heavy in a waistless way; only her thin nose was pink, and her curves were neither joyous nor warm; her long hand lay in one's own like a length of suet just out of the icebox and her upper teeth preceded her smile. One glance at mother and daughter predicted their history; by producing a girl of such clearly unmarriageable aspect, the neatly turned Mrs. Leake had assured herself of a well-serviced life until her own death — at a probable eighty. After that, Ginny Doll's fate would have been clearer in Lenchburg, for the South has never lost its gentle, feudal way of absorbing its maiden ladies in one family sinecure or another. But up here in the amorphous North, there was no foretelling what might happen, much less what did.

Ginny Doll also had manners whose archaic elegance I remembered from down home — it was these that my mother had hoped I would reacquire — but unfortunately hers were accompanied by a slippery voice, with a half-gushy catch to it, that gave her a final touch of the ridiculous. Still, I found myself unable to desert her. It appeared that I was her only friend (although her importunities were always so restrained that it took a keen ear to hear the tremor in them), and after I had gone there a few times I felt guilty at not liking her better, because I felt so sorry for her.

For it appeared also that my father had been accorded a signal honor in being allowed past their threshold. Mrs. Leake was not a widow as we had assumed, but a deserted woman, and it was because of this that nothing more masculine than the old pug, which she sometimes boarded for a rich sister-in-law, was ever allowed past her door. According to Ginny Doll, her mother had done nothing to merit desertion, unless it was having committed the *faux pas* of marrying a Texan. Indeed, her position was so honorable that conscience money from the sister-in-law, the husband's sister, was the means by which she was quite adequately supported. Still, there was a stain upon them — it was the fact that Mr. Leake still lived. Somehow this fact committed them to an infinite circumspection, and was responsible for the exhausted, yet virulent femininity of their ménage. It was also to blame for Mrs. Leake's one perverted economy, for which Ginny Doll was never to forgive her — her refusal to get Ginny Doll's teeth straightened. When approached by the sister-in-law, Aunt Tot, on this matter, she would reply that she wouldn't use conscience money to tamper with the work of the Lord. When approached by Ginny Doll, her reply came nearer the truth: "You didn't get them from me." As I came to know the Leakes better, I concluded that the stain was increased by the fact that Mr. Leake not only was, but was happy somewhere. Although Ginny Doll never spoke of him, I saw him clearly — a man still robust, with the slight coarseness of the too-far-south South, a man barreling along somewhere careless and carefree, a man who knew how to get peach fuzz off his hands.

By this time the household had won me, as it was to win so many — in later years I could well understand Ginny Doll's unique position in the Party. How it must have salved Party spirits, after a hot day in the trenches of the *Daily Worker*, to enter an authentic version of that Southern parlor inside whose closed circle one sits so cozened and élite, pleating time's fan! Our famed hospitality consists really of a welcome whose stylized warmth is even more affecting than genuine interest, plus the kind of stately consideration for the trivial that makes everybody feel importantly human — Ginny Doll did both to perfection. In my case, it was summertime when I met the Leakes, and our people do have a genius for hot weather. Inside their living room the shades were drawn cool and gray, white dust covers were slippery under bare legs, and a music box was set purling. No one was ever there long before Ida, a frustrated artist with only two to feed, came in bearing an enormous, tinkling tea which she replenished at intervals, urging us to keep up our strength. When, during the first of my visits, Ginny Doll happened to remark, "Your father is truly handsome; with that ahn-gree hair of his and that pahful nose, I declare he looks just like a sheik!" I took it for more of her Lenchburg manners. It was only later that I saw how the *idée fixe* "Men!" was the pivot from which, in opposite ways, the two Leakes swung.

When I was sixteen, my parents gave me a coming-out dance. After a carefully primed phone call to Mrs. Leake by my father, Ginny Doll was allowed to attend, on the stipulation that he bring her home at the stroke of twelve. At the dance I was too busy to pay her much mind, but later I heard my parents talking in their bedroom.

"She ought to take that girl back to Lenchburg," said my father. "Up here, they don't understand such takin' ways, 'less a pretty face goes with 'em. That girl'll get herself misunderstood — if she gets the chance."

"Taking ways!" said my mother. "Why she followed the boys around as if they were unicorns! As if she'd never seen one before!"

My father's shoes hit the floor. "Reckon not," he said.

The next day, Ginny Doll telephoned, eager for postmortems on the dance, but I'd already been through that with several of my own crowd, and I didn't get to see her until the end of the week. I found that she had spent the interval noting down the names of all the boys she had met at my house — out of a list of forty she had remembered twenty-nine names and some characteristic of each of the others, such as "real short, and serious, kind of like the Little Minister." Opening her leather diary, she revealed that ever since their arrival in New York, she had kept a list of every male she had met; my dance had been a strike of the first magnitude, bringing her total, with the inclusion of two doctors, the landlord and a grocery boy, almost to fifty. And in a special column opposite each name she had recorded the owner's type, much as an anthropologist might note "brachycephalic," except that Ginny Doll's categories were all culled from their "library," that collection of safely post-Augustan classics, bound *Harper's*, Thomas Nelson Page and E. P. Roe which used to be on half the musty bookshelves in the Valley of Virginia. There was a Charles Brandon, a Henry Esmond (one of the doctors), a Marlborough and a Bonnie Prince Charlie, as well as several other princes and chevaliers I'd never heard of before. A boy named Bobbie Locke, who'd brought a flask and made a general show of himself, was down as D'Artagnan, and my own beau, a nice quiet boy from St. Mark's, was down as Gawain. My father was down as Rasselas, Prince of Abyssinia.

I remember being impressed at first; in Richmond we had been taught to admire "great readers," even when female, and almost every family we knew had, or had had, at least one. But I also felt a faint, squirmy disquiet. Many of the girls I knew kept movie-star books, or had pashes on Gene Tunney or Admiral Byrd, but we never mixed up these legendary figures with the boys who took us to Huyler's. I was uncomfortably reminded of my father's cousin, old Miss Lavalette Buchanan, who still used more rouge than you could buy on Main Street, and wore gilt bows in her hair even to the Busy Bee.

From then on, my intimacy with Ginny Doll dwindled. Now and then I dropped by on a hot summer day when no one else was around and I simply had to talk about a new beau. For on this score she was the perfect confidante, of course, hanging breathless on every detail. After each time, I swore never to go back. It was embarrassing where there was no exchange. Besides, she drove me nuts with that list, bringing it out like an old set of dominoes, teasing me about my fickleness to "Gawain." I couldn't seem to get it through her head that this was New York, not Lenchburg, and that I hadn't seen any of those boys for years.

By the time I'd been away at college for a year, I was finished with her. Ginny Doll hadn't gone — Mrs. Leake thought it made you hard. My mother occasionally met Ginny Doll on the avenue, and reported her as pursuing a round that was awesomely unchanged — errands for Mamma, dinners with the aunts, meetings of the Sons and Daughters — even the pug was the same. The Leakes, my father said once, had brought the art of the status quo to a hyaline perfection that was a rarity in New York, but one not much prized there. Who could have dreamed of the direction from which honor would one day be paid?

The last time I saw her was shortly after my engagement had

been announced, when I received a formal note from the Leakes, requesting the pleasure of my and my fiancé's company on an afternoon. I remembered with a shock that long ago, "down South," as we had learned to say now, within that circle of friends whom one did not shuffle but lost only to feud or death, a round of such visits was *de rigueur*. I went alone, unwilling to face the prospect of Ginny Doll studying my future husband for noble analogues, and found the two Leakes behind a loaded tea table.

Mrs. Leake seemed the same, except for a rigidly "at home" manner that she kept between us like a fire screen, as if my coming alliance with a man rendered me incendiary, and she was there to protect her own interests from flame. Ginny Doll's teeth had perhaps a more ivory polish from the constant, vain effort of her lips to close over them, and her dress had already taken a spinster step toward surplice necklines and battleship colors; it was hard to believe that she was, like myself, twenty-three. We were alone together only once, when I went to the bathroom and she followed me in, muttering something about hand towels, of which there were already a dozen or so lace-encrusted ones on the rod.

Once inside, she faced me eagerly, with the tight, held-in smile that always made her look as if she were holding a mashed daisy in her mouth. "It's so exciting," she said. "Tell me all about it!"

"I have," I said, referring to the stingy facts that had been extracted over the tea table — that we were both history instructors and were going to teach in Istanbul next year, that no, I had no picture with me, but he was "medium" and dark, and from "up here."

"I mean — it's been so long," she said. "And Mamma made me dispose of my book." It took me a minute to realize what she meant.

She looked down at the handkerchief she always carried, worrying the shred of cambric with the ball of her thumb, the way one worries a ticket to somewhere. "I wondered," she said. "Is he one of the ones *we* knew?"

The Leakes sent us a Lenox vase for a wedding present, and my thank-you note was followed by one from Ginny Doll, saying that I just must come by some afternoon and tell her about the wedding trip; Mamma napped every day at three and it would be just like old times. I never did, of course. I was afraid it would be.

Ten years passed, fifteen. We had long since returned from abroad and settled in Easthampton. My parents had died. The vase had been broken by the first of the children. I hadn't thought of Ginny Doll in years.

Then, one blinding August afternoon, I was walking along, of all places, Fourteenth Street, cursing the mood that had sent me into the city on such a day, to shop for things I didn't need and wouldn't find. I hadn't found them, but the rising masochism that whelms women at the height of an unsuccessful shopping tour had impelled me down here to check sewing-machine prices at a discount house someone had mentioned a year ago, on whose door I'd just found a sign saying "Closed Month of August." In another moment I would rouse and hail a cab, eager enough for the green routines I had fled that morning. Meanwhile I walked slowly west, the wrong way, still hunting for something, anything, peering into one after the other of the huge glass bays of the cheap shoe stores. Not long since, there had still been a chocolate shop down here, that had survived to serve teas in a cleanliness which was elegance for these parts, but I wouldn't find it either. New York lay flat, pooped, in air the color of sweat, but a slatternly nostalgia rose from it, as happens in the dead end of summer, for those who spent their youth there. This trip was a seasonal purge; it would be unwise to find anything.

"Why, Charlotte Mary! I do declare!"

I think I knew who it was before I turned. It was my youth speaking. Since my parents died, no one had addressed me in that double-barreled way in years.

"Why — why Ginny Doll!" Had she not spoken, I would have passed her; she was dressed in that black, short-sleeved convention which city women were just beginning to use and looked, at first glance, almost like anyone. But at the gaspy catch of that voice I remembered everything about her. Here was the one mortal who must have stayed as much the same as anyone could, preserved in the amber of her status quo.

"Why, believe it or not, I was just thinking of you!" I said. It wasn't strictly true; I had been thinking of Huyler's, of old, expunged summers to which she faintly belonged. But early breeding stays with one, returning at odd times like an accent. I can still tell a half-lie, for the sake of someone else's pleasure, as gracefully as anybody in Virginia.

While she extracted the number and names of my children, I revised my first impression of her. Age had improved her, as it does some unattractive girls — we were both thirty-seven. She still stooped heavily, as if the weight of her bust dragged at the high, thin shoulders, but she was better corseted, and had an arty look of heavy earrings and variegated bracelets, not Greenwich Village modern, but the chains of moonstones set in silver, links of carnelians and cameos that ladies used to bring back from Florence — I remembered Aunt Tot.

Something about her face had changed, however, and at first I thought it was merely the effect of her enormous hat (how had I missed it?) — the wide-brimmed "picture" hat, with an overcomplicated crown, often affected by women who fancied a touch of Mata Hari, or by aging demi-mondaines. Later, I was to find that this hat was Ginny Doll's trademark, made for her in costume colors by the obscure family milliner to whom she still was loyal, whose fumbling, side-street touch saved the model from its own aspirations and kept it the hat of a lady. At the moment I thought only of how much it was just what Ginny Doll grown up would wear — one of those swooping discs under which romantic spinsters could visualize themselves leaning across a restaurant table at the not-impossible man, hats whose subfusc shadows came too heavy on the faces beneath them, and, well, too late. Here was her old aura of the ridiculous, brought to maturity.

"And how is your mother?" I asked, seeing Mrs. Leake as she still must be — tiny, deathless companion fly.

"Mamma?" She smiled, an odd smile, wide and lifted, but closed, and then I saw the real difference in her face. Her teeth had been pulled in. She had had them straightened. "Mamma's *dead*," said Ginny Doll.

"Oh, I'm sorry; I hadn't heard — "

"Six years ago. It was her heart after all, think of it. And then I came into Aunt Tot's money." She smiled on, like a pleased child; until the day of her death, as I was to find, she never tired of the wonder of smiling.

"But don't let's stand here in this awful heat," she said. "Come on up to the house, and Ida'll give us some iced tea. Oh, honey, there's so much to tell you!"

"Ida," I said, enchanted. "Still Ida? Oh I wish I could, but I'm afraid I haven't time to go all the way up there. I'll miss my train."

"But I don't live uptown any more, darlin', I live right down here. Come on." I gave in, and instinctively turned east. Toward Gramercy Park, it would surely be, or Irving Place.

"No, this way." She turned me west. "Right here on Fourteenth."

I followed her, wondering, used as I was to the odd crannies that New Yorkers often seized upon with a gleefully inverted assumption of style. From Union Square just east of us, westward for several long blocks, this was an arid neighborhood even for tenements, an area of cranky shops being superseded by huge bargain chains, of lofts, piano factories, and the blind, shielded windows of textile agents. Nobody, really nobody lived here.

We turned in at the battered doorway of a loft building. Above us, I heard the chattering of machines. To the left, the grimy buff wall held a signboard with a row of company names in smudged gilt. Ginny Doll took out a key and opened a mailbox beneath. I was close enough to read the white calling card on it — *Ginevra Leake*.

At that moment she turned, holding a huge wad of mail. "Honey, I guess I ought to tell you something about me, before you go upstairs," she said. "In case it might make a difference to you."

In a flash I'd tied it all together — the hat, the neighborhood, the flossy new name, my mother's long-gone remark about unicorns. It wouldn't be need of money. She had simply gone one Freudian step past Miss Lavalette Buchanan. She'd become a tart. A tart with Ida in the background to serve iced tea, as a Darley Leake would.

"I — what did you say?" I said.

She looked down tenderly at her clutch of mail. "I've joined the Party," she said.

Familiar as the phrase had become to us all, for the moment I swear I thought she meant the Republican Party. "What's that got —" I said, and then I stopped, understanding.

"Honey love," she said. The moonstones rose, shining, on her breast. "I mean the Communist Party."

"Ginny Doll Leake! You haven't!"

"Cross my heart, I have!" she said, falling, as I had, into the overtones of our teens. "Cross my heart hope to die or kiss a pig!" And taking my silence for consent, she tossed her head gaily and led me up, past the Miller Bodice Lining, past the Apex Art Trays, to the top floor.

Ida opened the door, still in her white uniform, and greeted

me warmly, chortling "Miss Charlotte! Miss Charlotte!" over
and over before she released me. I don't know what I expected
to find behind her — divans perhaps, and the interchangeable
furniture of Utopia built by R. H. Macy — certainly not what
confronted me. For what I saw, gazing from the foyer where
the abalone-shell lamp and the card tray reposed on the credenza as they had always done, was the old sitting room on
Madison Avenue. Royal Doulton nymph vases, Chinese lamps,
loveseats, "ladies" chairs, and luster candelabras, it was all
there, even to the Bruxelles curtains through which filtered the
felt-tasting air of Fourteenth Street. Obviously the place had
been a huge loft, reclaimed with much expense and the utmost
fidelity, "Lenchburg" Ascendant, wherever it might be. Even
the positions of the furniture had been retained, with no mantel, but with the same feeling of orientation toward a nonexistent one. In the bathroom the rod held the same weight of
ancestral embroidery. The only change I could discern was in
the bedroom, where Ginny Doll's nursery chintz and painted
rattan had been replaced by Mrs. Leake's walnut wedding
suite and her point d'esprit spread.

I returned to the parlor and sat down on the loveseat, where
I had always sat, watching, bemused, while Ida bore in the
tray as if she had been waiting all that time in the wings. "The
music box," I asked. "Do you still have it?" Of course they did,
and while it purled, I listened to Ginny Doll's story.

After Mrs. Leake's death, Aunt Tot had intended to take
Ginny Doll on a world cruise, but had herself unfortunately
died. For a whole year Ginny Doll had sat on in the old place,
all Aunt Tot's money waiting in front of her like a Jack Horner
pie whose strands she dared not pull. Above all she craved to
belong to a "crowd"; she spent hours weakly dreaming of suddenly being asked to join some "set" less deliquescent than the
First Families of Virginia, but the active world seemed closed
against her, an impenetrable crystal ball. Finally the family

doctor insisted on her getting away. She had grasped at the only place she could think of, an orderly mountain retreat run by a neo-spiritualistic group known as Unity, two of whose Town Hall lectures she had attended with an ardently converted Daughter. The old doctor, kindly insisting on taking charge of arrangements, had mistakenly booked her at a "Camp Unity" in the Poconos. It had turned out to be a vacation camp, run, with a transparent disguise to which no one paid any attention, by the Communist Party.

"It was destiny," said Ginny Doll, smiling absently at a wall on which hung, among other relics, a red-white-and-blue embroidered tribute to a distaff uncle who had been mayor of Memphis. "Destiny."

I had to agree with her. From her ingenuous account, and from my own knowledge of the social habits of certain "progressives" at my husband's college, I could see her clearly, expanding like a *Magnolia grandiflora* in that bouncingly dedicated air. In a place where the really eminent were noncommittal and aliases were worn like medals, no one questioned her presence or affiliation; each group, absorbed in the general charivari, assumed her to be part of another. In the end she achieved the *réclame* that was to grow. She was a Southerner, and a moneyed woman. They had few of either, and she delighted them with her vigorous enmity toward the status quo. Meanwhile her heart recognized their romantic use of the bogus; she bloomed in this atmosphere so full of categories, and of men. In the end she had found, if briefly, a categorical man.

"Yes, it must have been destiny," I said. Only kismet could have seen to it that Ginny Doll should meet, in the last, dialectic-dusted rays of a Pocono sunset, a man named Lee. "Lighthorse Harry" or "Robert E.," I wondered, but she never told me whether it was his first name or last, or gave any of the usual details, although in the years to come she often alluded to what he had said, with the tenacious memory of the woman who had once, perhaps only once, been preferred. It was not fantasy; I believed her. It had been one of those summer affairs of tents and flashlights, ending when "Party work" reclaimed him, this kind of work apparently being as useful for such purpose as any other. But it had made her a woman of experience, misunderstood at last, able to participate in female talk with the rueful ease of the star-crossed — and to wear those hats.

"I'm not bitter," she said. He had left her for the Party, and also to it. Her days had become as happily prescribed as a belle's, her mail as full. She had found her "set."

"And then — you know I went through analysis?" she said. She had chanced upon the Party during its great psychiatric era, when everybody was having his property-warped libido rearranged. Hers had resulted in the rearrangement of her teeth.

"The phases I went through!" She had gone through a period of wearing her hair in coronet braids; under her analyst's guidance she cut it. With his approval — he was a Party member — she had changed her name to Ginevra. He would have preferred her to keep the teeth as they were, as a symbol that she no longer hankered after the frivolities of class. But they were the one piece of inherited property for which she had no sentiment. Too impatient for orthodontia, she had had them extracted, and a bridge inserted. "And do you know what I did with them?" she said. "He said I could, if I had to, and I did."

"With the teeth?"

She giggled. "Honey, I put them in a bitty box, and I had the florist put a wreath around it. And I flew down to Lenchburg and put them on Mamma's grave."

Something moved under my feet, and I gave a slight scream. It wasn't because of what she had just said. Down home, many a good family has its Poe touch of the weirdie, my own as well, and I quite understood. But something was looking out at me from under the sofa, with old, rheumy eyes. It was the pug.

"It's Junius! But it can't be!" I said.

"Basket, Junius! Go back to your basket!" she said. "It's not the one you knew, of course. It's that one's child. Let's see, she married her own brother, so I guess this one's her cousin as well." Her tone was rambling and genealogical, the same in which my old aunt still defined a cousinship as once, twice or thrice removed. And I saw that the tip of her nose could still blush. "Old Junius was really a lady, you know," she said.

When I rose to leave, Ida followed us to the hallway. "You come back, Miss Charlotte," she said. "You come back, hear? And bring your family with you. I'll cook 'em a dinner. Be right nice to have you, 'stead all these tacky people Miss Ginny so took up with."

"Now Ida," said Ginny Doll. "Charlotte," she said, "if there's one thing I've learned —" Her moonstones glittered again, in the mirror over the credenza. It was the single time she ever expounded theory. "If there's one thing I've learned — it's that real people *are* tacky."

I did go back of course, and now it was she who gave the social confidences, I who listened with fascination. Once or twice she had me to dinner with some of her "set," not at all to convert me, but rather as a reigning hostess invites the quiet friend of other days to a brief glimpse of her larger orbit, the better to be able to talk about it later. For, as everyone now knows, she had become a great Party hostess. She gave little dinners, huge receptions, the *ton* of which was just as she would have kept it anywhere — excellent food, notable liqueurs and the Edwardian solicitude to which she had been born. As a Daughter and a D.A.R., she had a special exhibit value as well. Visiting dignitaries were brought to her as a matter of course; rising functionaries, when bidden there, knew how far they had risen. Her parlor was the scene of innumerable Young Communist weddings, and dozens of Marxian babies embarked on life with one of her silver spoons. The Party had had its Mother Bloor. Ginny Doll became its Aunt.

Meanwhile we kept each other on as extramural relaxation, the way people do keep the friend who knew them "when." Just because it was so unlikely for either of us (I was teaching again), we sometimes sewed together, took in a matinée. But I had enough glimpses of her other world to know what she ignored in it. No doubt she enjoyed the sense of conspiracy — her hats grew a trifle larger each year. And she did her share of other activities — if always on the entertainment committee. But her heart held no ruse other than the pretty guile of the Virginian, and I never heard her utter a dialectical word. Had she had the luck to achieve a similar success in "Lenchburg" her response would have been the same — here, within a circle somewhat larger but still closed, the julep was minted for all. She lived for her friends, who happened to be carrying cards instead of leaving them.

She did *not,* however, die for her friends. Every newspaper reader, of course, knows how she died. She was blown up in that explosion in a union hall on Nineteenth Street, the one that also wrecked a delicatessen, a launderette and Mr. Kravetz's tailoring shop next door. The union had had fierce anti-pro-Communist troubles for years, with beatings and disappearances for years, and when Ginny Doll's remains, not much but enough, were found, it was taken for granted that she had died in the Party. The Communist press did nothing to deny this. Some maintained that she had been wiped out by the other side; others awarded her a higher martyrdom, claiming that she had gone there equipped like a matronly Kamikaze, having made of herself a living bomb. Memorial services were held, the Ginevra Leake Camp Fund was set going, and she was awarded an Order of Stalin, second class. She is a part of their hagiolatry forever.

But I happen to know otherwise. I happen to know that she was on Nineteenth Street because it was her shopping neighborhood, and because I had spoken to her on the telephone not an hour before. She was just going to drop a blouse by at Mr. Kravetz's, she said, then she'd meet me at 2:30 at McCutcheon's, where we were going to pick out some gros-point she wanted to make for her Flint & Horner chairs.

I remember waiting for her for over an hour, thinking that she must be sweet-talking Mr. Kravetz, who was an indifferent tailor but a real person. Then I phoned Ida, who knew nothing, and finally caught my train. We left on vacation the next day, saw no papers, and I didn't hear of Ginny Doll's death until my return.

When I went down to see Ida, she was already packing for Lynchburg. She had been left all Ginny Doll's worldly goods and an annuity; the rest of Aunt Tot's money must have gone you-know-where.

"Miss Charlotte, you pick yourself a momento," said Ida. We were standing in the bedroom, and I saw Ida's glance stray to the bureau, where two objects reposed in *nature morte*. "I just could'n leave 'em at the morgue, Miss Charlotte," she said. "An' now I can't take 'em, I can't throw 'em out." It was Ginny Doll's hat, floated clear of the blast, and her false teeth.

I knew Ida wanted me to take them. But I'm human. I chose the music box. As I wrapped it, I felt Ida's eye on me. She knew what *noblesse oblige* meant, better than her betters. So I compromised, and popped the teeth in too.

When I got home, I hid them. I knew that the children, scavengers all, would sooner or later come upon them, but it seemed too dreadful to chuck them out. Finally, it came to me. I taped them in a bitty box, masqued with a black chiffon rose, and took them to our local florist, who sent them to a florist in Lynchburg, to be wreathed and set on Mrs. Leake's grave.

Nevertheless, whenever I heard the children playing the music box, I felt guilty. I had somehow failed Ginny Doll, and the children too. Then, when Mr. Khrushchev's speech came along, I knew why. I saw that no one but me could clear Ginny Doll's name, and give her the manifesto she deserves.

Comrades! Fellow members of Bourgeois Society! Let there be indignation in the hall! It is my duty to tell you that Ginevra Leake, alias Virginia Darley, alias Ginny Doll, was never an enemy of Our People at all. She never deserted us, but died properly in the gracious world she was born to, inside whose charmed circle everyone, even the Juniuses, are cousins of one another! She was an arch-individualist, just as much as Stalin. She was a Southern Lady.

And now I can look my children in the eye again. The Russians needn't think themselves the only ones to rehabilitate people posthumously. We Southrons can take care of our own.

# So Many Rings to the Show

HE and Esther walked out of the marriage clerk's office, past the other waiting couples and the wedding parties, out into the open air. Down here, the air had a remembered municipal grayness, as if its natural color had long since been gritted over with a light statistical dust. In 1949, though, surely he and Marie had gone to a different place to be married — or else this one had been remodeled. Jim recalled a dirty brownish cubicle stained with the tobacco-juice whiff of small-time political stews, and a clerk with a whine and a conniving eye. This afternoon, the office had shone with a kind of cleanly bureaucracy, and the clerk, cool and dentifriced, had refused Jim's large tip with a grave, ritual shake of the head.

Jim took Esther's elbow and guided her through the corridors, down the steps to the pavement, where still more couples stood about in uncertain tableaux. Dingily new, the city edifices pressed too near, as if seen gigantically close in an opera glass, and looking at one façade, one felt another at the small of one's back. Built in the hope of a Roman dignity, they had managed only a republican durability. They're too close together, he thought — that's it. There's not enough space between them for majesty.

He hailed a cab, and got in after her. The driver looked inquiringly over a shoulder. "Drive uptown — up Fifth," Jim said. The driver shrugged and started off.

Jim settled back and felt for Esther's hand. As soon as they were away, out of that neighborhood, he would be released from his compulsion to compare, to remember. From here on, it would all be new. He was half aware that his unwilling memories were the more painful because his first marriage had been embarked upon in the same golden warmth and faith, the same sense of inevitability. It had been an October day, that day full of scudding cloud and changeableness, and this day, more than twelve years later, was all moist and May, with a muffled vibrato of approaching summer. But in essence each day held the same fixed dream of rightness, of an incredibly lucky voyage with the one person without whom the world dulled. In essence, one day had been, and one day was, the happiest day of his life. It was as if, carefully putting away a freshly inked guaranty in a drawer, he had come upon another, gilt-scrolled and bright and ridiculously voided by time.

He looked at Esther, her serenely musing profile nodding faintly up and down with the movement of the cab. He was beyond seeing her, he knew, in any literal terms as a tall, good-looking girl with dark-blond hair, with features whose imbalance, stopping just short of strangeness, struck one on further scrutiny with their curiously personal beauty. For four years now, from the very beginning of the affair, she had seemed to him a medal struck once, and superbly, for him. Now she looked, as always, fresh and lovely. She always dressed, with wise chic, for the second glance, but today, in a gray dress he had seen once before, and a small spray of veil, she had been perhaps especially careful to avoid the flowery smirk of the bride. Neither of them had brought any huge emphasis to bear on today's ceremony, held as they had been by an unspoken agreement that for two who had so long been lovers this would be silly, perhaps gross. On their way downtown, stopping around the corner from her place to buy her a camellia at the florist shop they always went to, he had found a pleasing element of continuity, almost a safety, in the benedictory smile of the Greek, in the way he handed the flower, as usual, to Jim, and watched, bowing a little, while Jim handed the flower to Esther.

She was wearing it pinned not on her shoulder but on her belt.

She looked around at him now with a smile, a slight pressure of the hand in his, then returned to her wide-eyed contemplation of the driver's back, and he saw with a rush of warmth that she was surrounded by her own dream of rightness. If she was thinking of her own first wedding — that phlox-and-roses still life of a Connecticut lawn more than ten years back — he did not begrudge her this. Framed in black, it could lie in her memory only with the finality of a mourning card. The house and lawn of her parents had long since been sold; the boy, with whom she had never shared a house, dead within two months in Korea, could only tug importunately now and then at the rim of her remembrance. In a frightening way, he envied her this cameo of a memory, which must have for her the perfect finish given only by death. For her, there was no Marie, no young Jimmie, standing forever wounded, forever suppliant, on the fringe of conscience.

He opened his mouth to speak, because one of them must soon speak, and closed it again, in fear of the random significance of the first thing to be said. It was a feeling like that on the birthdays of his boyhood, when he had hesitated, wary, at the childish chant "If you do it on your birthday, you do it all year around — if you cry on your birthday, you cry the whole year round." The long affair had been an idyll, hardly shaken by the long divorce, so sure had they been of themselves and of the deep morality of the end in view. Now that they had it, he wanted to touch wood. He had never been more sure of the end; only the beginning troubled him a little.

"Decided where to, Mister?" the driver asked.

Jim looked over at Esther. She turned the palms of her hands upward, then clasped them lightly in her lap. "Where to . . ." she said, smiling, certain. He gave the driver the address of her apartment and leaned back, stretching his legs.

The cab turned down her street — still hers, even though he

had come there for years and his things were there now. "Maybe we should have gone off to the country somewhere," he said. "Would you have liked that?"

"No." She shook her head slowly. "I like us just as we are."

He kissed her and let his face rest for a moment on her shoulder, lazily breathing her perfume, watching the sun and shade dapple her lap. When he had paid off the cab, he followed her down the steps to the dark-blue door, flanked with potted shrubs, through which one entered her building, and they stood in the areaway for a minute, looking down the two streets that converged before it. Spaced along the sidewalks, small, wire-bracketed trees had put out every straining leaf, each trunk holding its rosette of branches like a child's head too heavy for the delicate stalk of neck. "What a day!" she said. "Isn't it a lovely day!" She spun on her heel, and put her hands in his.

"Lovely!" he said. It was the kind of day when the season, poised for the summer plunge, enclosed the city in a golden bubble whose faintly rounded walls distorted everything into a curve of beauty. Down the far distance, where the stores were, windows dazzled into cataracts, signs flew like pennants.

"Spring's the nearsighted season," Esther said softly, and it was true that although he had his glasses on, everything did look blurred, merged, as if he might just have taken them off, except for the door, on whose knob she had put her hand. Over the years of evenings when he had walked toward it in light-footed, sensuous quickening, the door had become the image that had halved his life, first as a rendezvous, with all the giddy charade the word implied, later with urgency and conflict, and finally as a symbol of what he wanted to walk toward forever. During the business days before the nights when he was to see her, it had always been this he had gone toward in his mind, so much so that if anyone had casually asked, "You know Esther King, don't you?" he would have been able to answer indifferently, but if anyone had said, "Do you know a house with a blue door?" he would have been left stammering and undone. Until the very last, when they had had to wrench themselves out into the open, once he had closed it behind him no one else had known where he was, nothing had been able to reach him, shuttered there in secrecy and love.

"Well?" She smiled and twisted her hand on the knob, and again he was back in a forgotten birthday, standing in a clutter of wrapping paper, looking, choked and prayerful, at the largest and most beautiful box of all.

"Too nice to go up yet," he said. "What do you say we have a drink at Rolo's?"

"Yes, let's," she said. "Let's go get a drink at Rolo's," she said singsong, tucking her hand under his arm, urging him back up the steps, as if this had been her idea, almost as if his thought had been hers.

"Strange, isn't it?" she said. She was sauntering along, eyes half closed, smiling. "Not to see you for a month, and then all of a sudden — this. I can't believe it. I can't believe you're not going to have to — go."

He squeezed the arm with her hand in it against his side. During the last weeks, they had kept apart; she had gone out of town while the decree became final and he went through the series of small obsequies — dreadful because they were so small — that had attended his final rupture with the house in New Canaan. Esther had wanted them to start clear, she had said, obsessed by a sudden, wistful grasp at propriety, and they had done so. On his last visit to the house, to get his summer clothes out of the attic and back to the hotel where he was staying, he had come down the attic stairs with his arms full, thinking, Was it only last summer — was it only *last* summer — that he had been living here? And he had run straight into Marie, who had always been carefully absent when he came before, on similar forays or for an appointed outing with young Jim. She had turned quickly into a room, shutting the door behind her, but not before he felt the same oddly monogamous twinge of guilt that had made his continued life there impossible. For it had been guilt, and a monogamous one — but its allegiance had been to Esther.

"Down this way. Remember?" Esther said, and stopped him from continuing past Second Avenue. The bar, Rolo's, was half-way down the block. It was a place they had first gone to one afternoon years before, out of a deep need to show their love in the company of someone. Little by little, as it became the one spot where they let themselves be seen, the magic comfort of such places gathered in its grimy red shadows, for here they were known to belong together. Here they had their own corner and their special drink; and their status, though never commented upon, had been well surmised and appraised — and this, too, made them happy. Finally, even the "characters" in the bar became dear to them, for in the eyes of these, they themselves were characters in their own romance.

At the door of the bar, Jim hesitated. Perhaps she would be hurt, after all, if there were not some celebration, some tiny bursting of the rose, even if only among the supernumeraries here. "As we were?" he asked.

"As we were." She touched a finger to her lips, and the smile was still upon them.

As we still are, he thought, following her in. He nodded to Tom, the bartender, raised two fingers, pulled out Esther's chair, sat down in his own, and nodded again, this time to Lydia Matthews, a white-haired beauty of fifty, who returned the nod with the dainty, spectral smile of her five-o'clock Martini swoon. The bartender, coming over to their table to set down their vermouth-cassis, glanced back at her with a pitying shrug.

Jim clinked his glass against Esther's. "To things as they are," he said. With a forefinger, he stroked the back of her hand. Over the raised rim of her glass, her eyes filled with tears.

They sat there for a long time; they had supper there while

the window behind them turned into a great ox eye of blue. When the bar was crowded, the place full, Lydia left, as she always did. They watched her thread her way out, a hostess speeding her guests, pausing here and there to lean over a table and drop the same muted phrases from the wry, aging dimple of her mouth. She stopped to speak to a couple at the table next to theirs. "Found your boy?" she asked the woman. "That's right, darling. That's everything there is." The woman laughed.

Lydia leaned over Esther. "Found your boy," she said, nodding like a pink, ruined, grandmotherly girl.

She drew herself up, her head queenly, her purse clasped tight in front of her. "Night, ducks," she said, her voice round and warm, and walked past them, out the door, treading lightly on the civet flow of the Martinis, her head held high in the regency of drink.

Glancing at each other, they rose, too, with intuitive rhythm, and left the place, walking silently through the blue element of the evening. And now he caught her around the hip and urged her, laughing, running, to the corner of their street. There they slackened, breathless, and again he urged her forward. On the brink of the steps, they teetered, then ran down them in unison; he flung the door open, pushed her inside, and caught her in his arms, listening with satisfaction to the door soothing shut behind them.

"Oh, Lord!" she said, laughing, picking the spray of veil from her hair and hanging its circlet on her wrist, falling silent as he still held her. Together they looked through the lozenge of window set high in the door, thick glass through which the world outside appeared tiny, distorted, clever — a world in a bull's-eye mirror. The young trees were holding their brave rosettes cleverly on high, the day was ending in an extraordinary gentleness, as if someone were pouring over it a knowing wash of dark, and he and she, standing close in its lambent shadow, were the cleverest of all.

"I'll just get the mail." She darted a quick kiss at him and bent to fumble in her purse for the mailbox key. He felt in a pocket for his key to the inside door, opened it, and, when she had got the mail, pushed her childishly up the stairs in front of him, hearing, with another flicker of satisfaction, the inner door click closed below.

Once inside the familiar oval of her one room, he sank down into a chair, winded and replete, watching her as she went about the room, turned a lamp on, then off, put her hands idly to her hair, flung open the casement, and leaned there, looking out. It was a room that he had never once returned to without feeling grateful that he was there again, another lap won. Now he sat there dizzy with gratitude, assessing each familiar symbol — the ashtray with the two deer beneath the glaze, the copper pot in which she made *espresso* coffee for them, the jar that variously held rhododendron and chrysanthemum, and now had willow in it. He almost resented the willow, because it was new, placed there in his absence, until he remembered that he would never have to resent change in this room again; he would always know what was in the jar.

"Smell it," she said, leaning out. "How can it smell like that — almost like the country? It's like syringa, or honeysuckle."

"It's the spring-blooming neons," he said. "The lovely neon smell."

"A little dusty." She stood up and brushed her hands together, then came and put her head down on him for a moment before she sat down across from him and looked through the mail. He sat watching, in his wonderful sloth of anticipation, thinking of what a remarkable rhythm women had for situation, and how they moved best, to some delicate inner pulse, in the situation of love. He found a moment of pity for the crude young couples they had seen at the marriage bureau, the visionary girls, the red, stammering boys, staring not at each other but past each other at some rigid pantomime of sex. This

room was burned into his mind, and now that he sat in its
center, it was lit from behind by all the banked hours that
started up, once he set foot here, percussive as drums.

She raised her head from an open letter on the pile in her
lap. "From my brother. All good wishes — and they want us
down for a weekend next month. The twentieth."

Jim took the letter she passed him, only skimming the wel-
coming words in his relief that now, and so easily, the strands
were beginning to knit — all the good, associative strands of
dinner with these, Sunday with those. *We look for you two on
the twentieth.*

"Why, and here's one for you," she said. "Forwarded from
the hotel." She handed it to him with a little flourish that said
it was his first letter here, that she, too, had her satisfactions.

One glance at the large, smudged envelope told him that it
was from Jimmie. Thin at the crease, worn, with an old business address of his own in the upper corner, it was one of a
stock of leftover letterheads that had been kept in the desk at
New Canaan. The inscription was printed in purple indelible
pencil. *Mr. James Nevis,* it said, then Esther's address, in ink,
above the canceled address of the hotel, and then: *New York
City. The United States. The World. The Universe.*

"The World, The Universe," she said, leaning over him. "Ah,
I used to do that, didn't you?"

"He always signs himself 'your favorite child,' " Jim said.
"Joke. Because he's the only one." He heard his tone, the careful deprecation with which parents boast to strangers of their
heart's blood.

"His pictures are so like — " she said. "I want so much to —
Jim, now we can have him visit here, can't we?"

"Yes," Jim said. "We can have him." He slit the letter open.
*Dear Jim,* it said. *This is to remine you the last time Ringling
Brothers Barnum and Bailey, the circus, the last time is Sun-
day May 10. Hoping to here from you. Your favorite child.*

*James R. Nevis.* A clipping of a circus ad was attached, stuck on with Scotch tape.

"But that was yesterday," he said. "Oh, God damn! That was yesterday."

"What, dear?"

He handed her the letter. A final sinking of the light outside the window sent prisms into the room, touching the wall, the jar, her bent head.

"Oh, Jim!" she looked up, clutching the letter, then patted it tenderly straight and handed it back to him. "Oh, the poor — I wouldn't have had it happen for the — "

"Neither would I."

"Had you promised?" she asked.

He nodded. "When I was up there last time," he said. "I came downstairs and found him playing outside, but I'd bumped into Marie upstairs, and I just wanted to get out of there. Later on, it must have slipped my mind."

He had come down the path, heavy with the unreasoning irritation the house always forced upon him lately, his arms clumsy with the clothes he was carrying, and Jimmie, dropping his ball, had rushed him, butting him in the stomach and uttering one of those comic-book noises that are the Esperanto of eight-year-olds: "Boinng!" Jim had replied feebly, "Playing ball?"

Jimmie had followed him to the car, talking excitedly. Jim had stuffed the clothes hurriedly into the car, promised, and driven away.

"I could have taken him yesterday," Jim said. "I just hung around the hotel. It rained yesterday, though. Didn't it rain yesterday?"

"Yes. But they have it in the Garden."

"Oh, sure," he said. "Sure, that's right."

Last year, Marie and the boy had been in Reno, but the spring before that Jim had taken him for the first time, not to a circus like the cheap-Jack traveling tents of his boyhood but to Madison Square Garden, where the big top was so far up that it was not there at all, and there were no cracks to admit the sky. He had been amused to find how girly the show had grown, but there had still been the all-powerful smell of horse. There had been so many rings in that circus that the most loving gaze could not do them all justice. He had given up, content to watch Jimmie, his head turning like a thatched brown bun, on the rack of delight.

"Call him," Esther said. "Why don't you call him now?"

"What could I say? No, I'll call him tomorrow. I'll think of something." He weighed the letter on his palm. "Besides, he'll be asleep by now." Surely he would be asleep by now, deaf to The World and The Universe, his vigil over. "No. I'll call him tomorrow," Jim said.

She sighed and stood up, looking down at him, her mouth rueful and soft. "Think I'll take a shower," she said. "Unless you want one first."

"No, go ahead."

The bathroom door closed behind her. He reached for his pipe, then chose a cigarette from a table. He turned on a lamp, and the room sprang up, limned and clear. Yes, they would have him come here. Marriage is a small room, too, Jim thought. She does not know that yet. And I have just begun to remember.

When she padded out of the bathroom, flushed and lovely, she had on a housecoat he had never seen. She sat down opposite him for his notice, folding her hands in her lap, childishly hiding her feet under the stiff silk. He lit a cigarette and passed it to her. After a while, she leaned toward him, drew the letter from his fingers, and tucked it out of sight behind the jar of willows. She sat back, her lids lowered, her chin cupped in her hands. Her hair was loose on her shoulders and her face had the vulnerable look this gives to women. So many rings to the show now, he thought. And the loving heart must do each justice.

He knelt and put his head in her lap, kneading his face against her knees. Once, he raised it, as if he heard something waning in the distance. She stretched out a draped arm then, and turned out the lamp. But in the darkness his eyes retained the room in perfect memory, with that finish given only by death. So, in the darkness, he clung to her for a moment not as a lover but as he might cling to some foolish crony who had once been there together with him in the Arcady of the past.

# The Night Club in the Woods

WE first saw her, Mrs. Hawthorn, sitting alone, the first one down in the tender that waited to take us off the Bermuda boat. She was wearing a quilted taffeta suit, expensively flared at shoulder and hip, and a matching hat — one of those deep, real hats we were all wearing in the fall of 1935 — and her arms were full, crammed full of tea roses. Under a city marquee, she would have had an enviable chic, but on the white deck of the tender, in the buttery Bermuda sun, she looked outlandishly urban for that travel-folder scene. As the rest of us climbed down into the tender, she made room for us with an apologetic shifting of the roses, but one could see, as she nestled her long, rouge-assisted face into the buds, that she was pleased with them.

Later on, in the week that followed, we saw her at our hotel, and Luke and I, drifting in the ambience of our honeymooners' table, idly watched her dinner entrances. Each evening, appearing late but consciously unflurried, in a different gown — one always too dominantly colorful and sparkling for the off-season crowd — she crossed to the table reserved for her and her companion, a dark, pear-shaped man, shorter than she, who received her with an anxious, hesitant courtesy.

On the first evening, Luke, nudging me, had pointed to the single bird-of-paradise bud with which the hotel kept the tables adorned, each beaked bloom soaring from its coarse glass holder like an immoderately hued bird, and every evening thereafter, the analogy had kept us amused. One evening, however, as she passed us, her tall, haggard figure sheathed in green sequins that boomeranged the light, a child at a nearby table cried out: "Look, Mommy! Christmas tree!" As she stopped, and bent toward the child, the sequins not quite concealing the middle-aged line from breast to hip, we heard her say, in a mellow voice, as if she were indulgently amused at both the child and herself — "Yes, darling! Christmas tree!" — and we felt ashamed, and liked her.

We met the two of them again, as we were all herded docilely into one of the glass-bottomed sightseeing boats, and she told us her name. The little man, tentative and deferential in the background, was one of those hovering people whose names one never catches, and we never did, although she told us it too. Again we saw her, alone on the beach in front of the hotel, in a maillot that was still somewhat scandalous for that time. We were a little embarrassed for her, not at the suit, but at its cruel, sagging revelation, and I remember that both of us, looking away with the instinctive distaste of the young for the fading, glanced down with satisfaction at our own bodies. One of her arms was almost covered from wrist to elbow with diamond and sapphire bracelets, and she must have seen me staring at them, or trying not to. She laughed, on the same mellow note.

"I'd feel naked without them." She turned, and slid into the water. She swam well, better than either of us, her long, water-sallowed face, which once must have been very handsome, sinking deep into the fervid blue of the water, the one mailed arm flashing in the sun.

In those days, the thing to do was to go down on the *Monarch* and come back on the *Queen*. The little stenographers squandering their vacation on off-season rates, an "interchangeable" wardrobe, and one shattering evening dress, the honeymooners, intent on seeming otherwise, all said it airily: "We came down on the *Monarch* and will go back on the *Queen*." On the return voyage, we met Mrs. Hawthorn and her vague companion again. The ship had run into bad weather, the usual October storms of the Caribbean, and at dinnertime, the little stenographers had been unable to appear in their evening dresses after all.

Luke had been affected too, although I was not. After dinner alone, I wandered into one of the ornate lounges that hollowed the ship. Seated in one of the gold chairs, her lamé gown blending so well that at first I did not see her, was Mrs. Hawthorn. She beckoned to me.

"I see you're a good sailor, too," she said. "I never get sick. Dave — the friend who is traveling with me — is down in his cabin." There was the slightest emphasis on "his." "Women are the stronger sex, I always say. You two are newlyweds, aren't you?"

"Yes."

"Look," she said. "Why don't you and your husband come up to my stateroom and have champagne. It's the best thing in the world for seasickness — and after all we really should celebrate for you two. Yes, do! We really must!"

I went down to our cabin, and roused Luke. "You think you're inveigling me," he said. "But it's really Mrs. Hawthorn who intrigues me."

We climbed the ladders from D deck to A. Up there, with no feel of more ship above us, the ocean, silhouetted against the looming slant of the stacks, seemed to shift its dark obliques more pervasively near us.

"The water seems more intimate up here with the rich, doesn't it?" I said.

"Hmmm," said Luke, "but it's not an intimacy I care to develop at the moment." I giggled, and lurching together, hip to hip, half with love, half with the movement of the deck, we entered Mrs. Hawthorn's stateroom.

The room was banked with flowers. Mrs. Hawthorn and her companion were waiting for us, sitting stiffly in the center of the blooms like unintroduced visitors in the anteroom of a

funeral chapel. Wedged behind a coffee table blocked with
bottles, Mrs. Hawthorn did not rise, but we greeted each other
with that air of confederate gaiety adopted by hostess and
guest at parties of whose success neither is sure. Across from
her, behind an imitation hearth, a gas log burned insolently,
as if a fireplace burning in the middle of the sea might serve
to keep the elements in their place.

"Life on the hypotenuse," said Luke. He retrieved a bunch
of gladioli, and set them back on the erring horizontal of a
table.

Mrs. Hawthorn shifted her bracelets. "Dave is the florist in
our home town — Hawthornton, Connecticut. I needed a rest,
so Dave came down with me. Senator Hawthorn couldn't get
away. He's the senator from there, you know."

Luke and I nodded, eager to let her see that we took her
explanation at its face value, unwilling to appear abashed at
the malpractices of the rich and worn. I imagined her life —
the idle, probably childless woman, burdened with an exuber-
ance no longer matched by her exterior, drawing toward her,
with the sequins of wealth and difference, the self-conscious
little man, who was doggedly trying to fill the gap between
them with the only largesse at his command — his abracadabra
of flowers. Luke and I exchanged looks across the flowers,
secure in our cocoon of beginnings, seeing before us an itiner-
ary that repudiated compromise, and made no concessions to
the temporal.

As we drank, the fraudulent solidity of the room was displaced now and again by a deep, visceral sway that drained
the chair arms from beneath our digging fingers, and the wine
seemed only to accentuate the irrationality of the four of us
so transiently, so unsuitably met. At one point, Mrs. Hawthorn told the blond, mild-featured Luke that he had a "sul-
phurous" look, which roused us all to unsteady laughter, and

again I remember her asking, with the gaucherie so denied by her appearance, if he were a "college man."

Then, suddenly, with an incredulous look on his face, Dave, the little man, stood up. Edging backwards, he felt for the doorknob, caught it, and disappeared around it. Ignoring his defection, the three of us sat on; then Luke, with a wild look at me, lurched through the flapping door and was gone.

Mrs. Hawthorn and I sat on for a moment, united in that smug matriarchy which joins women whose men have acted similarly and disgracefully. The heat from the burning log brought out the reek of the flowers, until it seemed to me that I had drunk perfume instead of champagne. Slowly the log up-ended and pointed toward the ceiling, but this too had slid far to the right, so that the room hung in a momentary armistice with the storm, the implacable hearth still glowing in its center. I stood up, and moved toward the door. It sidled toward me, and I achieved the corridor, but not before I had caught a last glimpse of Mrs. Hawthorn. She was sitting there like one of those children one often sees at dusk in the playground or the corner lot, still concentrated in fierce, solitary energy on the spinning top or the chalked squares of the deserted game, unwilling to admit the default of the others who have wilted, conceded in the afternoon's end, and acquiescently gone home.

By the time Luke and I had made our separate ways to the cabin, the ship had ridden out the storm area and was running smoothly. We would dock next morning in New York Harbor. We greeted each other, and slid limply into bed. Luke put his arms around me with a protectiveness tinged, I could not help thinking, with a relief that I had not proved so indomitable after all. For a second, I held him at arm's length. "Tell me first," I said. "Are you a college man?" Then we nestled together, in the excluding, sure laughter of the young.

At the docking the next day, we got through the lines early, without seeing anyone we knew. We had exchanged addresses with Mrs. Hawthorn, never really expecting to see her again, and in the busy weeks after, during which we returned to our jobs and our life together, we forgot her completely.

About a month later, sometime in November, we got a note from her, written in a large, wasteful hand on highly colored, expensive notepaper, and followed, when we did not immediately answer, by a phone call, during which her voice came over the wire as gaily insistent as before. Would we come up for dinner and stay the night? We accepted without particular consideration, partly out of a reawakened interest in her and what she would be like at home with the Senator, and partly because it was a place to go with the Chevvie — and no sense of the stringency of time had led us as yet to a carping evaluation of the people with whom we spent it.

On the way up that Saturday, a run of about seventy miles, we drove steadily through a long, umber autumn afternoon. At our left the sun dropped slowly, a red disc without penumbra. Along the country roads, the escarpments of pines and firs were black-green, with the somber deadness of a tyro's painting of Italy. Lights popped up in the soiled gray backs of towns, and a presage of winter tingled in our minds, its remembered icicle sliding down our spines. I was twenty-two, free, still catching up with a childhood where hot dogs had been forbidden. I made Luke stop for them twice. After that we drove silently, my head on Luke's shoulder. Inside the chugging little car, the heater warmed us; we were each with the one necessary person; we had made love the night before.

At seven, when we were expected, we were still twenty miles away. Luke stopped to phone. He came back to the car. "She says dinner will wait for us, not to rush. We're to go on to a night club afterwards."

In a second my mind had raked over everything in my suitcase, had placed me at the dinner table — perhaps not quite at the Senator's right — had moved me on to the little round table on the dance floor.

"I just remembered," I said. "I didn't put in my evening shoes."

"I just remembered," said Luke. "I didn't bring a proper tie."

We burst into laughter, "We'll swing round by way of New London," said Luke. "We can get things there."

When we got to the main street of the town, it was crowded, but the clothing stores were closing. Luke rushed into a haberdashery shop and came out with a tie. At the dark end of the shopping district we found a shoe store whose proprietor, counting stock in his dim interior, opened his locked door. I bought a pair of silver, girl-graduate sandals, the first pair he showed me. "Gee, lady," he said, as we whisked out of his shop, "I wish every lady was as quick as you."

Smiling to ourselves, we reentered the car. There was a charm that hung about us then, and we were not insensible of it, even aware that it had more to do with our situation than ourselves. We were still guests in the adult world of "lady" and "gentleman"; lightly we rode anchor in their harbor, partook of its perquisites, and escaped again to our enviable truancy. The rest of the world — we saw it in their faces — would be like us if it could. On the way through Hawthornton, I looked for a florist shop, but we passed too quickly by.

Five miles through the woodland of the Hawthorns' private road brought us to the house. There had been no others along the way. But the house that loomed before us, in a cleared area rather bleak and shrubless after the woods behind us, had no baronial mystery about it. By the lights under its porte-cochere, it looked to be about forty years old — one of those rambling, tasteless houses, half timbered, with thick stone porches, which "comfortably off" people built around the turn of the century, more for summer use, but providently made habitable for all year round. As we came to a stop under the porte-cochere, and the coupe's engine died, I heard the rushing sound of water, and saw that we seemed to be on the tip of a promontory that ended several hundred feet beyond.

"We on a lake?"

"Only the Atlantic," said Luke. "Don't you ever know where you are? We've been driving toward it all afternoon."

"Hardly ever," I said. "But we seem to be fated to meet Mrs. H. on one ocean or another."

A capped maid opened the door. Mrs. Hawthorn stood at the foot of the stairs to greet us. It was the first time I had seen her in black, a very low-cut, smart black, enlivened only by the cuff of bracelets on her right arm. It made her seem less of a "character," placing her almost in my mother's generation, although she may not have been quite that, and a little unsettling me. In my world, the different generations did not much visit each other, at least did not seek each other's company as she had ours.

She made a breezy stir of our welcome, giving us each a hand, directing the houseman as to our bags, referring us to separate corners for a wash. "Drinks in the dining room. See you there."

When we entered, she was seated at the long dining table, alone. Three places were set, not at the head, but down toward the middle, ours opposite hers. There was no evidence that anyone else was to dine, or had.

I remember nothing of the room, except my surprise. As we clicked glasses, were served, I tried to recall her voice as it had come over the wire to New York; certainly her airy chitchat had given me the impression that we were to be members of a house party. Otherwise, considering the gap between us of situation, money, age — how odd it was of her to have singled us out! Her conversation seemed to be newly flecked with slang, a kind of slang she perhaps thought we used. "That way for the johns," she had said, directing us to the bathrooms, and now, speaking of Bermuda, she asked us if we had not thought it "simply terrif." She had found European travel "rather a frost."

"I get more of a boot out of cutting a dash at home," she said, grinning.

A second manservant and maid were serving us. "I keep the estate staffed the way it's always been," she said. "Even though a good bit of the time it's only just me. Of course we've had to draw in our horns in lots of ways, like everyone else. But I've washed enough dishes in Hawthornton, I always say." She smiled down at her bracelets.

"Have you always lived in Hawthornton?" said Luke.

She nodded. "The Senator's people have always had the mills here. The Hawthorn Knitting Mills. And my father was the town parson — also the town drunk. But I married the mill-owner's son." She chuckled, and we had to laugh with her, at the picture she drew for us. It was the same with all her allusions to her possessions — allusions which were frequent and childlike. As they ballooned into boasting, she pricked them, careful to show that she claimed no kind of eminence because of them. What she did claim was the puzzling thing, for I felt that "the estate" meant something to her beyond the ordinary, and that her choice of our company was somehow connected with that meaning. Certainly she was shrewd enough to see that our scale of living was not hers, although for a while I dallied with the idea that a real social ignorance — that of the daughter of the down-at-the-heel parson, suddenly transmuted into the millowner's wife — had kept her insensitive to all the economic gradations between, had made her assume that because we were "college people," had been on the Bermuda boat, and had an anonymous East Side address, our jobs and our battered Chevvie were only our way of drawing in our horns. But she did not seem to be really interested in who we were, or what our parents had been. Something about what we had, or were now, had drawn her to us; in her queer little overtures of slang she seemed to be wistfully ranging herself on our side. But I did not know what she imagined "our side" to be.

We took our coffee in what she referred to as "the big room" — at first it was hard to categorize as anything else. Large as a hotel lounge, it had something of the same imperviousness to personality. Sofas and club chairs, stodgy but solid, filled its middle spaces; there was a grand piano at either end, and all along the edges, beneath the irregularly nooked windows, there were many worn wicker-and-chintz settees. But, looking further, I saw the dark bookshelves filled with Elbert Hubbard editions, the burnt-leather cushions, of the kind that last a lifetime, scattering the wicker, the ponderous floor lamps, whose parchment umbrella shades were bound with fringe — and I began to recognize the room for what it was. This was a room from which the stags' heads, the Tiffany glass had been cleared, perhaps, but it was still that room which lurked in albums and memoirs, behind pictures labeled *The Family at* ———. *Summer of 1910. Bottom row my son Ned, later to fall in the Ardennes, daughters Julie and Christine, and their school friend, Mary X, now wife of my son George.*

"I never did much to this room except put in the pianos," said Mrs. Hawthorn. "It's practically the same as when we got married, the year Harry's mother died, and he came back from France. We had some helluva parties here, though. Wonderful!" And now, as I followed her glance, I fancied that I detected in the room a faint, raffish overglaze of the early twenties, when I was too young to go to parties — here and there a hassock, still loudly black-and-white, a few of those ballerina book ends everyone used to have, and yes, there, hung in a corner, a couple of old batiks. Dozens of people could have sprawled here, the young men with their bell-bottomed trousers, the girls with their Tutankhamen ear-drops, pointed pumps, and orange-ice-colored silk knees. The weathered wicker would have absorbed the spilled drinks without comment, and cigarette burns would have been hilariously added to the burnt-leather cushions. Yes, it could have been a hell of a room for a party.

Mrs. Hawthorn led us to the windows and pointed out into the dark, staring through it with the sure, commanding eye of the householder. "You can't see, of course, but we're on three bodies of water here — the river, the Sound, and the ocean. There's the end of the dock — the Coast Guard still ties up there once in a while, although we don't keep it up any more. When I was a kid, it used to be fitted out like a summer hotel. I used to swim around the point and watch them." Then, I thought, she would not have been one of the three little girls in the bottom row of the picture — she would never have been in that picture at all.

She closed the curtain. "Let me show you your room, then we'll be off." She led us upstairs, into a comfortable, nondescript bedroom. "That's my door, across the hall. Knock when you're ready."

"Oh, it won't take a minute to change," I said.

"Change? Dear, you don't have to change."

"Oh, but we've brought our evening things," I said. "It'll only take us a minute." There was a slight wail to my voice.

"Really it won't," said Luke. "We're awfully sorry if we've delayed you, but we'll rush."

We continued our protests for a minute, standing there in the hall. She leaned down and patted my shoulder, looking at me with that musing smile older women wore when they leaned over baby carriages. I had encountered that look often that year, among my mother's friends. "No, run along, and never mind," she said. "Nobody else is going to be there."

In front of the mirror in our room, I ran a comb through

my curls. "Nobody who *is* anybody, I suppose she meant. I can't imagine why else she picked on us. And when I think of those awful shoes!"

"You can wear them at home," said Luke. "I like women to be flashy around the house. Come on, you look wonderful."

"I'm going to change to them anyway. They'll dance better."

"You'll only have to dance half the dances."

"Luke — " I slid my feet into the shoes and twisted to check my stocking seams. "Do you suppose that little man, Dave, will be there? Do you suppose we're being used as a sort of *cover?*"

He laughed. "I don't know. Come on."

"Don't you think it's funny she doesn't say where the Senator is? At least make his excuses or something?"

"Away on business, probably."

"Well, why isn't she in Washington with him, then? I would be — if it were you."

"Thank *you*," he said. "But how come you got through college? There's no Connecticut senator to Washington named Hawthorn."

"Luke! I knew there was something fishy! Maybe there isn't any Senator. Or maybe he's divorced her, and nobody around here will know her. Or maybe she's a little off, from his being dead, and wants to go on pretending he's alive. With people like us — who wouldn't know."

He put back his head in laughter. "Now I know how you did get through college." He kissed the back of my neck, and pushed me through the door. "State senator, dope," he whispered, as we knocked at Mrs. Hawthorn's.

"Ready?" She opened the door and held it back in such a way that we knew we were to look in. "This is the only room I changed," she said. "I had it done again last year, the same way. I thought the man from Sloane would drop in his tracks when I insisted on the same thing. All that pink. Ninety yards of it in the curtains alone." She laughed, as she had done at the child in Bermuda. "Of course I had no idea back then . . . I thought it was lovely, so help me. And now I'm used to it."

We looked around. All that pink, as she had said. The room, from its shape, must be directly above the big room below; its great windows jutted out like a huge pink prow, overlooking the three bodies of water. Chairs with the sickly sheen of hard candy pursed their Louis Quatorze legs on a rose madder rug, under lamps the tinge of old powder puffs. There were a few glossy prints on the walls — nymphs couched like bonbons in ambiguous verdure. Marble putti held back the curtains, and each morning, between ninety yards of rosy lingerie, there would rise the craggy, seamed face of the sea.

Mrs. Hawthorn put her hand on one of the cherubs, and looked out. "We sailed from there on our honeymoon," she said. "On the old Hawthorns' yacht, right from the end of the dock. I remember thinking it would give, there were so many people on the end of it." She took a fur from a chair, slung it around her shoulders, and walked to the door. At the door, she turned back and surveyed the room. "Ain't it orful!" she said, in her normal voice. "Harry can't bear it."

She had two voices, I thought, as we followed her downstairs and got in the car she referred to as her runabout, that she'd made Harry give her in place of the chauffeur-driven Rolls. One voice for that tranced tale of first possession — when the house, the dock, the boudoir, Harry were new. And one for now — slangy, agnostic, amused.

She drove well, the way she swam, with a crisp, physical intensity. There had been bridle paths through these woods, she told us, but she hadn't really minded giving up the horses; swimming was the only thing she liked to do alone. She swam every day; it kept her weight down to the same as when she married. "You'll be having to pick yourself some exercise now too, honey," she said, sighing. "And stick to it the rest of your days."

We would turn on to the main road soon, I thought, probably to one of those roadhouses full of Saturday night daters such as Luke and I had been the year before, spinning out the evening on the cover charge and a couple of setups, and looking down our noses at the fat middle-agers who did not have to watch the tab, but were such a nuisance on the floor.

The car veered suddenly to the left, and reduced speed. Now we seemed to be riding on one of the overgrown paths. Twigs whipped through the open window and slurred out again as we passed. Beside me, Luke rolled up the window. We were all in the front seat together. No one spoke.

We stopped. We must be in the heart of the woods, I thought. There was nothing except the blind probe of the headlamps against leaves, the scraping of the November wind.

"Guess the switch from the house doesn't work any more," she said, half to herself. She took a flashlight from the compartment. "Wait here," she said, and got out of the car. After she had gone, I opened the window and leaned across Luke, holding on to his hand. Above me, the stars were enlarged by the pure air. Off somewhere to the right, the flashlight made a weak, disappearing nimbus.

Then, suddenly, the woods were *en fête*. Festoons of lights spattered from tree to tree. Ahead of us, necromanced from the dark wood, the pattern of a house sprang on the air. After a moment our slow eyes saw that strings of lights garlanded its low log-cabin eaves, and twined up the two thick thrusts of chimney at either end. The flashlight wigwagged to us. We got out of the car, and walked toward it. Mrs. Hawthorn was leaning against one of the illuminated trees, looking up at the house. The furs slung back from her shoulders in a conqueror's arc. As we approached, she shook her head, in a swimmer's shake. "Well, ladies and gents," she said, in the cool, the vinaigrette voice, "here it is."

"Is it — is this the night club?" I said.

"This is it, baby," she said, and the way she said it made me feel as if she had reached down and ruffled my curls. Instead, she reached up, and pressed a fuse box attached to the tree. For a minute, the red dazzle of the sign on the roof of the house made us blink. GINGER AND HARRY'S it said. There were one or two gaps in GINGER, and the second R of HARRY'S was gone, but the AND was perfect.

"Woods are death on electric lines," she said. Leading the way up the flagged path to the door, she bent down, muttering, and twitched at the weeds that had pushed up between the flags.

She unlocked the door. "We no longer heat it, of course. The pipes are drained. But I had them build fires this afternoon."

It was cold in the vestibule, just as it often was in the box-like entrances of the roadhouses we knew, and, with its bare wood and plaster, it was just like them too — as if the flash and jump were reserved for the sure customers inside. To our right was the hat-check stall, with its brass tags hung on hooks, and a white dish for quarters and dimes.

"I never had any servants around here," said Mrs. Haw-thorn. "The girls used to take turns in the cloakroom, and the men used to tumble over themselves for a chance to tend bar, or be bouncer. Lord, it was fun. We had a kid from Holly-wood here one night, one of the Wampas stars, and we sneaked her in as ladies' matron, before anyone knew who she was. What a stampede there was, when the boys found out!"

I bent down to decipher a tiled plaque in the plaster, with three initials and a date — 1918. Mrs. Hawthorn saw me look-ing at it.

"As my mother used to say," she said. "Never have your picture taken in a hat."

Inside, she showed us the lounges for the men and the women — the men's in red leather, hunting prints, and green baize. In the powder room, done in magenta and blue, with girandoles and ball fringe, with poufs and mirrored dressing tables, someone had hit even more precisely the exact note of the smart public retiring room — every woman a Pompadour, for ten minutes between dances.

"I did this all myself," she said. "From top to bottom. Harry had a bad leg when he came back — he was in an army hospital before we got married. He gave me my wedding present ahead of time — enough to remodel the old place, or build a new one. I surprised him. I built this place instead."

"Is his leg all right now?" I said.

"What?" she said.

"His leg. Is it all right now?"

"Yes, of course. That was donkey's years ago." She was vague, as if about a different person. Behind her, Luke shook his head at me.

"And now . . ." she said. "Now . . . come in where it's warm." And this time my ear picked up that tone of hers as it might a motif — that deep, rubato tone of possession fired by memory. She opened the door for us, but for a scant moment before, with her hand on the knob, she approached it as a curator might pause before his Cellini, or a hostess before the lion of her afternoon.

And here it was. The two fires burned at either end; the sultry hooded sidelights reflected here and there on the pale, unscarred dance floor. The little round tables were neatly stacked at its edge, all but one table that was set for service as if now that it was 3 A.M. or four, the fat proprietor and her headwaiter might just be sitting down for their morning bowl of soup. On the wall, behind the tables, flickered the eternal mural, elongated bal-masqué figures and vaudeville backdrops, painted dim even when new, and never meant to be really seen.

It could be the one of the harlequin-faced young men with top hats and canes, doing a soft-shoe routine against an after-dark sky. Or it might be the one of the tapering Venuses with the not-quite bodies, behind prussian-blue intimations of Versailles. It did not matter. Here was the "Inn," the "Club," the "Spot," the Glen Island, where one danced to Ozzie Nelson, the Log Cabin at Armonk, the one near Rumson, with the hot guitarist, the innumerable ones where, for an evening or a week of evenings, Vincent Lopez's teeth glinted like piano keys under his mustache. The names would have varied somewhat from these names of the thirties, but here it was, with the orchestra shell waiting — the podium a little toward one end, so that the leader might ride sidesaddle, his suave cheek for the tables, his talented wrist for the band. Only the air was different, pure and still, without the hot, confectionery smell of the crowd. And the twin fires, though they were burning true and red, had fallen in a little, fallen back before the chill advance of the woods.

So, for the second time, we sat down to champagne with Mrs. Hawthorn. There was a big phonograph hidden in a corner; after a while she set it going, and we danced, Luke first with her, then with me. And now, as the champagne went to our heads, it was not the logs, or the chair arms that moved, but we who moved, looping and twirling to the succulent long-phrased music, laughing and excited with the extraordinary freedom of the floor. I thought of Dave, the little man, but Mrs. Hawthorn never mentioned his name. She was warm, gay — "like a young girl" — as I had heard it said now and then of an older woman. I had thought that this could ot be so without grotesquerie, but now, with the wisdom of the wine, I imagined that it could — if it came from inside. She had the sudden, firm bloom of those people who really expand only in their own homes. For the first time, we were seeing her there.

Toward the evening's height, she brought out some old jazz records, made specially for her, with the drum and cymbal parts left out, and from the wings back of the podium she drew out the traps, the cymbals, and the snare. In the old days, she told us, everybody who came did a turn. The turn with the drums had been hers. We made her play some of the songs for us, songs I remembered, or thought I remembered, from childhood, things like *Dardanella* and *Jadda Jadda Jing Jing Jing*. She had some almost new ones too — *Melancholy Baby*, and *Those Little White Lies*. We gave her a big hand.

Then, just as we began to speak of tiring, of going to bed because we had to drive back early the next day, she let the drumsticks fall, and put her fingers to her mouth. "Why, I forgot it!" she said. "I almost forgot to show you the best thing of all!" She reached up with the other hand, and turned off the big spotlight over the orchestra shell.

Once more, only the sidelights glowed, behind their tinted shades. Then the center ceiling light began to move. I hadn't noticed it before; it was so much like what one expected of these places. That was the point — that it was. It was one of those fixtures made of several tiers of stained glass, with concealed slots of lights focused in some way, so that as it revolved, and the dancers revolved under it, bubbles of color would slide over their faces, run in chromatic patches over the tables, and dot the far corners of the room.

"Dance under it," she said. "I'll play for you." Obediently, we put our arms around one another, and danced. She played *Good Night, Ladies*. The drums hardly sounded at all. When it was over, she let the sticks rest in her lap. The chandelie turned, silently. Oval blobs of light passed over her face, green ing it and flushing it like long, colored tears. Between the lights, I imagined that she was looking at us, as if she knew something about us that we ourselves did not know. "It was

lovely," she said. "That first year." And this time I could not
have said which of her two voices she had used.

We left early the next morning. By prearrangement, she was
to sleep late and not bother about us, and in a sense we did not
see her again. But, as we drove down the private road, we
stopped for a moment at a gap in the trees, to see the sun
shining, great, over the sea. There was a tall, gray matchstick
figure on the end of the dock. As we watched, it dove. She
could not have seen us; probably she would not have wanted to.
She was doing the exercise to keep her weight down, perhaps,
or swimming around the dock, as she had done as a child. Or
perhaps she was doing the only thing she cared to do alone. It
was certainly she. For as the figure came up, we saw its arm —
the one mailed arm, flashing in the sun.

During the next few years I often used to tell the story of our
visit to Hawthornton. So many casual topics brought it up so
naturally — Bermuda, the people one meets when one travels,
the magnified eccentricities of the rich. When it became fashionable to see the twenties as the great arterial spurt of the
century's youth, I even told it that way, making her seem a
symbol, a denizen of that time. I no longer speculated on why
she had invited us; I never made that the point of the story.
But for some time now I have known why, and now that I do,
I know how to tell her story at last. For now that I know why,
it is no longer Mrs. Hawthorn's story. It is ours.

It is almost eighteen years since we were at Mrs. Hawthorn's, just as it was then almost eighteen years since Harry
had come back from France. I was never to meet anyone who
knew them, nor was I ever to see her again. But I know now
that there was never any special mystery about her and Harry.
Only the ordinary mystery of the distance that seeps between
people, even while they live and lie together as close as knives.

Luke is in the garden now. His face passes the window,
intent on raking the leaves. Yet he is as far from me now

as ever Harry was from Hawthornton, wherever Harry was that day. He and I are not rich; we do not have the externalizations of the rich. Yet, silently, silently, we too have drawn in our horns.

So, sometimes, when I walk in the woods near our house, it is to a night club that I walk. I sit down on a patch of moss, and I am sitting at the little round table on the unscarred floor. I fold my hands. Above me, the glass dome turns. I watch them — the two people, about whom I know something they themselves do not know. This is what I see:

It is a long, umber autumn afternoon. To the left the sun drops slowly, a red disc without penumbra. Along the country roads, the pines and firs are black-green, with the somber deadness of a tyro's painting of Italy. Lights pop up in the soiled gray backs of towns. Inside the chugging little car the heater warms them; they are each with the one necessary person; they have made love the night before. The rest of the world, if it could, would be like them.

# The Seacoast of Bohemia

THROUGH the carnival loops of the beginning of the bridge the cars, shining suddenly, crept slowly on their way to Manhattan. Back of their packed lines, the dark smear of Jersey, pricked with itinerant sparkles, gained mystery as it was left behind, but never enough to challenge the great swag of coastline that hung on the blackness opposite.

In front of Sam Boardman's car the lines inched forward and stopped.

"Look at that!" he said. He leaned on his motionless wheel and stared south. "Will you look at that!"

Bee's nearer earring, tiny, hard and excellent, flexed with light.

"There she is," he said. "Just past your earring. One of the wonders of the world. If I live to be a hundred, I'll never get tired of it."

Or of knowing I have a piece of it, he thought. The city was his hero, the only one he had ever had or would have. Born into it, funneled through its schools and its cynical, enchanting streets, he was still as tranced by it as all the boys and girls from out of town who ate it up with their eyes and hearts and were themselves eaten in the hunt for a piece of it. There it was, he thought, the seacoast of Bohemia, moving always a little forward as you went toward it, so that even now, when he saw his listing in the telephone directory, *Samuel Boardman atty 351 5 Av, Residence 75 Cent Pk W,* he could hardly believe that he was an accredited citizen of the mirage.

"Give thanks you don't have to look at it from Englewood,"

she said. She lit a cigarette and blew vigorously on her furs. "How Irv and Dolly — of all people. . . ."

Because of the kids, he thought, as they moved forward a few feet. We know damn well it was because of the kids. All the New Yorkers who grew up there as tough as weeds were convincing themselves that their children couldn't have sound teeth or sound psyches unless they moved them to the country. Perhaps it was the last gesture, the final axing of the cocktail hour and the theater-ticket agency, by those who didn't want to stay in town unless they could go on being on the town. Or perhaps it *was* decentralization — not of cities, but the last, the final decentralization — of the ego. At least they said it was because of the kids, and you didn't say this aloud to a woman who had been trying to have one for ten years. You took pleasure, instead, in the quietly serviced apartment with the expansible dining nook and the contractible servant; and you were careful to voice this on occasion, perhaps at the little evening ritual when you were proffered the faultless drink from the crumbless table, and you reached around to pat the behind, flat as a ghost's, of the woman who had not let herself go.

Ahead of him, the lines melted slightly; he eased into a better lane and picked up some speed as they neared the city side. Through the surge of Irv's after-dinner highballs, he shied away from the image of Bee, her platformed shoes tucked stiffly to one side on the toy-strewn rug, her blond wool lap held politely defenseless against the sticky advances of Irv's twins. After all, there was a certain phoniness in the people who tweeded up and donned couturier brogues just because they were visiting the country; Bee's bravura Saturday night chic was more honest. And she had patted the twins' round fists and held on to them, if a little away from the lap, and had referred to herself as Aunt Bee.

"Talk about wonders," she said. "To see Irv and Dolly Miller knee-deep in paint and dirt is one of them. Two months out of Sutton Place. And that gem of an apartment."

"You realize they're the fourth in a year?" he said. "The Kaufmans, in Stamford. Bill and Chick, in Roslyn. And the Baileys, in Pound Ridge."

"Oh, it's the same difference," she said. "A perpetual stew of wallpapering."

He slowed up for the traffic on the New York side. It was true, he thought; it was about the same difference. Country coy, all of them, as soon as they hit a mortgage — they made a morality of acreage and a virtue of inconvenience. In Stamford and Roslyn the "doing it over" might be less obsessively home-grown, perhaps, and at the Baileys' there would be brandy instead of highballs after dinner — the glasses thinning appropriately with the neighborhoods, all along the way.

Even in the city though, the conversations of their friends were more and more loaded with the impedimenta of the parent. "That's just like my Bobby" and "If you can just remember it's a phase" floated above the bridge tables, and when the men coagulated in a corner afterward, even there, the inverted boasting of the successful male was likely to be expressed in terms of what it had been necessary to pay the orthodontist. When he and Bee met downtown for dinner these days, it was more and more often in a foursome with some couple older than they, some pair admiringly ticked off by others as "so devoted to one another" or "very close" — with only the faintest of innuendoes that this might be because there had been nothing else to come between.

Of a sudden, he turned away from the entrance to the express highway and wheeled up the entrance marked LOCAL TRAFFIC.

"Aren't you going down the highway?"

"Just thought I'd like to go by the old neighborhood."

In front of them, Broadway jigged like a peddler's market. Tonight, Saturday, it would be streaming with the hot, seeking

current of young couples walking hand in hand, as Bee and he
had once done, picking their futures on the cheap from the
glassed-in cornucopias of the stores. He felt an immediate
throb of intimacy with these buildings, their fronts pocked with
bright store-cubicles, their gray, nameless stone comfortably
sooted over with living. From the ocher and malachite entrance of the building where Bee and he lived now, one walked,
every pore revealed, into a fluorescent sea of light tolerable
only to those who had in some manner arrived — the man
jingling pocket change he would never dream of counting, the
woman swinging lightly from her shoulders the stole of success. Most of the houses here would have small, bleared hall-
ways with an alcove under the stairs, and on each of the five
or six flights above there would be a landing where a boy and
a girl, scuffling apart or leaning together, could smell, from
their paint-rank corner, the indescribable attar of what might
be.

He touched the hydromatic foot pedal as they reached a stop
light.

"Not bad for a couple of kids from around here," he said,
slapping his free hand on the duvetyn seat.

"Not bad." She smiled up at him eagerly, two lines on
either side of her mouth slightly frogging her cheeks. Her almost gross hunger for compliment always touched him nevertheless; she seemed to need to amass his every approving remark
— either personal or marginal — as evidence that their life together was what he wanted it to be. He watched her as she
looked out the window and squinted slightly for lack of the
glasses she would never wear except at home. If you had put
the Bee of tonight in a red dress with too much braid on it
and had substituted a hairdresser's springy weekend curls for
her present casually planed coiffure, she would be very like
the girl who had ridden uptown from City College with him,
with whom he had walked these streets on countless Saturday

nights. Still, with the years, a woman had a choice of either spreading or withering, and behind her quick, compulsive smile he sometimes caught a glimpse of what she might be at fifty. It was less frightening to see only age in the face of someone you loved, than to see the kind of aging it could be. He saw her at fifty — one of those women like shrunken nymphs, all slenderness and simulacrum from the rear, who, turning, met your glance with faces like crushed valentines.

"Where on earth are you going?" she asked.

They had left the vivid, delicatessen reek of the main street, and were traveling slowly down a street that dead-ended on the Harlem River. He stopped the car on a street with a few furtive secondhand stores on the west and a murky fuzz of unregenerated park on the east. None of it had changed with the years.

"There's High Bridge," he said. "And there's the water tower." He was only half aware of her moving sharply to the far end of the seat.

He could just see the water tower, a dun cylinder that had never been much more than a neighborhood mark in the city's proliferating stone. There it was though, a dingy minaret above the brush of the park. Any one of a number of paths led to its base, at the foot of which Bee and he had slept together one night, the first time for each, the only time before they had married. He could scarcely remember the innocence of that urban hedgerow lovemaking. Its details were lost forever, buried under hundreds of superimposed nights in bed. What he remembered was the imperative sense of "now," which had been shuffled off somewhere along the way. And he remembered the city, assisting like a third presence — the river steaming softly behind them in the mosquito-bitten night, and the occasional start of the tugs.

It was early November now, but the air had a delayed softness, the doomed, uneasy gentleness of fall. He put a hand on her lap and found her gloved hand.

"Want to take a walk?"

"No."

"Just for a minute. There's an entrance down there."

"Don't be silly."

"Come on."

"Sam . . . you tight?"

"Look, he said, "I meant a *walk*." He pressed her glove back on her lap and left it there.

Two capped men passed by, looking sideways at the car from vaguely identical foreign faces, and continued down the block, their feet slapping echoes on the dead street.

She watched them through her window, huddling into her furs. "I want to go home."

"You didn't used to be afraid of — neighborhoods," he said.

She sat still for a minute. "Took you twelve years. To throw that at me."

"Oh, look," he said, "I just want to talk to you. Before we get back to that damned apartment."

"I thought you liked the apartment."

"We're not so old we always have to be — inside places," he said.

"God in heaven. Is this what comes of going to Englewood?"

He pulled out a cigarette and pressed the lighter on the dash. Through the windshield, as he leaned forward, he could sense the special outdoors of the city, its compound of peculiar, incessant harvestings from parks muted with dust and pavements oscillating with power.

He lit the cigarette. "I spoke to that woman in Tennessee yesterday. The agency woman."

"You called Tennessee!"

"I figured, cut through the red tape. Look, Bee — we've had all the pictures and stuff. She can come in two weeks. She can bring either the four-month-old girl, or the nine months' boy."

"But I told you I wouldn't . . . not from down there. It isn't safe!"

"What's *safe?*" he said. "Ten years ago it was the war. Before that — the depression. But the streets are still full of them."

"That happens to be a different thing." She averted her chin, in a way familiar to him. For the first time, he noted how familiar it was.

"It's no one's fault we had to rule that out," he said gently.

"You can cut the chivalry," she said. "And start the car."

"Ahhh . . . damn," he said.

"Sam — "

"Look," he said, "are we people who want a kid, or — or comparison shoppers? We've gone along on all the proper lists in town for three years, and every year older we go down the list — not up. We're thirty-six years old. We need one now — before it has to wheel us around."

She sat up straight. "Need? Or want?"

"Take your choice," he muttered.

"Maybe I will," she said. "But not from the Ozarks."

He started the car then, and they swept away from the curb in a dangerous arc and an ooze of gas, only to be stopped at the next corner by a red light.

"For your information," he said, "they're all born without shoes."

He let her out in silence at their entrance, drove the car to the garage off Amsterdam, and slowly walked his way back. Even now, he was excited, as he never failed to be by those violent shifts of neighborhood which succeeded one another without warning everywhere in the city. Instruction lurked these streets, and in the end, evaded.

As he walked into his own building, he turned down the collar of his coat. The place was a decorator's cave, so effectively contrived to deny the elements that not to cooperate seemed coarse. Like the apartment upstairs, to which Bee gave so much concentration, it made cunning use of all the sensuous affirmations of safety. In front of the elevator, which was actually self-service, a uniformed attendant lounged nevertheless, reduced to the level of that accessory given to people who had everything. Above the man's head a SHELTER sign pointed, like a rude thumb.

He let himself into the apartment. In the long living room whose every possession schemed toward its perfect one — a casement framing Central Park — a few lamps glowed, but not too many, and the table in the bay held a plate of sandwiches, glasses, a decanter, a bottle of beer and an opener, as if Bee were saying to him: "This is my talent . . . don't despise it . . . don't be angry." Long draperies, in a nervous pattern of darts and runs that he had once dubbed "thrills and chills," and thereafter always referred to thus, had been slid across the window. People like themselves had so many pet names for things, so many terrible mutual coynesses. He pulled the draperies back. There it was — the diorama that never switched off. As he took off his coat, still looking at it, the hem caught the beer bottle, which slipped to the rug unbroken. Bending to pick it up from the soft pile, he saw that the bedroom door was open a crack, shedding light into the hall off the far end of the room.

"Bee. Come on in here."

She came in, almost at once. With her, to be caught disheveled was to be caught out; even when ill, she managed it with patient artistry, covering up, under a feverish flow of perfumes and bed-jackets, the less savory fevers of the body. Now, in her pink robe, she looked as if she had put their quarrel under a hot shower, and had powdered over it. She picked up his hat and coat from the sofa where he had tossed them and hung them away in the quilted closet. He watched her until she came and sat down across the table from him, as they had sat together in the oval of thousands of evenings.

"O.K.," he said. "Now we're — inside."

They sat on, in silence.

"You going to make me do it all, Bee?" he said.

"I want you just to see that woman," he said. "See those kids. "I'll get her to bring both, if you want. I'll get Parker to check them, test them." His voice trailed off.

"God in heaven!" he said. "It's not usually the *man*. . . ."

She got up from the table then and leaned against the window, her back to him.

"So it's a risk," he said. "Look out there. The whole world has a shelter sign on it. It always has. Some kind of a one.

"Bee." He went over to her and put an arm around her. "It's why people have kids." He rocked her gently back and forth. "Their own gamble."

"But it wouldn't be ours!" she said, and stiffened away from him. "It would never be ours!"

His arm, still on the shape of her, dropped to his side.

"Sit with them in the park sometime," she said. "All those women. Like I do with Lil. They lean over the carriage and say, 'Who does it take after?' And I wouldn't know."

In the black and gold pane, her image, vague and beveled, looked back at him. "I'd get to love it — and all the time I'd be thinking . . . where's the woman who had it . . . who's the father? Even if we knew.

"Sure I'd love it," she said, "but I'd always be *watching* it. Because it wasn't mine."

"Turn around," he said. "*Turn around.*"

She turned.

"Those lists," he said. "All those lists!"

She put out her hand, a short wheedling distance.

"Suppose we'd gotten to the top of one of those?" he said. "You want the truth?"

He looked at her face unrefracted by glass. "If you happen to have some with you."

Under the rosy cast of the lamps and her robe, the tears that immediately crumpled her eyes would be pink too, if he neared them. "I kept telling myself I could — that it would all iron out . . . when I got there."

She reached into the pocket of the robe. It would be there — the handkerchief. It was there. "When you know you can't handle something — isn't it better to know beforehand?"

"Sure," he said, "if you only want what you're sure you can handle."

"All right then. I'm sorry. Then I'm not big enough." She put the handkerchief to her mouth. "Either way!" she said, and ran past him to the bedroom door. He watched her turn there.

"Sam. It's not as if we weren't close. Closer than most people."

He looked at her, across the aisle of wood and leather and arranged cloth that was hers. "Give us time," he said. "A few years — and nobody'll be able to tell us apart. Just give us time."

In the interval before the door closed there was no shading, nothing, between him and what he saw. Not even air.

After a time, he opened the door and walked down the hall. As he stood there, he could hear the tub running in the bathroom off the bedroom. Her remedy for everything, he thought. A washing away. A change of clothes, a lift of heart. His eyes felt hot. What had she done, what had she managed, all these years?

Stop it, he thought. It wasn't so. Even without the endless roster of doctors, he knew that it wasn't. If he was tempted to believe anything of her now, it was only because up to now he had believed everything. There was a raw, terminal sadness in it for them both, in that she had had to be the one to point out to him what her real limits were. And she had not so much concealed these as, briefly and pitiably, risen to an awareness of them — as a marionette might, for one extraordinary instant, see the strings that held it and achieve, in that same mourning instant, the moment when it stood alone.

He walked into the dining nook and poured himself a stiff drink from a cellarette in a corner. Carrying the drink with him, he walked the length of the living room, turning out lamps as he went. With each lamp that went out the city advanced toward him, until, with the last, it stood in the room — a presence — brilliant, and third.

He drank, watching it. It neither extorted nor gave. It was one of the wonders of the world, and had merely to be there. If its Bohemia had, after all, no seacoasts, this would hardly be noticed now, in a world that had all but deserted the horizontal laziness of ships. One could hanker there all one's days and hardly notice that the piece of it earned had come out of oneself.

It was a vertical place for people like them, in which the only way out was up. He watched the two of them, a couple named Sam and Bee, climbing from tower to tower, in a gilt-edged monkeydom of closeness, to the spheric music of the brandy glasses that would get thinner along the climb.

He drank, watching them. Opposite him, against a sky humbled to a perpetual nude, the towers waited, like slowly fizzing rockets that never went out — or soared away.

# Time, Gentlemen!

MY FATHER, born in 1862, and old enough to be my grandfather when I entered the world a year after his marriage to a woman twenty-two years younger than he, was by birth therefore a late Victorian. By 1900 he had already been of an age to have emigrated long since from South to North, and to have acquired both a business successful enough to permit him to celebrate the Diamond Jubilee at his usual haunts of Mouquin's and Delmonico's, and a rheumatism fashionable enough to require recuperation at Mount Clemens Spa. But like so many youngest sons of those large families whose fortunes have either declined or not been built, he had from the first shown a precocious, Alger-like energy that — in his case combined with some of the bright fairy-tale luck that comes to the third sons in Grimm — was to keep him all his life younger in appearance and temperament than others of his span, pushing him constantly toward modernity, even while he dragged his feet, protesting. During the nineteen-twenties and thirties, when I knew him best, he was, at the very least, early Edwardian.

Since he was the youngest of a family so long-lived that he and his sisters and brothers, all close to seventy, still had their mother, and one so close-knit that all its branches lived within round-the-corner call of each other in Manhattan, I spent the indoor part of my childhood with old people — people old enough to regard my mother, in her thirties and forties, as a young person of promise who still owed them deference but might now and then be admitted to the family councils in a listening capacity. Her own fluttering efforts, either to freshen the décor of the anciently cluttered household she had married into, or to cling weakly to some of the habits of her contemporaries, were looked upon somewhat as the *art nouveau* bric-a-brac of an incoming bride might be regarded by the chatelaines of a manor house — with the tolerant knowledge that all this nonsense would eventually disappear.

Down at the bottom, a pebble at the roots of this banyan tree, was I, leading a curious double life, half of me in one century, the other half very nearly in the one preceding it. Once out of the house, on my way to school or in the long, spinning afternoons, I had the urchin street-freedom that descends upon the middle-class apartment-dweller's child at the age of seven or eight, when the nursemaid is passed on to the younger ones. As I whizzed around the block, one of a scabby-legged pack of skaters with two-wheelers clamped on their high brown shoes, or tore through forbidden cellars macaronied with steam pipes and elevator cables, leaving behind me shreds of plaid and a trail of bone underwear-buttons, I was as much a child of my sector of the new century as any other. Yet, once the brown metal, fireproof door of our apartment closed behind me and I stood listening in the foyer, whose dark air had a dried olive smell from the books musting double-rowed on the shelves, and a black-leather tint from the davenport that gloomed in the shadows, I stepped, without ever questioning it, into another element, one not present in the home-worlds of my fellows.

Entering this element, the raw light of the new decade had to humble itself past towering cabinets, through bead-crowded, wood-carved space in order to glint on the round, gold-wired spectacles of elderly people as they sat endlessly over coffee that streamed like a continuous soothing syrup from the kitchen. From there the light had to cool itself against much marble and be strained through many yards of lace, before it might arrive, collected and plain once more, at the calm blue and white of my bedroom. Even then, it might have to rest resignedly on what someone had had the relentless patience to cut, sew and starch — my two weeks' supply of fourteen white organdy sashes.

The "element" itself, however, was composed of much more — of all the ways that people had found to carve intaglio from the smaller moments of their lives, and more significantly, of all the spaces in between, when they found nothing to do at all, and did not seem to notice or mind. Within it, all the violent temperaments in our family, the daily puppet-clashes and doge intrigues, lay swaddled in a fleece of security, where life might recompose itself in the thick texture of those novels whose un-demanding dramas flamed at writing desks and petered out in morning rooms. This element was, of course, the Victorian sense of time.

Possibly the best way to describe how it worked, or rather — since there was no sense of anything working — how things were, would be to chronicle the daily phenomenon known in our household as "getting Father off." As a young man, my father had acquired a decorous old business that dealt wholesale in perfumes, soaps, complexion powders, essences and po-matums for the toilette, a trade of enough French frivolity to give his personality that tinge of the panache which it might not have had, had he dealt in staples. Since he was the owner, had long since placed the factory side under the supervision of one brother, the office under another, and had various cousins and brothers-in-law at a straggle of desks in between, he felt himself under no obligation to get downtown at any particular hour. Indeed, since he was a man of the most delicate family feelings and could not have borne to have any of his relatives think that he wished to lord it over them, it was probable that he preferred to schedule his arrival at the office at an hour late enough to keep him from ever knowing the hour of theirs.

My mother, however, although she had never been in the business world, had certain convictions about it which would have done her credit in a later era. She believed that a business run with such unpressurized ease, even enjoyment, must be well on its way to ruin, that one so nepotically staffed could survive only at the price of eternal vigilance, and that even if my father had managed to do very well for years before he met her, he now owed it to her self-respect, to his own Dun & Bradstreet rating, and to their joint children, to give at least the appearance of frenzied toil. She was a woman who would have felt much safer breathing hard and fast in the wake of one of those lunchless men whose race with their calendar ends only with death. And she was never to comprehend the real truth: that people loved to do business with my father because, in an already accelerating age, his dandified air of the coffeehouse, his relaxed and charmingly circuitous tongue — which dwelt much on anecdote but only lightly on orders or due dates — and above all, his trust in the "plenty" of time, made them feel participants in a commercial romance, gentlemen met by chance on the Rialto, who had decided to nurture a little affair.

But since she did *not* understand, each morning at home was a contest, a parable in which Conscientious Practicality, my mother, strove to get Imaginative Indolence, my father, out of the house somewhat nearer nine than noon. Imaginative always won, partly by refusing to notice the strategic lines of force sent out constantly, all morning, by Conscientious, and partly, as I came to believe, because Time itself, elsewhere being made to skip so violently, was coming to lean more and more sympathetically on my father's side.

I awake then, on a certain morning, almost any morning in the nineteen-twenties. Perhaps the milkman's clop-clopping horse has already been replaced by a rubber-tired van, but I hope not, since the horse's reflective, frequently interrupted pace is so much more suitable to what is going to follow. It is somewhere between six and seven o'clock back there; Josie, the maid, is still curled in her central cubicle in the angle of the long, wandering L that is our apartment; my grandmother sleeps, as she will for hours yet, in her separate wing; even my mother and my two-year-old brother, those disciples of *Achtung,* are still fast on their pillows.

But my father, strangely enough, as you might think, for a man who is always reassuring people that he and they have "all the time in the world," is already up and about, puttering in the kitchen for himself, as he loves to do. Not strange at all — he who is at home in Time rises with interest at the prospect of a new stretch of it; only its minions need to bury their heads. And if there is a little of the insomnia of the aging in his early habit, then it is never fretful, but spry and accepting, like a man who has been offered more food than he is hungry for, but will do what he can.

I get up too and go to the kitchen and we look at one another, each in our pajamas. And now a nice thing happens. He says nothing — no probing for the day's beginning or for me, as I re-form myself out of dream — but merely reaches behind him, fumbling in a collection of brown paper bags he brought home last night, brings out a blood orange, of the kind he knows fascinates me, and hands it to me. Were my mother here she would say, "Say Good Morning to Your Father, say Thank You!", not to me really, but to serve notice to the world that she is ready for her obligations, *en garde* for all the sword-thrusts of the day.

But she is much younger than we are. Two of a kind, we enter the dining room without saying a word. He is carrying the pot of coffee he has made, a low thing for a man in his position to do, as we both know, and akin to the smelly kippers he will toast for breakfast if not watched, and to that itinerant hobnobbing in delicatessens which produces the brown paper bags.

Saturdays, when my mother returns in a flurry of delivery boys, her beaver toque askew over cheeks fretted rosy from her plundering of the shops, and exclaims, "Done for the week, for the entire week!" my father may reply mildly, "A cuisine should saunter, m'dear. From day to day." He is thinking then perhaps of his old housekeeper in New Orleans, who used to cuddle his pears in tissue paper and reverse his wine bottles of an evening; but he will say nothing, because of the cheese he hid and forgot, that my mother found last week, that waved in a blossom of maggots when she lifted the sweating, china dome — and because she believes that wine makes you drunk. It is difficult, he knows, for a woman to have married an old man so full of comparisons. But it is difficult too — although this he never says — to have married out of one's century.

Now, however, in this hour while the morning freshens at the window, and some of the lamps that are always left burning to chart our household through the night are still on, Time moves for him as it should, like treacle, or even, as in my child's world, not at all.

Then, all at once as it seems, the morning paper thumps outside the hall door, the veteran clock in the hall gives its strangled cluck for the half hour, Josie lets fly the flush handle in her bathroom with a bang that can be heard all over the house, the weakening lamps give up the ghost, my brother roars. My father gives me an untranslatable look that I understand perfectly. The century, this one, has spoken; the contest has begun.

Mrs. Huber, my brother's nurse, who is as much on my mother's side as Josie, if anywhere, can be said to be on ours, passes us, bottle in hand, on her way to the kitchen, giving us a starched, thermometric nod for the tacky pair we are.

"Run, stop the paper boy," my father says to me. "I want to pay him." He ambles after me, and I leave them deep in confab at the hall door. I return to the table, at which I find my mother, in her morning chain-mail of ribbon and lace. She wears a boudoir cap to match, shaped like an upside-down ruffled spittoon, but beneath it, her voice is edged with modernity.

"Whom can he have found to talk to already!" she says.

When my father returns he has some paper greenery that he tries to stuff into the nonexistent pants pocket of his pajamas. Tickets for the Irish Sweepstakes, it develops, that McDonough, the paper boy, has sold him. My mother sits still for a moment, then says in a stifled voice that of all the fifty heads of families in this building, it is probable that only my father has the time to learn the name of every mendicant who plies its halls, and hadn't he got a similar packet of tickets last week? — to which my father incautiously replies that the more coverage the better in any gamble. Gamble is one of the money words which produce a known response in my mother; when it does not come as usual I say it for her, since I have my own reasons for currying her favor this morning, and I know by heart all the public expressions of her private terrors.

"Everything going out," I say, "nothing coming in."

My father's reaction to this is such as requires her telling him not to encourage me, and her commanding me to dress at once, or else I shall be late for school.

"Nonsense!" he says, for secretly he resents the school for daring to impose temporal restrictions on any flesh of his flesh. "She has plenty of time." And such is my faith in his faith that, although he has thus made me late morning after morning, and I am consistently punished in the school world for being also a resident of his, it will be years before I am willing to admit that it was he who was out of step with them.

"What time is it?" says my mother, and in the same instant closes her eyes and puts the back of her hand against her capped brow. For there are at least eight running clocks in our house in addition to broken ones in drawers and antique ones with stopped faces — almost one for every room — and not one agrees with any other. And this is so not only in our house, but in the houses of all the uncles and aunts on my paternal side. They all have something in their blood that slows clocks, my mother claims, but this is not true, for one clock we have breaks into rowdy tarantellas in the night and must be forcibly calmed — it is more probable that they confuse them. I do not mind our eight — it gives one such a choice.

"Oh, do *you* have a headache *too*," I say quickly. At once my father's hand, dry with years, is at my forehead, as I knew it would be, feeling for temperature. I droop cooperatively and let him see that I, nicknamed "hungry Henrietta," have pushed aside my plate. Death is a word never spoken in our family, since there are so many of an age to expect it, but my father, who will thus deny his own mortality, is always hearing its dragon breath snuffing near the heads of his children, as if he fears that Providence will surely snatch from him early what he neglected to take from it until so late.

"Now, Joe," says my mother, "you know as well as I do that she will recover like magic as soon as it's safely ten o'clock!"

"Ah, now, now," he replies, his hand holding safe my cheek, "you know you'd never forgive yourself, if . . ."

My mother throws up her hands, and I see that this will not be one of the mornings when, enraged, she will threaten castor oil or the enema, or when, half convinced, she will suggest citrate of magnesia or Feenamint, or any other of those mild unspecifics she claps down us to warn the dark powers that she is aware. She gives me up, the better to concentrate on him. "Tailor came last night," she says. "He brought back your pearl-gray."

My father accepts the prod with grace, having won the first round, and goes off with a tuneless whistle, although he is not a whistling man. This means that even he does not believe me this morning. It is an expression also of his refusal to truckle to schools on principle, on the grounds that they are coarse instruments for the shaping of such quality material as he sends them. Above all, it means that his day has begun as a proper day should, easing itself so gently into the whorls of circumstance that it can scarcely be said to have moved, and with the first prerequisite of a Victorian household — with *everybody home*.

My mother has barely time enough to dress and to make one rapid round-trip through the apartment, setting higher the fires under everybody's caldron, and there he is back at the table — shaved, spatted, cologne on handkerchief, stickpin in lilac tie. And this provokes her most of all, that while his long view of life is so deliberate, he is not at all dilatory about its detail; it is hardly to be borne that of the thousands of trains he has had to make in his life he has, by not only the neatest but the calmest of margins, never missed one. Time is her enemy, and, she knows, the natural enemy of us all; it is not fair that my father's naïve trust in it works for him as pragmatically as some people's trust in God. She sits at table, thinking of the enviable tohu-bohu of shaving cuts and indigestion in which the other fifty fathers have long since whirled away, and wonders if this morning, just this morning, after the incontestable interval of the *Tribune* and the grapefruit, she might not be able to get him off with a couple of three-minute eggs.

"Fix you some calfs-brains, Misser Joe?" This is Josie, bearing the first cup of coffee, and one of the clocks has just struck ten. My mother flinches — calves' brains have to be poached, and after the poaching, breaded, and after the breading, fried.

"Mmmm," he says, "and with black butter, eh Josie? Black butter, not brown."

Another clock — sometimes they do their best to be helpful — strikes the hour, and my mother murmurs rapidly and bitterly of all the duties before her, including the fact that she must be off to the bank, to which my father says nothing, for he knows that she will not leave the house before him, although he does not know why. It is because she must protect his reputation, since he will not, and she considers it infinitely low-class for a woman to be seen up and abroad when her man is still lounging at home. Forgotten by them, I listen, incognito unless I turn healthy before noon. Nested in the shawls that have been mustered against disease, I mull over which of them is the aristocrat, which the low, over why it is so hard to love the worthy, so warming to be in the presence of one who will allow himself to be deceived. Above all, I wonder which of them is right about Time, not knowing that it is more than my mother and father who do battle here. Contra, contra I hear their dividing voices, as, with a Eurasian aching, I hear them yet.

The doorbell rings and now my father rises, eager, nostrils sniffing the true pursuit of the morning. For the second prerequisite for a Victorian household is that all morning long its doors, front and back, be applied to by processions of those who either bring special services or require them. Before noon we will have had, besides our regular shipment of eggs from coquettishly pastoral places with names like Robin Roost, of French Vichy from the drugstore, and panatela cigars from the little Spaniard in Harlem, also various but unvarying visits from upholsterers, dressmakers, opticians, even a bootlegger whose *ton*, like all the others, so remarkably suits us — a rococo little man, trapped like us, between two eras, who carries a cardcase and deals only in wine. In between come the variables, perhaps a former servant girl with her new baby, or a long-lost cousin with her old debts (both of them aware that petitions will not do as well in the afternoon, which is my mother's dominion), or perhaps an old-clothes man who does not yet know that we never ever sell anything off, we only buy. Even he is detained long enough to learn that he has one commodity for which my father will find some way to reward him — conversation.

"It's the Walker-Gordon man," my mother says, in triumph, and my father sits down. This is the man who delivers the special acidophilus milk for my brother, a routine meant to cease in the first month after birth but prolonged by my father so that the heir may have his traditions too. In other respects it has been a failure — the Walker-Gordon man will not stop to talk.

Providentially, Mrs. Huber enters to say that if my father wishes to pay his usual visit to the nursery, will he kindly do so at once, so that she may get her charge out in the sun "while it is high." As soon as he is gone, my mother puts on her hat, not that he will take the hint, but it makes her feel better, and besides, since there is no routine left to him now except his half hour's reading to my grandmother, and since this has been an exceptionally reasonable morning so far, it is just possible that, if no bells ring, she may get him off by eleven, which is at least a half hour better than par.

I am quite used to seeing her go about her housewifery for hours on end thus hatted; she was wearing one on that extraordinary day when, in a similar period of waiting, she suddenly lifted her petticoats, revealing to my pleased eye that although she had laughed at my yellow satin Christmas garters she sometimes wore them, took three steps back, and kicked the dining-room clock. There is red in her eye now as she looks in on me in passing, but she will kick no more clocks. The subsequent sal volatile and sweeping-up provided my father with an hour's valid delay, and the clock returned from repair "same like ever" just as the old watchmaker had promised, that is, running ten minutes later than the one in the hall.

But joy of joys, here he is and it is only eleven, and he has actually already completed his devoirs to his mother, his matins to his son — it must be the spring, ding-a-ding, for matters 'gin arise, time's on the run, and father makes for the hatrack, on which his bowler lies. . . . And two bells ring.

At the front door. At the back. And now there is no device of wit, verb or cachinnation by which I can follow the final counterpoint of my father, the *a cappella* exits and returns by which he halts, circles, hedges, rises to the high C of delay, and ultimately, coda, goes.

Let me try. The ring at the front door belongs to Mr. Krauss the cabinetmaker, who comes to us once a month, to feed the furniture. There is nothing *outré* about this; we have masses of elderly wood and veneer that apartment-house heat withers, and Mr. Krauss spends an earnest day feeding linseed oil and casauba to our parched gargoyles, griffons and lion-footed tables, never troubled by any fantasy that he might do as well by placing his supplies in the center of the arena and quickly taking his leave. He is a tall, cavernous German, full of Hegelian pauses through which occasionally climbs one memorable phrase — the kind of old-fashioned workingman whose society is always courted by urban men like my father. The ring at the back door belongs to Cyril, one of the West Indian elevator boys, who can also talk Creole. He has come to borrow my father's roulette wheel, and this I shall not bother to explain; if by now it does not seem perfectly natural, there is no more to be done. No, better to leave them at once, the three of them bogged there forever, Cyril's winsome causerie on one side, Krauss's silence on the other, and my father somewhere in between them, with his foot on the stile.

He goes at last, of course, although I never seem to see him do it, only hearing his parting, customary cry. It is his one mock-fierce threat, one so gay, so mild, so aptly like him, yet its *frisson* always travels up my spine as no threat of the cat-o'-nine-tails could. "Be a good girl!" he always cries. "Else I'll throw you into the middle of next week!"

Now my mother is left in her bevy of women, free to chivy us back into her century. As dusk advances, her siege of him will be renewed by telephone, and pointed the other way, toward us, as she begins to doubt that he will ever again come in the door she was at such pains to get him out of; for an office where there is plenty of time is just as hard to leave, and all the way up the avenue from the subway station there are cracker-barrels which know Mr. Joe. Now, however, she rests. One more morning has passed without realizing her worst fear — that the dreadful, shiftless day will come when he will still be there for lunch.

But he comes, and evening with him, and all his clan gathered to him from block and cranny, and then his star rises to its full. For in the end he draws us all back with him into his calm antipodes. Supper-talk is slowed, appetites dreamy, now may our griffons protect us, our curtains swaddle. Even my mother has stopped her White Queen running and sinks in her chair, a little muzzy with life, as at those times when she can be persuaded to a single glass of ruby claret. I fall asleep on the davenport, smelling its ageless, mummy leather, hearing the murmur of the elders. The last thing I see is my father, his eyes sweet with triumph. The vital threads of existence are blending, yet endless, the furniture is fed. We are all together with him in the now, rocking in the upholstered moment, in the fur-lined teacup of Time. The lamps are lit for the night, against that death which is change. And tomorrow, *da capo*, it is all to do over again.

And now I am awake on another night, tonight. Thirty years have gone by, and I no longer hear the murmuring of the elders. All around me, as I slept back there, my own century was coming to the fore. Flappers, streaking by me in Stutzes and Auburns, were already disappearing over the edge of their era; each day the stock market climbed like the horses of Apollo, yet at nightfall had not come down. Later would come the false stillness of the thirties when hands hung heavy; then, with a proletarian clanking of machinery we would be off again, into a war, into the self-induced palpitations of the forties, as, pit-a-pat, pit-a-pat, we changed matter into light, outdistanced sound, and came roaring out upon the strait turnpike of the fifties in our new pink cars.

And now there is nothing left to outdistance, except Time. I am awake wherever I am; is it on the rim of the world, the lip of the Time-machine? All around me there is a cold, sublunary glare, the sourceless light of science fiction, that greens the skin, divorces cell from cell.

I know where I am now. If there are any gods in this place I must pray to them, as once one could to the comfortable old evils of Ra or Baal. I must pray to s-s-s, or b-oom. For this place is the middle of next week.

Then, from over the rim of the world, I hear voices, the dividing voices.

"Run! Run!" says my mother. "Can't you run a little faster!"

And then I hear my father's voice, Rhadamanthine, serene.

"You have time," says my father. "All the time in the world."

And from the pinpoint where I stand, I can see it, the old place, lit up bravely as a fish bowl against the dark shadows of eternity, moving slowly while it persuades itself that it stands still — the whole improbable shebang, falling through the clear ether silently, with all its house lights on.

# May-ry

MY FATHER, born in Richmond about the time Grant took it, was a Southerner therefore, but a very kind man. All of us — children of his sixties, with abolitionist consciences — knew that. The limits of his malice extended to flies, and to people who hit children or mistreated the helpless anywhere. His pocket was always to be picked by any applicant, and no matter how many times my mother, much more of a grenadier, pointed out where they did him in, he remained the softest touch in the world.

His manners were persistently tender to everyone, and perhaps because he looked and dressed somewhat like Mark Twain and shared a small, redeeming slice of Twain's humor, nobody ever seemed to find this saccharine. He was, for instance, the only person I ever knew who could chuck a carriage baby under its chin and goo at it — "Coo-chee-coo!" — without making anybody gag at the sight, or doubt for one minute that it was done out of pure spontaneity and love. Yes, he was the kindest man in the world. Yet, when the time came, it was my father who was purely unkind to our colored maid Mary — May-ry.

May-ry, who must have been about thirty at the time I speak of, was no old family retainer; she had come to work for us, her first job in New York, through an ad in the *Times* ten years back, when I was very little. Even then, our family had already been forty years away from the South. But my father's memories of the first twenty years of his youth there were deep and final. At bedtime he would often tell us of Awnt Nell, the mammy who had brought him up, although he never mentioned her in public — "too many Southern colonels around already." Awnt Nell had been a freedwoman; even before the War our grandmother, his mother, would never have servants of any other description. He was so firmly proud of this that when I found, flattened away in the old Richmond Bible, a receipt made out to my grandfather for insurance on a slave, I slipped it back and never taxed him with it.

In any case, all that our tradition had boiled down to was my father's insistence that my mother always keep colored help. This was hard on her, since, being German, she could never quite manage or understand them. She had an inflexibly either-or attitude toward trust, plus a certain jealousy of other people's hardships, that made her stiff with those who had more of them. Also, without any reason to be, she was always a bit afraid of May-ry, referring to her whenever she could as *"Die Schwarze."* My father did not like this, and often caught her up on it. And nobody, at any time, ever said "nigger" in our house.

Meanwhile, May-ry and my father kept up their special allegiances. There were of course a thousand ways in which he knew the life she had come from, and she "knew" us. Whenever he could be heard embarking on one of the ritually flamboyant regional anecdotes that my mother couldn't bear, May-ry usually was to be seen edging closer to the company, only as decorous as a uniform could make her, her mouth drawn out like a tulip ready to burst at the familiar denouement — which brought shriek after shriek of her released laughter, followed, under my mother's glance, by a quick retirement. But she and my father also shared more particular sympathy, or professed to, over the rheumatism. As a young man, he had had to take an eighteen-week cure for his at Mount Clemens Spa, and like many diseases contracted early, it had kept him youthful, healthy, and appreciated; on a dull day a loud twinge of it would suddenly announce itself to the house — and to his best audience.

May-ry's rheumatism was of another sort. It was her euphemism for the fact that, periodically, she drank. Whenever she felt a long attack coming on, about every four months or so, she always absented herself from our house on a short trip to Roanoke, where she could lay up in the sun a little. We all were aware of the probable truth — that she was holing up in Harlem with one or the other of the people she had originally come up here with in the wake of the preacher who had brought them all North together. My father knew she drank, and she knew that he knew, but the fiction of Roanoke was always maintained. She was a child — and he loved all children. Just so long as she kept herself seemly in front of him (and she never did anything else), she was only doing what was expected of her, and he the same. "What you recommend I do for *my* rheumatiz, May-ry?" he might sometimes tease, but this was as far as he ever went.

Once a year, on her paid vacation, May-ry did go to Roanoke. We knew this because just before she was due back, a case of jars of home-canned peaches always arrived. She liked to use them during the year and tell us something about the farm as each jar was opened; these were her anecdotes, and I knew all of the characters in them, from Mooma and Daddy Gobbo down to the cow that always stood with its head over the gate, like a cow in a primer. On rheumatism vacations no jars ever came; only, of a sudden, there would be May-ry back again, scrubbing at the moldings as if these had to be whitened like her sins, cooking up for my father everything she could sink in the brown butter he adored. Between these times, once in a while she failed to come back from her Thursday night off until Monday; when she returned, it would not be she who had been sick, but one of the friends "over on One Hundred and Twenty-ninth Street." But someone else there always had

to phone for her, so we knew. On these occasions my mother
would be furious. She wanted a German girl whose docile allegiance would be to her, whose ins and outs she would know the
way my father knew May-ry's. Patiently, he would explain these
to her. "They're children, that's all. They can't stand up to us.
Never have been able to. Never will. But if you just give them
their head a little, they're the best servants in the world. And
the loyalest."

Then came Somus. May-ry had always been allowed to enter-
tain her many suitors, evenings and Sundays if she wished, in
our kitchen, Father sometimes stopping in to chat with them,
to let them know on what terms they were welcome, to have a
little Southern cracker-barrel time — and to see that they were
the right sort for May-ry. With Somus, this all vanished. Somus
was the son of that same preacher of the Abyssinian Church
of God who had brought May-ry up here, and he was the real
reason (besides us, she said) why she had never married; she'd
been in love with him, hopelessly until now, ever since they'd
spatted mud pies together down home. Somus had quarreled
with his own father almost from the moment they all came up
here and had been away studying for a long time. Now he was
here to take his civil-service examinations.

Somus turned out to be just as handsome as she'd said he
was. Rebel from the church he might be, but I could never
see him, black in his black suit, without thinking Biblically,
things like "the ram of God" and "His nose is as the tower of
Lebanon that looketh forth toward Damascus." There was not
an inch of ornament upon him, beyond the strict ivory of his
teeth, the white glare of his eye. Not that I saw much of him.
When Somus took May-ry out, he did just that, took her *out*,
never sat in our kitchen or ate in it; later on we knew that
she'd had a bad time getting him to ring at the back door.

Somus. Why he loved May-ry was not hard to tell, quite apart
from the fact that she too was handsome, with a shapely mouth,

a sweet breadth of brow and eye. She drank — and he didn't approve of that. She dressed high and loud, not even in the New York way but in the bandanna bush colors that antedated Roanoke — and he was forever trying to get her to imitate that sister of his who wore navy blue with round organdy collars. She liked to dance at the Club Savoy — and it pained Somus to find himself still that good at it. Worst of all, she was the staunchest and most literal of Bible beaters, and to an emancipated man, this opium of his people must have been as the devil. So, all told, love between them was foreordained.

She adored him, of course. He was just like his father, strong, dour, and, like many ministers' sons before him, with the genes of faith coming up in him just as hot and strong in other ways — in the very form of his unbelief.

I remember just when the trouble came. It could have been the red spring dress that sparked it. "Kah-whew!" I said, when she showed it to me. It was almost purple, and still trying. "Never get to heaven in that!" Heaven was a great topic between us. "Besides, it'll run."

"Sho' will." She stuck out her chin, pushing her smile almost up to her nose, her nostrils taking deep draughts of the dress, as if it, all by itself, were perfume. "And me with it. All the way."

"May-ry, tell us about heaven." It was a dull day.

Always willing, she answered me, explicit as if it were Roanoke, as if we had just opened the largest peach jar of all. It was a nice fleshly style of heaven but not rowdy; a touch of the Savoy maybe, but enough pasture for the cow. Triumphant, in the red dress, she entered it.

"Where's Somus? Isn't he there? Where he gonna be?" In these exchanges, exactly like my father, I used to fall into her language.

She cast her head down, furred up her brows under a forehead as smooth as a melon. "He be there," she said after a while, in a low voice. Pushing out her chin again, she asserted it. "You just wait and see. He be!" And in the same moment she whirled around and caught me at the icebox, my hand in the evening dessert. Washing my hand at the tap, she warned me, "You go on like you been doing, you gonna come to no good end."

"If I do — how'm I gonna be up *there*, to see *him!*" She and I loved to crow at each other that way, to cap each other's smart remarks, in the silly sequiturs of childhood. But this day, something else teased at me to tease her. It wasn't my own unbelief; that had already been around for some time. But in other ways I could feel how I was going on, and I didn't like it either. I was growing out of my childhood. Maybe, like somebody else, I envied her the perfection of hers.

"Listen, May-ry," I said, squinting. "Suppose . . . when you get there . . . it isn't at all like you said it was. Suppose they don't let you sashay around in any red dress — suppose they just hump you over your Bible in a plain old white one. No music either, except maybe a harp. Oh, *May-ry* — what the Sam Hill you gonna do if they give you a harp?"

Once more, she considered. The dignity with which she mulled my cheap dialectic already smote me. She raised up and looked at me. "Then I *wears* my white dress, and I *plays* my harp," she said, her lip trembling, "and I praises the Lord God."

I ran and kissed her. "You'll look just as beautiful, I bet. You'll look pyorely beautiful, pretty as pie."

"You hush," she said, sharp and starched. "Stop that talking like a nigger, you hear?" Yes, I forgot to mention that. She was the only one who ever said it in our house.

The next night, Thursday, Somus came to call for her. I was peeping, to see her in the dress, and that was the last time I saw him. Ram of God again, height six cubits and a span. May-ry looked beautiful. But in about an hour she came back alone, then went out again. I was the only one who saw her. We had the phone call the next morning, one of the several voices never identified but familiar. May-ry's Mooma was taken bad. May-ry was already on her way down there.

The Saturday afternoon she returned, nine days later, my mother was out, as May-ry had known she would be. I heard May-ry's voice, talking low to my father, in the parlor. Usually the sight of the place, left to the mercies of the day cleaners from the agencies, would enrage her at once, emboldening her enough to fling off her good clothes for her cleaning smock, bind up her hair, and set to work, meeting no one's eye and loudly scolding the air. But this time, I could see by peeping that she was sitting in the stiffest chair and had not even removed her gloves.

"No, Mr. Joe," she was saying, nervously holding on to her pocketbook. "No, suh — no." No. She had to leave us. Somus say he wouldn't marry her unless she did.

I heard my father "remonstrate" with her, as he always called it. This meant that he was using the same comfort voice that he used on us when delegated by Mother to punish us, the voice with which he helped us toward the first stage of being good again, by mending the *amour-propre* that we ourselves had injured in being bad.

It was all right, he was saying. Why, it was going to be all right! Whoever expected a girl like her to stay single? Especially when she was being spoken for by a fine boy like Somus. But what was all the fuss about? Mustn't she know that all along we had expected it — that some day or other she was going to want to get married and live out? He put his hands on his spread knees and leaned back, shaking his speckled ruff of hair at her. "Lord, what you women won't do to get a little torment." This too was part of the comfort, to put the offense as quickly as possible in the realm of human nature.

She didn't answer him, although she opened and closed her mouth several times.

"I see," he said after a while, biting at his mustache, "Somus doesn't want you to work at all."

Oh nossuh, it wasn't that. She was able to say this clearly; then she fell to mumbling, her head all the way down. Then she was silent again. He had a hard time getting it out of her. It wasn't that, she said at last. She and Somus would surely have to count on her doing day work. But Somus say what the use of her being up North if she work for *home* folks? Somus say she won't really *be* up North until she stop working for people from home.

And now my father really was nonplussed at first, then angry enough to stomp around the room. "Why, good God in heaven, girl!" (This was just what he always said to me at such times.) What in the name of the Lord had got her into such monkey-shines? Was she going to let that boy sell her down the river? Who was going to treat her better than us — not to mention pay! Didn't she know right well, from talking to the other maids on the roof when she hung out the washing, how some people treated colored folks up here?

Yes, she knew. She said it in a voice like the Victrola's when something was wrong with its insides, her head hanging down. She didn't expect to be as well off, she said. And she would never forget his kindness — us. But Somus.

So, at last, my father played trumps.

He was standing over her by this time, looking down. "Day job or not, you're going to want some kind of steady *family* people, aren't you?" He said "ain't you" really, or close to it. "Don't tell me he wants to make you into one of those pitiful agency creatures working from dawn to dusk, getting somebody else's piled-up dirt every day!"

No suh. For the first time, she looked at the moldings.

"Then —" he said, and hesitated. "Now then, May-ry —"

His voice dropped to a conspirator's. He rubbed the red spot left on his nose by his pince-nez, as always when he was embarrassed. "Now then, May-ry, what about . . . what about Roanoke? You know you got to go there, times you get laid up. You know right well not everybody going to give you the time off we do."

Yes, Mr. Joe. She whispered it. And this was the point at which she stood up, stopped her hands from their fooling with each other, and looked straight ahead of her, as if she were going to speak a piece, or were attending a wedding. "Somus say I got to have that out with you too." She spoke quietly, but she could not look at him. "I never did go there but once a year, on my vacation. And you all knowed it."

He actually put up a hand to ward her off. "Now, now, don't you go and say anything foolish, girl. No need to do what you might regret later on."

"It's true," she said. Even her accent had shifted, hardening toward something like Somus's — who, by some steady effort, had almost none. "I get drunk." Then she turned gray, and started to shiver.

My father stepped back, and he too changed color. It was almost as if she had touched him.

Then a most peculiar scene took place. My father positively refused to consider, to treat, to discuss, to *tolerate* a hint of what she wanted to tell him and he knew as well as she did. That she'd been lying all these years and wanted the dear privilege of saying so. And she followed him around the room in circles after him, snuffling her "Mr. Joe" at him, all the time growing more halfhearted, confused — ever so often looking over her shoulder to see if Somus, that tower of strength, mightn't have appeared there. But he hadn't. He'd told her what she must do, and left her to it. He was a stern man, Somus, and a smart one — and he understood my father right down to the ground.

Finally, she stopped in the middle of the room and screamed

it, exactly like a baby repudiating the universe, her face all maw. "I never was down there but once a year, and you know it. I was getting drunk over on One Hun' Twenny-ninth Street. And you know it, and you know it." Rocking back and forth, she beat her foot on the ground. "I'm going there now. And I'm not coming back." But by this time she was crying like a baby too.

When my father took her to the back elevator, she was still weeping. "Now, now, we'll just forget everything you said," he said. "We'll just forget this whole afternoon. Why, getting married is a serious thing, girl — no wonder you all upset." His voice took on the dreaminess with which he told us our good-nights. "Hush now, hush. You just have yourself a good rest down there in Roanoke." By the time he rang the bell for her, she was already nodding.

When the elevator door opened, she turned back to him. "I'd ruther . . . ruther — " But then she choked up again, and we never did hear what.

"Hush now," he said, patting her into the elevator. "And when you come back . . . it'll be just like always, hear? Meantime, you send us up some of those peach jars." As the door closed, she was still nodding.

In the succeeding weeks, my mother and father kept a bet on. "You'll see," he'd say, even after the time had long since stretched beyond what May-ry had ever been away before. "She'll have her jobs — and she'll lose them. Nobody up here's going to appreciate enough what she does do — and what she can't. And she knows it, she knows it." It was almost as if he were echoing May-ry, in a way. Other times, he just worried it aloud. He loved taking care of people. "Who's going to take care of her like us?"

Then, one morning, the box of jars came — the herald. But when the box was opened, the jars were found to be of grape —

grape conserve. Now, grapes were all over the shops right here, at the time — it was October. "Idiots," said my father. "What was the address on the outer wrapping?" But it had already gone down the dumbwaiter with the trash. I think my mother knew, but she never said. She was never much for children really. Except for my father. And after that, as more weeks went by and we began the endless series of German "girls" whom I never quite liked or my father either, he submitted, and spoke no more of colored help, or of May-ry. My mother had won, it appeared — and Somus.

But I still yearned sometimes, and wondered. *Did* she go back to Roanoke? I tried hard as I could to recollect whether there had ever been talk of grape arbors on Fox Road in Roanoke — in the tales that had come out of the peach jars. There had been damson, I knew, and elderberry. Damson too sour for you folks, and all the berries goes to the wine. Had she ever said there were grapes? I couldn't remember, though every now and again for years I tried. Had she sent them from there, or from Harlem? I knew well enough what the box meant, though, same as my father had. It meant pure spontaneity, and love.

Later on, years later when I was teaching in college, there was a girl who looked so much like May-ry — her eyes and that brow — that I had all I could do not to go up and speak to her, ask her who was her mother. Of course I couldn't. How could I be sure, these days, of terms that would be pleasing to her? Besides, I never knew May-ry's last name — or Somus's. That was the way it was, in those days. So I'll never know for sure whether Somus did marry May-ry and she got emancipated, at least enough to work for Northerners, and send that girl on to college. Or whether, by now, she's only been emancipated as far as heaven. If so, I hope she has the dress she wants, and maybe even a little snifter after dinner — and I'm purely sorry I ever was mean enough to insinuate that heaven might be anything else. People should be able to get freed without having to be perfect for it beforehand. Maybe even Somus knows that now. I'm even big-hearted enough to hope that he's with her, either here or there, and has been all along. She'd never be happy without him, so he must be. For if anything had gone wrong, she'd always know whom to come to. And it's been a long time. It's been thirty years now, and she hasn't come back yet.

# Saturday Night

THAT Saturday afternoon, after he had left the analyst's office for what might be the last time, he stopped in at the elegant little Viennese bakery in the same block, and bought a mocha cake for his wife. Although, even five years ago, Dorothy had been one of those out-of-towners who slipped into the ways of the city with only a little more emphasis than was natural, she had never lost her glee over the complicated, alien tidbits which were such a contrast to the pies and hefty layer cakes of her native Utica. The huge new "housing development" in which they had been lucky enough to get an apartment quartered only several glittering chain shops, which she had long since learned to snub.

Waiting absently at the counter for his change, he found that actually he could not fully realign Dorothy's face in his memory. Although he could summon a hundred images of their life together, before and now — the curve of her back as she offered the spoon to the child, the tilt of her head as she slumped, reading, in a chair — in full focus her face evaded him, remaining always in the rear, or to one side. A common enough occurrence, he knew. Nevertheless it left a curious hollow in his new-found assurance.

As he left the store, he turned a last look on the block to which he had been coming for almost three years now. Although, when away from it, he could not have told between which two of the line of houses the one he visited was precisely located, the whole of the block reared itself in his mind like a composition, an entity whose significance had become the foreground of his life. Up three steps, in at the gray entrance, into one of those self-service elevators within whose clicking, measured suspension one rode always with a sense of doom, no matter to what event. Then the anonymous room, whose stepped-down colors and noncommittal furniture offered only the neuter comfort of no stimulus to either approval or dislike. Then, finally, another installment in the long, delicate auscultation of himself, during which, sometimes clamped in resistance, sometimes irrigated with relief, he had been free to pursue the quality of his fear.

Turning away, he walked down to the corner and joined the vague group waiting for a bus. Wherever you went, at almost any time, on almost every corner, there would be such a group assembled. It was a deceptively impressive fact which, when elaborated on, he had long since learned, led nowhere. It was part of the provocative pulse of a city, of a world in which, if you did not learn to deflect the thousand casual contacts strewn at you, without attempting to seize upon them, to weld them into some philosophy of destination, you were lost indeed.

He wedged himself onto the bus, carefully protecting the cake. Looking down at the white box, he thought tiredly of what a funny symbol it was of that daily switch-off in which, laying aside the engrossing thread of himself, he bought a cake, he took a bus, and — rapped smartly back into the secondary — he deserted for another day the re-creation of himself as a working being. As a working being, he cautioned himself, he heard himself being cautioned by the dry voice from behind him in the anonymous room. For if the whole process had not helped him to hold himself untremulously at last in a world where others managed, what had it been but an infinitely seductive excursion into ego, after which, as cut off from others as he had been in the beginning, he would find himself twice alone, holding together the explored corners of himself?

Clutching the box in his cramped hand, he got off the bus

at his stop. Less than a year ago, down here, there had been nothing but the great cylindrical gas tanks, nuzzled by tenements, slotted shops, and the exhausted outbuildings natural to the wharflike streets near an old river. Now the "housing development" loomed upward before him, an incredible collage pasted against the sky. Even remembering the excavations and the swarmed signs of contractors, even forcibly recalling the scores of families who were inside it going through their daily paces like tidy, trotting simulacra of each other, it was hard to believe that the whole organism had not been stroked from a lamp. Looking at it, the eye seemed always to be trying to wipe it away.

He and Dorothy had already been drawn into the imitatively suburban life of the young couples who lived there. Dorothy, of course, he thought, much more than he — since whatever time he had away from his university job was already so prescribed. Again he strove for a better picture of her, brushing aside the recurrent blankness. In the mornings, waving to her as he passed the playground on the way to his classes, he had seen her sitting talking or reading or sewing with the other mothers, watching Libby as she played with the other beplaided and corduroyed toddlers in the austerely planned sandpit, already cluttered with buried rakes and spoons and lost tin fish. All of the mothers, still slender and attractive, looked like thirty-year-old versions of the college girls they once had been. Many of them had had careers or talents that marriage and children had interrupted or aborted, and to the memory of these they paid insistent and bitter homage, constantly totting up the frustrations of housewifery in remarks which were like a kind of bleak, allusive shorthand understood by them all. For now that they were women of the home, they felt an inferiority to their former selves, and so, too, they had constructed a technical patter full of words like "preschool" and "security" and references to "Gesell-and-Ilg," as if by this subaqueous jargon they would return motherhood, with all its inconvenient secretions and scullion duties, to the status of a profession.

With Dorothy, however, he thought thankfully, this defeated prattling never had been more than part of her half naïve acceptance of the New York "line." She had been reared in a town where people, particularly the women, expected that life would deal with them according to those archaic truisms which, if no longer so hallowed as once, came to them, at least, without the friction of disappointment. It had been this certainty in her which had drawn him as much as her mild blond good looks, whose exact lineaments so curiously evaded him now; it had been to this sureness that he, already deeply flawed with irresolution, had clung and married himself, in the sick hope of transference.

How was he to have foreseen, he thought now, that this very ability of hers to cope, this health, would become formidable between them, sending him further into his cowl of preoccupation, leaving her beached on normality, so that, strangers now, too far apart even for conflict, they had gone on sharing the terrible binding familiarities of the joint board, the joint child, and, less and less often, the graceless despair of the common bed?

For in the world of the normal, he knew now — he heard the dry voice say — to those whose qualms were always based on the tangible, the active, the real, how could he have seemed otherwise than intransigent, when he had insisted that in his world there was a basic, roiling chaos, over which the footage was never more than a series of staircases that dissolved as one trod them, in the midst of which alternatives faced one like knives — and people were only alternatives?

He walked on through the circuitous approaches to his own building. Light skittered, noise faceted from the hived buildings about him, lazily compounding a day, redolent of livelier Saturdays and more expectant springs, which was like a percussive recall to health. Fear was all right, it said to him, as long as one could bring it out into the light and give it a name. He was almost up out of the ditch now, almost up on the other, the safe side, with Dorothy and all the people who knew where they were going, and could manage.

He turned in at Number 6 Village Drive, noting, as always, the cozy term applied to the massive clinical building whose entrance halls, all of nude beige marble enlivened only by buttons, held the etherized silence of a museum. It was difficult to believe that on its upper floors hundreds of doors opened on interiors rumpled with living and the intimate sediment of people, on kitchens checkered with the aftermath of meals, bathrooms, clotted with diapers and cream pots, at whose windows stockings hung swinging in the dust motes and the sun.

The door opened to his key and he stepped into the apartment, receiving the familiar impingement of the pictures, the chairs, the books serried just as he had left them. Everything waited for him like a box full of stale attitudes, old grooves in which he both fitted and chafed. As always on Saturdays, the room had a cleanliness almost pitiable in view of the way Sunday's lax living jarred and crumbled it — almost as if Dorothy expected someone — or something. He hoped she was not going to expect too much of him at first. He hadn't really thought, he hadn't had time to think of it during these years, visualizing her, when at all, as a man in a ward visualizes the ordinary ones, cumbered with health, who wait patiently in the anterooms of hospitals.

In the bedroom, Libby lay on his bed, her face locked fast in the upturned purity of sleep. Dorothy, face down on her own bed, turned her head toward him as he came in. Her mouth, drawn down at the corners at first, in the half-drugged enmity of the dreamer coarsely awakened, quivered faintly in greeting.

Of course, he thought, feeling foolishly relieved. This is she. This is the way she is.

"Hi," he said softly, because of Libby.

"Hi."

He looked down at Libby, who was in pajamas. "She in for the night?"

She nodded. "I gave her an early supper. You know how it is otherwise." She raised herself up on her elbow and pushed back her hair.

"Mmm," he said. He knew how it was. In her voice, her attitude, he heard the echoing plaint of the other women: "If you don't let them nap then they're cranky, and if you do then they never want to go to bed later on — and you have them on your hands till nine!" Nobody seems to enjoy or glory in his children any more, he thought. We're always plotting, calculating how to have a personal life in spite of them.

"Thought you might want to go shopping or something," he said, trying on a smile. In his mood, composed half of his release, half of the infectious rhythm of Saturday expectancy, he found himself thinking of the Saturday afternoons she used to love — in the early days of their marriage, or when Libby had been a woollen-wrapped bundle carried jauntily on his shoulder — when they had been part of all the other families idling through the stores, trekking through Sears, perhaps — and coming out of that array of rose trellises and tires with a pair of curtains or a kitchen tool, they had returned home heartened and gay and somehow conquerors, through that device so feminine, so American — the purchase.

"I've done the shopping," she said, with a faint look of surprise. "The Ewarts asked us upstairs for the usual. I thought we could come down once in a while to check. It's too late for a sitter."

"Mmm." He put the cake-box down on the night table, stretching his cramped hand. "Mocha," he said.

"Thanks." She awarded it a brief, listless smile.

He sat down carefully on the side of her bed. His hand,

braced on the bed, was near her waist. She edged away politely, careful not to interpret affection into the casual gesture. For both of them it had become a matter of pride not to admit, to solicit for the shaming need that was no longer closeness. Nightly, the tense waiting for the hand which did not come had sagged more and more often into sleep; in the infinitesimal edgings away they had built the routine of remoteness.

He put his hand in his lap, inspected it. "I'm through," he said. "At the doctor's." He gave her a quick, guilty look, and concentrated again on the hand. Except for the first of the month, when the bills came in, it had been a matter of rigid convention never to mention the doctor.

"For good?" she said.

"He thinks. I hope."

She swung her legs down to the floor on the other side of the bed. After a minute, she padded around in front of him and sat down at the dressing table with her back to him, opened a drawer, took out a hairbrush, ran a finger over the bristles. He waited for her to speak, turn at least, but she began brushing her hair, slapping the brush against her head with a tired halfhearted stroke.

He gave a self-conscious laugh, and again, the surreptitious look. "Ring out, wild bells," he said.

"I'm sorry —" She turned. He waited, he told himself, for her to drop the damn brush.

"I'm sorry," she repeated, "sorry I can't be more . . . oh well —" She looked down at the brush. "I know you expected me to be . . . well . . . waiting." Then she put down the brush and the words came with a rush, a bitterness. "At the door. Or a street corner, maybe. With a lei, or something."

The quick acid of the words surprised him. She was slow and honest in all she did, with no deft talent either with the paring knife or the tongue.

"Forget it," he said, the dread of a scene opening like a funnel before him.

"No," she said, laboring now. "I suppose . . . in a way I *was* waiting." She raised her head. "Did you ever ask your doctor that . . . ask him what happens to people waiting on the sidelines for people like you to — ?" She stopped.

"To what?"

"To get over their love affair — with themselves."

"Love affair!"

"Ah, you know you loved it," she said. "Spinning out yourself. Because meanwhile you didn't have to *do* anything — about anything or anybody."

"Would it have been better if I'd had T.B.? Something that showed?"

She put a hand out toward him, almost touching his knee, then drew it back. "I kept thinking of them all the time — all the wives, and husbands, and parents of the people going to your doctor. On the outside all the time, smoothing things over, picking up the pieces — holding their breath. What are we supposed to do? Stop living?"

"If you felt like that, why didn't you say some — "

"Oh no," she said quickly. "I wasn't supposed to interrupt — or intrude!"

It was true, he thought. What she had represented these three years had been the damaging real — which he had avoided even as he fought his way toward it.

"I know it hasn't been easy for you," he said humbly. "Perhaps that was part of my trouble . . . that I didn't think enough about that. But now — "

"What's 'now'?" She looked down at her clenched hands. "People like me will always be on the outside . . . with people like you."

He got up heavily from the bed and crossed to the window. God save us, he thought, us — the equivocal ones — from the ones who see life steadily, and see it whole. From those who can't bury or evade the truth, but have to drag it out and beat it like a carpet. Who can say the raw, the open thing, that can never be glozed over again.

He stared out the window, twisting one hand around and around in his pants pocket. "Come on," he said. "Let's go up to the Ewarts'."

"No. I don't want to go after all."

"Well, for God's sake," he said, sore with his new effort, "you're always the one who's trying to drag me!"

"Because it was better than being alone together." She shrugged, smiling crookedly up at him. "Besides . . . Saturday night . . . one always hopes for the best."

"Come on then." He met the smile with a placating one of his own.

"No, It's just more of the same."

"The same?"

"You know," she said. "Like a record we all play once a week. Jim, hanging around, waiting for Esther to get drunk enough so she'll go home, and Karen watching Lou for her reasons, and me watching you for mine. I just don't want any part of it any more."

He watched it almost jealously, that soft, flexible look of hers, which concealed the enviable certitude, the stubborn strength to reject, to decide.

"Well, what do you want to do?"

She looked away from him consciously. "I thought I'd go back home for a while. If you're really on your feet now."

"For a while? Or for good?" he said. For good, he thought. That's what she asked, only a little while ago.

She was silent.

"What makes you think Utica, or any other place, isn't more of the same, these days?" he said.

"It doesn't matter where. I just can't go on being an adjunct — any more!"

"And Libby?" He softened his voice suddenly, as if their joint concern might wake her, where their forgetfulness had not.

She put her head down in her hands, rubbing her concealed face back and forth. She'll cry now, he thought, although he could not remember when he had last seen her cry, and he waited, almost with relief, for with women, the lucky women, this meant the dissolving of an issue, the haggled end of emotion — but she went on defeatedly rocking.

"Come on," he said, after a moment. "I'll fix us a drink." He waited, and then put a hand on her shoulder. "We'll have a party by ourselves."

In the kitchen, his hands took over the mixing of the Martinis, picking out and combining the gin, the vermouth, the lemon peel, with disembodied competence. "This is real enough for you!" he thought. "Isn't it? Isn't it?" he said defensively to the dry voice in the anonymous room.

He thought of the crowd upstairs now at the Ewarts', in the pattern, as Dorothy had said, pooling all their uncertainties of the week, drowning them in the fabricated bonhomie of Saturday night. The Ewarts, Syl and Harry, were a few years older than the average couple in the building and were both "in business"; perhaps it was a combination of these facts which led them into great spurts of energy, in which droves of people must be enlisted to help them kill the weekend's frightening acreage of time. To their coarse-grained parties there came, patronizingly, the fledgling physicists, the writers on their way to a foothold, the confused but verbose young men with their foetally promising jobs in the government, in the State Department, or, like himself, in the universities. They came because they were at loose ends, or at odds with themselves or the wife, or roughened with the loneliness of the city, or, let it be said, because the Ewarts could serve the liquor they themselves could infrequently afford. And with each of them came the wife, in the new hair-do, the primary colored dress with its attempted primary appeal — all the intelligent, frustrated girls, fleeing from the diapers toward an evening in which they could forget their altered conceptions of themselves.

He held the Martini mixer up to the light, and stirred, forestalling the thought of Dorothy and himself with critical thoughts of the others. It's true, what she said, he thought. Esther, having to drink herself into insensibility more and more often, with Jim doggedly watching, and Karen, flitting grimly, unobtrusively into the kitchen now and then to see that Lou's reflex skirt-chasing doesn't get him in more trouble than he can handle. And me, wrapped up in a corner. "For once let's not think about me!" he said defiantly to the voice in the repudiated room. And through it all the Ewarts hurried like high-class orderlies, bright with reassurances to the sufferers, administering glasses, plates of food, or winks in the direction of the bathroom.

The sufferers, he thought. The prowlers in retreat from themselves. He put two glasses on a tray and looked at the light through the mixer for a last delaying time. It stared back at him like an unanswerable, viscous, lemon-watery eye.

He walked back with it into the bedroom. Dorothy was stretched out on the bed again, staring into the pillow.

"Want to go in the other room, or stay here?"

"Oh leave me be. Leave me be."

He put the tray on the dressing table and sat down beside her with a brisk, overemphasized resolve.

"Come on," he said, urging her up to a sitting position. "This'll fix you up. We'll rustle up some dinner later."

They sat on the side of the bed together, sipping, not saying anything, as if they both sucked desperately at some potion of last resource. After a while he put a drink-loosened arm around her, using his other arm to refill the glasses, and they sat on in the growing dark, finishing the second drink, the third, watching with careful fixity the lambent points of their cigarettes. Outside the window, the light-studded evening converged, ramified, without them.

A tremor in her shoulder made him know, suddenly, that she was crying, and trying to conceal it. He was cleft with pity, and even a kind of possessive pride because she was the sort of woman who did not cry for show.

"Ah don't," he said. "Ah don't."

She gave her head an angry, backward shake. "I'm not trying to . . . oh you know!" she said, in a strangled whisper.

"I know." He tightened the arm that was around her, and put his other hand blindly toward her. It met her face. She moved her face back and forth in his palm, and he felt the hot sidle of tears through his fingers.

"I'm afraid," she said. "That's all it is."

"Afraid?" he said, delicately handling the sharp tool of the word. "What are you afraid of?"

"That's it. I don't know. I never used to be."

He held her as she sobbed, knowing that for this, on which of all things he should have been most knowledgeable, there was no answer that he could give. But it seemed to him that the edged word, coming through the sweetish, gin-fogged air, came like a bond, a link which slit through the cocoon around himself. He began to kiss her with a kind of heavy sympathy for them both. Turning, they stretched out on the bed and made use of one another in a final spasm of escape.

Long after she slept he lay awake in the dark, which had a pallid incompleteness from the deflected street lights outside. After a while he got up noiselessly and looked at the glowing disc of the clock. It was only nine o'clock. He crossed to the other bed, his own, near the window, and picked up the sleeping child. Holding her, on his way to the crib in her own room, her warm, inert weight seemed to him like a burden he was inadequate to carry. "Parents like us!" he thought. This must be why we avoid them, the children, because they are the mirror we make for ourselves. They are the alternative of no evasion, on whose knife we are impaled. He put her down, tucking the light blanket carefully around her, and went back into the other room.

Through the window he saw and heard it — the Saturday night pattern — its neon blotted by haze, its multiplying, loose roar jingled into softness by the tricky distances of spring. It seemed to him that he heard in it, in that heightened blend of the hundreds of gurgling, cheeping noises of daily living, some of which were quickened for him by memories of aspiration or love, but now never more than quickened — that he heard all around him the endless echolalia of his time, his world, his trap. They were all down in the ditch with him, the prowlers, and the weak alarums of their malaise lacked even the dignity of the old ecclesiastical cry: "Father, what are we? And whither do we go?" For, in our cleverness, he thought, we know what we are, and in the sadness of no mystery, we know where we are going.

He looked down at the other sleeping figure, wondering what there was in the construction, the being of a face, that had once made it his vital necessity, and that now, by some combination of circumstance and familiarity as brutal as it was quiet, had been attenuated past recall. He looked down, waiting, wishing for a sense of ruin. For ruin implied salvage; it implied the loss of something dear. Where there was a sense of ruin, there might also be a sense of hope.

# What a Thing, to Keep
# a Wolf in a Cage!

MRS. BOWMAN, the small, dark American woman walking up the Via Aurelia Antica in the sauterne Roman sunlight, was glad that she had worn the good brown pumps with the low French heels. "Take the Monteverdi bus from the Piazza Fiume," Mrs. Wigham, the British journalist resident in Rome, had said on the phone. "After that, it's a twenty-minute walk." But of course it was turning out to be a very British twenty-minute walk, as the American had suspected it might.

Visiting Italian villas, if one had no car and must watch long cab fares, had a technique of its own. One had to be dressed to cope with the crammed *filobus*, the dodging between motorcycles on the steep walk afterward, the long, cobbled approaches to the houses themselves. But once there the *amour-propre* might have to cope with a room full of signoras dressed with their usual black and white graffito perfection or, worse still, with those of one's own countrywomen who traveled preserved in some mysterious, transportable amber of their own native conveniences. Well, the new coat and the brown shoes would about do. She smiled to herself, remembering that she had read somewhere that a lady always traveled in brown.

The road was walled on each side, so that the sun scarcely glinted on the occasional green Vespa, red Lambretta or on herself, the only pedestrian. Here was a door set tight in the wall — number four, and number three had been minutes back. Number twenty-two might well be another mile away. Well, time is not *time* in Italy, she reminded herself. "My time is your time," she sang under her breath, and walked on. After a while she came to the top of a hill and saw four priests approaching from the opposite direction, walking along in their inevitably coupled way. From above, the four black discs of their hats, with the round, center hubs of crown, looked like the flattened-out wheels of some ancient bas-relief vehicle. The wheels of the church, she thought, and crossed the road.

"Per favore," she faltered. "Il numero ventidue — é lontano?" In a flood of smiles and gestures they waved her on. High above her head the embankments hid the greenery, making the way seem endless. From the dust of the road came the deciduous, stony smell of antiquity. Her lowered eyes caught sight of a pebble, smooth and egg-shaped, rather like the white jelly-bean stones her younger boy at home in the States had in his collection. She passed it, hesitated, and went back for it. I found it on the Via Aurelia Antica, she would tell him. On Easter Sunday afternoon.

At home it would still be morning. Her boys, released from the school chapel, would be at dinner in the commons or horsing in the yard. It was a habit she had not been able to break, these six months away — this counting back to what time it was over there. She hadn't wanted to go, she hadn't. But "Go!" all the others on the faculty had said. After all — a sabbatical. Once in seven years. "And four of those a widow," they must have whispered behind her. "Perhaps . . . over there . . ." Well, they would find her the same as before her sea change. At forty, forty-one, to range the world like a honing girl, the eye liquid, the breast a cave, was no more decent abroad than it would have been at home. One learned to be alone over here, as one had back there. It was like baggage. She slipped the stone into her pocket and went on.

At last she came to the high iron gates of number twenty-two. They swung open, released by the invisible keeper in the hut

at the side, and at the end of a driveway shorter than most
she came to the house — nothing of museum grandeur about
it, like others she had visited, but low, extended in a comfortable way and about the size of her house at home. No one was
about. "*Ciao!*" she would have liked to have called, but did
not. "Hello?" she said, and waited. "Hell-lo-o."

Mrs. Wigham came round the corner of her house, neatly
gray-haired, sweatered and skirted in dun, a sensible English-
woman at home in her garden, in whatever country that garden
might be. "Ah, Mrs. Bowman, so happy to meet you," she
said. "The Maywoods wrote me about you. On leave from your
post, they tell me." They shook hands. "Sociology, is it not?"
said Mrs. Wigham. "Are you going to be studying us for a
book?"

"No," said the American, laughing. "I tell myself I'm seeing
and being."

"Oh, well. No one ever does much work in Rome." Mrs.
Wigham led the way, past potting sheds, up a brief staircase,
into the house and out again. "Two of your compatriots are
here this afternoon," she said. "A lady from Hollywood, perhaps you know her? Her husband owns a film company, something like that." She mentioned a name, one of the pioneer,
supercolossal names.

"Oh, yes, of course. No — I don't know her," said Mrs. Bowman.

"She's here with a friend of hers sent me by our film man
in London. A lady who writes for the films, I believe." Mrs.
Wigham, correspondent for a London daily, had that pale,
weathered glance which was perhaps *de rigueur* for middle-aged
British lady journalists. It had never seen mascara perhaps but,
in a quietly topographical way, it had seen almost everything
else. It rested thoughtfully now on Jane Bowman. "You know
of *her*, possibly? A Miss Francine Moon?"

"No," said Jane Bowman. "I, er — I've never been to Hollywood." There, she thought. Was that snobbery or modesty? Have I established myself as sufficiently Eastern seaboard and impecunious? When abroad alone, particularly on one's first trip, one had constantly to stifle this terrible desire to establish oneself, knowing full well that, with the British, any overtness about this would establish one all too well. She stared at Mrs. Wigham's back as it led the way to the terrace. The most map-conscious people in the world, they were, yet they still alluded to the States as once they might have to Kenya — as to one of those vast but cozy terrae incognitae where certainly everybody knew everybody else.

But when they came out on the terrace and she was presented to the three ladies seated there in the magnificent light that made paintable even the debris of afternoon tea, she was less certain that "the States" was not the intimate terrain that her hostess had presumed it. On their left, the pleasant-faced elderly woman who had answered to the name of Miss Hulme with a brisk "Dew!" was surely English — hatted and caned and wrapped in woollens whose lines one was not meant to pursue. But it was the nearer of the two hatless American women opposite who caught her eye, who was limned in the light with a precision that defeated any tenderizing chiaroscuro of Roman air.

But of course, I do in a way know her, thought Jane. If I were sleepwalking in Arabia deserta and I opened my eyes on her image, I would know her. Gray tailleur, a "Ford" as Seventh Avenue calls it, lapel pin so expensively junk that it does not have to be real. Enormous alligator bag — for this is one of the things that must not be counterfeited — and yes, there are the matching shoes. Gold of bangled wrist, flint of ageless figure, perhaps forty, hair irrefragably gold and coiffed not ten minutes before, butterfly glasses with this year's line of twisted gold at the bridge. How should I not know her — this artifact of North

America, authentic in its way as the pebble I picked up back there on the road?

"Francine Moon," said this person, reinforcing their hostess's hummed introduction. One felt her to be a person who established herself immediately.

"Mrs. Bowman has been living in London for the past six months," said Mrs. Wigham. She looked from one American to the other with the bright teatime glance of those for whom conversation was still an accredited pursuit.

"London!" said Miss Moon, attaching the word to herself as she might hook another trinket to the polyglot baubles at her wrist. She was still leaning forward, partially screening the second Californian, a sullenly handsome woman of about the same age, who had acknowledged Jane with a single dead-pan, dark blink, returning to brood behind a lean brown hand afire with one astounding jewel. "Where did you live when you were in London? I had the loveliest flat — on Hay Hill."

"Oh, Pimlico, Chelsea," said Jane. "But most of the time with friends in the Middle Temple," she added demurely. Miss Moon looked doubtfully, then shrewdly at the two British women, suspecting that her own Mayfair-tempered armor might have been pierced in some recondite way.

"In the Law Courts!" said Miss Hulme. "But how — how delightful!" But "How amazing" was what she had begun to say. She and Mrs. Wigham exchanged glances. The Americans; they are everywhere. One has grown used, in the last fifty years, to their heiresses unlocking our dukedoms. But now, even into our sanctuaries they fall, topside up on their incredibly neat, unlineaged legs. Even into the Middle Temple have they fallen, blunt and indiscriminate as the bombs.

"You've just come down from Florence, have you not?" said Mrs. Wigham.

"Ah . . . Florence. I shall not manage it this time," said Miss Hulme. Over her simple, elderly-sweet profile there passed that basking glaze which, at the mention of Florence, crept over the faces of all Londoners old enough to remember the days before the pound-sterling travel restrictions — a moment's Zoroastrian magic, sluicing through fog.

"Florence!" said Miss Moon. "I've been up there for two weeks. Doing some research. Historical stuff. They're all mad for Italy on the Coast, you know."

"The Coast?" said Miss Hulme.

"The West Coast of America, Enid," said Mrs. Wigham.

"Well," said Miss Moon. "I was getting some simply marvelous stuff for my people when Mira here wired me from Garmisch, insisting that I come and stand by her in Rome. She gets so bored, you know — where there's no skiing."

Mira, impassive, blinked once, an animal pricking slightly to the mention of its name. It was enough of a movement to refract the stone that studded her hand like a king's seal. This then was the wife of that California magnate who perhaps had caught an imported starlet as she rose, or had been caught by her as she faded. Under its wiry, black karakul hair, this was a face that had never been personal enough for real beauty perhaps and was now a little too worn for lushness. But, short-nosed and impenetrably planed, it had been that central European cat-face which did well with pictures and with men, which one saw now and then framed in marabou on little girls sitting like spoiled goddesses next to their mothers on the East Bronx train. She wore a coat clipped by couturier scissors but dusty, even dirty, and her scuffed sandals showed a split in one sole. Visiting people of no importance to her, she had abjured even conventional grooming, but the seedlets that hung from her ears had an ineffable grape-bloom and were, Jane saw suddenly, black pearls. It was a pity that Mrs. Wigham, obviously not one for the nuances of dress, might not know how subtly she was being insulted. For this woman was dressed, in a way that the Miss Moons would never dare, with the down-at-the-heel effrontery of the woman who, even in her bath, wears a diamond as big as the Ritz.

"Rome has its attractions," said Mrs. Wigham. "But I fear skiing is not one of them."

"Rome!" said Miss Moon. "I have to keep telling Mira now it's got it all over poor Paris. Sixteen times she's crossed, and this is the first time anybody's been able to drag her here."

"More tea?" said Mrs. Wigham to Mira.

"She hates tea," said Miss Moon. Again Mira blinked, and this time it was as if she had twitched a ridge of skin to remove a fly. "When she's skiing she won't even smoke. She's marvelous at it. Dedicated." She turned to shake her head at Mira, to look enviously at the body, still good, still lithe, that moved now, with the humility of the admired, in its rattan chair. Suddenly Mira took out a mirror and stared at it intensely, moving one hand around her eye sockets. Her face pursed in a spasm of regret. She put the mirror away.

"Tarrible for the skin," she said.

"What . . . tea?" said Miss Hulme.

"The wind and the sun on the slopes, you know," said Miss Moon. "But she will do it." And leaning forward, they could all see the white mask left by the goggles and, radiating through it, the lines of strain, flash burns from the agony of the sport.

"But faces are more interesting as they gather life-lines, don't you think?" said Miss Hulme.

Mira stared, unflickering, into space. Then she stood up, flinging out a hip, in a voiceless sex-contempt for women whom nature had not permitted to know what else a face may gather. She spoke, apparently to Miss Moon. "They have ordered that cab yet? You know I have a date at six-thirty."

From Mrs. Wigham's flush it was clear that "they" had been "she," but her face retained its smile with only a slight shift, as if she had quickly substituted a spare. "Giuseppe is ringing about now, I should imagine. One doesn't order anything ahead here, don't you see. Italians don't have our sense of promptness. Miss Moon will have found all this out, I fancy." The rapid flutter of her tongue was meant to imply that she had perceived rudeness and risen above it, but now it was she, Jane thought, who wasted a nuance.

"I alwess like to rest before a date," said Mira. The word "date" seemed to stir her to an anticipatory sleekness. She stretched a long leg in front of her, reared her chin and bosom. Then, uneasily, her fingers returned to explore her eye sockets, as if she were learning an unwelcome Braille. Not once had she looked at anyone directly. Jane had never seen a woman whom it was possible to observe so indiscreetly, without danger of the counterglance, the sudden swerve of rapport.

"Mira's husband phones her every night," said Miss Moon. "Think of it!" Behind the great, clear wings of her glasses she appraised the other women, their dowdy innocence, with marmoset eyes. "Every single night she's been away! All the way from Beverly Hills!"

"Indeed!" said Mrs. Wigham, who was the friend of more than one dexterous marchesa and had looked on Mussolini's paramour hanging wry-mouthed in the public square. She rose. "Let us take a look at the garden until the cab arrives," she said firmly. "I must show you our irrigation system. It's quite unique."

"Ah yes, how lovely," said Miss Hulme, rising also. "I hope to persuade your Giuseppe to sell me an oleander. I must have a present for my little Signorina Necci before I leave for home."

"No!" said Mira. She kicked one shoe against a chair leg, dislodging some gravel from the sole. "I must be back at the hotel at six!"

But Mrs. Wigham had already handed Miss Hulme her cane. "Oh, yes," she murmured. "Giuseppe has developed a very good nursery business on his own." And somehow, between the vague smoke of her chitchat and a guerrilla flanking of Miss Hulme's cane, the three Americans found themselves maneuvered off the terrace, onto a path that meandered far and bournless into the flat surrounding field.

It was a narrow path, hardly more than a rut in the yellow earth, hedged by currant bushes hair-do high and by low clouds of European daisies, their delicate nets set at nylon level, their perfect, flock-pattern faces, scratchier than in Botticelli, tipped ingenuously toward the sun. Miss Hulme headed the line, and her progress was slow. Her cane probed; her enthusiasm, inflected with the remorseless lilt of *solfège*, paused at each planting. Behind her, Mira stumped, taking a step from the hip, when she was able. Miss Moon followed, placing each spike heel with safari decision, turning to flash encouragement to Mrs. Wigham and Jane.

Moving thus crabwise, she was still able to give them a précis of herself. Hearing Jane tell Mrs. Wigham that she had two boys in school, Miss Moon remarked that she had once been a housewife herself. "Married to a script-writer," she said. "Years and years of never using my mind!" Then she had chanced to make some suggestions on a script and it had turned out that she was a born natural. "Ah, then you are one of those writer-teams," said Mrs. Wigham. But it seemed that Miss Moon had ditched the husband — who had not been a natural. She had been in pictures ever since. The work she was doing now was really a luxury of the intellect that she had had to allow herself at last. For, said Miss Moon, whacking viciously at an artichoke plant that had caught her skirt on a spire, her mind was having its revenge for all those fallow years. It had become an instrument that gave her no rest.

"Take Mira," she said. Ahead Mira, face lowered as if to butt, breathed mutinously near Miss Hulme. "There's a girl who knows four languages. And one of those real low singing voices.

But all she wants to do is ski like mad and dance all night. Never reads a book or uses her mind."

Mrs. Wigham peered watchfully at Mira, so very near, so extremely close to Miss Hulme. "Sounds frightfully nice," she said. "Don't you think so, Mrs. Bowman?"

"Yes, indeed I do," said Jane.

"Well, of course, she goes in for domesticity like mad at home." Miss Moon's tone was huffy. "Her husband's a great stickler for maturity. Everybody is, with us."

Suddenly the path ended abruptly and they found themselves in front of a large, dirty green pool, the path having led them to the front of the house.

"Dear me," said Mrs. Wigham. "You have left *us* so far behind." She hurried toward the two women ahead at the brink of the pool, and it was thus impossible to say to whom she had addressed this last. Slipping neatly between Mira and Miss Hulme, she embarked on an explanation of the pool as a vestige of the great hydraulic systems of antiquity; waving a brisk hand, she displayed the horizon, on whose line one might just see, or imagine, the worn arches of the aqueducts, marching with ruined step toward classical Rome.

Mira gazed morosely at a stone faun that reared from the center of the pool and made a modest return of water to it on a basic principle. She inhaled ominously in her throat, so that one saw the fine, black ciliar fur of her nostrils. "Francine. Here is not yet that cab."

A white-jacketed servingman came from the house, a Maltese cat nosing between his legs. Mrs. Wigham questioned him in Italian. He spread his hands. Mrs. Wigham sighed and took out a handkerchief. Dabbing her lips with it, as if to blot them free of the hopelessly sweet jelly of Italian, she turned to Mira. "It will take a little time. Meanwhile . . . perhaps you'd like to see the house."

"Yes, may we?" said Jane, with the smoothness of the tourist who knows the rates of exchange. She wondered whether the others knew that they were being asked if they wished to wash their hands.

At that moment the cat, rubbing against Mrs. Wigham's legs, slid also against Mira's. With an electric recoil, Mira screamed and kicked it. The cat, flung several paces, humped and spat. Giuseppe, his mouth open, ran forward and picked it up in his arms.

Mrs. Wigham, immobile, used the handkerchief again to press her lips together. But it was too much for Miss Hulme, who rose telescopic in her suddenly military woollens, her hat a shako, her cheeks a murderous pink. "Really," she said, "but really this cannot be b — !" Her fist rose, the fist with the cane. Ah, thought Jane. She is. She is going to. The cane came down, an inch into the ground, missing Mira's foot by a hair.

There was a moment's silence. For Jane it was a moment of the deepest overtone, that ecstasy of the traveler who realizes that for once he is looking at what he came for. In a moment of almost alcoholic percipience she saw all the inward threads of the *mise en scène*; she saw the Reuters world of Mrs. Wigham, with a fringe of Vatican red; she saw the metro-golden shine of California knocked against the Bayswater Road; down at the bottom she saw even her own little East Coast eye.

And now, it seemed almost as if Mira were going to make apology. Her head dropped to one side, her shoulder moved circularly, as if it wished to rub against Mrs. Wigham as had the cat. "I hate them," she said. "On the plane a woman have one in a box, and it claw me from hip to thigh." She bent and peeled her skirt upward to the waist, extending the thigh as a queen might her hand at levee. "On the United Air Lines," she said.

Behind Mrs. Wigham, Giuseppe stared with interest over the head of the cat. Mrs. Wigham moved indefinably, and Giuseppe retired in haste, leaving the door open behind him. Since she had not turned her head, her manner too had its touch of the royal. "Do let us go in," she said. "Cyril and James will have got back from their walk. They will be so delighted to meet you. And perhaps you would sing for us. Your friend tells us you have a charming voice."

Mira dropped her skirt down.

"Do," said Miss Hulme, rallying, although her hat retained its outrage. She paused to right it, to make amends. "A little Purcell, perhaps. I do so love the old madrigals. Or a ballad?"

Mira swung her head suspiciously to one side. She thinks she is being chivied, thought Jane. Or like an animal that must be persuaded it has not behaved badly.

Mrs. Wigham moved the door in invitation. Through it Jane saw the room beyond, recognizing the tone of the afternoon that might have been had she and Mrs. Wigham been alone. Tables confused under books, worn couches blotted with pillows and stained with periodicals, all the familiar droppings of the intellect, in the international sitting room of the mind. From an unseen corner came the sounds of gentlemen.

Mira stirred unexpectedly. "All right, I will sing." Her head rose, in the diva's pause. "I will sing — Bhramss' Lullaby." She advanced for entry, and Mrs. Wigham and Miss Hulme moved politely aside. She bent her head. "It is not needful," she said, almost jovial, and it seemed she was awkwardly attempting a joke. "It is not needful to wait for me because I am the star." And, as mutely, they all turned to follow her in, there at last was the cab.

Mira crossed to it without ceremony, leaving their farewells to Miss Moon. "Yes, perhaps so," said Mrs. Wigham to Jane, who thought it wise to share the cab. "We must have our chat another time." As the cab door closed, she leaned across Jane, to the others. "Cyril will be *desolate* not to have met you. And I have *so* enjoyed our afternoon." And from her smile, wide as a salmon's, as the cab drove off, it appeared that he would, that she had.

They rode down through Trastevere in silence. A darkness invested the cab, as if they rode through the white, siesta-stricken streets on the black, plangent core of Mira's impatience. As they crossed the Tiber she muttered, "I like to *rest* before a date!" and Miss Moon replied, "Well, you are resting. In the cab," in that reasonable tone, half-toady, half-governess, which made Jane wonder at the exact terms of her standing by Mira in Rome. As they rounded the immense white sugar loaf of the Victor Emanuel monument, Miss Moon remarked that they were not far from where the Roman wolf was kept in its cage. Because of Romulus and Remus — of course, they knew that story? Mira shook her head, intent on twisting her ring in time to the wheels. Miss Moon told the story of Romulus and Remus. "And so, ever since," she concluded, "they keep a wolf, a female wolf, in a cage in the middle of Rome."

"What you mean a wolf!" Mira turned from the window. She stopped twisting the ring. That's what gives her such a queer intentness, thought Jane. She only does one thing at a time.

"What I said, dear. A real she-wolf, just like the one Romulus and Remus had. In a cage in the heart of Rome."

Mira grunted. "What hearts, these people! She does not give suck now, yes?"

"Well, of course not!" said Miss Moon. "It's just a symbol, dear. And they only keep one."

"Fine people!" said Mira. "What a thing!"

"Mira has the dearest little girl at home," said Miss Moon, as if to explain this tenderness on the part of one who had just kicked a cat. "The dearest little four-and-a-half-year-old girl.

Just crazy for her mummy. Just pining for her mummy to come home."

Well, no six-o'clock cab will get her *there*, thought Jane. She rubbed the stone in her pocket with a secret, appeasing touch.

Mira ignored this, bristling with some dark, libertarian sympathy that was as powerful as had been her impatience. "Crazy people!" she said. "What a thing!" When the cab drew up at the entrance of the Excelsior, she stood by unheeding while Miss Moon, over Jane's protest and with the alertness of a lady in waiting, paid the very large fare. As they stood on the steps twilight fawned upon them, tangling their lashes with yellow, and from inside the hotel they heard, like a finger drawn across the backbone, the fine tinkle of evening pursuits. Mira blinked, breathing hard. "What a thing!" she said, deep in her throat, before she turned and went inside. "What a thing, to keep a wolf in a cage!"

Left together on the steps of the gleaming entrance, Miss Moon and Jane each turned, hand held out, ready to make off. For there was nothing, each said to herself with an oblique inward glance, certainly nothing that they had in common.

"Well — " said Miss Moon.

"So pleased — " said Jane.

But it was that perilously soft hour of all great cities in the spring, when the evening rises to a sound like the tearing of silk and it is better not to be alone, to have some plan.

"Care to join me in a drink?" said Miss Moon.

"Well — perhaps just one," said Jane. I can't refuse, she told herself. I must buy her a drink, because of that fare. After that it will be time for the eight o'clock sitting at the *pensione*. And after that I can sit on the balcony, on the pretty side, the Pincio side, and write letters home. Or I can ask that nice girl at the next table to have a *granita di caffè* at Doney's. "Shall we go next door to the Flore?" she said. "Or if you'd like a walk — perhaps the Café Greco?" She was faintly proud of knowing both.

"Oh, no, let's go in here," said Miss Moon. As they entered the Excelsior her face brightened. "All California's here on spring location," she said, sotto voce, as she led Jane to a table near the door of the huge lounge, and they sat down. "And this is the bar that gets the play."

At the bar itself there was only a solitary young man, his tall legs wrapped around the bar stool, his blond, "clean-cut American" good looks bent in moody profile over his glass, his tweed back turned away from the groups settled here and there in cushioned niches, as if he uncomfortably knew none of them. It was clear that these others all knew, or knew of, each other. Not that everyone talked to everyone else. But as new people entered conversations were arrested: foursomes spoke deeply among themselves but their glances were asymmetric, and as couples rose, scattering nods, and strode from the arena, a buzz formed behind them. And to the careful watcher, there was still another unity. The women — the wives, that is, for most left hands bore a shock of light — were not all young, but they were younger. The men were beautifully textured as puddings in their minimizing pin-stripe cases, and their cheeks were flanks freshly pummeled by the steam bath, but their wives were their daughters. Opposite them the women sat narrow in luminous sheaths, their shoulders soft explosions of fur, their faces unclenching and closing, automatic as fans.

"Look! There's Sylvia Fairchild!" Miss Moon spoke out of the side of her mouth. She raised her sharp chin with a brilliant smile that faded as it was doubtfully returned. Quickly she redistributed the smile to one far corner, waved briefly to another. She took a vengeful sip of her Martini. "Believe it or not — she used to do my nails at Marshall Field's." The Martini sank farther, and she leaned back with a sigh. "Pretty soon

I'll have to go upstairs and pound that typewriter. I simply have to lock myself in."

"Oh, you're staying here?" said Jane.

"Well, no, but I have a place to work in Mira's suite. She gets in a dreadful state when there's no — when she gets bored. And I like to be where the play is, you never know." One of the chattering groups strolled by, and Miss Moon leaned brightly toward Jane, speaking very distinctly. "For instance, I was just going to do a book, when I meet Mat Zipp, of Decca. Why do a book, he says, there's more money in lyrics, and they're shorter. So I do, and it turns out I'm a natural." The group passed. She waved to the waiter for another drink. "So then," she said in a lower tone, "so then what does he do but go and die on me, in a cab on the way to work. With my stuff in his briefcase, right there in the cab."

"Oh, my," said Jane. In her childhood she had been much at the mercy of a little girl who was always wanting to play house. Now you just be old Mrs. Brown, Jane, and I'll be Elise Harper, just married, and come to tea.

"So I do a narrative, weave all the stuff together, and almost sell Dolin and Markova on the idea of a ballet." She took a sip of the second Martini. "Then they split up."

"Oh, dear," said Jane. It struck her that she was still not a very good Mrs. Brown.

Behind Miss Moon, at some distance, there was a mirror in which Jane could just see herself — rather unvarnished, tailored and small against all this princely down. Not quite plain Jane though, she told herself, and not quite yet, she thought, looking her age. At home, when she put on a bare-necked summer cotton and served gin-and-tonic to the sprightlier clique of the faculty, it was often hardly credited that she was the mother of those two enormous boys.

"So then," said Miss Moon heavily, "I'm at the Park Lane, and who do I bump into but Grofé. Get him for music and you're set for the Festival Hall, everybody says. The English are suckers for Americana."

Behind her own image in the mirror, Jane saw the bent head of the young man. He bit his lip and recrossed his legs, still staring into his drink. Alone and out of place here, she thought, like me. It would be nice to talk to him, although the idea was, of course, absurd. That was the worst of being on one's own too long in a strange country, so far from the base of affections that steadied one at home. One dried up without some personal emotion; that was all it was. One could not forever be a lens. And at certain hours of the day one found oneself lingering with anyone, as she lingered here.

"Surely you know who Grofé is," said Miss Moon.

"Oh, yes, of course," said Jane. "Philip Morris. I mean the commercial. And isn't he Vladimir Dukelsky for classical — oh, no, of course not — that's Vernon Duke." She thinks me an idiot, she thought, and I am to sit on here, waiting to hear how it was they didn't get Grofé. For from the grim, antiphonal way Miss Moon drew on her glass, it was clear that they hadn't.

"So then," said Miss Moon, but she interrupted herself to twinkle a hand at someone who passed, to murmur an indistinct name.

I'll grab the check and go now, thought Jane. For it was no longer funny to watch Miss Moon. It was like seeing those women who hovered secretly at other women's dressing tables, to spray themselves avidly and cheaply with another person's scent.

I'll take the check and go now. She glanced at her watch. It was seven, that hour here when even the windows of *pensione* bedrooms were violet frames that turned one inside to say Look! to the empty room, to lie face downward, ears stopped against the bell-shake of evening, and say Listen! to the vacant bed. The hour when an experienced traveler knows better than to corner himself there. The hour when the lens turns upon oneself.

"And . . . so then?" said Jane.

But Miss Moon was looking elsewhere again, and this time with such a different, such an unrehearsed expression that Jane looked around too. It was Mira, standing at the entrance. Groomed now for people of importance, she had made herself, as women did, to be as like them as possible. Her dress was luminous too, cut with pale cleverness to conceal where it could no longer insist, and she stood encircled in a huge riband of fur. She looked sleeker and, in a powdery way, older. Perhaps she had seen this in some mirror before leaving, for now she reached up uncertainly and rumpled her tamed hair, as if to declare the girl she had been against the woman she was. She walked forward with a mannequin's glide, her smile full for the room, then turned her back to it and, with an eager, a crescent leaning, slipped her hand through the arm of the young man at the bar.

He looked up, then stood up, and on his face, handsomer even than in profile, one saw the snow marks of the goggles on the brown skin. But where the white circles on Mira's face were fretted like rose windows, his were still smooth. He was about thirty, that age when, with Americans, one often glimpses the young man looking through the palings of the man, and in his look, lightened with relief but somehow hangdog, one caught this now. As he and Mira left the bar, Mira saw the two women, Jane and Miss Moon. For the first time she really saw them. She looked directly into their eyes and she smiled. Then she and the young man passed by them, walking slowly down the long room, and although Mira, nodding here and there with narrowed eyes, clung softly and proudly to the crook of his arm, it seemed almost that he was paraded on hers. A buzz formed behind them.

"She's a fool." Miss Moon breathed this to herself. Behind

her glasses her eyes were bright and fixed. "It'll be all over the Coast in twenty-four hours."

Now the couple neared them again, in their return passage down the room. The young man's face was warm. Mira was still faintly smiling, and although this time the smile, fixed on the door, was for neither of the two women, to Jane, trembling suddenly in her tailored suit with a shock that was bitter and sororal, it came as if it was. Almost a grimace, it showed its teeth to an invisible mirror, denying with the lips the secret lines that a body must gather — the crow's feet of the armpit, the dented apple of the belly, the mapped crease, fine leather too long folded, that forms between the breasts. As Mira passed her on the arm of the young man, her scent remained for a moment behind. It rested on Jane as if it were her own.

At the door, Mira and the young man paused. A rush of lilac came to them from the outside, and Mira's fur slid from shoulder to waist, a dropped calyx. The young man replaced it carefully. Her lips parted, watching him. It was a beautiful fur, manipulable as smoke. Before the arts of the furrier had dappled it, it might have been just the color of wolf.

Left together by the flicking of the door, the two women stared at one another.

"Traveling alone?" said Miss Moon.

Jane nodded.

"Divorced too?"

"No," said Jane. "I'm a widow." Her head lifted. "I have two boys."

Miss Moon seemed not to have heard this last. "Care to — join forces for dinner?"

No, thought Jane. Don't settle for anybody's company. As she does. As she has. Not yet. She gazed past Miss Moon, saw herself in the mirror, and looked quickly away. "Thanks," she said, and her voice was kind. "I'm afraid . . . I have work to do too."

"Oh, you work," said Miss Moon eagerly. "What do *you* do?"

"I teach," said Jane. "In a university." I teach, an echo said inside her, and of course at home I have the two boys. And suddenly the echo, her breath, something, rammed itself hard against her chest, inside. Not enough, it said, beating behind the mapped crease between her breasts. Not enough. What a thing, it said, crying. What a thing!

"Well, back to the salt mines for us, eh?" said Miss Moon. Her voice was matey, unbearable. Just as if she too had smelled the scent, had heard the thing crying. As if she knew too that Jane, staring into the big, winged glasses, could see the two poor eyes beating against the glass.

And now they stood up quickly, gathered their purses and signaled for the waiter. When he came, they paid him with a dispatch unusual to women, and the lire notes left lying in his saucer were large enough for anybody here. For now they could not part quickly enough. For now, each said to herself, the other's company was no longer to be borne. No, it was not to be borne. Not now. Now that they both knew what it was they had in common.

# The Hollow Boy

WHEN I was in high school, my best friend for almost a year was another boy of about the same age by the name of Werner Hauser, who disappeared from his home one night and never came back. I am reminded of him indirectly sometimes, in a place like Luchow's or Cavanagh's or Hans Jaeger's, when I am waited on by one of those rachitic-looking German waiters with narrow features, faded hair, and bad teeth, who serve one with an omniscience verging on contempt. Then I wonder whether Mr. Hauser, Werner's father, ever got his own restaurant. I am never reminded directly of Werner by anybody, because I haven't the slightest idea what he may have become, wherever he is. As for Mrs. Hauser, Werner's mother — she was in a class by herself. I've never met anybody at all like her, and I don't expect to.

Although Werner and I went to the same high school, like all the boys in the neighborhood except the dummies who had to go to trade school or the smart alecks who were picked for Townsend Harris, we were really friends because both our families had back apartments in the same house on Hamilton Terrace, a street which angled up a hill off Broadway and had nothing else very terrace-like about it, except that its five-story tan apartment buildings had no store fronts on the ground floors. Nowadays that part of Washington Heights is almost all Puerto Rican, but in those days nobody in particular lived around there. My parents had moved there supposedly because it was a little nearer to their jobs in the Seventh Avenue garment district than the Bronx had been — my father worked in the fur district on Twenty-eighth Street, and my mother still got work as a finisher when the season was on — but actually they had come on the insistence of my Aunt Luba, who lived nearby — a sister of my mother's, of whom she was exceptionally fond and could not go a day without seeing.

When Luba talked about the Heights being higher-class than the Bronx, my parents got very annoyed. Like a lot of the garment workers of that day they were members of the Socialist Labor Party, although they no longer worked very hard at it. Occasionally, still, of an evening, after my father had gotten all worked up playing the violin with two or three of his cronies in the chamber music sessions that he loved, there would be a vibrant discussion over the cold cuts, with my mother, flushed and gay, putting in a sharp retort now and then as she handed round the wine; then too my older sister had been named after Ibsen's Nora — which sounded pretty damn funny with a name like Rosenbloom — and of course nobody in the family ever went to a synagogue. That's about all their radicalism had amounted to. My younger sister was named Carol.

The Hausers had been in the building for a month when we moved in on the regular moving day, October first; later a neighbor told my mother that they had gotten September rent-free as a month's concession on a year's lease — a practice which only became common in the next few years of the depression, and, as I heard my mother say, a neater trick than the Rosenblooms would ever think of. Shortly after they came, a sign was put up to the left of the house entrance — Mrs. Hauser had argued down the landlord on this too. The sign said *Erna Hauser. Weddings. Receptions. Parties*, and maybe the landlord was mollified after he saw it. It was black enamel and gold leaf under glass, and about twice the size of the dentist's. When I got to know Werner, at the time of those first frank questions with which boys place one another, he told me that ever since he and his mother had been sent for to come from Germany five years before, the family had been living in Yorkville in a furnished "housekeeping" room slightly larger than the one Mr. Hauser had occupied during the eight years he had been in the United States alone. Now Mrs. Hauser would have her own kitchen and a place to receive her clientele, mostly ladies from the well-to-do Jewish families of the upper West Side, for whom she had hitherto "helped out" at parties and dinners in their homes. From now on she would no longer "help out" — she would cater.

Most of what I learned about Werner, though, I didn't learn from Werner. He would answer a question readily enough, but very precisely, very much within the limits of the question, and no overtones thrown in. I guess I learned about him because he was my friend, by sucking it out of the air the way kids do, during the times I was in his house before he was forbidden to hang around with me, and during the dozens of times before and after, when he sneaked up to our place. He was at our place as often as he could get away.

Up there, a casual visitor might have taken him for one of the family, since he was blond and short-featured, like my mother and me. He was a head taller than me, though, with a good build on him that was surprising if you had already seen his father's sunken, nutcracker face and bent-kneed waiter's shuffle. It wasn't that he had the special quiet of the very stupid or the very smart, or that he had any language difficulty; he spoke English as well as I did and got mostly nineties at school, where he made no bones about plugging hard and was held up as an example because he had only been in the country five years. It was just that he had almost no informal conversation. Because of this I never felt very close to him, even when we talked sex or smoked on the sly, and sometimes I had an uneasy feeling because I couldn't tell whether he was stupid or smart. I suppose we were friends mostly out of convenience, the way boys in a neighborhood are. Our apartments partly faced each other at opposite sides of the small circular rear court of the building; by opening his bedroom window and our dining-room window we could shout to each other to come over, or to meet out in front. I could, that is, although my mother used to grumble about acting up like riffraff. He was not allowed to; once, even before the edict, I saw the window shut down hard on his shoulders by someone from behind. After the edict we used to raise the windows very slightly and whistle. Even then, I never felt really close to him until the day after he was gone.

Saturday mornings, when I was that age, seemed to have a special glow; surely there must have been rainy ones, but I remember them all in a powerful golden light, spattered with the gabble of the vegetable men as they sparred with women at the open stalls outside their stores, and ringing with the loud, pre-Sunday clang of the ash cans as the garbage collectors hoisted them into the trucks and the trucks moved on in a warm smell of settling ash. It was a Saturday morning when I first went up to the Hausers', to see if Werner could get off to take the Dyckman Ferry with me for a hike along the Palisades. I already knew that he helped his mother with deliveries evenings and afternoons after school, but I had not yet learned how prescribed all his hours were. The hall door of the Hauser apartment was open a crack; through it came a yeasty current as strong as a bakery's. I flicked the bell.

"Come," said a firm, nasal voice. Or perhaps the word was "*Komm.*" I was never to hear Mrs. Hauser speak English except once, when Werner and I, who had not heard her come in, walked through the parlor where she was dealing with a lady who had come about a daughter's wedding. That was the occasion at which I saw her smile — at the lady — a fixed grimace which dusted lightly over the neat surface of her face like the powdered sugar she shook over her coffee cakes.

I walked in, almost directly into the kitchen. It was very like ours, small and badly lighted, but it had two stoves. Rows of copper molds and pans of all shapes hung on the walls. One graduated row was all of *Bund* pans, like one my mother had, but it was the first time I had seen utensils of copper, or seen them hung on walls. Supplies, everything was in rows; nothing wandered or went askew in that kitchen; even its choke-sweet odor had no domestic vagary about it, but clamped the room in a hot, professional pall. Werner and his mother, bent over opposite ends of a cloth-covered table, were carefully stretching at a large plaque of strudel dough which almost covered its surface. Both of them glanced up briefly and bent their heads again; the making of strudel is the most intense and delicate of operations, in which the last stretching of the dough, already rolled and pulled to tissue thinness, is done on the backs of the hands, and balances on an instinctive, feathery tension. I held my breath and watched. Luba and my mother made strudel about once a year, in an atmosphere of confused merriment and operatic anguish when the dough broke. As I watched, red crept up on Werner's face.

Almost opposite me, Mrs. Hauser bent and rose, angularly deft, but without grace. I had expected some meaty-armed *Hausfrau* trundling an ample bosom smeared with flour; here was the virginal silhouette of a governess, black and busked — a dressmaker's form collared in lace. From the side, her face had a thin economy, a handsomeness that had meagered and was further strained by the sparse hair spicked back in a pale bun.

Suddenly she straightened. The paste had reached the edges of the cloth; in a few whisked motions it was dabbed with butter, filled, rolled, cut, and done. She brushed her hands together, blew on the spotless front of her dress, and faced me.

She was not handsome at all. Her nose, blunt-ended, came out too far to meet one, her eyes protruded slightly with a lashless, committed stare, and the coinshaped mouth was too near the nose. She wore no make-up, and her face had the triumphant neatness of the woman who does not; next to it Luba's and my mother's would have looked vital, but messy. Her skin was too bloodless though, and her lips and the nails of her floured hands were tinged with lavender, almost stone-colored, as if she suffered from some attenuation of the heart.

Werner mumbled out my first name, and I mumbled back my errand.

Mrs. Hauser, holding her hands lightly in front of her, still gave me her stare, but it was to Werner that she spoke at last.

"*Sag ihm nein,*" she said, and turning on her heel, she left the room, still holding away from her dress the hands with the stone-colored nails.

After that, I knew enough not to go to Werner's unless he asked me to, usually on evenings when his father was on night duty in the restaurant where he worked, and Mrs. Hauser had an engagement, or on Sundays, when she had an especially fancy wedding and Mr. Hauser, dressed in his waiter's garb, went along to help her serve. I never got used to the way their apartment looked, compared with the way it smelled. When there was no cooking going on, and the hot fumes had a chance to separate and wander, then it was filled, furnished with enticing suggestions of cinnamon, vanilla, and anise, and the wonderful, warm caraway scent of little pastries stuffed with hot forcemeat — a specialty of Mrs. Hauser's, of which her customers could never get enough. Standing outside the door, I used to think it smelled the way the house in *Hansel and Gretel* looked, in the opera to which my parents had taken me years before — a house from whose cornices and lintels one might break off a piece and find one's mouth full of marzipan, an aerie promising happy troupes of children feasting within, in a blissful forever of maraschino and Nesselrode.

Actually, the four dim rooms, curtainless except for the blinds which the landlord supplied — one yellow, one dark green to a window — had an almost incredible lack of traces of personal occupancy, even after one knew that the Hausers never thought of the place as anything but temporary. It was furnished with a bleak minimum of tables and chairs like those in hired halls. Mrs. Hauser had procured everything from a restaurant supply house, all except the beds, which were little more than cots, and wore hard white cotton spreads of the kind seen in hotels. Here, in the bedrooms, some of the second-hand surfaces were protected with doilies, on which a few European family photographs had been placed. Years later, when I was staying in the luxurious house of a family which had managed to keep on its servants in the old-fashioned way, stumbling inadvertently into the servants' wing, one morning, I came upon a room that reminded me instantly of the Hausers', although even its dresser had a homely clutter of tawdry jewelry, dime-store boxes, and letters.

Even so, when Werner and I hung around awhile in his room, we never sat on the drill-neat bed. Usually we sat on the floor and leaned back against the bed. Except for the times we did our homework together, we either just talked or exchanged the contents of our pockets, for it was the kind of house in which there was simply nothing to do. Once or twice we smoked cigarettes there, carefully airing the room and chewing soda-mints afterward. I supplied both the cigarettes and the soda-mints, since it was an understood thing that Werner never had any money of his own; the considerable work he did for his mother was "for the business." The rows of cakes, frilled cookies, and tiny *quenelles* that we sometimes passed, going through the kitchen, were for the business too. I never got anything to eat there.

Usually, after we had been there a short while, Werner, wriggling his shoulders sheepishly, would say, "Let's go up to your place," or I would invite him up. I knew why Werner liked to be there, of course, why he could not keep from coming even after Mrs. Hauser had forbidden it. It may sound naïve to say so in this day and age, but we were an awfully happy family. We really were. And I never realized it more strongly than during the times I used to watch Werner Hauser up there.

I guess the best way I can explain the kind of family we were is to say that, although I was the only nonmusical one in a family that practically lived for music, I never felt criticized or left out. My father, although he tired quickly because of a shoulder broken when he was a boy and never properly healed, was the best musician, with faultless pitch and a concert-meister's memory for repertoire. Nora played the cello with a beautiful tone, although she wouldn't work for accuracy, and Carol could already play several wind instruments; it was a sight to watch that stringy kid of ten pursing her lips and worrying prissily about her "embouchure." Both Luba and my mother had had excellent training in piano, and sang even better than they played, although Luba would never concede to my father that she occasionally flatted. My mother, contrarily, tended to sing sharp, which so fitted her mock-acid ways that my father made endless plays on words about it. "Someday," he would add, striking his forehead with his fist, "I am going to find a woman who sings exactly in the middle; then I will steal the company's payroll, and take her to live at The Breakers in Atlantic City!"

"*Mir nix, dir nix,*" my mother would answer. "And what kind of music would be at The Breakers?"

"A string quartet," Luba would shout, "with a visiting accordion for the weekends!" Then the three of them would pound each other in laughter over the latest "visiting accordion" who had been to our house. All kinds of people were attracted to our house, many of whom had no conception of the professional quality of the music they heard there, and were forever introducing a protégé whom they had touted beforehand. Whenever these turned out to be violinists who had never heard of the Beethoven Quartets, or pianists who had progressed as far as a bravura rendition of the "Revolutionary Etude," our secret name for them was "a visiting accordion." Not even Carol was ever rude to any of these though; the musical part of the evening simply ended rather earlier than usual, and dissolved into that welter of sociable eating and talking which we all loved. When I say I wasn't musical, I don't mean I didn't know music or love it — no one in that family could help it — I could reproduce it and identify it quite accurately in my head, but I just couldn't make it with my hands or my voice. It had long ago been settled upon that I was the historian, the listener, the critic. "Ask Mr. Huneker here," my father would say, pointing to me with a smile (or Mr. Gilman, or Mrs. Downes, according to whatever commentator he had been reading). Sometimes, when in reading new music the group achieved a dissonance that harrowed him, he would turn on me: "We should all be like this one — Paganini today — Hoffman tomorrow — and all safe upstairs in the head." But the teasing took me in; it never left me out. That's what happened to Werner at our house. They took him in too.

We had our bad times of course. Often my father's suppertime accounts of his day on Seventh Avenue, usually reported with a deft, comedian's touch, turned to bitter invective, or were not forthcoming at all. Then we knew that the mood in which he regretted a life spent among values he despised had stolen over him, or else the money question was coming up again, and we ate in silence. Luba and my mother quarreled with the violence of people who differ and cannot live without one another; their cleavages and reunions followed a regular pattern, each stage of which pervaded the house as recognizably as what was simmering on the stove. My sister Nora, eighteen and beautiful, was having trouble with both these contingencies; each month, just before her periods, she filled the house with a richly alternating brooding and hysteria that set us all to slamming doors and leaving the house. A saint couldn't have lived with it. And Carol and I bickered, and had our pint-size troubles too.

I can see how we must have seemed to Werner though. No matter what was going on, our house had a kind of ruddiness and satisfaction about it. Partly its attraction was because there *was* always something going on. If anyone had asked me about the state of my innards in regard to my family, I guess I would have said that I felt full. Not full of life, or happiness, or riches, or any of those tiddly phrases. Just chock full. I would have said this, most likely, because, as I watched Werner hanging, reticent but dogged, to the edge of our family, watched him being stuffed by my mother, twitted by my father, saw him almost court being ignored by Nora and annoyed by Carol, I had the awful but persistent fancy that he must be absolutely hollow inside. Literally hollow, I mean. I could see them, his insides — as bleak as the apartment where his parents were either oppressively absent or oppressively around, and scattered with a few rag-tag doilies of feeling that had almost no reason to be there. There would be nothing inside him to make a feeling out of, unless it were the strong, tidal perfume of the goodies that were meant for the business.

One evening at the beginning of that summer, Werner was with us when my father scooped us all up and took us to the concert at the Stadium, only a few minutes' walk from home. We went often to those concerts, although, as everyone knows, open-air music can rarely have the finish of the concert hall. But there is something infinitely arresting, almost pathetic, in music heard in the open air. It is not only the sight of thousands of ordinary faces, tranced and quiet in a celebration of the unreal. It is because the music, even while it is clogged and drowned now and then by the rusty noises of the world outside the wall, is not contaminated by them; even while it states that beauty and the world are irreconcilable, it persists in a frail suggestion that the beauty abides.

Werner, at his first concert, sat straight-backed on one of the straw mats my father had rented for us, taking in the fragments of talk milling around us, with the alertness of a person at a dinner who watches how his neighbor selects his silver. During the first half, when an ambulance siren, combined with the grinding of the trolleys on Amsterdam Avenue, clouded over a pianissimo, he winced carefully, like some of those around him. But during the second half, which ended with the Beethoven Fifth, when a dirigible stealing overhead drew a thousand faces cupped upward, Werner, staring straight ahead with a sleepy, drained look, did not join them.

As we all walked down the hill afterward, Carol began whistling the Andante. As she came to that wonderful breakthrough in the sixteenth measure, Werner took it up in a low, hesitant, but pure whistle, and completed it. Carol stopped whistling, her mouth open, and my father turned his head. No one said anything though, and we kept on walking down the hill. Suddenly Werner whistled again, the repetition of that theme, twenty-three bars from the end, when, instead of descending to the A flat, it rises at last to the G.

My father stopped in his tracks. "You play, Werner?"

Werner shook his head.

"Somebody plays at your house?"

"*Nein*," said Werner. I don't think he realized that he had said it in German.

"How is it you know music?"

Werner rubbed his hand across his eyes. When he spoke, he sounded as if he were translating. "I did not know that I know it," he said.

In the next few weeks Werner came with us almost every time we went. I didn't know where he got the money, but he paid his own way. Once, when he hadn't come to go with us, we met him afterward, loitering at the exit we usually took, and he joined us on the walk home. I think he must have been listening from outside the Stadium wall.

He always listened with a ravenous lack of preference. Once he turned to me at the intermission and said with awe, "I could hear them both together. The themes. At the *same* time." When I spoke sophomorically of what I didn't like, he used to look at me with pity, although at the end of a concert which closed with the "Venusberg," he turned to me, bewildered, and said. "It *is* possible not to like it." I laughed, but I did feel pretty comfortable with him just then. I always hated those triangles in the "Venusberg."

Then, one time, he did not come around for over a week, and when I saw him in the street he was definitely avoiding me. I thought of asking why he was sore at me, but then I thought: The hell with it. Anyway, that Sunday morning, as my father and I started out for a walk on Riverside Drive, we met Werner and his mother in the elevator. Mrs. Hauser carried some packages and Werner had two large cartons which he had rested on the floor. It was a tight squeeze, but the two of us got in, and after the door closed my father succeeded in raising his hat to Mrs. Hauser, but got no acknowledgment. My father replaced his hat on his fan-shaped wedge of salt-and-pepper hair. He chewed his lips back and forth thoughtfully under his large, mournful nose, but said nothing. When the door opened, we had to get out first. They passed ahead of us quickly, but not before we heard what Mrs. Hauser muttered to Werner. *"Was hab' ich gesagt?"* she said. *"Sie sind Juden!"*

Anybody who knows Yiddish can understand quite a lot of German too. My father and I walked a long way that day, not on the upper Drive, where the Sunday strollers were, but on those little paths, punctuated with iron street lamps but with a weak hint of country lane about them, where the city petered out into the river. We walked along, not saying much of anything, all the way up to the lighthouse at Inspiration Point. Then we climbed the hill to Broadway, where my father stopped to buy some cold cuts and a cheese cake, and took the subway home. Once, when my father was paying my fare, he let his hand rest on my shoulder before he waved me ahead of him through the turnstile, and once he caught himself whistling something, looked at me quickly, and closed his mouth. I didn't have a chance to recognize what he whistled.

We were at the table eating when the doorbell rang. Carol ran to answer it; she was the kind of kid who was always darting to answer the phone or the door, although it was almost never for her. She came back to the table and flounced into her seat.

"It's Werner. We wants to see you. He won't come in."

I went to the door. He wasn't lounging against the door frame, the way he usually did. He was standing a couple of paces away from it.

"Please come for a walk," he said. He was looking at his shoes.

"Gee, whyn't you come in?" I said. "I'm dead."

"Please," he said, "I want you please to come for a walk."

I was practically finished eating anyway. I went back to the table, grabbed up a hard roll and some pastrami, and followed him downstairs.

Summer in the city affects me the same way as open air music. I guess it's because both of them have such a hard time. Even when the evening breeze smells of nothing but hot brick, you get the feeling that people are carrying around leaves in their hearts. Werner and I walked down to our usual spot on the river, to a low stone wall, which we jumped, over to a little collection of bushes and some grass, on the other side. It was an open enough spot, but it reacted on us more or less like a private cave; we never said much of anything till we got there. This time it was up to Werner to speak. I had the sandwich, so I finished that.

The electric signs across the river on the Jersey side were already busy. Werner's face was turned parallel with the river, so that it looked as if the sign that gave the time signal were paying out its letters right out of his mouth. THE TIME IS NOW . . . 8:01 . . . Ordinarily I would have called his attention to this effect and changed seats with him so he could see it happen to me, but I didn't. The sign jazzed out something about salad oil, and then paid out another minute.

Werner turned his head. "You heard . . . this morning in the elevator?"

I nodded.

"Your father heard too?"

I nodded again.

He pressed his knuckles against his teeth. His words came through them with a chewed sound. "It is because they are servants," he said.

"Who do you mean?"

"My father and mother."

"You mean . . . they don't like Jews because they have to work for them sometimes?"

"Maybe," said Werner, "but it is not what I mean."

"It's no disgrace, what anybody works at, over here." I wasn't sure I believed this, but it was what one was told. "Besides, they have the business."

Werner turned his back on me, his shoulders humped

up against the Palisades. "Inside them, they are servants."

He turned back to face me, the words tumbling out with the torn confiding of the closemouthed. "They do not care about the *quality* of anything." His voice lingered on the word. He jerked his head at the Mazola sign. "Butter maybe, instead of lard. But only because it is good for the business."

"Everybody has something wrong with his family," I muttered.

Werner folded his arms almost triumphantly and looked at me. "But we are not a family," he said.

I got up and walked around the little grass plot. The way he had spoken the word *quality* stayed with me; it popped into my mind the time in spring when he and I had been sitting near the same old stone wall and two scarlet tanagers lit on it and strutted for a minute against the blue. You aren't supposed to see tanagers in New York City. Sooner or later, though, you'll see almost everything in New York. You'll have almost every lousy kind of feeling too.

The river had a dark shine to it now. It smelled like a packinghouse for fish, but it looked like the melted, dark eyes of a million girls.

"I wish we were going up to the country this year," I said. "I'd like to be there right now."

"I hate the country!" Werner said. "That's where they're going to have the restaurant. They have almost enough money now."

Then it all came out — in a rush. "Come on back," he said. "They're out. I want to show you something."

All the way up the hill he talked: how his mother had worked as a housekeeper for a rich merchant after his father had left for America; how he had always been the child in the basement, allowed to play neither with the town children nor the merchant's; how his mother would not agree to come over until his father had saved a certain sum, and then required that it be sent to her in dollars before she would sail. Then, in Yorkville, where they had only taken a larger room because the landlady insisted, they used to walk the garish streets sometimes, listening to the din from the cafés — "*Ist das nicht ein . . . ? Ja, das ist ein . . .*" — but never going in for a snack or a glass of beer. "We breathed quiet," I remember him saying, "so we would not have to use up too much air."

And always, everything was for the restaurant. At Christmastime and birthdays they did not give each other presents, but bought copper pans, cutlery, equipment for the restaurant. They had their eye on an actual place, on a side road not too far from some of the fancy towns in Jersey; it was owned by a man whose wife was a cousin of Mrs. Hauser's. It already had a clientele of connoisseurs who came to eat slowly, to wait reverently in a waft of roasting coffee, for the *Perlhuhn* and the *Kaiser-Schmarren*. The cousins were smart — they knew that Americans would pay the best for the best, and even wait a little long for it, in order to be thought European. But they had let the place get seedy; they did not have enough discipline for the long, sluggish day before the customers arrived, and they had not learned that while the Americans might wait out of snobbishness, they would not do so because the owners were getting drunk in the kitchen. The Hausers would be smarter still. They would serve everything of the best, at a suitably stately pace for such quality, and they would not get drunk in the kitchen.

He stopped talking when we got to his door. The whole time, he hadn't raised his voice, but had talked on and on in a voice like shavings being rubbed together.

His room was dark and full of the cloying smell. He stood in front of the window, not turning the light on, and I saw that he was looking over at our place. I saw how it looked to him.

That was the summer radios first really came in. Almost

everyone had one now. We hadn't got one yet, but one of Nora's boy friends had given her a small table model. There were a couple of them playing now at cross purposes, from different places on the court.

"Thursday nights they are broadcasting the concerts, did you know?" he said softly. "Sometimes someone tunes in on it, and I can hear, if I keep the window open. The echoes are bad . . . and all the other noises. Sometimes, of course, no one tunes it in."

I wondered what he had to show me, and why he did not turn on the light.

"Today was my birthday," he said. "I asked them for a radio, but of course I did not expect it. I am to get working papers. When they leave, I am to leave the high school."

He walked away from the window and turned on the light. The objects on the bed sprang into sharp black and white: the tie disposed on the starched shirt, which lay neatly between the black jacket and pants. That's what it was. It was a waiter's suit.

"Of course I did not expect it," he said. "I did not."

It was after this that Werner, when he whistled across the court, started using themes from here and there. Sometimes it was that last little mocking bit from *Till Eulenspiegel* when Till's feet kick, sometimes it was the Ho-yo-to-ho from *Valkyrie*, sometimes the horns from the "Waltz of the Flowers." It was always something we had heard at the Stadium, something we had heard together. When my father, to whom I had blabbed most of that evening with Werner, heard the whistle, his face would sometimes change red, as if he were holding his breath in anger against someone; then this would be displaced by the sunk, beaten look he sometimes brought home from Seventh Avenue, and he would shrug and turn away. He never said anything to Werner or to me.

The last night, the night it must have happened, was a Thursday a few weeks later. It was one of those humid nights when the rain just will not come, and even the hair on your head seems too much to carry around with you. We were all sitting in the dining room, brushing limply now and then at our foreheads. Nora was in one of her moods — the boy who had given her the radio had not phoned. She had it turned on and sat glowering in front of it, as if she might evoke him from it.

My father was standing at the window, looking up at the sky. The court had its usual noises, children crying, a couple of other radios, and the rumble from the streets. Once or twice some kid catcalled from a higher floor, and a light bulb exploded on the alley below.

My father leaned forward suddenly, and looked across the court, watching intently. Then he walked slowly over to the radio, stood in front of it a moment, and turned it on loud. We all looked at him in surprise. He didn't think much of the thing, and never monkeyed with it.

I looked across the court at Werner's window. I couldn't see into its shadows, but it was open. I thought of the look on his face when he met us outside the Stadium walls and of his voice saying, "Sometimes no one tunes it in." I would have whistled to him, but I couldn't have been heard over the music — *Scheherazade,* it was — which was sweeping out loud and strong into the uneasy air.

My mother whispered a reproach to my father, then took a side look at his face, and subsided. I glanced around at Carol, Nora, all of us sitting there joined together, and for some reason or other I felt sick. It's the weather, I thought, and wiped my forehead.

Then, in the square across the court, the blackness merged and moved. The window began to grind down. And then we heard Werner's voice, high and desperate, louder even than the

plashing waves of the Princess's story — a long, loud wail.
"No! Please! Scheherazade is speaking!"

Then there were two figures at the window, and the window
was flung up again. My mother clapped her hand against her
face, ran over to the radio and turned it down low, and stood
bent over with her back against it, her fist to her mouth. So it
was that we heard Werner again, his words squeezed out,
hoarse, but clear. *"Bitte, Mutter. Lass mich hören. Scheherazade spricht."*

Then the window came down.

The next evening the house was like a hive with what had
happened. The Hausers had gone to the police. There had been
one really personal thing in their house after all, and Werner
had taken it with him. He had taken the whole of the cache
in the wall safe, the whole two thousand dollars for the
restaurant.

The detectives came around to question me — two pleasant
enough Dutch uncles who had some idea that Werner might
have made a pact with me, or that I could give them some
clues as to what had been going on inside him. I couldn't tell
them much of use. I wasn't going to tell them to look over at
the Stadium, either outside or in, although for years afterward
I myself used to scan the crowds there. And I wasn't fool
enough to try to explain to them what I had hardly figured out
yet myself — that nature abhors the vacuums men shape, and
sooner or later pushes the hollow in.

Mr. and Mrs. Hauser stayed on, and as far as anyone could
tell, kept on with their usual routine. They were still there
when we moved — Luba had decided the air was better in
Hollis, Queens. During the months while we were still at
Hamilton Terrace though, my father acquired an odd habit.
If he happened to pass the open dining room window when
our large new radio was playing, he was likely to pause there,

and look out across the court. Sometimes he shut the sash down hard, and sometimes he let it be, but he always stood there for a time. I never decided whether the look on his face was guilty or proud. I knew well enough why he stood there though. For it was from our house that the music had come. It was from our window that Scheherazade spoke.

# Mrs. Fay Dines on Zebra

ARIETTA MINOT FAY, at thirty-seven, still lived in the house in which she, her father and all their known male forebears but the first had been born, a white, Hudson River-bracketed house, much winged and gabled but with a Revolutionary cottage at its core, set in a tiny village, once only a road, on the west shore of the Hudson River, about twenty-five miles from New York. Arietta's first forebear, Yves Minot, had come to the States in the entourage of Lafayette (some said as a body-servant, although this had never been proved) and had managed to stay near the general's person throughout all the general's campaigns except Valley Forge. In 1779, when the general had gone back briefly to France, Yves had stayed behind, first to marry one of the local Dutch girls (receiving the cottage and a large parcel of land as her dowry) and later to leave her at home while he ventured into battle or other forays, whenever he was so minded. In 1824, when Lafayette returned to America for a final visit, Yves was still there, flourishing in all but sons (because of land inheritance, the Minot line usually ran carefully to one) and had accompanied the general on his famous triumphal tour, again in some capacity typical of the Minots, something unidentifiable, profitable and without a doubt enjoyable.

Arietta, if asked to hazard a guess as to what this might have been, usually replied, with the family talent for presenting itself accurately, that Yves's function probably had something to do with a cap and bells. For, all the Minots took for granted what they had been, were, and hoped to go on being. They were jesters, *fonctionnaires* attending the private person only, quarter-masters supplying the ego, minor affections and spirits of those who were rich enough to keep living standards equal to their own *bon viveur* tastes, had the intelligence to relish the thrusts of which they were wisely capable, and above all were important enough to enable the Minots to admire them. This was the Minot vanity and their backbone through the years: that managing always to attach themselves to the most honorable patrons, they had meanwhile restricted their own knavish tricks to the surface diablerie required of their profession — that is, to entertainment only. Beneath the skin they were not knaves, beyond a certain French clarity as to the main chance, which in turn had instructed them that a supernormal honesty, shrewdly displayed, was invaluable to him who lived on perquisites.

For no Minot had ever had a salary, or had gone, as the phrase is, "to work." Every male Minot had attended a university as a matter of course, to be refined for his trade, and occasionally to pick up there some symbiotic relationship that had lasted him for life. Arietta's father, of the first generation to have no sons, had done his best by sending her to Vassar, where three members of the Rensselaer (an old dining-club of which he was secretary) had sent their girls that same year — the three men representing respectively money with family, money with politics, and — since the Minots had had to lower their standards along with the rest of the world, though belatedly — money with money. For until her father's time — and he, poor man, was in no way responsible for the monstrous change in the world — all had gone marvelously well with the Minots in both comfort and reputation. And deservedly, for all had worked hard. Although their perquisites had often been extraordinarily vague, ranging from small properties given them to manage and subsequently inherited either in part or in toto, from careers as retainers (they retained so gracefully) or as incumbents of benefices that never had to be explained to them or by them, all the way down to the latter-day vulgarities of stockmarket tips — no Minot had ever boondoggled at the earning of what he received. Until well past the First World War, one could imagine two important men murmuring of a third, as in another context they might mention that his chef was the great-nephew of Brillat-Savarin — "Lucky man, he has a Minot."

Even in the non-Venetian world of post-'29, the world that had begun to be so hard on those useful types for which there never seemed to be any but foreign names: the *cavalière servante*, the *fidus Achates*, the *condottiere*, the . . . Minot — the family had still managed, amiably using its talents where there was still scope for them, but for the first time dangerously using its resources when there was not. Over a hundred years in this country had weakened their French pith, making them less antipathetic than they should have been to eating their capital and selling their land. Marrying by inclination had been an even earlier symptom to appear, but here perhaps they had been lucky, for like so many reared nobly, their inclinations had always been a little bit coarse — and this had kept the line remarkably healthy. This meant that Arietta, when she came on the market, did so from a long line of non-idiots, non-hemophili-acs with a minimum life-expectancy of eighty. It also meant that, with one thing and another, she hadn't much expectancy of anything else except the uses to which she might put her share of Minot temperament — that merriment spiked with truth-telling, suppleness just short of servility, and love of ease combined with a wonderfully circuitous energy for pursuing it. Like so many of her ancestors, Arietta was willing to burn any number of ergs in the process, as long as neither dishonor nor the usual channels of attainment were involved.

On this particular summer Saturday evening at about seven o'clock, Arietta, dressed to go out in her one still respectable cocktail dress, sat in the dimming upstairs parlor of the house that had been hers since the death a year ago, within a few months of each other, of her father and her husband, and gazed out on the river, musing, moodily for her, on the narrow area of play offered that temperament by the modern world. Saturday was shopping day for the week, and that morning, hold back as she might on things like paper napkins — they would use the linen ones — she had not been able to avoid spending eighteen dollars on food. Her nine-year-old son Roger, away for the night at a friends house, would consume that almost unaided during the school week. One of the sweet-voiced robot-ladies from the telephone company had phoned twice during the past few days, and even the Light & Power, usually so kindly, had begun to press her about last winter's heating bill. This week, to the bewilderment of her friends, she had taken to answering the phone in French, ready to aver that "Madame" was away. There had been no cleaning-woman for a year. Behind her, the rooms, receding wing on wing into the hillside with the depressed elegance of a miniature château, showed, besides the distinguished stainings of a hundred and fifty years, the thin, gradual grime of amateur care. The house, free and clear for a century until the thirties, was hers thanks to her father's single quirk of hereditary thrift, hidden from them until the otherwise worthless will was read — mortgage insurance. It was worth about twenty thousand dollars, possibly a little more to one of that new race of antiquarians who had debouched upon these hills aching to "restore" some old place electrically, and able to — viz. the Lampeys, where she was going that evening. But its sale, if she could bring herself to sell, would be slow. Here she sat in it then, in the richest country in the world. In addition to the house, she had a few marketable "old pieces," small ones to be culled from among the massive bedsteads and armoires, but nothing on which to rear a nine-year-old boy. She was sitting at Great-grandmother Marie-Claire's tambour desk; Roger could eat it in two months. She had the pawn tickets for Marie-Claire's rose-diamonds, and for Marie-Claire's daughter-in-law's épergne. And she had $126.35 in the bank.

And in addition she had, of course, herself. It had been her only dowry, and until some six months ago she had never seriously attempted to draw upon it. "What a pity," her golden-haired Uncle Victor — elder brother of her father and the last successful one of his generation — had remarked of her when she was eight, what a pity that Arietta wasn't male, for she seemed to have all the Minot talents, including a marked facial resemblance to the founder of the line. Victor had died, from an overdose of his patron's pheasant and Lafitte, at the minimal age of eighty, spared from knowing that it was even more of a pity that she wasn't a nineteenth-century male. But here she was, and she was neither. The room where she sat now was the *petit salon* that held the conglomeration of family pictures, and without turning to look at that descending gallery of honorable rogues, she could trace in them not only the decline of the private patron — of which all the world was aware — but of his factotum — small, tragic, subdominant theme that the world had ignored.

Above the mantel was Yves, done on ivory, full-length too, which was unusual for the medium. Legend had it that he had insisted on this because, knee-breeched to the end of his life, he had declared a man to be incomplete without a show of calf; certainly their japing angle went with the face above. It was a triangular face in which all the lines went up, a minstrel face whose nose, long for its tilt, must have moved, as hers did, with speech. The enamelist had even managed to indicate in *couleur-de-rose* those same crab-apple bumps of cheek she had when she smiled. Next to him was the Dutch wife, shown in conventional oval to the waist, of which there was much, a great blonde, serene in all but her stays. Beneath the two, depending on lengths of velvet ribbon in the tree of life, were their heirs direct and collateral, daguerreotype to Brownie, spilling from the mantel to the side walls. As a curious phenomenon, one could see one or the other of the two progenitors always recurring, often with such fidelity that there had long been family slang for the two types — "the beefies" for the Dutch ones, and *"les maigres"* for those *mince* creatures who were true Minots. Although there had been no intermarrying, one type had usually managed to marry the other, and his children tended to be his opposites as well.

Yes, it is all very interesting, thought Arietta — we are a fascinating lot, rather like the green and yellow peas in Mendel — and her father had often dined out on that story. In time, if there was time, she might dine out on it too. Meanwhile, brooding on the three pictures between Yves and the wedding portrait of herself and Carolingus Fay, deceased, she traced a history much more in Gibbon's line.

Beneath Yves came his son Claude, a "beefy," of whom it might have been said (as Henry Adams had said of himself) that "as far as he had a function in life, it was as a stable-companion to statesmen, whether they liked it or not." In Claude's case they had. Next came Louis, her grandfather, who had switched to railroad barons — a light sprig of a man who had passed on, full in years and benefices, while accompanying home the equally aged body of his baron, on the Union Pacific somewhere between Ogden and Omaha, in a private car. Under him, in the sepia gloss of the eighties, were his sons, beefies again: her father in his teens, in the deerstalker's cap so prophetic of his later years, and Victor, already a man with a beautiful Flemish jowl. Victor had already been with "munitions" at the time. At the minimal age of eighty he had died (her father used to joke) not of pheasant but of pique, because his patron's son, seduced by the increasingly corporate air of Delaware, had entered Victor's exquisitely intangible services on a tax sheet, had actually tried to incorporate *him*. If so, it had still been death in the high style, and of it. But with her father, the long descent, gradual as the grime on her bric-a-brac, was clear. He had still had the hereditary talent, but he had been fifteen years younger than Victor. Patrons herded in groups now instead of carrying on singly, and preferred the distressingly plebeian admiration of the many to the fine, patrician allegiance of the one. And gaiety, the mark of the personal, was suspect in a sociological world. Ergo her father. When a Minot was stripped of his devotion and of the truth-telling that was its honorable underside, when he was reduced to picking up crumbs of "contact" wherever he could, to making public show of his charms like anyone else, then he did so in the only way he knew. Her father had become a diner-out. It was some consolation that, under many lambent chandeliers and between many long-stemmed rows of pink and tawny glasses, he had dined so well.

She glanced at her wrist, remembered that she no longer had a watch, and looked at the river, estimating the seasonal angle of light on the opposite shore. Still too early to walk the short distance to the Lampeys, who, much as they adored her company, touted it, still preferred their guests to arrive, sharply gala, at eight. And these days Arietta aimed to please, had in fact aimed so steadily these past months and so far from her usual haunts, the shabby Saturday night parties of the real denizens of these hills, that it was no wonder if these were already remarking how unexpected it was of Arietta — slated one would have said for years yet to the memory of Carolingus — to be openly hunting a husband, and in such circles as the Lampeys, too. How surprised they would be if they knew that all she was hunting was a job. A job, to be sure, for a Minot — a sinecure not for sloth, but for the spirit. With, of course, perks enough to feed a healthy nine-year-old boy.

She rose and went to the mantel, staring up at Yves — one "*maigre*" looking at another. She was four velvet ribbons re-

moved from him, and — except for Roger, who would be nothing for years yet — the last hope of his line. If from his vantage
point he could have approved the resemblance, would he have
expected her, a female, nevertheless to do something in his line?
Being female, what she had done was, twelve years ago, to
marry Carolingus Fay. After Vassar had come a year in Italy
with one of the daughters of her father's three friends; the girl
had married there, and Arietta, after attending her in a horse-
hair hat, had returned home. Next, the second girl, married to
an Englishman who farmed in Nigeria, had invited her there.
Against her father's wishes — it was not cautious for a woman
to become too *déracinée* — she had gone, and in her lightsome
way had enjoyed it, but marooned there, she had missed much
of the war and most of the eligible men. In any case, esprit, or
whatever it was she had, was difficult in a woman if it wasn't
so much accompanied by looks as contributed to by them. Returning home, with her laugh-lines baked deeper than they
should have been for her age, and with some knowledge of
cacao and palm oil added to the magpie lore of her clan, she
had vegetated in the Hudson Valley for a few restless months —
her father's profession so seldom left him home to be cooked
for — and then had gone to Baltimore to visit an old cousin.

And there she had met Carolingus. Eighteen years older than
she, he had still seemed a man whom many might be glad to
marry — a very fine "beefy" with proconsular manners and
profile, and all his curls. Actually he had been a cliché, poor
dear Carolingus — old Baltimore French, old poor, old hat —
and he had been very glad to marry her. For, by heredity, and
unfortunately nothing else, he was a patron — an even sadder
case than hers. They had recognized each other, or loved — in
time it seemed the same thing — at once. The only way he
could afford to retain her was to come live in her house, which
he did, to her father's delight — their mutual recognition too
was a touching affair. Carolingus had been too shy to dine out

(he had only the dispensing talent), and in time, with her and her father's full acquiescence, the house and what it held might have been taken by any casual guest to be his. At eighty her father retired, and the two men could not have been happier, jogging along in a life of aristocratic pattern gone native, shooting over their two acres for rabbit instead of grouse, and serving up the game with an excellent dandelion wine. And in their contentment Arietta had been happy too. It was so difficult for a Minot not to be happy, not to see, in whatever dried facts and kernels of incident the day provided, the possibility of a soufflé. Even when Carolingus had not long survived her father, she could not avoid thinking that he was better so, just as she could not help seeing, as the long, curlicued, taupe coffin went down the front steps, that it looked exactly like the éclairs of which he had always been so fond.

And then of course, it had become her turn — to dine out. She had let no one know her real situation; she would have been plied with all usually offered an untrained widow — "rent your lovely rooms to teachers; become a nursery school aide" — all the genteel solutions that would trap her forever. No, she was still child enough of her race to risk all on its chimera: that somewhere there was a post where one might exercise an airy, impalpable training which could never be put down on any resumé, somewhere even in this taxable world.

So far, her efforts to renew her father's contacts in New York had shown her only how faded they were, and how even those old and well-bred enough to remember the breed she sprang from, its always delicate aims, tended to misinterpret when the diner-out was female, however plain. These last months she had been looking about her in the Valley, among people like the Lampeys, whose kindness had the practicality which went with money still fresh in the till. Tonight, for instance, they were having her in to meet a Miss Bissle from Delaware, who was devoting to a state-wide program of hedge roses and bird sanctuaries her one-twenty-fifth share in a great-grandfather's fortune in explosives, and whose secretary-companion had just died. The Lampeys, drawing Arietta out for Miss Bissle's benefit, would no doubt ask her to repeat the story they particularly loved — about the time a zebra, a real zebra, had appeared in her garden — although she had other anecdotes she herself preferred. A humanist, she liked stories about people, and the zebra one was bad art besides, having no ending really, and an explanation that was sadly mundane. She would much rather tell about Claude and Henry Clay, about one of the Great Compromiser's compromises that had never reached the historians. Or about Louis's patron, a philanthropist who gave in kind only, and who, on being approached at his door by a panhandler who wanted money for a glass eye, was able to invite him into a *cabinet de travail* where he had a box of them. But considering the roses and birds, possibly the zebra was more in line.

Across the river, the last evening light shone on the silver roof of a New York Central streamliner; she had a few minutes' walk and it was time. Courage, she said to herself, thinking of Roger. You are learning your trade a little late, that is all. You still have $126.35 worth of time. And maybe Miss Bissle would be a jolly hedonist who wanted a "good companion," although this was not often the conclusion one drew from watching people who watched birds. Remember, in any case, that when the artist is good, it is still the patron who is on trial. Reaching up toward Yves, she blew the dust from his frame. Why should our art, she thought, the art of happiness, be such a drug on the market these days? On that note, she tilted her head and went out, swinging the skirt of her dress, luckily so dateless, and tapping sharply, almost as if she scolded it, the tambour desk.

Meanwhile, a few minutes away, the Lampeys and their houseguests, Miss Bissle and her second cousin Robert, were speaking of Arietta. Parker and Helen Lampey, a white-haired couple in their sixties, had started life together at Christian College, Missouri, but long since, owing to Parker's rise to the extreme altitudes of international law, had accustomed themselves to the ponderous social mixture to be found there — Swiss bankers, German industrialists, American judge advocates and solid rich like the Bissles. Thirty years of moving intercontinentally had not made them raffish — so far as was known they had never felt an expatriate tingle. What it had done was to give them the eternally pink-cheeked, good-tempered look of summer people; they had in fact been summer people all over the world. By native standards they should have been suffering from all the ills of cosmopolitan riches and ease; actually money, comfort and change had kept them amiable, enabling them to be as kindly as they looked, though considerably more worldly. Parker held several directorships adjacent to Robert, whose share in the family fortune was much larger than Miss Bissle's, and it was through him they had heard of her needs. And had at once thought of Arietta.

"I made Robert come with me," said Miss Bissle, "because Mary Thrace, the last one, you know — drank." She was a large, gray pachyderm of a woman whose eyes blinked slowly. "And I don't at all. You would think that would make it easier to notice in others, wouldn't you? But it doesn't. So I brought Robert."

"Well, I do," said her cousin, looking at his drink through the lower half of his bifocals. "Steadily. So you did just right."

Parker smiled. He knew Robert, a quiet, abstemious sort, widowed early and childless, devoted to rather *sec* philanthropies since. One of those mild, almost expunged men for whom second or third generation fortune was a conscience, not a release.

"Why do men always make themselves out more colorful

than they are?" said Miss Bissle, for whom Robert, past fifty, was still a younger cousin.

Helen Lampey glanced at Miss Bissle's shoes, the flat, self-assured feet of a woman who would never know why. Her cousin looked the way most people who wore glasses like that did — round and tame.

"Is this Mrs. Fay outdoorsy?" said Miss Bissle. "Mary Thrace wasn't."

"I don't know that one thinks of her as 'out' or 'in,'" said Helen slowly. "What would you say, Parker?"

"Delightful either place. In Arietta's company, where you are always seems just where you want to be. The father was just the same."

Helen could see Miss Bissle thinking that this was not the way one got things *done*. "She had a year in Africa," she said hastily. "I should think one would have to be . . . outdoorsy . . . there. And of course she grew up right here in the Hudson Valley — why, they caught a copperhead on their place only last year."

"Still has the old place. Old family hereabouts, the Minots," said Parker, rising to replenish the drinks.

"Minot!" Robert said softly. "Did you say — Minot?"

"Yes, ever know any of them? Understand they were quite a family at one time." Busy with the drinks, he did not note Robert's lack of response, covered in any case by Miss Bissle.

"*Trigonocephalous contortrix*," she said. "They don't eat birds."

Robert sat back in his chair. Yes, I knew a Minot, he thought. I knew Victor. Probably isn't the same family; chances are it couldn't be. Still, what Lampey had just said about the woman they were expecting — that was just the way Victor had been, turning life rosy and immediate wherever he was, and for adults too, as could be seen in the aureole that went round a room with him — not merely for Robert, the small boy on whom he had occasionally shone his great face, fair, hot and flame-colored as Falstaff's sun. Looking back on Victor now from the modern distance, it seemed to Robert that he must have dreamed him — that day on the Brandywine for instance, 1912 it must have been, when Victor had taken him fishing, the same day he had insisted on letting Robert join the men lunching at Robert's grandfather's table before the stockholders' meeting, and had fed the boy wine. Robert could see him now, jutting like a Rubens from even that portly group, the starched ears of the napkin he had tied around his cravat shining blue in the water-light reflected from walls that were white instead of walnut because of his choice, the napkin flecked, as lunch went on, with sauces Victor had conspired with the cook, the heavy company meanwhile tasting him with the same negligent appreciation they gave the food, as now and then he sent a sally rolling down the table like a prism, or bent over Robert, saying, "A little more claret with the water, Robert? . . . And now, if you please — a little more water with the claret." After lunch, Robert had seen him give his grandfather a sheaf of papers, saying, "Here they are, Bi — Robert and I are going out after turtle." As they left, one of the men said, "Bi — where do you get your cigars?" — it was Victor who had started people calling Robert's grandfather Bi. "Victor gets them for me in Philadelphia." At the man's murmured envy, his grandfather had taken a careful puff, gently guarding the long, firm ash, and had smiled.

And that afternoon on the dock, sitting over the lines that the caramel-colored Negroes in the shack behind them had lent them, had been a time he had remembered always, like a recurrent dream — a day on which absolutely nothing had happened except sun, water and the lax blush of the wine in his limbs. And Victor — doing nothing all afternoon except what he did everywhere, making one feel that whatever you and he were doing at the moment was "it," that where you were was "here." They had caught, Robert recalled, two turtles; he remembered being warned of their bite, and informed, lovingly, of their soup. "Victor," he had asked suddenly, "what are you in?" — meaning chemicals, cotton, tin, this being the way men in those days, at that table, had spoken of what they did. "Oh I'm not 'in'" had been the laughing answer. "You might say I'm — *with*." Breathing hard, Victor had been peering in at the hamper that held the turtles. Robert had looked down at him. "So shall I be," he had said. "Oh no you won't. You're already stuck with it, like these chaps. You're already *in*." Victor had risen, puffing. "Best you'll be able to do is to have somebody around like me — way Bi does." Robert had considered. "I'll have you then if I may," he had said.

Victor's face had been in shadow, the sun behind him, but after more than forty years Robert could still sense in him the unnameable quality that had sent him fishing in his cravat. "Mmm. If your father doesn't get to you first," he said. And Robert's father had got to him first, as, in Victor's old age, he had got to Victor. Not a hard man, his father, but a dull one, of the powerful new breed that cherished its dullness for its safety, and meant to impose that, along with the rest of its worldly goods, on its sons. "Like that brew we had at lunch?" Victor had said, as they trotted the hamper along the shore. "And well you might," he said, mentioning a name, a year. "Pity I've only daughters," he sighed. "Women've no palate. Perfume kills it." Above them, atop the green dunes of lawn that swept to the water's edge, a small figure waved at them, his grandfather, guests sped, sauntering the veranda alone. "Will I have one, d'ya think?" asked Robert. "Mmm, can't tell yet." Robert considered. His grandfather, colorless and quiet, seemed to him much like his father, who drank only Saratoga water. "Does Bi?" he said with interest. Victor smiled, waving back. "He's got me," he said.

And Grandfather was like me really, not like Father, thought

Robert, returning to the Lampeys', where conversation, as so often happened elsewhere, had rippled on without him. He was a dull man too, as I am, but like me with the different and often painful dimension of not valuing it, of knowing that somewhere, sometimes in the same room, conversation twinkled past him like a prism, a rosier life went by. Grandfather was like me. But Grandfather had Victor.

And looking at the door through which Emily's possibility was to come, telling himself that it was midsummer madness — of Victor's daughters one was dead and the other last heard of years ago in a nursing order in Louisiana — he still told himself that he would not be surprised, not at all, if the woman who came through the door were to be huge and serenely fair, a great Flemish barmaid of a woman, with Victor's florid curls.

When Arietta walked through the door, he was surprised, at the depth of his disappointment. For what he saw was a slight woman, almost tiny, whose hair, sugared now like preserved ginger, might once, at youth's best, have been russet, a small creature whose oddly tweaked face — one of those pulled noses, cheeks that looked as if each held the secret cherry of some joke — was the farthest possible from the classic sun-face he remembered. Even if she were some relation, she was nothing like. There was no point in asking, in opening a private memory to future rakings over whenever he paid a duty call on Emily. For what he was looking at, he reminded himself, all he was looking at was Emily's future companion.

As the evening progressed, he was not so sure. For the Lampeys' protégée remained dumb. From their baffled glances he judged that this was not usual; he himself would have guessed that Mrs. Fay's ordinary manner, if she had any, was more mobile. But for whatever reason, her eyes remained veiled, her hands folded in the lap of her pale, somewhat archaic skirt. A certain stubborn aura spread from her, but nothing else, certainly nothing of the subtle emanation they had been promised, and but rarely a word. Only Emily, impervious to this as she was to so much, noticed nothing, intent on numbering the occasional sips Mrs. Fay took of her wine.

Nor could Arietta have explained. She could have said only that almost at once she had felt Miss Bissle to be a person she could never admire. Or tell the truth to, the truth about Miss Bissle being what it was. Not because Miss Bissle was dull — the best patrons necessarily had almost as much dullness as money — but that she did not suffer from it, whereas the real patrons, all the great ones, had a sweetening tremor of self-doubt at the core. If dullness was what had made them keep Minots, then this human (and useful) sweetening was what had made Minots keep them. But I must, thought Arietta. Roger, she said to herself. $126.35. Nevertheless, when Parker deftly introduced Nigeria, on which he had often heard her entertain, she heard herself furnish him three sentences on the cultivation of the cocoa nib, then fall still. It must be stage fright, her first professional engagement. Her father should have told her that the artist's very piety and scruples were a considerable hindrance when the artist came down to dining out. In desperation she gulped the rest of her wine. Opposite her Miss Bissle blinked slowly at Robert, as if to say "I count on you."

"Arietta!" said Helen Lampey. It was half command, half plea. "Do tell us the story about your zebra."

"Zebra?" said Robert. "Have you hunted them, Mrs. Fay?"

"No." Mrs. Fay addressed her small, clenched hands. "That's equatorial Africa." She heard Helen sigh. "Have you?"

Now, what none of them, what no one knew about Robert Bissle was that once in a while, under certain conditions, he lied. Not on the Exchange of course, or in any real situation. It was his only valve, his sole vice, and it escaped him, with the wistful sound of steam from an air-locked radiator, only when, as tonight, he deemed himself in the safe company of those even duller than he. He leaned back — on these occasions he always did. "Zebras are very beautiful creatures. I never molested them save to procure specimens for the museums, or food for the porters, who liked their rather rank flesh."

Mrs. Fay, for almost the first time, raised her eyes and looked closely at him. "Yes?" she said. Her nose, he observed, moved with speech. "Do go on."

"The hartebeest," he said slowly. "Coke's hartebeest, known locally by the Swahili name of kongoni — were at least as plentiful and almost as tame."

"Why Robert!" said Miss Bissle. "I never knew you were in Africa."

"Oh yes," he said, still looking at his neighbor, in whose odd face — he had not noticed until now — all the lines went up. "One year when your back was turned." He plunged on. "A few months before my arrival, a mixed herd of zebra and hartebeest rushed through the streets of Nairobi, several being killed by the inhabitants, and one of the victims falling just outside the Episcopal church."

"Handy," said Helen Lampey, in spite of having been informed that the Episcopal was Miss Bissle's own. She was watching Arietta and Robert — Arietta *with* Robert, smiling her pawkiest smile at him, and saying, "Yes, yes, do go on."

Robert took off his glasses. No, there was no resemblance, not even if he imagined a napkin tied round her neck, although for a moment there he had almost fancied an echo saying, "and now, a little more claret." He shook his head. The company, whatever it was, was not as safe as he had thought. "Your turn," he said. "Your zebra."

Arietta unfolded her hands. They trembled slightly. Miss Bissle's cousin, and even richer one had heard — and even more. One of the old breed, she was sure of it — and she had almost missed him. "My zebra?" she said. "Mine was — " She had been about to say *real*. But one let people see one knew the truth about them only after one had won them, sometimes long after. And particularly these people. "Mine was — here," she said. "Right here in the Hudson Valley. In our garden."

"So help me it was," said Parker. "I saw it. Go on, Arietta."

So she did. It had been a Saturday morning, she said, and she had been sitting in her bath, when Roger, seven then, had knocked at her door and said there were policemen in the garden and she had called back, "Tell Daddy." Minutes later, Roger had knocked again and said, "Mum, there's a zebra in the garden," and she had replied — "Tell Daddy." "Now," said Arietta, "Roger is not a fey child. I should have known." She knew every periphrasis of this story, every calculated inflection and aside; this was the point where everyone always began to smile expectantly, and pausing, she saw that they had. "I've never been able to afford to disbelieve him since." For then Carolingus had come up the stairs. "He looked," said Mrs. Fay, delaying softly, expertly, "well — like a man who has just seen a zebra in his garden." As, according to him, he had. She went downstairs — and so had he. She made them see the scene just as she had, the two policemen, Mack Sennett characters both of them, yelling "Stand back there!" from a point well behind Carolingus, and there, cornered in a cul-de-sac near the carriage house, flashing and snorting, the zebra, ribanded in the rhododendrons like a beast out of the *douanier* Rousseau.

"The policemen," she said, "had had no breakfast, so there I found myself, carrying a tray with sugar and cream and my best coffee cake — luckily I had baked on Friday — to two policemen and a zebra, in a back yard twenty-five miles from New York." She rose, circled the room, holding the scene with her hands pressed lightly together, and as if absent-mindedly, poured Parker some coffee out of the Lampeys' silver pot. Outside, in the Lampeys' garden, a barn owl hooted — it was the atmosphere, conspiring gently with her as usual. She waited. At this point someone always asked, "But how?"

"But *how?*" said Miss Bissle.

"Ah, now," said Mrs. Fay, "I have to double back. I have to tell you that across from us, in one of those very modern houses with the kitchen set just under the crown of the road, the family gets up very early. They garden, and the mother-in-law is a past president of the Audubon Society of Atlanta, Georgia." Still circling the room, a diseuse gently fabricating her own spotlight, Mrs. Fay rested one hand, a brief wand, on Miss Bissle's shoulder as she passed her. Robert watched, enthralled. There was nothing to it, yet she held them all. They sat like marionettes whom she was awakening slowly to a mild, quizzical sensation like the pleasure-pain in a sleeping foot. "And at about six o'clock that morning, the head of the County Police picked up the phone and heard a cultivated Southern voice say, 'Ah should like to repo't that jus' now, as we wuh setten at breakfas', we saw a zebra payss bah on the Rivuh Road.'" Parker laughed, and Mrs. Fay picked it up, wove him in quickly. "Ah yes," she said, "can't you hear her? And the chief thought to himself that the River Road is rather the bohemian part of his parish, and that Saturday morning comes, well — after Friday night. So he calls our policeman and says, 'George, people down your neck of the woods seeing zebras.' George decides to wait until, well, two or more people see it. Then Joe Zucca, the old caretaker at Fagan's, telephones, babbling that a striped horse is crashing around his conservatory. And the chase is on. And they bring it to bay in our garden."

Parker guffawed. "There are zebras at the bottom of my garden."

Arietta, reaching her own chair, sat down in it. Someone always said that too. She looked round at their faces. Yes, she had them, particularly one. Quickly, quickly now, wind it up. And in a long, virtuoso breath, she wound it all up — how the village had filled the yard, a gold mine if she'd just had the lollipop concession, how her smart-aleck neighbor had stopped by the front gate, offering a drive to town, and when she'd said, "Wait a bit, Tom, we've got a zebra in the back yard," had smirked and said "Yeah, I heard that one at Armando's — and the horse said, 'I've been trying to get it to take its pajamas off all night.'" And how it had been one of the great satisfactions in life to be able to lead him round to the carriage house. And how the cops had finally got hold of the Hudson River Cowboys Association — yes there was one, those kids in white satin chaps and ten-gallon hats who always rode palominos in the Independence Day Parade — and how they'd come, out of costume alas, but with their horse trailer, and how Carolingus and the cops had finally jockeyed the beast in, using a three-man lasso. And how, at the height of it — children screaming, yokels gaping, three heated men hanging on ropes, the whole garden spiraling like a circus suddenly descended from the sky, and in the center of it all, the *louche* and striped, the incredible — how Arietta's eighty-five-year-old Cousin Beck from Port Washington, a once-a-year and always unheralded visitor, had steamed up the driveway in her ancient Lincoln, into the center of it all. "Oh, Cousine Beck," she'd stammered — in French, she never knew why — "you find us a little *en deshabille*, we have us *un zèbre*." And how Beck, taking one look, had eased her old limbs out of the car and grunted, "Arietta, you *are* dependable. Just bring me a chair."

Mrs. Fay folded her hands. Now someone would ask the other question. She gave a sigh. Next to her, her neighbor marveled. No, she was nothing like — no aureole. This one whisked herself in and out, like a conjuror's pocket handkerchief. But the effect was the same. Small sensations, usually ignored, made themselves known, piped like a brigade of mice from their holes. There was a confused keenness in the ear . . . nose . . . air? One saw the draperies, peach-fleshed velour, and waited for their smell. The chandelier tinkled, an owl hooted, and a man could hear his own breath. The present, drawn from all its crevices, was here.

"But where did the beast come from?" said Miss Bissle.

Yes, it would be she, thought Arietta. The cousin, his glasses still off, was staring at her with eyes that were bright and vague. "A runaway," she said in a cross voice. It always made her sulky to have to end the fun this way, with no punch line but fact. "There's an animal importer up the mountain; we found out later. He buys them for zoos." She turned pertly to the cousin. "Perhaps it was one of yours."

"I can't think when, Robert," said Miss Bissle. "I've always known exactly where you were."

Robert, before he replaced his glasses, had a vague impression that Mrs. Fay looked guilty, but she spoke so quickly that he must have been wrong.

"Parker," she said, "did you and Helen ever hear about Great-grandfather Claude, and Mr. Henry Clay?"

They hadn't. Nor had they heard about Louis's patron's glass eye. Robert, saved, sank deeper in his chair. He was his father's son after all, trained to fear the sycophant, and he brooded now on whether Mrs. Fay wanted something of him. Look how she had got round the Lampeys. Was she honest? Victor's tonic honesty, he remembered, had spared no one; he never flattered individually but merely opened to dullards the gross, fine flattery of life alone. And what did he, Robert, want of her? If he closed his eyes, prisms of laughter floated past him, flick-flack, down the long cloth of another table; he could feel, there and here, the lax blush of the present in his limbs. He slouched in it, while Arietta told how, when Carolingus spoke for her, her father had said, "You know she has no *dot*." And how Carolingus, who was slightly deaf, had replied, "I've no dough either." And how in after years, both always amiably purported to be unsure of who had said which.

And then Robert sat up in his chair. For Arietta was telling the story of the "beefies" and *"les maigres."*

So that's it, he thought. I knew it, I knew it all the time.

And in the recesses of his mind he felt that same rare satisfaction which came to him whenever he was able to add to a small fund he had kept in a downtown savings bank almost since boyhood, money separate from inheritance, made by his own acumen, on his own. I recognized her, he thought, and the feeling grew on him, as it had been growing all evening, that in the right company he was not such a dullard after all. He leaned back now and watched her — quiet now after her sally, unobtrusive whenever she chose. It was not wit she pretended to; her materials were as simple as a child's. What was the quality she shared with Victor, born to it as the Bissles were born to money, that the others here felt too, for there was Lampey, murmuring ingenuously into his brandy-cup "Wonderful stuff, this, isn't it?" — quite oblivious of the fact that it was his own — and there even was Emily, her broad feet lifted from the floor? Whatever Mrs. Fay did, its effect was as Victor's had been, to peel some secondary skin from the ordinary, making wherever one was — if one was with her — loom like an object under a magnifying glass — large, majestic and there. She made one live in the now, as, time out of mind it seemed, he had once done for himself. But he did not know how she did it. Or whether she did. Watching her rise from her chair, begin to make her adieu, the thought came to him that he would not mind spending a lifetime finding out.

"Let me go with you," he said, standing up. "Let me drive you home."

But Emily had arisen too. "Mrs. Fay," she said, her blinking fluttered, "have you had any experience with birds?"

Arietta smiled between them. How lucky she had recognized him, the real thing, poor dear, even if his sad little blague — out of *African Game Trails* of course, old Teddy Roosevelt, on half the bookshelves in Nigeria — was not.

"Do," she said to him, "but let's walk." She turned to Miss Bissle, and let the truth escape from her with gusto. After all it was her own. "No, not really. Of course — I've shot them."

On the short way home, the river, lapping blandly, made conversation. Robert spoke once. "I don't really think Emily would have suited you," he said, and Mrs. Fay replied that it was nice of him to put it that way round.

At Arietta's doorway, they paused. But it was imperative that she find out what was on his mind. Or put something there.

"I'd ask you in," she said, "but I've nothing but dandelion wine."

"I've never had any," said Robert. "I'd like to try it."

She led him through the hall, past the rack where Carolingus's leather jacket hung, and her father's, and the squirrel-skin weskit they had cured for Roger, then through the softly ruined downstairs rooms, up the stairs and into the little salon. It was an educative tour; it told him a great deal. And this was the family room; he sensed the intimate patchouli that always clung to the center of a house, even before he looked up and saw them all above the mantel, hanging on their velvet tree. While Arietta went for the wine, he moved forward to examine them. What a higgler's collection they were, in their grim descent from ivory to pasteboard to Kodak, yet a firm insouciance went from face to face, as if each knew that its small idiom was an indispensable footnote to history, to the Sargents, Laverys, de Lászlós that people like him had at home. And *there*, in that small brown-tone. Yes, there.

"Take me round the portraits," he said when she returned, and here too, since she also was on the wall, he learned. He saw that Carolingus must have been of an age near his own. "And who are they?" he said. "You missed that one." They were sitting at a small escritoire on which she had placed the wine, and if he stretched a hand he could touch the faded brown-tone.

"That's my father as a boy, and his older brother, Victor."

What an absurd feeling happiness was. That must be its

name. To feel as if such a sum, such a round sum had been deposited in that bank that he need never go there again. Not if he stayed here. As, in time, he thought, he could arrange.

Opposite him, Arietta fingered a drawer inside which the name of the desk's first owner was inscribed — Marie-Claire, who had married for inclination but had got the rose-diamonds too. She stole a glance at her vis-à-vis. After all, she had recognized him, and in time, as she did remember, this and inclination could come to be almost the same. It was strange that he was no "beefy," but she had already had one — and no doubt her tribe, along with the rest of the world, must move on. And he was very responsive. In time, she thought, the house would come to seem to him like his own.

"Wonderful stuff," he was saying, holding up to the light one of the old green bottles into which Carolingus and her father had put the wine.

"Is it really?" said Arietta. "I was never any help to them on it."

"What it wants," he said, "is to be decanted, for the sediment. One does it against a candle flame. I was thinking — I might come by tomorrow. And show you."

"Do — for company," said Mrs. Fay. "Actually, one wine seems to me much like any other. I've got no palate for it. Women don't, my father always used to say."

"No, they don't." He was looking at her so deeply that she was startled. "Perfume kills it," he said, and so intensely that, odd averral as it was, it hung over them both like an avowal of love.

Downstairs, she let him out the front door, and watched him to the end of the lane. Roger's spaniel yipped, and over the hill another dog set up an answering cry. In the darkness, as she closed the door, she smiled, one of old Teddy's sentences lumbering through her mind. "The hunter who wanders these lands sees the monstrous river-horse snorting, the snarling leopard

and the coiled python, the zebras barking in the moonlight."
As she went back up the stairs, she wondered whether she
would ever tell him. Some truths, as an honest companion, one
spoke in jest; others, as a woman, one kept to oneself. At the
moment it didn't matter. Standing in the doorway of the little
salon, she stretched her arms. "I've dined out!" she said to the
pictures, to herself. "I've dined on zebra, and on hartebeest, and
yes, I think, on . . . husband. I've dined well."

Outside the hedge at the end of the lane, Robert watched
the door close. He knew just how it would begin tomorrow; he
would begin by asking her, as he had never asked anyone, to
call him "Bi." There would always be a temptation to say
more — who, for instance, would understand about that day
on the Brandywine better than she? But he must remember;
with all she was — she was also a woman. They liked to be
chosen for themselves. He must always be as mindful of that
as of his incredible luck. And what utter luck it was! He swelled
with the urge to tell someone about it. But there were not
many in the world today who could appreciate precisely its
nature. It was even possible that he himself was the last one
extant of all those who once had. Standing in the shadow of
the hedge, he whispered it to himself, as once a man had
whispered it to his grandfather, over the cigar. "Lucky man,"
he said to himself, "you have a Minot!"

# The Coreopsis Kid

O N an afternoon late in the Indian summer of 1918, on the lawn of the house from which the Elkin family was returning to the city the next day, a garden party was ending, and the talk there was all of the war, which was ending too. But inside the house — in a room called the "music" room because it held chairs in which no one could settle, a piano on which no one played, and a broken guitar slanted in a corner like a stricken figure — the Elkin child, Hester, lay on the floor, wishing that the war would never end and that a little old couple called the Katzes had never come to the party at all.

Outside, in the pink, operatic light, all the town guests, most of them Mr. Elkin's elderly retainers, had just gone, looking almost rakish out of their city serge, in the foulards, pongees, and sere straws they had thought proper to the occasion. Her father, who was the head of the family and of the business which supported it, attracted retainers — as her mother often said — as if he were royalty. Even when they were no kin and useless to the point of impossibility, like old Mr. Katz, they swam knowingly toward him out of the sea of incompetents, and he kept them on, out of sympathy, some vanity, and an utter lack of the executive violence necessary to have off with their heads.

Today, all of them had eaten greedily of cakes whose scarce ingredients had been so happily procured, had partaken reverently of Mr. Elkin's claret — meanwhile chattering thinly of what the end of the war boom might do to such claret-consuming incomes as the one which maintained them — and ancient relatives whom Hester had never before seen out of chairs had sat daringly on the grass. Toward the end of the party, Mr. Katz (thought of by Hester as her Mr. Katz), who had drunk no claret, had nevertheless been found sitting on the grass too, dazedly preoccupied in wrapping remnants of cake and ice cream, plates and all, in some napkins and a length of string, yards of which projected from a ball in his pants pocket and coiled fecklessly in his lap. He and his wife had just gone, gathered up and reassembled by Miss Lil, Mr. Elkin's forelady, a tall old woman with dead-black hair and a face like a white Jordan almond, who had shepherded them into a taxi, flapped her draperies officiously over their humbled, retreating backs, and climbed in after them with a great show of agility, as one whose competence age had not affected.

Outside the window now, Hester's mother and Mr. Elkin's sisters, Aunt Mamie and Aunt Flora, clinked and murmured over retrospective cups of coffee. The aunts, as per custom, had come out from the city the night before, to "help" in their peculiar way — Flora to check interminably on Mrs. Elkin: "What you have to pay for this chicken, your butter, these berries, Hattie?" and to cap each of her sister-in-law's responses with some triumphantly cawed instance of her own shrewdness in such matters. Mamie would clog the air with vague recipes out of their Southern girlhood, recipes which she seemed to think had an extra and regional delicacy either because these scorned Yankee exactitude for "a pinch" of this and "a piece the size of a walnut" of that, or had some little trick she could never quite recall — "a wild geranium leaf, I think it was" — or had no pertinence whatever to the occasion at hand, like okra soup, when the question was afternoon tea. In addition, both had to squelch any assumption on the part of the maid that they might be poor relations, and this they did by handily assuming any of Mrs. Elkin's duties which were merely verbal,

and by their keenly critical acceptance of service at one magpie sit-down snack after another.

"Good coffee," said Flora.

"The last of the Mocha Joe got from his importer friend,"
said Hester's mother. It was in the nature of things that Flora's
remark was tinctured with disapproval, and Mrs. Elkin's with
a hint of scarcities to come.

"I mustn't eat another thing," added her mother. "Kozak
says I'm not to gain another ounce beforehand. Did you know
— I ate a pound and a half of Seckel pears the night before
Hester was born!"

"No wonder she's so greenish," said Mamie's pecking voice.

"I know, I know," said her mother. "The summer hasn't
done a thing for her. Autointoxication, Kozak says. He thinks
I ought to put her on a farm, let her get built up. I thought
maybe next spring, when the time comes. Or afterwards."

Hester inched closer to the window. The family had made
the transition from Manhattan to White Plains very late this
summer, because of that ailing of Mrs. Elkin's which Hester
knew to be connected with the impending birth of a baby. She
had guessed this, just as she had long ago concluded that what
her parents really wanted, and what they must have wanted her
to be, was a boy. To the aunts, and Mr. Elkin's brothers, all
girls had been born. At fifty, Mr. Elkin had produced Hester,
last in a line of six girl first cousins, the other five of whom —
Isabelle, Lucille, Jessamine, Gertrude, and Caroline — were
sitting in their own group on the lawn now. All of these were
flamboyantly handsome young women, to whom the nine-year-
old Hester had never once been likened except, ruefully, in the
matter of sex. If the women in her family (as, possibly, in the
world) seemed to be of peculiarly dominant natures, it might
be because they must never admit to a value somewhat lowered because there were so many of them.

"I've set my foot down with Joe," said Mrs. Elkin. A cup

rang decisively in a saucer. "We're not going to take on this place another summer, with the war ending, and nobody knowing what business will do. Now he's even talking about a trained nurse, instead of a practical. When we should be cutting down — all along the line."

"My brother's extravagances are never for himself," said Flora.

"No," said Mrs. Elkin. "No, *indeed*."

"The way he lets people run on at the factory!" Mamie put in hastily. "A place that size, without a proper chemist! But he lets that Lil, who I remember when she was nothing but the head girl . . . and now she won't even tell Joe himself the formulas!"

Oakley and Company, as Mr. Elkin's business was known, were wholesale purveyors of finely milled hand soaps, individually wrapped in paper printed with testimonials so genteel, so familiar to the devoted users, and in such fine type, that these were rarely read. In addition they had several lines of talcums and toilet water — old-fashioned essences of lilac, rose, coreopsis, lily of the valley, and violet, favored mostly by that trade which had once been carriage: gentlemen whose tastes had retired with their incomes, and *grandes dames* living in rooms already overheated with the floral essence of the past. As for the company itself — much of its staff was as old as its clientele.

"And Katz!" said Flora. "My God, Hattie, isn't Joe going to do something about Katz? It's a wonder the firm isn't a laughingstock to the trade!"

"I keep telling him," said Mrs. Elkin. "I had it out with him that awful day we came down here."

That day, the trip had been made, as usual, in a touring car hired with driver for the occasion, and as usual it had been a caravan of hampers, floating motor veils, and hindsight ejaculations. At the last minute, the two aunts had arrived uninvited, with a bland coincidence that had overreached itself in their already having donned veils. At that minute which inevitably followed the very last one, "old man Katz," the messenger boy attached to Mr. Elkin's office, had arrived with a folder of money, checks, and notes that he seemed unwilling to surrender, standing there with an amnesia to which he was subject at times so apparent on his bewildered, age-spotted face that they had been afraid to leave him there on the street, and had wedged him in, too. Hester, squeezed in next to him for the long ride, sneaking looks at his shaky, almost luminous hands with the blue veins and the brown cemetery spots, had felt that he and she were kin. He and she were the worthless people, whom the practical people could not forever afford.

With her father, she and Katz were safe. Mr. Elkin, when pressed for an indulgence, might counter, "Money doesn't grow on trees, daughter!" but this was a joke promptly nullified by the indulgence itself, provoking only a delightful image of a tree from which, in ropes and ribbons and spangles, money did somehow hang. But from her mother's arpeggios of background complaint came another portent, tied to the lurking references to the baby, and focused not so much on living expenses as on the particular objects of Mr. Elkin's headstrong altruism — of which Hester felt herself to be one. For with her father, one had only to be. But with Mrs. Elkin, some businesslike reason for being was expected. With her there was a status to be earned, either by a displayable beauty, like that of those cousins to whom Hester was never compared, or by some competence, of which, in company with Katz, Hester had only the lack. Lately, the predicted end of the war and the arrival of the baby had joined in Hester's mind as the probable end of a halcyon time, after which expenses like herself and Katz, unless they could justify themselves in the meantime, might not be rescuable, even by her father, from her mother's measurement of worth. All that uneasy summer she had listened with concern to the fluctuating dinner-table destiny of Katz, appraising it silently, feeling that it involved her own.

Today though, at the party's beginning, Mrs. Elkin had sat in its midst in a peaceful mood that had thickened upon her of late, letting others do the bothering, with a *laissez faire* that was for her, and for them all, the ultimate extravagance. With the most lavish, reassuring touch of all — she had invited Mr. and Mrs. Katz.

Therefore, when Mr. and Mrs. Katz had trotted up the path this afternoon, it had at first seemed an augury of the best for them and Hester also, for expendables everywhere. For, judged by the least worldly of standards, the market value of the Katzes must be doubtful indeed. With matching white wool hair, stunted twin statures of something under five feet each, and flat, cartilaginous faces nodding, blanched and puzzled, over their hard Sunday black, they looked like two elderly lambs, somewhere between full size and mantelpiece. Lambs, moreover, between whom there must be a preliminary agreement that Mr. Katz was to do the gamboling for the family, and Mrs. Katz the baaing. While Mr. Katz, whisking back and forth between the guests, his hands tremulous with cake plates and cups, seemed determined to prove that his rickety legs and understanding were still capable of infinite errands, Mrs. Katz plodded from the edge of one group to another, looking up at the faces of the conversationalists until she caught a declarative sentence, which she would thereupon confirm with a loud, assenting "Annnnh!" Watching them, Hester thought it cheering that two of such small wit had not only found each other, but managed to grow old. Later, watching her mother, as Mr. Katz was uncoiled from his string, wiped, and sped on his way, she had seen that her mother had not been cheered.

Now she stretched out an arm and scuffed the strings of the guitar, which let out a plangent sigh.

"Hester! Come out in the open air!"

Outside, clouds of motes gyrated in the lustrous, Indian heat. Her mother bent again over her embroidery hoop. Aunt Mamie was crocheting in nervous jerks, and Aunt Flora was stringing the bronze beads and jet passementerie with which she would later adorn her front. Near them, in a circlet of their own, the five cousins were doing no fancywork, but such was the twiddling of curls by ringed fingers, the fluttering of chiffon kerchiefs drooped from airy wrists, that one had almost an impression that they were.

Behind the casement Hester stuck out a wrist and shook it, but the effect was not the same. She picked up the guitar, hugging it to her like a doll, and walked outside. Standing near the older women, she listened to the ripple of the cousins, the stirred flounces, the round-robin lilt of "the Casino," "the Island," "the Turkey Trot," that went from velvety head to head of those five who so resembled one another in their dark-fanned eyes, fair necks, and cheeks that curved with rose.

"Will you look at that hem line," said her mother. "Half up from her knees again!" Hester sat down, looking at herself. One was to be built up, yet one's hem lines were to stay the same. There was no pleasing them — the practical ones. Yet they had to be pleased.

She looked over at the cousins. They are a wreath, she thought. They are like a rosy wreath. They were as closed to her as if they had locked hands against her, meanwhile interchanging the soft passwords of their pet names — Belle, Cile, Jessy, Trudy, Lina.

"Mother," she said. "Why don't I have a nickname? Why don't I?"

Her mother's needle speared a French knot. "Oh — I don't know." She held her work critically at arm's length. "Daddy and I are just not a nickname family, maybe."

"Nicknames come natural," said Aunt Flora. "Drink more

milk. Maybe one'll float up." She looked over at her Belle, her mouth smug.

Hester took a breath. "When the baby comes — will Daddy keep Mr. Katz?"

"Why, whatever put . . . ?" Her mother glanced at the aunts, who looked down in their laps. "Why, that has nothing to . . . ." Mrs. Elkin expelled her breath in a chiding sigh, as if at some unknown transgressor. "There's a limit to what one can do for some people. Sometimes it isn't even a kindness to do it." Reddened, she stared at Hester, with severity, as if some of the unseen offender's guilt had rubbed off on her.

Hester stood up. At the far end of the lawn, her father and the uncles were talking business, ratifying their words with large, blue puffs from their long cigars. She walked toward them.

"What do you know!" said her mother behind her.

"Out of the mouths!" said Mamie. "Out of the mouths."

Hester sat down on the grass near her father's chair. He was lighting a fresh cigar, and absently passed her the band. "Coronas!" her mother had said this morning, watching her father carefully slit a brown box. "Nothing too good for them, I suppose. Coronas!" But during the week her father smoked Garcia Vegas. "Here's a quarter, Hester. Run down and get me three Garcia Vegas."

Bending over, she saw her face in the shiny guitar, sallow, shuttered, and long. It must lack some endearing lineament, against which people and language might cuddle. For it, a nickname was a status to be earned. Leaning against her father's chair, she fell asleep, rocking the guitar. Sometimes, in her doze, it was Mr. Katz she rocked, sometimes it was herself.

During the next days, after the Elkins' return to the city, all New York seemed brimming with more than the autumn season. At school assemblies, teachers rehearsed "The Red Cross Nurse," "There's a Long, Long Trail A-Winding," "In Flanders Field," with a zest that lilted through and contravened even the saddest days. During the day, street corners knotted up with chattering crowds, and at night, Hester, dreaming uneasily of farms, was awakened by the sound of windows upflung to the halloos of newsboys who ran below with indistinct, curdled wails.

On the morning of the Armistice, racing home from school declared off for the day, she was certain that this morning, in her absence, the baby must have been born, too. Her mother however was there as usual in toque and wide, shapeless coat edged in martin, waiting for Hester to eat her creamed carrots and change into her pink crepe. It was dancing-school day, and they were to go, though, because of traffic and people already shoaling the streets, they were to leave early and take a cab.

They were an hour getting to the place, normally a short ride away, for not only were cars and buses creeping bumper to bumper, but people trailed heedlessly between them, poking their grin-split faces into cars, swarming on the platforms and roofs of the buses, as if on this one day bodies were more indestructible than machines. Inside the brownstone which housed the dancing academy there was an air of desertion. The little anterooms where private pupils received coaching in "toe," or young men and women initiated each other into the wicked mysteries of the Turkey Trot, were dark and quiet. In the grand ballroom, the rows of gilt chairs, where the mothers usually knitted and watched, were empty, but a few mothers clustered around Mr. Duryea, a loose-jointed, very tall man whose length seemed the more exaggerated because all significant detail — toupee, dental plate, ribboned eyeglass — was crowded together at the top. Now he detached himself from the twittering group, clapped his hands, and the lesson began. No commotion in the street was to interfere with the verity of the two-step, the waltz. At the end of the lesson, however, Mr. Duryea, pairing off the pupils, presented the girl of each couple with a single American

Beauty rose, from the long stem of which dripped streamers of red, white, and blue. As often had been the case before, he had left out Hester to dance with himself. With a nod to the pianist they were off, for chorus after chorus of a bounding, exultant waltz, Mr. Duryea bending low so that Hester might approximate the correct position with her arms, in her fist the rose of peace.

Back in the returning cab, Hester held the bruised rose thoughtfully against her skirt, as one who was not easily to be tricked into believing that pink crepe and roses were her just and personal due. She glanced over at her mother. Sirens and whistles were keening overhead; as they drove slowly past a church they heard the continuous shrike-shrike of its bell. Her mother, holding her coat tightly around her, stared out fearfully at the crowds which caromed in the streets. Hester would not have been surprised if she had said, "Now that this has happened I must see about getting the baby born," but her mother said nothing.

"Is the war really and truly over?" said Hester.

"Indeed it is, indeed it is," said her mother, still looking out the window. Several people had been pushed off the curb nearest the cab. One of them, an elderly man, rose painfully, scrabbling for his hat.

Hester's fingers tightened on the mauled rose. She put her hand on the fur band of her mother's sleeve, then drew it back. There was no use asking her again about Mr. Katz. Just before they got out of the cab at their door, her hand crept out again and touched the sleeve. "Do you suppose . . . do you suppose it's because I'm the *best* — that Mr. Duryea dances with me?"

Her mother, fumbling for change, looked up as if she were looking over the rims of eyeglasses, although she wore none. "Might be," she said, and gave her a pat to hurry her out of the cab. "But it's more likely because you're far and away the tallest."

In the weeks after the Armistice, the city faded slowly through an anticlimactic New Year into the liverish restlessness of off-season. It was now that almost weatherless time when even the sparrows seemed to idle in the trees, and through days the color of flat soda water one saw more clearly the chapped curbstones of the streets. At the Elkins' there was quiet, too; even the number of family visitors had fallen off. A nurse had come to stay, whose only function seemed to be the arranging in the spare room of packages which arrived constantly, or to watch, squinting, while Mrs. Elkin, who spent most of her days in a wrapper, sat nibbling shamefacedly from little plates, or even from paper bags. Mornings Mr. Elkin could hardly be got out of the house, and he came home earlier and earlier, stopping to kiss Hester as she played, for the first time unsupervised, with the gangs of children in the streets.

There, as in the papers read aloud at the Elkin dinner table, the talk was all of a great victory parade with which the city was to greet General O'Ryan and the victorious Twenty-seventh. At Madison Square, statues and pylons of plaster were to form a Court of the Honored Dead. The Washington Arch was to be transformed into an electrified version of the Arc de Triomphe. Fifth Avenue was to have arches hung with glass jewels, in front of the longest continuous grandstand in history. And here, in the matter of the grandstand, history reached out to the Elkins' dinner table. For according to the outcry in the papers, in spite of all that welter of plaster and wood and glass, no seats in the grandstand had been provided for those wounded soldiers who had been returned to their country in a condition which prevented their being honored either as part of the line of march — or in Madison Square. A group of merchants whose places of business fronted on Fifth Avenue had arranged, angrily and proudly, to accommodate these. Oakley and Company had been allotted four.

On the morning of the parade, Hester, waking before it was

light, heard the milkman's horse clopping in the street below. By the time she reached the window it had vanished, but she could still pick out the fading tramp of its hoofs and the lurch of the wagon as it stopped far down the block. The growing morning had a glinting change in it; there was a green tricki- ness in the March air, and paper scraps scuffled high above the streets. She dressed hurriedly, without calling for help in but- toning the backs of her camisole and sailor dress. Dragging a chair to the closet, she took from a high shelf a blue serge cape and a Milan straw hat with a broad band trailing from its rear. With luck, since her mother was not to be of the party watch- ing the parade from the Oakley and Company premises, no one would notice that Hester was not wearing her winter coat and had substituted for woolen knee socks the short, pale silk ones which were always the true demarcation of spring.

At the breakfast table, occupied only by her father and the nurse, no one spoke. The nurse looked at them with that slit- eyed remoteness with which she regarded their family life, as if she were telling herself and them, "My concern, after all, is for my patient." Mr. Elkin ate abstractedly, fidgeting without his newspaper, which had not yet arrived. They were to go in the touring car, for which they had a special permit. The streets were to be closed to all downtown traffic by eight.

Downstairs, the open car was waiting, the two aunts, here this time by invitation, already in the back seat. Hester got in between them, noting with disappointment that, except for the veils, they were dressed much as usual: Flora in the violent stripings and trembling arrays of jet on which hardly any extra would be noticeable, and Mamie in that lofty dowdiness which exempted her from style.

"How's Hattie?" said Flora.

"Wish I didn't have to go," said Mr. Elkin, getting in with the driver, "but the nurse is with her."

"Any time?"

"Any time."

"Isn't this child dressed rather thin?" said Mamie.

The car started, drowning out Mamie's remark. Hester squeezed down as far as possible between the aunts. Near her left ear, the tiny percussions of Flora's jet went on and on in a rhythm that aped the car's, then paused.

"What are we stopping for?" said Flora.

Hester, sitting up, saw that they had pulled up in front of one of the tenements on Amsterdam Avenue.

"I thought I better get the Katzes there with us," said Mr. Elkin.

"Oh good *God*, Joe," said Flora.

"I know, I know," he answered. "Pull down those two extra seats, will you. Hester, you go on in and tell them we're here. It's the ground floor right." He pointed up at a window. "Just knock and tell them. I don't think there's a bell."

Hester went up the stoop and into a vestibule floored with linoleum, in it a great worn hole. The door groaned closed and she was left almost in the dark. Stairs rose sharply in front of her, their risers just visible. Far above, at least four flights higher, a skylight glimmered. There was no definite sound, but the building murmured, nevertheless, with the unseen nearness of people. The riband hanging down her back rustled in a steady, poking draught, and she flipped it quickly forward over her shoulder. A door at the right had a glass pane at the top, over which lozenge-patterned paper had been pasted. She knocked. She heard the tinkle of a plate or a spoon being pushed back, a creak, a tread — all the noises, begging for mystery, which sounded so exciting from behind closed doors.

The door opened and Mrs. Katz stuck her head out on a level with Hester's. Her woolly fringe caught on the brim of the straw hat, and Hester looked for a moment straight through Mrs. Katz's spectacles at eyes which rolled like large blue immies behind them.

"Annnnh!" said Mrs. Katz, clapping her hands. She patted Hester into the room and shut the door. "Katz! Katz, they are here. The child is here. Come, Katz!"

In the room, there was so much, so fantastically much, that at first Hester could not untangle Mr. Katz from the rest. This was not merely the furniture, which seemed to consist of innumerable small mounds, so swagged with throws and coverlets and scarves that tables could not be told from chairs. The walls, the surfaces of the mounds, the ceiling, from which objects hung on strings, the very air was crammed with such a miscellany that Hester's eyes could not take it in, but had to stop, blinking, on one thing, until recognition set in. This thing resolved itself into Mr. Katz, who lay on one of the larger mounds, looking vaguely in front of him. He was dressed as he had been at the garden party, except for a wide collar of flannel which was tied around his neck with two long ears sticking up behind.

"Annnnh," said Mrs. Katz, nodding and smiling at Hester. "He has with the throat." Still nodding, she scuttled to Mr. Katz's side and began pecking at him with little croons and pats. "Up, Katz. Come. Up!"

Hester stared at one of the walls of the corner in which Mr. Katz lay. It was tacked from top to bottom with scraps of lace, colored and plain, pleated and flat, fanned out straight or puffed in bows that quivered with dust. On a shelf above his head, several yards of it were festooned over drapery cards. Between these there was a signed picture of the banquet variety, and a placard which said *Henkel Brothers. Fine Laces and Veilings.* Beneath the shelf, almost touched by one of Mr. Katz's flannel ears, there was a collar and cuff set, tacked in dainty alignment, as if waiting for a neck and two wrists to sprout neatly into place out of the wall.

Hester looked at the other side of the corner. This wall was crosshatched with narrow shelves, dozens of them, on which there were ranged, almost there tinkled, an army of china trifles: Dutch boys, pagodas, slippers filled with pincushions, tankards and bud vases gilded with the names of towns or painted with simpering girls whose ringlets ended in a curl flowing artlessly over a shoulder. Among these, too, there were pictures, and one large placard — *Weinstein and Gaby. Jobbers to the trade.*

Hester turned on her heel. Here was a far corner devoted to buttons, there, beyond it, objects she could not identify. Each section had its photographs and placards. Even among the things which swung from the ceiling — an assortment of feathers — there was a sizable plume to which a placard had been pinned. On the mantelpiece, arranged as in a showcase, there was something — familiar.

"Katz!" said the crooning voice behind her. "Mr. Elkin is waiting. On you he *depends*, Katz."

At the sound of her father's name, the array on the mantelpiece merged and made sense. Set there, exactly as in the anteroom of Oakley and Company, were samples of all its products. Here were the bottles with their intricate labels: Lilac, Parma Violet, Coreopsis of Japan, and Triple Essence of California Rose. On tripods between them were the "compacts," small rounds of satin centered with moiré rosebuds, each box containing a hard cake of powder, or a flaming oval of orange or purplish rouge. There was even a display of one of Mr. Elkin's transient ventures — tiny vials of rosy or greenish liquid (each with a brass clip at its back), which had been designed to hook onto a lady's corselette or inside the lacy masses of her *décolletage*, there to dispel a mysterious fragrance as she breathed — but which, Hester knew, had somehow or other "not caught on." Set in the center of all this, flanked by many gilded cardboard trade-marks, were two pictures.

She moved nearer. One was a picture of the Oakley office. The other was a picture of herself. It was a replica of one on her father's desk downtown — of herself at the age of three, in white corduroy bonnet with lining frilling her solemn face, coat with belt absurdly far below the waist, the hem just touching the kid uppers of her patent boots. Scrawled in her father's fancy hand, on this copy, however, an inscription ran right across the boots: *To Mr. and Mrs. Katz. Regards. From the Coreopsis Kid.*

"Annnnh. Now!" said Mrs. Katz in a failing voice. Hester turned. Mr. Katz was on his feet. He still had a vague look of waiting for instruction, but he was vertical.

"Come," said Mrs. Katz. She stepped nimbly in front of Mr. Katz, as if she were used to shielding him from notice. "You looking samples?" She pointed a knotty paw. "When Katz was in Lace." She pointed again. "When he was Souvenirs."

"What are those?" Hester indicated the far corner.

"Findings," said Mrs. Katz. "Ledder Findings. Was before Buttons." She followed Hester's gaze to the mantel. "Annnnh," said Mrs. Katz, folding her hands. "The *Company*."

Behind her, Mr. Katz jackknifed so suddenly that Hester thought he had fallen over, until she saw that he was tugging at several packages which were piled on the floor under the mantel.

"Nah, nah, Katz." said Mrs. Katz, with a fretful sob. She tweaked at the flannel. "Today is holiday, remember, Katz?"

There was a sharp rat-a-tat at the door.

"Annnnh, *Gott*," Mrs. Katz sighed, and pulled Mr. Katz upright. She pressed her face close to Hester's "Sometimes Katz cannot think how to come any place but home. *Versteh?*" she whispered. "So he brings them here, the bundles, and we go out togedder. Him to carry. Me to show where."

There was another, louder knock at the door. "Like podnership, see?" whispered Mrs. Katz. She put a blunt forefinger against her pleading, wrinkled muzzle. "Sh-h-h. You are good girl, *nu?*" Then she scurried to the door. "Yes, yes! We are ready!" she cried, and flung the door open, bobbing low behind it, almost in a curtsy.

"Well, please come on then," said Mr. Elkin, in a voice more indulgent than his expression. "Or we'll never get there." He looked at Mr. Katz, shook his head, then took Katz by the arm and led him out the door.

Hester and Mrs. Katz waited on the stoop while Mr. Katz was inserted in the front seat of the car, next to the driver. Mrs. Katz put a hand on Hester's upper arm and squeezed it. "Big strong girl," she muttered. She nodded closer, so that Hester again looked through the spectacles at the round, swimming eyes. "Sometimes I carry, too," whispered Mrs. Katz.

Mrs. Katz was to have shared the back seat with the aunts, but with the mulishness of the timid, she pleaded the anxiety of her "podnership" and was finally allowed to get up front. From the back seat only her nodding bonnet was visible, next to the tartan shawl she had wrapped carefully around Katz.

Mr. Elkin got in one of the small seats facing the back, turning around to hand the driver a large engraved card. "Drive down to Washington Square and back up, whichever way they'll let you go," he said. "I think this will get you through." He sat Hester on the little seat next to him and cradled her hand in his lap. "I want Hester to see the Arch."

It was still very early. The car made good headway, creeping along the battered streets near the East River.

"How many boys will you have, Joe?" said Flora.

"Four, they said."

"They say some of them . . ." Mamie said nervously. "*Basket* cases."

"Oh, no, nothing like that, Mamie." Mr. Elkin gnawed his mustache. "They wouldn't."

Hester saw the soldiers in her mind, baskets over their poor, mad heads, with holes woven for the strange, lucent eyes.

"Joe," Flora's voice cracked, parrotlike, above the motor hum.

She motioned with her chin toward the front seat. "Is he always like that?" she said, lowering her voice. "Really, you ought to realize."

"On and off," said her father. "He's not much use around the office any more. Still pretty fair on deliveries, though."

Hester lowered her eyes to the hand held in her father's and counted her breaths. In, out. In, out.

"Couldn't you mail?" said Mamie.

"Oh . . ." said her father, looking vaguely out the window. "There's always something."

"You mean you see to it there's something," said Flora. "That business will collapse of its own dead weight one of these days."

Mr. Elkin looked patiently back at the two who had been part of the dead weight for years. "They haven't a soul. I'm trying to get them into a home."

"Daddy," said Hester, "what is the Corylopsis Kid?"

"The Coreopsis Kid?" Mr. Elkin squeezed her hand with an absent smile. "That's you, m'dear."

"Me?"

Mr. Elkin nodded over her head at the aunts. "Louis Orenstein, wasn't it, who started it with that telegram the day she was born. 'Three cheers for the Coreopsis Kid.'"

"What a fool you were that day, Joe," said Flora, her jet quivering with chuckles. "What an old fool."

"Why not?" said Mr. Elkin. "I'd waited a long time for that day."

"And the telegrams *you* sent out later," said Mamie with a pursed smile. "Eight hundred of them. 'Greetings, from Oakley and Company and the Coreopsis Kid.'"

"Well, the line's known from coast to coast," said Mr. Elkin. "And so am I." He looked down at Hester. "And so is Hester. When I'm on the road I get it all the time. 'How's the Coreopsis Kid, Joe?'"

Suddenly, turning a corner, they were at the Arch. It gleamed in front of them like an enormous croquet wicket massed with jewels. Then it was hidden by the blue bulk of a policeman. When he saw the card, his face cleared. "I'll get you over to the curb, sir. You'll have to wait there a bit, but we'll get you through."

At the curb, the people packed swelling behind the barrier looked enviously into the long car. The two aunts held up their bosoms, looking stiffly ahead with the hauteur of influence. The car edged into a line of others and stopped, pointing straight at the Arch. To the north, south, and west, phalanx after phalanx of waiting uniforms quivered in the early morning sun. Here and there commands sparked suddenly above a continuous surf of sound. To the left of the car, a horse curvetted and was reined in, his nostrils distended but still.

Hester looked at the Arch. Hung with a dazzle of light, it swayed with the sound of thousands of colors chiming softly together. It kept time with the dazzle in her chest, inside of which a music box tintinnabulated over and over, "Coreopsis . . . Coreopsis . . . Coreopsis Kid."

She stood up, and stepped on Mamie's foot. At Mamie's sharp yelp, she sat down again.

"When that baby comes," said Mamie, nursing her foot, "I know someone whose nose is going to be out of joint."

"Mamie," said Mr. Elkin, "sometimes you haven't the sense of a mule."

Hester stared at Mamie. Idly, she noted how well her aunt's triangular mouth suited her sly bird-speech, was perhaps too small for anything more, but her own answer came from far below the stare. "I don't know," she said. "I guess Daddy can afford us all."

A murmur from the crowd drowned out her father's guffaw. The lines of soldiers tautened, each to a single glitter. Waves of brass washed over them, and the glitter moved with the drums. Now everyone in the crowd was throwing something —

packs of cigarettes, oranges, paper rosettes, and streamers of
*tricolore.* The aunts dug down in a hamper and brought out
things to throw, too. From the windows around the Square,
confetti flaked and fell through the air. Some of the brilliant
bits spiraled onto the car, and Hester, leaning against her father,
raised her face to receive them, as she did in winter with the
first, slow feathers of snow. Her father held her, as he would
uphold them all. And there was no other quite so dashing name
in the whole Oakley and Company line.

Then the band converged upon them. Its clangor invaded
her chest. She burst into tears.

"What . . . what?" said her father, bending down.

"I loved it," she whispered back. "I loved the war." But her
father shook his head, his smile half turning into a frown.

Mrs. Katz leaned over the back seat. Her arms and hands
were crammed full, and her muzzle was pleated with glee, with
the joy of having things to throw away. She pressed an orange
into Hester's hand.

"Throw!" she said, nodding her woolen lamb-curls. "Throw!"

Hester cupped the orange in her hand. It was round, perfect,
like the world at this moment. If there was a flaw in it, it could
not yet be seen. She held onto it for as long as she could.
Then, closing her eyes tight, she threw it.

# The Scream on
# Fifty-seventh Street

WHEN the scream came, from downstairs in the street five flights below her bedroom window, Mrs. Hazlitt, who in her month's tenancy of the flat had become the lightest of sleepers, stumbled up, groped her way past the empty second twin bed that stood nearer the window, and looked out. There was nothing to be seen of course — the apartment house she was in, though smartly kept up to the standards of the neighborhood, dated from the era of front fire escapes, and the sound, if it had come at all, had come from directly beneath them. From other half-insomniac nights she knew that the hour must be somewhere between three and four in the morning. The "all-night" doorman who guarded the huge façade of the apartment house opposite had retired, per custom, to some region behind its canopy; the one down the block at the corner of First, who blew his taxi-whistle so incessantly that she had for some nights mistaken it for a traffic policeman's, had been quiet for a long time. Even the white-shaded lamp that burned all day and most of the night on the top floor of the little gray town house sandwiched between the tall buildings across the way — an invalid's light perhaps — had been quenched. At this hour the wide expanse of the avenue, Fifty-seventh Street at its easternmost end, looked calm, reassuring and amazingly silent for one of the main arteries of the city. The cross-town bus service had long since ceased; the truck traffic over on First made only an occasional dim rumble. If she went into the next room, where there was a French window opening like a double door, and leaned out, absurd idea, in her nightgown, she would see, far down to the right, the lamps of a portion of the Queensboro Bridge, quietly necklaced on the night. In the blur beneath them, out of range but comfortable to imagine, the beautiful cul-de-sac of Sutton Square must be musing, Edwardian in the starlight, its one antique bow-front jutting over the river shimmering below. And in the façades opposite her, lights were still spotted here and there, as was always the case, even in the small hours, in New York. Other consciousnesses were awake, a vigil of anonymous neighbors whom she would never know, that still gave one the hive-sense of never being utterly alone.

All was silent. No, she must have dreamed it, reinterpreted in her doze some routine sound, perhaps the siren of the police car that often keened through this street but never stopped, no doubt on its way to the more tumultuous West Side. Until the death of her husband, companion of twenty years, eight months ago, her ability to sleep had always been healthy and immediate; since then it had gradually, not unnaturally deteriorated, but this was the worst; she had never done this before. For she could still hear very clearly the character of the sound, or rather its lack of one — a long, oddly sustained note, then a shorter one, both perfectly even, not discernible as a man's or a woman's, and without — yes, without the color of any emotion — surely the sound that one heard in dreams. Never a woman of small midnight fears in either city or country, as a girl she had done settlement work on some of this city's blackest streets, as a mining engineer's wife had nestled peacefully within the shrieking velvet of an Andes night. Not to give herself special marks for this, it was still all the more reason why what she had heard, or thought she had heard, must have been hallucinatory. A harsh word, but she must be stern with herself at the very beginnings of any such, of what could presage the sort of disintegrating widowhood, full of the mouse-fears and softening self-indulgences of the manless, that she could not, would not abide. Scarcely a second or two could have elapsed between that long — yes, that was it, soulless — cry, and her arrival at the window. And look, down there on the street and upward, everything remained motionless. Not a soul, in answer, had erupted from a doorway. All the fanlights of the lobbies shone serenely. Up above, no one leaned, not a window had flapped wide. After twenty years of living outside of the city, she could still flatter herself that she knew New York down to the ground — she had been born here, and raised. Secretly mourning it, missing it through all the happiest suburban years, she had kept up with it like a scholar, building a red-book of it for herself even through all its savage, incontinent rebuilding. She still knew all its neighborhoods. She knew. And this was one in which such a sound would be policed at once, such a cry serviced at once, if only by doormen running. No, the fault, the disturbance, must be hers.

Reaching into the pretty, built-in wardrobe on her right — the flat, with so many features that made it more like a house, fireplace, high ceilings, had attracted her from the first for this reason — she took out a warm dressing gown and sat down on the bed to put on her slippers. The window was wide open and she meant to leave it that way; country living had made unbearable the steam heat of her youth. There was no point to winter otherwise, and she — she and Sam — had always been ones to enjoy the weather as it came. Perhaps she had been unwise to give up the dog, excuse for walks early and late, outlet for talking aloud — the city was full of them. Unwise too, in the self-denuding impulse of loss, to have made herself that solitary in readiness for a city where she would have to remake friends, and no longer had kin. And charming as this flat was, wooed as she increasingly was by the delicately winning personality of its unknown, absent owner, Mrs. Berry, by her bric-a-brac, her cookbooks, even by her widowhood, almost as recent as Mrs. Hazlitt's own — perhaps it would be best to do something about getting the empty second twin bed removed from this room. No doubt Mrs. Berry, fled to London, possibly even residing in the rooms of yet a third woman in search of recommended change, would understand. Mrs. Hazlitt stretched her arms, able to smile at this imagined procession of women inhabiting each other's rooms, fallen one against the other like a pack of playing cards. How could she have forgotten what anyone who had reached middle age through the normal amount of trouble should know, that the very horizontal position itself of sleep, when one could not, laid one open to every attack from within, on a couch with no psychiatrist to listen but oneself. The best way to meet the horrors was on two feet, vertical. What she meant to do now was to fix herself a sensible hot drink, not coffee, reminiscent of shared midnight snacks, not even tea, but a nursery drink, cocoa. In a lifetime, she thought, there are probably two eras of the sleep that is utterly sound: the nursery sleep (if one had the lucky kind of childhood I did) and the sleep next or near the heart and body of the one permanently loved and loving, if one has been lucky enough for that too. I must learn from within, as well as without, that both are over. She stood up, tying her sash more firmly. And at that moment the scream came again.

She listened, rigid. It came exactly as remembered, one shrilled long note, then the shorter second, like a cut-off Amen to the first and of the same timbre, dreadful in its cool, a madness expended almost with calm, near the edge of joy. No wonder she had thought of the siren; this had the same note of terror controlled. One could not tell whether it sped toward a victim or from one. As before, it seemed to come from directly below.

Shaking, she leaned out, could see nothing because of the high sill, ran into the next room, opened the French window and all but stood on the fire escape. As she did so, the sound, certainly human, had just ceased; at the same moment a cab, going

slowly down the middle of the avenue, its toplight up, veered
directly toward her, as if the driver too had heard, poised there
beneath her with its nose pointed toward the curb, then
veered sharply back to the center of the street, gathered speed,
and drove on. Immediately behind it another cab, toplight
off, slowed up, performed exactly the same orbit, then it too,
with a hasty squeal of brakes, made for the center street and
sped away. In the confusion of noises she thought she heard
the grind of a window-sash coming down, then a slam —
perhaps the downstairs door of the adjoining set of flats, or
of this one. Dropping to her knees, she leaned both palms on
the floor-level lintel of the window and peered down through
the iron slats of her fire escape and the successive ones below.
Crouched that way, she could see straight back to the building
line. To the left, a streetlamp cast a pale, even glow on empty
sidewalk and the free space of curb either side of a hydrant; to
the right, the shadows were obscure, but motionless. She saw
nothing to conjure into a half-expected human bundle lying
still, heard no footfall staggering or slipping away. Not more
than a minute or two could have elapsed since she had heard
the cry. Tilting her head up at the façades opposite, she saw
that their simple pattern of lit windows seemed the same.
While she stared, one of the squares blotted out, then another,
both on floors not too high to have heard. Would no one, having heard, attend? Would she?

Standing up, her hand on the hasp of the French window,
she felt herself still shaking, not with fear, but with the effort
to keep herself from in some way heeding that cry. Again she
told herself that she had been born here, knew the city's ways,
had not the *auslander's* incredulity about some of them. These
ways had hardened since her day, people had warned her, to an
indifference beyond that of any civilized city; there were no
"good" neighborhoods now, none of any kind really, except
the half-hostile enclosure that each family must build for itself.

She had discounted this, knowing unsentimentally what city life was; even in the tender version of it that was her childhood there had been noises, human ones, that the most responsible people, the kindest, had shrugged away, saying, "Nothing, dear. Something outside." What she had not taken into account was her own twenty years of living elsewhere, where such a cry in the night would be succored at once if only for gossip's sake, if only because one gave up privacy — anonymity — forever, when one went to live in a house on a road. If only, she thought, holding herself rigid to stop her trembling, because it would be the cry of someone one knew. Nevertheless, it took all her strength not to rush downstairs, to hang on to the handle, while in her mind's eye she ran out of her apartment door, remembering to take the key, pressed the elevator button and waited, went down at the car's deliberate pace. After that there would be the inner, buzzer door to open, then at last the door to the outside. No, it would take too long, and it was already too late for the phone, by the time police could come or she could find the number of the superintendent in his back basement — and when either answered, what would she say? She looked at the fire escape. Not counting hers, there must be three others between herself and the street. Whether there was a ladder extending from the lowest one she could not remember; possibly one hung by one's hands and dropped to the ground. Years ago there had been more of them, even the better houses had had them in their rear areaways, but she had never in her life seen one used. And this one fronted direct on the avenue. It was this that brought her to her senses — the vision of herself in her blue robe creeping down the front of a building on Fifty-seventh street, hanging by her hands until she dropped to the ground. She shut the long window quickly, leaning her weight against it to help the slightly swollen frame into place, and turned the handle counterclockwise, shooting the long vertical bolt. The bolt fell into place with a thump she had never noticed before but already seemed familiar. Probably, she thought, sighing, it was the kind of sound — old hardware on old wood — that more often went with a house.

In the kitchen, over her cocoa, she shook herself with a reminiscent tremble, in the way one did after a narrow escape. It was a gesture made more often to a companion, an auditor. Easy enough to make the larger gestures involved in cutting down one's life to the pattern of the single; the selling of a house, the arranging of income or new occupation. Even the abnegation of sex had a drama that lent one strength, made one hold up one's head as one saw oneself traveling a clear, melancholy line. It was the small gestures for which there was no possible sublimation, the sudden phrase, posture — to no auditor, the constant clueing of identity in another's — its cessation. "Dear me," she would have said — they would have come to town for the winter months as they had often planned, and he would have just returned from an overnight business trip — "what do you suppose I'd have done, Sam, if I'd gone all the way, in my housecoat, really found myself outside? Funny how the distinction between outdoors and in breaks down in the country. I'd forgotten how absolute it is here — with so many barriers between." Of course, she thought, that's the simple reason why here, in the city, the sense of responsibility has to weaken. Who could maintain it, through a door, an elevator, a door and a door, toward everyone, anyone, who screamed? Perhaps that was the real reason she had come here, she thought, washing the cup under the faucet. Where the walls are soundproofed there are no more "people next door" with their ready "casserole" pity, at worst with the harbored glow of their own family life peering from their averted eyelids like the lamplight from under their eaves. Perhaps she had known all along that the best way to learn how to live alone was to come to the place where people really were.

She set the cup out for the morning and added a plate and a

spoon. It was wiser not to let herself deteriorate to the utterly casual; besides, the sight of them always gave her a certain pleasure, like a greeting, if only from herself of the night before. Tomorrow she had a meeting, of one of the two hospital boards on which, luckily for now, she had served for years. There was plenty more of that kind of useful occupation available and no one would care a hoot whether what once she had done for conscience' sake she now did for her own. The meeting was not scheduled until two. Before that she would manage to inquire very discreetly, careful not to appear either eccentric or too friendly, both of which made city people uneasy, as to whether anyone else in the building had heard what she had. This too she would do for discipline's sake. There was no longer any doubt that the sound had been real.

The next morning at eight-thirty, dressed to go out except for her coat, she waited just inside her door for one or the other of the tenants on her floor to emerge. Her heart pounded at the very queerness of what she was doing, but she overruled it; if she did feel somewhat too interested, too much as if she were embarking on a chase, then let her get it out of her system at once, and have done. How to do so was precisely what she had considered while dressing. The problem was not to make too many inquiries, too earnest ones, and not to seem to be making any personal overture, from which people would naturally withdraw. One did not make inconvenient, hothouse friendships in the place one lived in, here. Therefore she had decided to limit her approaches to three — the first to the girl who lived in the adjacent apartment, who could usually be encountered at this hour and was the only tenant she knew for sure lived in the front of the building — back tenants were less likely to have heard. For the rest, she must trust to luck. And whatever the outcome, she would not let herself pursue the matter beyond today.

She opened the door a crack and listened. Still too early.

Actually the place, being small — six floors of four or five flats each — had a more intimate feeling than most. According to the super's wife, Mrs. Stump, with whom she had had a chat or two in the hall, many of the tenants, clinging to ceiling rents in what had become a fancier district, had been here for years, a few for the thirty since the place had been built. This would account for so many middle-aged and elderly, seemingly either single or the remnants of families — besides various quiet, well-mannered women who, like herself, did not work, she had noticed at times two men who were obviously father and son, two others who, from their ages and nameplate, noticed at mailtime, might be brothers, and a mother with the only child in the place — a subdued little girl of about eight. As soon as a tenant of long standing vacated or died, Mrs. Stump had added, the larger units were converted to smaller, and this would account for the substratum of slightly showier or younger occupants: two modish blondes, a couple of homburged "decorator" types — all more in keeping with the newly sub-theatrical, antique-shop character of the neighborhood — as well as for the "career girl" on her floor. Mrs. Berry, who from evidences in the flat should be something past forty like herself, belonged to the first group, having been here, with her husband of course until recently, since just after the war. A pity that she, Mrs. Berry, who from her books, her one charming letter, her own situation, might have been just the person to understand, even share Mrs. Hazlitt's reaction to the event of last night, was not here. But this was nonsense; if she were, then she, Mrs. Hazlitt, would not be. She thought again of the chain of women, sighed, and immediately chid herself for this new habit of sighing, as well as for this alarming mound of gratuitous information she seemed to have acquired, in less than a month, about people with whom she was in no way concerned. At that moment she heard the door next hers creak open. Quickly she put on her coat, opened her door and bent to pick up the morning paper. The girl coming out stepped back, dropping one of a pile of boxes she was carrying. Mrs. Hazlitt returned it to her, pressed the button for the elevator, and when it came, held the door. It was the girl she had seen twice before; for the first time they had a nice exchange of smiles.

"Whoops, I'm late," said the girl, craning to look at her watch.

"Me too," said Mrs. Hazlitt, as the cage slid slowly down. She drew breath. "Overslept, once I did get to sleep. Rather a noisy night outside — did you hear all that fuss, must have been around three or four?" She waited hopefully for the answer: Why yes indeed, what on earth was it, did you?

"Uh-uh," said the girl, shaking her head serenely. " 'Fraid the three of us sleep like a log, that's the trouble. My roommates are still at it, lucky stiffs." She checked her watch again, was first out of the elevator, nodded her thanks when Mrs. Hazlitt hurried to hold the buzzer door for her because of the boxes, managed the outer door herself, and departed.

Mrs. Hazlitt walked briskly around the corner to the bakery, came back with her bag of two brioches, and reentered. Imagine, there are three of them, she thought, and I never knew. Well, I envy them their log. The inner door, usually locked, was propped open. Mrs. Stump was on her knees just behind it, washing the marble floor, as she did every day. It was certainly a tidy house, not luxurious but up to a firmly well-bred standard, just the sort a woman like Mrs. Berry would have, that she herself, when the sublease was over, would like to find. Nodding to Mrs. Stump, she went past her to the row of brass mail slots, pretending to search her own although she knew it was too early, weighing whether she ought to risk wasting one of her three chances on her.

"Mail don't come till ten," said Mrs. Stump from behind her.

"Yes, I know," said Mrs. Hazlitt, recalling suddenly that they had had this exchange before. "But I forgot to check yesterday."

"Yesterday vass holiday."

"Oh, so it was." Guiltily Mrs. Hazlitt entered the elevator and faced the door, relieved when it closed. The truth was that she had known yesterday was a holiday and had checked the mail anyway. The truth was that she often did this even on Sundays here, often even more than once. It made an errand in the long expanse of a day when she either flinched from the daily walk that was too dreary to do alone on Sunday, or had not provided herself with a ticket to something. One had to tidy one's hair, spruce a bit for the possible regard of someone in the hall, and when she did see someone, although of course they never spoke, she always returned feeling refreshed, reaffirmed.

Upstairs again, she felt that way now; her day had begun in the eyes of others, as a day should. She made a few phone calls to laundry and bank, and felt even better. Curious how, when one lived alone, one began to feel that only one's own consciousness held up the world, and at the very same time that only an incursion into the world, or a recognition from it, made one continue to exist at all. There was another phone call she might make, to a friend up in the country, who had broken an ankle, but she would save that for a time when she needed it more. This was yet another discipline — not to become a phone bore. The era when she herself had been a victim of such, had often thought of the phone as a nuisance, now seemed as distant as China. She looked at the clock — time enough to make another pot of coffee. With it she ate a brioche slowly, then with the pleasant sense of hurry she now had so seldom, another.

At ten sharp she went downstairs again, resolving to take her chance with whoever might be there. As she emerged from the elevator she saw that she was in luck; the owner of a big brown poodle — a tall, well set up man of sixty or so — was bent over his mail slot while the dog stood by. It was the simplest of matters to make on overture to the poodle, who was already politely nosing the palm she offered him, to expose her own love of the breed, remarking on this one's exceptional manners, to skip lightly on from the question of barking to noise in general, to a particular noise.

"Ah well, Coco's had stage training," said his owner, in answer to her compliments. She guessed that his owner might have had the same; he had that fine, bravura face which aging actors of another generation often had, a trifle shallow for its years perhaps but very fine, and he inclined toward her with the same majestic politeness as his dog, looking into her face very intently as she spoke, answering her in the slender, semi-British accent she recalled from matinee idols of her youth. She had to repeat her question on the noise. This time she firmly gave the sound its name — a scream, really rather an unusual scream.

"A scream?" The man straightened. She thought that for a moment he looked dismayed. Then he pursed his lips very judiciously, in almost an acting-out of that kind of respose. "Come to think of it, ye-es, I may have heard something." He squared his shoulders. "But no doubt I just turned over. And Coco's a city dog, very blasé fellow. Rather imagine he did too." He tipped his excellent homburg. "Good morning," he added, with sudden reserve, and turned away, giving a flick to the dog's leash that started the animal off with his master behind him.

"Good morning," she called after them, "and thanks for the tip on where to get one like Coco." Coco looked back at her, but his master, back turned, disentangling the leash from the doorknob, did not, and went out without answering.

So I've done it after all, she thought. Too friendly. Especially too friendly since I'm a woman. Her face grew hot at this probable estimate of her — gushy woman chattering over-brightly, lingering in the hall. Bore of a woman who heard things at night, no doubt looked under the bed before she got into it. No, she thought, there was something — when I mentioned the scream. At the aural memory of that latter, still clear, she felt her resolve stiffen. Also — what a dunce she was being — there were the taxis. Taxis, one of them occupied, did not veer, one after the other, on an empty street, without reason. Emboldened, she bent to look at the man's mailbox. The name, Reginald Warwick, certainly fitted her imaginary dossier, but that was not what gave her pause. Apartment 3A. Hers was 5A. He lived in the front, two floors beneath her, where he must have heard.

As she inserted the key in her apartment door, she heard the telephone ringing, fumbled the key and dropped it, then had to open the double lock up above. All part of the city picture, she thought resentfully, remembering their four doors, never locked, in the country — utterly foolhardy, never to be dreamed of here. Even if she had, there were Mrs. Berry's possessions to be considered, nothing extraordinary, but rather like the modest, crotchety bits of treasure she had inherited or acquired herself — in the matter of bric-a-brac alone there was really quite a kinship between them. The phone was still ringing as she entered. She raced toward it eagerly. It was the secretary of the hospital board, telling her that this afternoon's meeting was put off.

"Oh . . . oh dear," said Mrs. Hazlitt. "I mean — I'm so sorry to hear about Mrs. Levin. Hope it's nothing serious."

"I really couldn't say," said the secretary. "But we've enough for a quorum the week after." She rang off.

Mrs. Hazlitt put down the phone, alarmed at the sudden sinking of her heart over such a minor reversal. She had looked forward to seeing people of course, but particularly to spending an afternoon in the brightly capable impersonality of the board-room, among men and women who brought with them a sense of indefinable swathes of well-being extending behind them, of such a superfluity of it, from lives as full as their checkbooks, that they were met in that efficient room to dispense what overflowed. The meeting would have been an antidote to that dark, anarchic version of the city which had been obsessing her; it would have been a reminder that everywhere, on flight after flight of the city's high, brilliant floors, similar groups of the responsible were convening, could always be applied to, were in command. The phone gave a reminiscent tinkle as she pushed it aside, and she waited, but there was no further ring. She looked at her calendar, scribbled with domestic markings — the hairdresser on Tuesday, a fitting for her spring suit, the date when she must appear at the lawyer's for the closing on the sale of the house. Beyond that she had a dinner party with old acquaintances on the following Thursday, tickets with a woman friend for the Philharmonic on Saturday week. Certainly she was not destitute of either company or activity. But the facts were that within the next two weeks, she could look forward to only two occasions when she would be communicating on any terms of intimacy with people who, within limits, knew "who" she was. A default on either would be felt keenly — much more than the collapse of this afternoon's little — prop. Absently she twiddled the dial back and forth. Proportion was what went first "in solitary"; circling one's own small platform in space, the need for speech mute in one's own throat, one developed an abnormal concern over the night-cries of others. No, she thought, remembering the board meeting, those high convocations of the responsible, I've promised — Lord knows who, myself, somebody. She stood up and gave herself a smart slap on the buttock. "Come on, Millie," she said, using the nickname her husband always had. "Get on with it." She started to leave the room, then remained in its center, hand at her mouth, wondering. Talking aloud to oneself was more common than admitted; almost everyone did. It was merely that she could not decide whether or not she had.

Around eleven o'clock, making up a bundle of lingerie, she went down to the basement where there was a community washing machine, set the machine's cycle, and went back upstairs. Forty minutes later she went through the same routine, shifting the wet clothes to the dryer. At one o'clock she returned for the finished clothes and carried them up. This made six trips in all, but at no time had she met anyone en route; it was Saturday afternoon, perhaps a bad time. At two she went out to do her weekend shopping. The streets were buzzing, the women in the supermarket evidently laying in enough stores for a visitation of giants. Outside the market, a few kids from Third Avenue always waited in the hope of tips for carrying, and on impulse, although her load was small, she engaged a boy of about ten. On the way home, promising him extra for waiting, she stopped at the patisserie where she always lingered for the sheer gilt-and-chocolate gaiety of the place, bought her brioches for the morning, and, again on impulse, an éclair for the boy. Going up in the elevator they encountered the mother and small girl, but she had never found any pretext for addressing that glum pair, the mother engaged as usual in a low, toneless tongue-lashing of the child. Divorcée, Mrs. Hazlitt fancied, and no man in the offing, an inconvenient child. In the kitchen, she tipped the boy and offered him the pastry. After an astonished glance, he wolfed it with a practical air, peering at her furtively between bites, and darted off at once, looking askance over his shoulder at her "See you next Saturday, maybe." Obviously he had been brought up to believe that only witches dispensed free gingerbread. In front of the bathroom mirror, Mrs. Hazlitt, tidying up before her walk, almost ritual now, to Sutton Square, regarded her image, not yet a witch's but certainly a fool's, a country-cookie-jar fool's. "Oh well, you're company," she said, quite consciously aloud this time, and for some reason this cheered her. Before leaving, she went over face and costume with the laborious attention she always gave them nowadays before going anywhere outside.

Again, when she rode down, she met no one, but she walked with bracing step, making herself take a circuitous route for health's sake, all the way to Bloomingdale's, then on to Park and around again, along the Fifty-eighth Street bridge pass, the dejectedly frivolous shops that lurked near it, before she let herself approach the house with the niche with the little statue of Dante in it, then the Square. Sitting in the Square, the air rapidly blueing now, lapping her like reverie, she wondered whether any of the residents of the windows surrounding her had noticed her almost daily presence, half hoped they had. Before it became too much of a habit, of course, she would stop coming. Meanwhile, if she took off her distance glasses, the scene before her, seen through the tender, Whistlerian blur of myopia — misted gray bridge, blue and green lights of a barge going at its tranced pace downriver — was the very likeness of a corner of the Chelsea embankment, glimpsed throughout a winter of happy teatime windows seven years ago, from a certain angle below Battersea Bridge. Surely it was blameless to remember past happiness if one did so without self-pity, better still, of course, to be able to speak of it to someone in an even, healing voice. Idly she wondered where Mrs. Berry was living in London. The flat in Cheyne Walk would have just suited her. "Just the thing for you," she would have said to her had she known her. "The Sebrings still let it every season. We always meant to go back." Her watch said five and the air was chilling. She walked rapidly home through the evening scurry, the hour of appointments, catching its excitement as she too hurried, half-persuaded of her own appointment, mythical but still possible, with someone as yet unknown. Outside her own building she paused. All day long she had been entering it from the westerly side. Now, approaching from the east, she saw that the fire escape on this side of the entrance did end in a ladder,

about four feet above her. Anyone moderately tall, like herself, would have had an easy drop of it, as she would have done
last night. Shaking her head at that crazy image, she looked up
at the brilliant hives all around her. Lights were cramming in,
crowding on, but she knew too much now about their nighttime
progression, their gradual decline to a single indifferent string
on that rising, insomniac silence in which she might lie until
morning, dreading to hear again what no one else would appear
to have heard. Scaring myself to death, she thought (or muttered?), and in the same instant resolved to drop all limits, go
down to the basement and interrogate the Stumps, sit on the
bench in the lobby and accost anyone who came in, ring door-
bells if necessary, until she had confirmation — and not go upstairs until she had. "Excuse me," said someone. She turned. A
small, frail, elderly woman, smiling timidly, waited to get past
her through the outer door.

"Oh — sorry," said Mrs. Hazlitt. "Why — good evening!" she
added with a rush, an enormous rush of relief. "Here — let me,"
she said more quietly, opening the door with a numb sense of
gratitude for having been tugged back from the brink of what
she saw now, at the touch of a voice, had been panic. For here
was a tenant, unaccountably forgotten, with whom she was almost on speaking terms, a gentle old sort, badly crippled with
arthritis, for whom Mrs. Hazlitt had once or twice unlocked the
inner door. She did so now.

"Thank you, my dear — my hands are that knobbly." There
was the trace of brogue that Mrs. Hazlitt had noticed before.
The old woman, her gray hair sparse from the disease but freshly
done in the artfully messy arrangements used to conceal the
skulls of old ladies, her broadtail coat not new but excellently
maintained, gave off the comfortable essence, pleasing as rose-
water, of one who had been serenely protected all her life.
Unmarried, for she had that strangely deducible aura about
her even before one noted the lack of ring, she had also a

certain simpleness, now almost bygone, of those household women who had never gone to business — Mrs. Hazlitt had put her down as perhaps the relict sister of a contractor, or of a school superintendent of the days when the system had been Irish from top to bottom, at the top, of Irish of just this class. The old lady fumbled now with the minute key to her mailbox.

"May I?"

"Ah, if you would now. Couldn't manage it when I came down. The fingers don't seem to warm up until evening. It's 2B."

Mrs. Hazlitt, inserting the key, barely noticed the name — Finan. 2B would be a front apartment also, in the line adjacent to the A's.

"And you would be the lady in Mrs. Berry's. Such a nicely spoken woman, she was."

"Oh yes, isn't she," said Mrs. Hazlitt. "I mean . . . I just came through the agent. But when you live in a person's house — do you know her?"

"Just to speak. Half as long as me, they'd lived here. Fifteen years." The old lady took the one letter Mrs. Hazlitt passed her, the yellow-fronted rent bill whose duplicate she herself had received this morning. "Ah well, we're always sure of this one, aren't we?" Nodding her thanks, she shuffled toward the elevator on built-up shoes shaped like hods. "Still, it's a nice, quiet building, and lucky we are to be in it these days."

There was such a rickety bravery about her, of neat habit long overborne by the imprecisions of age, of dowager hat set slightly askew by fingers unable to deal with a key yet living alone, that Mrs. Hazlitt, reluctant to shake the poor, tottery dear further, had to remind herself of the moment before their encounter.

"Last night?" The old blue eyes looked blank, then brightened. "Ah no, I must have taken one of my Seconals. Otherwise I'd have heard it surely. 'Auntie, my niece always says —

what if there should be a fire, and you there sleeping away?'
Do what she says, I do sometimes, only to hear every pin drop
till morning." She shook her head, entering the elevator. "Going
up?"

"N-no," said Mrs. Hazlitt. "I — have to wait here for a minute." She sat down on the bench, the token bench that she had
never seen anybody sitting on, and watched the car door close
on the little figure still shaking its head, borne upward like a
fairy godmother, willing but unable to oblige. The car's hum
stopped, then its light glowed on again. Someone else was coming down. No, this is the nadir, Mrs. Hazlitt thought. Whether
I heard it or not, I'm obviously no longer myself. Sleeping pills
for me too, though I've never — and no more nonsense. And
no more questioning, no matter who.

The car door opened. "Wssht!" said Miss Finan, scuttling
out again. "I've just remembered. Not last night, but two weeks
ago. And once before that. A scream, you said?"

Mrs. Hazlitt stood up. Almost unable to speak, for the tears
that suddenly wrenched her throat, she described it.

"That's it, just what I told my niece on the phone next
morning. Like nothing human, and yet it was. I'd taken my
Seconal too early, so there I was wide awake again, lying there
just thinking, when it came. 'Auntie,' she tried to tell me, 'it
was just one of the sireens. Or hoodlums maybe.' " Miss Finan
reached up very slowly and settled her hat. "The city's gone
down, you know. Not what it was," she said in a reduced voice,
casting a glance over her shoulder, as if whatever the city now
was loomed behind her. "But I've laid awake on this street too
many years, I said, not to know what I hear." She leaned
forward. "But — she . . . they think I'm getting old, you
know," she said, in the whisper used to confide the unimagi-
nable. "So . . . well . . . when I heard it again I just didn't
tell her."

Mrs. Hazlitt grubbed for her handkerchief, found it and blew her nose. Breaking down, she thought — I never knew what a literal phrase it is. For she felt as if all the muscles that usually held her up, knee to ankle, had slipped their knots and were melting her, unless she could stop them, to the floor. "I'm not normally such a nervous woman," she managed to say. "But it was just that no one else seemed to — why, there were people with lights on, but they just seemed to ignore."

The old lady nodded absently. "Well, thank God my hearing's as good as ever. Hmm. Wait till I tell Jennie that!" She began making her painful way back to the car.

Mrs. Hazlitt put out a hand to delay her. "In case it — I mean, in case somebody ought to be notified — do you have any idea what it was?"

"Oh, I don't know. And what could we — ?" Miss Finan shrugged, eager to get along. Still, gossip was tempting. "I did think — " She paused, lowering her voice uneasily. "Like somebody in a fit, it was. We'd a sexton at church taken that way with epilepsy once. And it stopped short like that, just as if somebody'd clapped a hand over its mouth, poor devil. Then the next time I thought — no, more like a signal, like somebody calling. You know the things you'll think at night." She turned, clearly eager to get away.

"But, oughtn't we to inquire?" Mrs. Hazlitt thought of the taxis. "In case it came from this building?"

"This build — " For a moment Miss Finan looked scared, her chin trembling, eyes rounded in the misty, affronted stare that the old gave, not to physical danger, but to a new idea swum too late into their ken. Then she drew herself up, all five feet of her bowed backbone. "Not from here it wouldn't. Across from that big place, maybe. Lots of riffraff there, not used to their money. Or from Third Avenue, maybe. There's always been tenements there." She looked at Mrs. Hazlitt with an obtuse patronage that reminded her of an old nurse who had first instructed her on the social order, blandly mixing up all first causes — disease, money, poverty, snobbery — with a firm illogic that had still seemed somehow in possession — far more firmly so than her own good-hearted parents — of the crude facts. "New to the city, are you," she said, more kindly. "It takes a while."

This time they rode up together. "Now you remember," Miss Finan said, on leaving. "You've two locks on your door, one downstairs. Get a telephone put in by your bed. Snug as a bug in a rug you are then. Nothing to get at you but what's there already. That's what I always tell myself when I'm wakeful. Nothing to get at you then but the Old Nick."

The door closed on her. Watching her go, Mrs. Hazlitt envied her the simplicity, even the spinsterhood that had barred her from imagination as it had from experience. Even the narrowing-in of age would have its compensations, tenderly constricting the horizon as it cramped the fingers, adding the best of locks to Miss Finan's snugness, on her way by now to the triumphant phone call to Jennie.

But that was sinful, to wish for that too soon, what's more it was sentimental, in just the way she had vowed to avoid. Mrs. Hazlitt pushed the button for Down. Emerging from the building, she looked back at it from the corner, back at her day of contrived exits and entrances, abortive conversations. People were hurrying in and out now at a great rate. An invisible glass separated her from them; she was no longer in the fold.

Later that night, Mrs. Hazlitt, once more preparing for bed, peered down at the streets through the slats of the Venetian blind. Catching herself in the attitude of peering made her uneasy. Darkening the room behind her, she raised the blind. After dinner in one of the good French restaurants on Third Avenue and a Tati movie afterward — the French were such competent dispensers of gaiety — she could review her day more as a convalescent does his delirium — "Did I really say — do — that?" And even here she was addressing a vis-à-vis, so deeply was the habit ingrained. But she could see her self-imposed project now for what it was — only a hysterical seeking after conversation, the final breaking-point, like the old-fashioned "crisis" in pneumonia, of the long, low fever of loneliness unexpressed. Even the city, gazed at squarely, was really no anarchy, only a huge diffuseness that returned to the eye of the beholder, to the walker in its streets, even to the closed dream of its sleeper, his own mood, dark or light. Dozens of the solitary must be looking down at it with her, most of them with some *modus vivendi*, many of them booking themselves into life with the same painful intentness, the way the middle-aged sometimes set themselves to learning the tango. And a queer booking you gave yourself today, she told herself, the words lilting with Miss Finan's Irish, this being the last exchange of speech she had had. Testing the words aloud, she found her way with accents, always such a delight to Sam, as good as ever. Well, she had heard a scream, had discovered someone else who had heard it. And now to forget it as promised; the day was done. Prowling the room a bit, she took up her robe, draped it over her shoulders, still more providently put it on. "Oh Millie," she said, tossing the dark mirror a look of scorn as she passed it "you're such a *sensible* woman."

Wear out Mrs. Berry's carpet you will, Millie, she thought, twenty minutes later by the bedroom clock, but the accent, adulterated now by Sam's, had escaped her. Had the scream had an accent? The trouble was that the mind had its own discipline; one could remember, even with a smile, the story of the man promised all the gold in the world if he could but go for two minutes not thinking of the word "hippopotamus." She stopped in front of the mirror, seeking her smile, but it too had escaped. "Hippopotamus," she said, to her dark image. The knuckles of one hand rose, somnambulist, as she watched, and pressed against her teeth. She forced the hand, hers, down again. I will say it again, aloud, she thought, and while I am saying it I will be sure to say to myself that I am saying it aloud. She did so. "Hippopotamus." For a long moment she remained there, staring into the mirror. Then she turned and snapped on every light in the room.

Across from her, in another mirror, the full-length one, herself regarded her. She went forward to it, to that image so irritatingly familiar, so constant as life changed it, so necessarily dear. Fair hair, if maintained too late in life, too brightly, always made the most sensible of women look foolish. There was hers, allowed to gray gently, disordered no more than was natural in the boudoir, framing a face still rational, if strained. "Dear me," she said to it. "All you need is somebody to talk to, get it out of your system. Somebody like yourself." As if prodded, she turned and surveyed the room.

Even in the glare of the lights, the naked black projected from the window, the room sent out to her, in half a dozen pleasant little touches, the same sense of its compatible owner that she had had from the beginning. There, flung down, was Mrs. Berry's copy of *The Eustace Diamonds,* a book that she had always meant to read and had been delighted to find here, along with many others of its ilk and still others she herself owned. How many people knew good bisque and how cheaply it might still be collected, or could let it hobnob so amiably with grandmotherly bits of Tiffanyware, even with the chipped Quimper ashtrays that Mrs. Berry, like Mrs. Hazlitt at the time of her own marriage, must once have thought the cutest in the world. There were the white walls, with the silly, strawberry-mouthed Marie Laurencin just above the Beerbohm, the presence of good faded colors, the absence of the new or fauve. On the night table were the scissors, placed, like everything in the house, where Mrs. Hazlitt would have had them, near them a relic that winked of her own childhood — and kept on, she would wager, for the same reason — a magnifying glass exactly like her father's. Above them, the only floor lamp in the house, least offensive of its kind, towered above all the table ones, sign of a struggle between practicality and grace that she knew well, whose end she could applaud. Everywhere indeed there were the same signs of the struggles toward taste, the decline of taste into the prejudices of comfort, that went with a whole milieu and a generation — both hers. And over there was, even more personally, the second bed.

Mrs. Hazlitt sat down on it. If it were moved, into the study say, a few things out of storage with it, how sympathetically this flat might be shared. Nonsense, sheer fantasy to go on like this, to fancy herself embarking on the pitiable twin-life of leftover women, much less with a stranger. But was a woman a stranger if you happened to know that on her twelfth birthday she had received a copy of *Dr. Doolittle*, inscribed to Helena Nelson from her loving father, if you knew the secret, packrat place in the linen closet where she stuffed the neglected mending, of another, in a kitchen drawer, full of broken Mexican terrines and clipped recipes as shamefully grimy as your own cherished ones, if you knew that on 2/11/58 and on 7/25/57 a Dr. Burke had prescribed what looked to be sulfa pills, never used, that must have cured her at the point of purchase, as had embarrassingly happened time and again to yourself? If, in short, you knew almost every endearing thing about her, except her face?

Mrs. Hazlitt, blinking in the excessive light, looked sideways. She knew where there was a photograph album, tumbled once by accident from its shunted place in the bookshelf, and at once honorably replaced. She had seen enough to know that the snapshots, not pasted in separately, would have to be exhumed, one by one, from their packets. No, she told herself, she already knew more than enough of Mrs. Berry from all that had been so trustfully exposed here — enough to know that this was the sort of prying to which Mrs. Berry, like herself, would never stoop. Somehow this clinched it — their understanding. She could see them exchanging notes at some future meeting, Mrs. Berry saying, "Why, do you know — one night, when I was in London — " — herself, the vis-à-vis, nodding, their perfect rapprochement. Then what would be wrong in using, when so handily provided, so graciously awaiting her, such a comforting vis-à-vis, now?

Mrs. Hazlitt found herself standing, the room's glare pressing on her as if she were arraigned in a police line-up, as if, she reminded herself irritably, it were not self-imposed. She forced herself to make a circuit of the room, turning out each lamp with the crisp, no-nonsense flick of the wrist that nurses employed. At the one lamp still burning she hesitated, reluctant to cross over that last shadow-line. Then, with a shrug, she turned it out and sat down in the darkness, in one of the two opposing boudoir chairs. For long minutes she sat there. Once or twice she trembled on the verge of speech, covered it with a swallow. The conventions that guarded the mind in its strict relationship with the tongue were the hardest to flaunt. But this was the century of talk, of the long talk, in which all were healthily urged to confide. Even the children were encouraged toward, praised for, the imaginary companion. Why should the grown person, who for circumstance beyond his control had no other, be denied? As she watched the window, the light in the small gray house was extinguished. Some minutes later the doorman across the way disappeared. Without looking at the luminous dial of the clock, she could feel the silence aging, ripening. At last she bent forward to the opposite chair.

"Helena?" she said.

Her voice, clear-cut, surprised her. There was nothing so strange about it. The walls remained walls. No one could hear her, or cared to, and now, tucking her feet up, she could remember how cozy this could be, with someone opposite. "Helena," she said. "Wait till I tell you what happened while you were away."

She told her everything. At first she stumbled, went back, as if she were rehearsing in front of a mirror. Several times she froze, unsure whether a sentence had been spoken aloud entirely, or had begun, or terminated, unspoken, in the mind. But as she went on, this wavering borderline seemed only to resemble the clued conversation, meshed with silences, between two people who knew each other well. By the time she had finished her account she was almost at ease, settling back into the comfortably shared midnight post-mortem that always restored balance to the world — so nearly could she imagine the face, not unlike her own, in the chair opposite, smiling ruefully at her over the boy and his gingerbread fears, wondering mischievously with her as to in which of the shapes of temptation the Old Nick visited Miss Finan.

"That girl and her *log!*" said Mrs. Hazlitt. "You know how, when they're that young, you want to smash in the smugness. And yet, when you think of all they've got to go through, you feel so maternal. Even if — " Even if, came the nod, imperceptibly — you've never had children, like us.

For a while they were silent. "Warwick!" said Mrs. Hazlitt then. "Years ago there was an actor — Robert Warwick. I was in love with him — at about the age of eight." Then she smiled, bridling slightly, at the dark chair opposite, whose occupant would know her age. "Oh, all right then — twelve. But what is it, do you suppose, always makes old actors look seedy, even when they're not? Daylight maybe. Or all the pretenses." She ruminated. "Why . . . do you know," she said slowly, "I think I've got it. The way he looked in my face when I was speaking, and the way the dog turned back and he didn't. He was lip-reading. Why, the poor old boy is deaf!" She settled back, dropping her slippers one by one to the floor. "Of course, that's it. And he wouldn't want to admit that he couldn't have heard it. Probably doesn't dare wear an aid. Poor old boy, pretty dreary for him if he is an actor, and I'll bet he is." She

sighed, a luxury permitted now. "Ah, well. Frail reed — Miss
Finan. Lucky for me, though, that I stumbled on her." And on
you.

A police siren sounded, muffled less and less by distance, approaching. She was at the window in time to see the car's red
dome light streak by as it always did, its alarum dying behind it.
Nothing else was on the road. "And there were the taxis," she
said, looking down. "I don't know why I keep forgetting them.
Veering to the side like that, one right after the other, and one
had his light out, so it wasn't for a fare. Nothing on the curb
either. Then they both shot away, almost as if they'd caught
sight of something up here. And wanted no part of it — the way
people do in this town. Wish you could've seen them — it was
eerie." There was no response from behind her.

She sat down again. Yes, there was a response, for the first
time faintly contrary.

"No," she said. "It certainly was *not* the siren. I was up in a
flash. I'd have seen it." She found herself clenching the arms
of the chair. "Besides," she said, in a quieter voice, "don't
you remember? I heard it twice."

There was no answer. Glancing sideways, she saw the string
of lights opposite, not quite of last night's pattern. But the
silence was the same, opened to its perfect hour like a century
plant, multiple-rooted, that came of age every night. The
silence was in full bloom, and it had its own sound. Hark hark,
no dogs do bark. And there is nobody in the chair.

Never was, never had been. It was sad to be up at this hour
and sane. For now is the hour, now is the hour when all good
men are asleep. Her hand smoothed the rim of the waste-
basket, about the height from the floor of a dog's collar. Get
one tomorrow. But how to manage until then, with all this
silence speaking?

She made herself stretch out on the bed, close her eyes.
"Sam," she said at last, as she had sworn never to do in thought

or word, "I'm lonely." Listening vainly, she thought how wise her resolve had been. Too late, now she had tested his loss to the full, knew him for the void he was — far more of a one than Mrs. Berry, who, though unknown, was still somewhere. By using the name of love, when she had been ready to settle for anybody, she had sent him into the void forever. Opening her eyes, adjusted now to the sourceless city light that never ceased trickling on ceiling, lancing from mirrors, she turned her head right to left, left to right on the pillow, in a gesture to the one auditor who remained.

"No," she said, in the dry voice of correction. "I'm not lonely. I'm alone."

Almost at once she raised herself on her elbow, her head cocked. No, she had heard nothing from outside. But in her mind's ear she could hear the sound of the word she had just spoken, its final syllable twanging like a tuning fork, infinitely receding to octaves above itself, infinitely returning. In what seemed scarcely a stride, she was in the next room, at the French window, brought there by that thin, directional vibration which not necessarily even the blind would hear. For she had recognized it. She had identified the accent of the scream.

The long window frame, its swollen wood shoved tight by her the night before, at first would not budge; then, as she put both hands on the hasp and braced her knees, it gave slowly, grinding inward, the heavy man-high bolt thumping down. Both sounds, too, fell into their proper places. That's what I heard before, she thought, the noise of a window opening or closing, exactly like mine. Two lines of them, down the six floors of the building, made twelve possibles. But that was of no importance now. Stepping up on the lintel, she spread the casements wide.

Yes, there was the bridge, one small arc of it, sheering off into the mist, beautiful against the night, as all bridges were. Now that she was outside, past all barriers, she could hear, with her ordinary ear, faint nickings that marred the silence, but these were only the surface scratches on a record that still revolved one low, continuous tone. No dogs do bark. That was the key to it, that her own hand, smoothing a remembered dog-collar, had been trying to give her. There were certain dog-whistles, to be bought anywhere — one had hung, with the unused leash, on a hook near a door in the country — which blew a summons so high above the human range that only a dog could hear it. What had summoned her last night would have been that much higher, audible only to those tuned in by necessity — the thin, soaring decibel of those who were no longer in the fold. Alone-oh. Alone-oh. That would have been the shape of it, of silence expelled from the mouth in one long relieving note, cool, irrepressible, the second one clapped short by the hand. No dog would have heard it. No animal but one was ever that alone.

She stepped out onto the fire escape. There must be legions of them, of us, she thought, in the dim alleyways, the high, flashing terraces — each one of them come to the end of his bookings, circling his small platform in space. And who would hear such a person? Not the log-girls, not for years and years. None of any age who, body to body, bed to bed, either in love or in the mutual pluck-pluck of hate — like the little girl and her mother — were still nested down. Reginald Warwick, stoppered in his special quiet, might hear it, turn to his Coco for confirmation which did not come, and persuade himself once again that it was only his affliction. Others lying awake snug as a bug, listening for that Old Nick, death, would hear the thin, sororal signal and not know what they had heard. But an endless assemblage of others all over the city would be waiting for it — all those sitting in the dark void of the one lamp quenched, the one syllable spoken — who would start up, some from sleep, to their windows . . . or were already there.

A car passed below. Instinctively, she flattened against the casement, but the car traveled on. Last night someone, man or woman, would have been standing in one of the line of niches above and beneath hers — perhaps even a woman in a blue robe like her own. But literal distance or person would not matter; in that audience all would be the same. Looking up, she could see the tired, heated lavender of the mid-town sky, behind which lay that real imperial into which some men were already hurling their exquisitely signaling spheres. But this sound would come from breast to breast, at an altitude higher than any of those. She brought her fist to her mouth, in savage pride at having heard it, at belonging to a race some of whom could never adapt to any range less than that. *Some of us*, she thought, *are still responsible.*

Stepping forward, she leaned on the iron railing. At that moment, another car, traveling slowly by, hesitated opposite, its red dome light blinking. Mrs. Hazlitt stood very still. She watched until the police car went on again, inching ahead slowly, as if somebody inside were looking back. The two men inside there would never understand what she was waiting for. Hand clapped to her mouth, she herself had just understood. She was waiting for it — for its company. She was waiting for a second chance — to answer it. She was waiting for the scream to come again.

# Tale for the Mirror

WHEN Dr. Bhatta, the Hindu "neurologist," acquired the old Kuypers estate, which no one else would buy, and installed there his entourage of two faded, Western lady secretaries, a number of indeterminately transient guests, and a faintly rotten, saffron breeze of curry, the neighbors in the other old houses strung along the riverbank absorbed his advent with little more than mild comment. The river road, though deceptively near the city, was part boundary line of a county that brushed shadowy patroon-descended towns to the north, still sheltered, in its gentle ranges toward the west, tribal remnants with tattered Indian red in their cheeks, and had weathered many eccentrics in its time. Something about the county's topography of rear-guard hills, pooled with legend and only circularly accessible, of enormous level-land sunsets brought up short by palisades that dropped the river road below into darkness at four, had long since made it a natural pocket for queer birds, birds of privacy. Many of these were still there, appearing at yearly tax meetings as vestigially alive as the copperheads that sometimes forked before the nurserymen's neat spades in the spring. It was a landscape from which individuality still rose like smoke, in signal columns blue and separate and clear.

More than one of the houses along the river road had had a special history, of the tarnished kind that often clings longer than honest coats of arms. Houses of wood, white, with endless verandas and gabled bedrooms framed in carpenter's lace, they had been built by the dubiously theatrical or sporting rich of seventy or eighty years ago, whose habit had been to leave their trotting races on the Harlem of an afternoon, and to come, with a change of carriage, up the river, there to pursue, in champagne and blood and scandal, their uncloseted amours. And the capricious summer palaces they had had the native workmen build for them, though sturdy of timber, still showed, even in a new age, the shaky regality of seasonal money. From turrets made without ingress, balconies soared and died away. Iron weathervanes swung unheeded over "widow's walks" on which no rightful widow had ever paced, and at the ends of the grounds there was often a tiny pavilion, lodged like an innocent white afterthought among the romantically unpruned trees.

It was such a house that Dr. Bhatta had bought, acquiring it with some sleight of hand whereby the accompanying gunpowder pops of bill-collectors from the other places where he had lived were delayed for several weeks. When these too came, the neighbors were not surprised. Houses like the Kuypers estate had been harmonious even in decline. Descended through relatives who had not been deeded the income to keep them up, they seemed destined to be lost again by owners whose need of grandeur exceeded their incomes, often by those who needed grandeur in order to acquire income. Fakirs, healers, dealers in correspondence course faith — the river road had seen them come and go — all of them sharers in the circuitous faith that if one lived in a castle one could more easily attract devotees from whom one might then borrow money to pay for the milk. Idly the road decided that Bhatta's title of "doctor" was more than probably self-assumed, but this did not really matter. Charlatans, if one made it quickly clear that one would lend neither money nor credulity, often made very tractable neighbors. They could not afford to be like old Mrs. Patton, who had half a million but never painted her house, and let her lawn grow as high as her hedge. They painted quickly, lavishly, at least in all the spots that showed, and kept their sites trim for trade.

Not much was seen of the doctor that winter. It was an open winter, a mild one, but the doctor's tall, corpulent form only showed itself occasionally, on the broad steps underneath his porte-cochere, calling to his dog, Lili, or shuffling in his carpet slippers as far as the greened bronzed griffins that guarded the gate, where he always turned to look critically at the house, his long maroon overcoat flapping at his ankles, the sun running like brown butter on his dark jowls and on the bald pate with its muttonchop of black hair. Occasionally he was seen, still in the coat and slippers, in front of the chain-store in the village, waiting while his two ladies made their purchases inside. Of anyone else it might have been said that he looked, at times, disconsolately cold, but to John Garner, his immediate neighbor on the road, and to others who established a greeting basis with him, the doctor's comments on the world were always showily serene. Either he was a man of inner peace, or else his trade constrained him to appear so.

Whatever his trade was — and this had not been quite established, it was of too large a dignity to allow him to help "the ladies," as he always called them, load the car. These, Miss Leeby and Miss Daria, were both blond, both small, both of uncertain age, but life had faded them in different ways. Miss Leeby's hair and accent had a New England thinness and respectability, her pale eyes and stubby, broken-nailed hands the absent look of a worker uncomfortably away from her task. It was she who was seen from dawn to dusk on the grounds, grubbing and cutting, on the roof of the barn, hammering, and once, painting away on the cupola of the house itself. When encountered, she had the stifled voice, the ducking ways, of a tweeny. Conversely, if, as rumored, the ladies were not the doctor's secretaries but his consorts, then it was Miss Daria who gave herself the airs of the boss-wife. Her streaked hair fell to her shoulders in cinematic curls, her eyes were sunk in sockets blackened with experience, or kohl, or occasionally, as gossip had it, the doctor's fist. Under her haggard fur coat she wore blouses of no illusion, through which one saw the bright satin points of her brassieres. It was she who drove the car, since the doctor did not work with his hands, and managed the finances, since the doctor never handled money — some stores had already begun to complain that they had not yet handled any of his. But, as regarded the two women, he made no other distinction that anyone could see. When the dusty old car had been loaded, and sometimes pushed into starting, he detached himself from his stance against the wall, seated himself in the front seat between the two ladies, gave a portly nod, and was driven away.

But, with the earliest March thaw, activity burst its pod at the doctor's, in advance of any place else. Armies of crocuses snapped to attention on the vast lawn, burlap was unwrapped to display dozens of rosebushes that must have been planted the fall before and were already beginning to twine properly up the chipped columns of the veranda, and all over the grounds there were peeping green evidences that Miss Leeby had indeed grubbed well. A truck came and groaned up and down the horseshoe driveway all one afternoon, depositing a sparkling white carpet of crushed stone. After it came the two women, raking it smooth, bordering it with two lines of whitewashed rocks that they lugged from the barn. When the mailman's truck stopped at the gate, Miss Daria called to him, and with his dazed help a large, ugly cement urn was eased up the cellar stairs and dragged to the center of the lawn. When he left, with her nonchalant thanks, he looked angrily over his shoulder, and slammed hard the door of his truck, before he drove away. For, all that time, with eyes squinting happily in the tawny air, with powerful arms and chest revealed

by the short sleeves and Byronic collar of his shirt, the doctor
had been sitting on the stoop.

It was only during the next few days, however, that John
Garner, his neighbor to the north, began to take any consistent
notice of what was going on next door. Garner was no gossip;
in the city during the business day he was conversely rather
proud of the lazy, non-suburban tolerance of the road on which
he lived, but a man who owns property, or nearly, has a natural
vested interest in that of his neighbor. Ten years before, he
and his wife Amelia had been "that nice young university
couple" whom the cautious local bank had entrusted with a
surprisingly large mortgage on the big old house next to the
Kuyper place. Now they were "the Garners," with four children, two in school, and during all that time both the house
and the mortgage had remained a little too big for them.
Garner's father had been a trial lawyer who had enjoyed to the
full the strutting side of the law; Garner had passed for the bar,
married, and been in practice as a modestly salaried subordinate
of a small firm for some years before he had finally admitted to
himself that there was no side of the law that he would ever
enjoy, and that he would never be anything more at it than a
respectable drone.

Each work day, carrying the briefcase that had been given him
when he passed the bar, he took the seven-thirty bus to the city, a
tall man with thinning sandy hair, with cheeks whose tired creases
quirked pleasantly when he smiled, and each evening, at
half past six, he returned, a little thinner on top, a little more
creased than he had seemed the day before. His father's father
had been a farmer in the magnificently tilled lands above the
Finger Lakes, and when Garner, in his private shufflings of the
past, thought of what might have been, he always returned to
the same boyhood image of himself and the old man, his palm
in the old man's fist, and the two of them standing to watch
whatever might be going on at the moment on the farm. In the

evenings, the old man would sit at his roll-top desk in his catalogue-lined study, poring over his accounts, and it was the image of this too that Garner had retained, even more than the memory of the plump barns, and the tractor grooving the hills. It was a feeling of not "going to work," as his father had done, but of working where you lived, where you stood, and of standing on the land. But his father had made the break to the city all too well; the son, gentled to pavements and collars, listening to the valedictorian tell him that he was standing "on the threshold of choice," would have been as incredulous as the father at the idea that the grandfather's life might have been one such choice. Only, some five years later, during that same year when he had come to terms with his private assessment of himself, he had bought the property adjoining the Kuypers estate.

Both properties fronted on the river (although the Kuypers place had a seven hundred footage to his two), and the acreages of both places ran back in a straight line up and over the hill that rose sharply behind, and were lost in the woodland at the crest. Amelia, his wife, always assumed that they had made the move for the children's sake, and because here, just barely within commuting distance of the city, their bit of money had stretched to so much more than it could have done in a newer, neater suburb. Over the years, Garner had come to believe this himself. But certain references in the deed, surveyor's jargon that granted him a portion of ground under his feet, phrases like "riparian rights," that ceded him certain calculable powers over the river, also gave him an immeasurable delight. It was, obscurely, because of this that, although he left all other civic duties to Amelia, he had allowed himself to be voted in as a member of the road's zoning board, which met three times a year to ratify building permits, to consider and defer the problem of repaving the road, and to reaffirm its one holy gesture against the cellularly creeping city to the south — that no commerce, no multiple dwelling of any kind was ever to be allowed. He had long since forgotten that his own house, stolid relic of a history too colorless to survive, had once reminded him of his grandfather's place, and that when, on fine Sundays, he walked up the back acre to his part of the hilltop and looked down over the cascaded tips of the pines that still grew here, the great blue stare of the river, deceptively motionless and foreshortened by other hills, had a look of Lake Seneca. He was an indifferent gardener; he had never learned to pull salvation, like a turnip, from the soil. But each evening, when he crawled back from the multiple of multiples, there was a moment when he rested the briefcase on the porch steps, and plowed the river with his eyes.

It was at such a moment, at dusk on a Friday evening, when, turning from the river to note that his lawn should receive its first mowing in the morning, he saw that, over at the doctor's, they had boarded up the little hexagonal summerhouse that perched halfway up the hill. The tiny peaked roof fitted like a dropped handkerchief over the columns that formed the sides; it had been a simple job to fit long wooden shutters, of which most of the houses along the road had an abandoned stock in the cellar, in the airy spaces beneath. Between two trees, in a small clearing hacked out for it, above the ground-honeysuckle that matted the entire hill, it glimmered now like a wintering carousel.

Strange, he thought, for what purpose would they have done this now, in the spring, and as he did so, a figure came from behind the pavilion and started slowly along the skinny footpath that zigzagged down the hill. It was a woman, carrying honeysuckle cuttings, two big sheaves of them that lifted her arms at right angles and trailed behind her, dragging the ground like a train. She passed him, quite close on the other side of the hedge, coarsely cut gray hair, emaciated eyes in a face he had never seen before, and trailed on through the opening in the hedge, down to the riverbank, where she let the cuttings fall into the river, and stood while they were borne away. She wheeled, and came back up the path. Even as he nodded, tentatively, into the uninflected face, he saw, with an inner, breaking "Ah!" of pity, that she must be mad. The eyes told him first — set motionless, aghast, as in those drawings where the doubled face was wrenched apart, the full eye set staring in the profiled nose. But it was the arms that told him for certain, arms still extended, cross-like, above the empty shape of the honeysuckle, as she marched back up the hill. She made three trips through the darkening air, each trip preceded by the sound of her scythe up above. When Garner finally entered his house, she had stopped coming, but he could still hear the slashing of the scythe among the vines.

He said nothing to Amelia, eating in the kitchen with her and the four chattering children, grateful for the familiar, perky pottery dishes, for the room's bright chromium sanity. But that night, as they were undressing for bed, in their room that faced the hill, he told her, and they discussed it in low, troubled voices. "It's about the *children* that I'm . . ." said Amelia. She turned out the light, as she always did before she put on her nightgown, although there was no one up the hill to see. "Look!" she said, leaning on the window sill. The shutters that had been used to board up the summerhouse, Garner remembered, had been of the kind with a small half-moon cut out of the wood, and now, in each of them that made up the blank façade, there was a weak spot of light.

The next morning, he was leaning on his new power mower (almost paid for now), and looking at his shaved lawn with a warm sense of satisfaction, when the doctor emerged for his morning tour. To date, his and Garner's over-the-hedge interchanges had consisted mostly of Garner's murmured assents to the doctor's pronunciamentos on the beauties of what lay before them — Bhatta had a way of conversationally appropriating the glories of the universe, and pointing them out to his listener (as if the latter might not have noticed them without his help) that reminded Garner of some ministers he had known. Sometimes, at his approach, Garner, out of a shyness he would have phrased as not wanting to "get too thick" with neighbors, waved and moved on to a distant task, but today he stayed where he was.

"Good morning, Misser Garner." Bhatta advanced majestically. "I see you have been up early, and worked well." He waved an expansive hand. "Now comes the beautiful time, har? No fuel bills!"

Garner nodded, paying a moment's silent tribute to the landscape, in accordance with the doctor's gesture. "See you put in a fine lot of roses there."

"Yars. In my country, the cultivation is very simple. Plenty of manure, plenty of roses. But here there is only *chicken* manure — and very expensive. A commentary, har?" Bhatta smiled broadly.

Garner smiled also — an overcompensating smile of the kind one used with people who spoke a foreign language. He could never get over a feeling, of the worst provinciality, he knew, that Bhatta was not speaking English, even at the very moment he so excellently was. "See you closed up the summer-house."

"Yars." The doctor took another turn at the landscape.

"You, um . . . you moving your practice up here?"

"I do not have what you would call a pract-ice, Misser Garner."

"Oh . . . I see."

"Um." The doctor smiled again. "When I come to America to study medicine, I am very young, very enthusiastic. But when I finish, I find after all that I am not sufficiently — assimilated. For me, neurology is only part of a philosophy. I find I cannot sit in an office and take mo-ney for making cures. A little surgical, a little phar-maceutical housework — bang bang, one hundred dollars." He shook his head. "Unfortunately, I am not happy doing housework, Misser Garner."

"But you do take some patients?"

"For a while I do many things. I give lectures, I write books, one time I even have a restaurant. But everywhere people say, 'Bhatta, you have the secret of living, what is it?' I tell them that it is only because in India, where life is hard, we have to learn early the connection between work and love. I tell them that it is only here, where mo-ney churns butter, that people have time to suffer, because they do not have this connection. But they do not believe me. So I let them come up here and learn." He turned to look at Miss Leeby, who was standing on a ladder some yards away, clipping a hedge. "When they are grateful, they give gifts. For them it is therapy to give, and therefore it is possible for me to receive." He turned back to Garner. "You understand how this is, Misser Garner?"

Garner had no immediate answer, but he saw, from the doctor's expression, that a prompt one would have been a disappointment.

"Ah, you think it devious, perhaps," the doctor said quickly. He turned away from Garner again, looking downriver with a benignant smile. "The air is so clear in America," he said softly. "So very, very *clear*." He beckoned suddenly toward Miss Leeby, who started obediently down her ladder. "Come and see Misser Garner's beautiful new lawnmower," he called. "How that woman works!" he said, sotto voce. "How she loves flowers!"

Miss Leeby came and squatted down over the lawnmower, her work-split nails moving expertly over it, her bun and prim, altar-guild face odd over her man's shirt, dungarees, and dirty saddle-shoes.

"Is this not a beautiful machine, Leeby?" said the doctor.

"We ought to have one like it." She looked up at him

devoutly. "It would give me so much more time for the roses."

"Well, perhaps Misser Garner will show you how to run it, one day."

Garner nodded, half wondering whether the doctor would not suggest the wise therapy of his giving them the mower. Meanwhile, Miss Leeby had wandered over to Garner's peony bed, and was kneeling there. "Why, you're letting these choke!" she said, horror sharpening her high voice. "If you don't thin them, the ants will be all over the buds!" She stretched a compassionate hand toward them, she had already taken a trowel out of a pocket, she was already beginning on them.

"Now Leeby," said the doctor, shaking his head indulgently. "Cultivate our own garden, please." He watched her move back to her ladder, chuckles shaking his shoulders, his considerable belly. "A happy woman, Misser Garner. When she first came to me, she was stone-deaf. Only a case of psychological deafness, as her hundred-dollar man took care to tell me."

Over on the doctor's driveway, Miss Daria had backed out the old car, and leaving the motor running sluggishly, was stuffing a battered peach basket into the luggage compartment. In the bright morning air, with her black net stockings and very short skirt, with her long curls bobbing above the withered *femme fatale* make-up and the embarrassingly evident underwear, she looked like a grotesquely debased little girl, but she moved with stolid competence. The doctor squinted at her appreciatively, but made no revelations as to the history of her cure. "Ah, they need me for the shopping," he said. He waved. "They keep me stepping, those ladies. This morning, a lobster, no less, for the curry." He caressed his belt buckle. "How they love to spend mo-ney, those silly girls!" With a salute to Garner, he started off, then paused. "You are a lawyer, eh, Misser Garner?"

Garner nodded. By a fraction, he felt, he had prevented himself from adding "Yars."

"Ah, you must take curry with us some evening. I myself have a good many legal problems from time to time."

Garner roused himself from the rhythmic sloth into which the doctor's style of address had cast him. "Guess I'm like you, Doctor," he said, with a grin. " 'Fraid I don't have my own practice either."

But it was the doctor who had the last word. "Ah, how lucky!" he said. "How wise! You too have learned, then, how destroying it is to admit the connection between mo-ney and the work one loves!"

Garner watched him cross his lawn and enter the car. The car moved stertorously down the driveway and slowly past Garner. Bland between his two ladies, the doctor saluted once more. Garner leaned on his mower for a minute, then started rolling it toward his garage. It was not until he had emerged, empty-handed, looking absently about him for the next Saturday task, that he realized that he had not learned anything more about the woman on the hill.

That afternoon he went to the village to do the weekly shopping he and Amelia usually did together, leaving her immersed in preparations for the birthday party to be held for Sukey, their oldest, the next day. Ever since they had lived up here, a treasure hunt had been a traditional part of the children's fetes; in the dime store he gathered together a collection of prizes of that familiarity imposed by the ten-cent limit — crayons, bubble pipes, harmonicas, string bags of marbles and jacks, packets of green paper play-money with which the children could play store in Sukey's new cardboard grocery, some jointed plaster snakes, some rubber balls. At the last minute, groaning with lack of inspiration, he raised the limit to a quarter, and added some water pistols, and some pink plastic babies for the smaller girls. Then to the butcher's, for the order

Amelia had phoned in, and at last to the supermarket, where he scarcely needed Amelia's list. The order was always roughly the same, it seemed to him — enormous renewals on the breakfast foods, the bread and the canned tomatoes (Grade C, the canny list reminded him), boxes and boxes of frozen vegetables (these were no longer an economy except of time, Amelia had worriedly said last Saturday — now that they needed two of a kind for enough servings at a meal), the same list of staples, the two dozen eggs. Not pullets, he remembered, although this was not down on the list, for he had been a good pupil, and he knew now, among other bits of lore, that the cheaper pullets worked out to no eventual good, because of their size. Poor Amelia, he thought, it was not her fault if her prideful instructions on the arts of domestic evasion had become repetitive — it was not her fault if the evasions had always to be the same. "Butter — or oleo," the list said, leaving it up to him. Yes, perhaps it had better be an oleo week. He recalled the doctor's phrase about money churning butter. A little dig at America. Where the living is easy, he had in effect said, it was often hard on people. Garner chuckled. He was a sharp one, Dr. Bhatta, even if one could not quite tell whether his manner came from a lack of the language or a way with it. And a nervy one — to deliver that kind of sermon from a seat on the stoop.

Garner had finished his list, pushed his overflowing wire basket to the end of the long queue at the cashier's desk, and was idly betting with himself that his total would be somewhere between eighteen and nineteen dollars, when he saw, with a twinge, that he was directly behind Mr. and Mrs. Adrian Dee. The Dees were very thin, very old, and very poor — of a poverty that gentility held together like the black string tie that Mr. Dee wore to do his shopping, even in this weekend wilderness of sports shirts and dungarees. "Natives" — that is of the old Hudson Valley Dutch stock, as distinct from newcomers like Garner himself — they were, as cousins, both of a family that had given innumerable place-names to the county, but whose tenure had long since thinned with its blood. Mr. Dee had always worked hard in one of those clerkly jobs the exact nature of which no one ever remembered, other than that it had been in some outmoded business which had finally faded just as its outmoded employees needed it most. They lived now in the smallest house on the river road, a kind of baroque toolhouse, its tipsy turret supported by a wisteria vine thicker than either of the Dees, that was located on the edge of what probably had once been all Dee land. Cornered in this last briar patch of inheritance, Mr. Dee, county historian and fiercest member of the zoning board, upheld the conscience, ancient and present, of the road. For if he loved the town deeply, with the love that one gives only to the place that best knows who one is, he had an even more subterranean fright of the city, with whose approach his delicately guarded identity would no longer be known at all. And the town — and for this Garner too loved it — had been delicate with him indeed. It was aware that he had refused to register for Social Security, and no one had ever dared sound him on the subject of old age pensions. Quietly the town saw to it that he had a place on those important committees to which no suspicion of a fee could be attached; even more quietly it had made his name the sole contender for those still honorable civic duties for which he could be paid. He was a keeper of records, a taker of censuses, a watcher at polls. At one crisis in Mrs. Dee's health, the historical society had found itself in sudden need of a commissioned sesquicentennial report; at another, the library had found itself similarly helpless without a part-time custodial appointee. But still, altogether, the fees must be very small. Once before, Garner had found himself in the aisle of canned goods, behind the Dees, and had averted his eyes, his ears, from the two pairs of hands, pale as thorns, hovering past the salmon to the sardines, from the two hatted heads bent in secret consultation over the price on the bottom of a tin.

Now, above Garner's bulging basket and the Dees' sparsely tidy one, their glances met. "Mr. Garner sir, good morning!" Mr. Dee offered his handshake, ghostly version of one that must once have matched the office with the fumed oak, the black leather davenport, the wine-dark cigars. Behind him, Mrs. Dee, gloved hands clasped, nodded only; she belonged, by both personality and era, to those women who enhanced their husbands' dignity by echoing their actions but never equaling them.

"Well met, sir," said Mr. Dee. "On the part of the zoning committee, I was just about to get to you on the telephone."

Eighty, if he's a day, thought Garner. Not the man for the latter-day "Ring you," "Call you." Or, more probably, no phone of his own.

Mr. Dee leaned forward. "You know, perhaps, of your new neighbor's activities?" he whispered.

"Well . . . an unusual ménage, I gather."

"Oh, that!" Mr. Dee smiled primly, raising a milk-blue finger. "Not our concern, of course. We are not that kind of meddler here. But of late years — I have had to acquire the habit of reading the *Times'* real-estate section. Unfortunately, local transactions have grown beyond the local newspaper." He coughed, remembering gently that Garner, a former city man, must have had a history of just such a transaction, and fumbling in the watch-pocket of his vest, held out a clipping. Garner bent over it. Under the heading COUNTRY BOARD, he read: *Come to the house of the Pundit Bhatta. Great white house like castle. Crushed stone driveway. Roses everywhere you look. Build your own guest-house. Indian cookery and wisdom. Health through peaceable work. Contribution, $30 per week.*

"I thought you and I might talk to the gentleman, first," said Mr. Dee. "Explain to him that the tradition, in fact the law of the river road does not permit even two-family dwellings, much less any such communal development."

"From what I know of him, he'll do the talking," said Garner. He felt annoyed, suddenly and sharply, less by the threat to his own property — although the thought of other poor creatures like the woman in the summerhouse, all sweeping the hillside like the seven maids with seven mops, was an unnerving one — than by the humiliated feeling that in this morning's conversation with the doctor he had in some way been "sold," been "had." Some tricky sympathy in himself had responded to the kernel of what the man had said, had led him to conclude that if Bhatta sold nothing but confidence, he perhaps belonged, nevertheless, to that unique and complicated breed which believed in its own wares. He, Garner, had been "taken," like those who listened to the talented swindler purely out of admiration for the spiel but ended up with the mining shares after all.

"I doubt if we can force the boardinghouse issue, Mr. Dee," he said. "The road never has, you know. Because of the occasional hardship cases."

"But it's not that!" Mr. Dee pointed again to the ad, looking agitatedly around him, as if here, on this Rialto of screaming children, harried mothers, packhorse husbands, there were the very signs of the urban beast that waited, alert for the tip on a house that might be converted, a property that might be acquired as a wedge, a sudden amalgamation that might be made. "Build." he whispered. "You see what he says right here. *Build!*"

Back of Garner, the long line murmured, ahead of him the checker shrugged her impatience. "Oh I do beg all your pardons," said Mr. Dee. With a "No, allow me, dear," to his wife, who had once again moved a tentative glove, he emptied his basket on the counter. He took a five-dollar bill from his wallet, and paid. "Perhaps I could walk down to see you tomorrow, sir, after church?"

Garner nodded, busy emptying his own basket. Then, as the Dees filed out, he called after them. "Care to wait, I'll be glad to drop you and your things on the way."

"Oh, thank you," said Mr. Dee, "but Mrs. Borden has already been so kind." He raised his hat, including the checker in his nod, and went out, followed by a clerk carrying the small box of goods. Behind him, Mrs. Dee turned once, and smiled.

Mrs. Borden, Garner thought. That would be the old Mrs. Borden, whose vintage car and chauffeur were often to be seen parked only in front of those grocers who still sold over the counter. After he had lived in the county for a while, he had gradually become aware of some of the old, still traceable bloodlines, and although, in the course of things, he would never become acquainted with Mrs. Borden, or want to, there was somehow, because he did live here, a more than antiquarian or social interest in the knowledge that she had been a Van Schaick, that the Van Schaicks had held on to their land. No doubt she took care of the Dees quite regularly, in many little ways. For, below the stratum of couples like Amelia and himself, there was still discernible, in the bedrock of that very village which they would someday overwhelm, a faint vein of that other antique world of allegiance, still banding together against the irresistible now, still, in resentment or noblesse, taking care of its own.

That night, after the children were asleep, he and Amelia walked up the back hill, he swinging a lantern along the path, she carrying a basket of the toys for the treasure-hunt, which she had placed in the printed cotton bags they kept from year to year. Above them, the wood rose sharply, darkened even by day by an undergrowth of maple seedlings, dogwood, fern, by an ominous spreading of bush and brush whose names he did not even know. Thirty years ago, in the feudal time of gardeners and servants, the hillside had been worked and terraced, a carefully husbanded sampler of grape arbors and cold frames, of neatly curtailed dells. But now, in this suburban renaissance where people bought for the sake of the houses and the land was only extra and ignored, almost all the places along the road backed up against a dark encroachment like this one, where, here and there in the spring, an occasional old planting sparked with stunted fruit, or a sentinel iris pushed its spear through the honeysuckle, the sumac and the grass.

Just back of the house there was a large plateau where the garden officially ended, and it was here, in scuffed, already traditional places — in the hollow tree that held the swing, in the ledges behind the children's tent, in the dry channels of last year's squash vines, that he and Amelia cached the bags, not too well hidden, where the children might find them the next day. They looked lovely in the starlight, with their dim paisley scrolls and freckles — like the fey nesting of some wild and improbable bird. He swung the lantern in an arc above them — an efficient department store lantern, bought for those evening hours when he cadged a bit of time to chop wood, to fix the fan-belt on the pump. Silly or not, with its fake oil-lantern shape, it felt good to swing it in this ritual that their years here had already built for them, above these places which for the children were long since familiar and old.

Back at the kitchen door, Amelia stumbled in ahead of him, murmuring that the children had worn her to a frazzle, in and out of the house all day. He doused the lantern, and sat down on the porch steps, looking out at his acre, his back hill. At times it made him feel like an interloper, a defaulter. It came scratching at his door, not like the wilderness, but like a domestic animal, crying to be tended. This year he would have to burn back the brush, for sure.

Sometime before morning, he got up from bed to latch back a banging shutter. For a moment he thought he saw a figure move across the grass and merge behind the summerhouse. He waited, but saw nothing but the movement of the trees, stirring in the pre-dawn wind. He was about to go back to bed when he saw, down the long hall that led to the front windows, the first eastern flake of light. This was one of the privileges that went with living where he did, one dearly bought and seldom used, the privilege of watching the sun rise on the river from his own window, his own realm. He watched the yellow light shake itself into prisms on the leaves of his horse chestnut trees, waited until the red ball heaved itself out of the river at a spot where, if he remembered correctly, he had the right to seine shad. Then he went back to bed.

When Mr. Dee presented himself the next morning, Garner was alone, Amelia having gone to pick up Sukey at Sunday school, taking the others along for a ride. Neither Garner nor Amelia was a churchgoer, but Sukey's recent request to go had been acceded to at once, lest she be damaged in her natural craving "to belong." All the other city emigrés along the road were always making these little forays into the art of belonging — for this too was felt to be one of the privileges of living here. Watching as Mr. Dee picked his way toward him, carefully setting his freshly blacked shoes between the mud squelches that winter had raised on the poorly surfaced road, Garner wondered what it would feel like to be he, inhabitant of that lost steel-engraving world into which one had been born with all one's affiliations incised.

On the doctor's porch together, a few minutes later, they waited while the door chime sounded somewhere inside. It was an elaborate chime — a four- or five-tone affair.

"Dear me," said Mr. Dee, shaking his head. He stared up at the cathedral-like architraves of the front door. "My understanding is — someone *gave* him the place!" he whispered.

A second sound, of steady hammering, blended with the repeated peal of the chime. Mr. Dee blenched. He looked sideways at Garner's Sunday morning garb of T shirt, army surplus slacks, and sneakers, dropped his glance covertly to his own dark vest, carnelian seal. "I understand also, however," he whispered, "that his own credit is very infirm."

Miss Daria opened the door. Her gaze met Mr. Dee first, approximated him. "Good morning," she said, in a businesslike voice that went oddly with her waxed lashes, her dazzling blouse. "You've come to see about the rooms?"

"Indeed not!" said Mr. Dee, in a high voice. Garner, intervening, asked for the doctor.

"Come in," she said, unsmiling, and led the way like an usher, through a hallway formed by the first arc of a spiral staircase, into a vast double room, where, in a oasis of furniture set against portieres that divided the regulation sitting room and parlor of such houses, the doctor sat, drinking tea. He had, Garner thought, almost an air of being "discovered" drinking tea. Indeed there was an air of theatrical arrangement, a floridly seedy, "rented" flavor to the whole scene. Garner looked about him, reminded that Amelia would want to know. Kemtone paint, in a number of purposefully intense, but somehow failing colors — pink, orchid, acid green — had been applied to the imperially molded ceiling, the high, cracked walls, and had been wreathed, like tulle around the ravaged throatline of an old beauty, up the underpinning of the spiral stairs. On a hotel-Moorish table, set among several baronial but battered plush chairs, incense bloomed suddenly from a pot, as if it had just been set burning. There was a determined attempt at Oriental mystery, but except for two huge ivory-inlaid teakwood screens, it remained a fatally auction-room Oriental. It was, Garner decided, remembering Miss Daria's blouse, perhaps "the ladies' " idea of mystery.

"So, Misser Garner, you come to see me after all."

Garner introduced Mr. Dee, in the latter's capacity as board chairman.

"Ah, zoning," said the doctor. His nod was sage, managing to indicate that he drew upon a vast, physicianly stock of unsurprise. He shook Mr. Dee's hand, looked down at it searchingly for a moment, then gave it back to him. "Good arteries," he said. "You will probably live forever."

Mr. Dee, withdrawing slightly, bent down, not without a certain pride of spryness, to detach a bit of dried mud from his shoe.

"Very bad, yars, the road in front of my house," said Bhatta. "Perhaps now it is spring, the village plans to repair."

"On the contrary, sir." Mr. Dee straightened, squaring his frail shoulders. "Last thing we want here is the heavy, beer-truck kind of traffic. Let them go round by the state road."

"Ah?" said the doctor. "Of course, here in this house we do not smoke or drink. Alcoholism is a very character-istic symptom of Western neurosis. But I do not think it responds to superficial restraints." He moved a hand toward his cup. "Darjeeling. A very soothing type of addiction. You will join me?" He clapped his hands together, but the sound was barely audible above an increased din of hammering in the rear of the house. He looked sideways at Garner, veiling a brown gleam of amusement with one lowered eyelid. "T-t-t. Those busy ladies."

"You mistake me, sir," said Mr. Dee. "We guard only the community, nor its, er, personal habits. This is a unique preserve we have here. No coastal railway, one minor factory. On an international waterway, if you please, and *dangerously* near the city. One false step — why there are garden-apartment interests that watch us night and day. You have only to look at the other side of the river — "

Bhatta nodded, impressed not so much, Garner thought, by the phrase "the other side of the river," whose weight of local scorn he might not realize, as by Mr. Dee's competitive flow. He waved a slow hand toward the back of the house. "Well, as my unfortunate ears inform me, we are building our own

Eden here. All night Miss Leeby insists on finishing the new bathroom, for the arrival of some guests. We have this evening a double celebration. First, the anniversary of Indian independence. Second, the arrival of my nephew from Allahabad, who comes to study medicine. I will get Miss Leeby to stop and bring tea."

"No, really we can't stay," said Garner. A fluttering endorsement of this came from Mr. Dee. "We came merely to — "

"To be delightful and neighborly, of course. So you must allow me. Meanwhile make yourselves at home — there is material here and there that may interest you." Bhatta motioned toward the piano, toward a pile of books in a corner, various framed papers on the walls. "Also, I must hear more of this zoning. Like this gentleman, I am also an enemy of progress." He chuckled, and rose slowly. The plush chair fell backward from him, its withered ruffle exposing its bowed legs, like the comedy sprawl of an old character actress. "Not with his admirable structure, however." He tapped the back of one of his hands sadly with two fingers of the other. "Adipose. Hypertensive. Probable final history — embolism," he said, smiling, and left the room, leaving the chair upended behind him.

Mr. Dee moved closer to Garner. "Slippery," he whispered. Chin sunk in his hard collar, he meditated, delving further, perhaps, into the penny-dreadfuls of his boyhood. The carnelian seal rotated slowly. His peaked face came up, triumphant. "Very slippery article. We'll get nowhere with him. An injunction, I fear. If we can only find out precisely what his activities are." He moved along one wall, examining. At an exclamation from him, Garner followed. He was reading a long card, in elaborate but somewhat amateurish print, held to the wall by passepartout. It was a restaurant menu. Under the title NEW INDIA RESTAURANT, a long list of curries followed, using a number of badly spaced different kinds of type. *Maharajah Curry (for two)* $3.50 headed the array. Leaning closer, Garner de-

ciphered an italicized notation to the right. *With Turban $5.00.*
The list declined in rank, price, and size of print as one neared
the bottom, where it rose again with a final entry added in
typewritten capitals: *Mahatma Ghandi Curry — One Dollar.*

"Good God," said Mr. Dee. "Do you suppose he's running a
restaurant?"

Garner, his mind full of turbans — would they be in the
curry or on the customer? — was already standing in front of
the next display. It was a very ordinarily framed diploma,
granted in medicine to one Pandit Bhatta, from Iowa State
University.

"Dear me," said Mr. Dee. He looked up at Garner, his
wrinkles focusing shrewdly. "There is an Iowa State University?" On Garner's reassurance, his head sank. "Dear me."

Above an old upright piano there was a large poster drawing
of a veiled woman in an attitude of prayer, seated on a pedestal
formed by the block letters DESIRES. On the music rack below,
a single sheet of manuscript music lay carefully open, its
many migratory arpeggios blackening the page. Both poster
and music were signed *Bhatta.*

They had reached the pile in the corner, fifty or more copies
of the same book, a small volume, again by the Pandit, published by the Nirvana Press, with a flyleaf of other titles by the
same author. Entitled *Rose Loves,* it seemed to be half poem,
half paragraphs of meditation, apostrophes which had, here and
there, an oddly medical turn of phrase. A description of the
circulatory system swelled into diapason: *So the phagocytes
swarm in my veins, stars eating stars; the ganglia make little
rose-connections along the capillaries of the brain. I rise above.
Swung by my dervish blood, I can return to the tree-towns of
childhood, suspended above the city's begging bowls I swing
like a monkey from tree to tree.*

A folded piece of paper dropped from between the leaves of
the book. Garner picked it up, reinserted it, placed the book on

the pile of others, and pretended to be studying the ivory in-
lay in the nearer of the screens, as the doctor entered, followed
by the two women carrying the tea things, and a young man,
who ran to pick up the fallen chair.

"Ah, Misser Garner, you admire the screens?"

"Yes, very beautiful work."

"Yars. Very valuable . . . Miss Daria here wants me to sell
them. For three hundred dollars, although they are worth
much more than that. Eh, extravagant miss?" Miss Daria, engaged with Miss Leeby in settling Dee and Garner in chairs
and passing round the cups, kept her face bent, expressionless.
The doctor shook his head at her, including his guests in his
mirth. "Probably for . . . two hundred, she would sell them,
that girl!"

It was remarkable how, even as the two women served out
the tea, the doctor, with fluently hospitable gestures, maintained
the impression that he himself dispensed it. He introduced the
young man, his nephew, with a flourish that gave the effect of
the latter's having been created on the spot for this purpose.
The nephew, a slender brown young man in neat Western
clothes, exhausted his cup in two rapid inhalations, and was
quickly served again.

"He is very enthus-iastic," said the doctor, looking at him
meditatively. "Very anxious to get on."

"Gate on," said the young man, nodding repeatedly, with
the grinning intensity of the foreigner who wishes to make it
known that he understands. He rolled his eyes in an exquisite
spasm of comprehension. "Gate on!"

The doctor looked at Garner. Again his eyelid drooped. "It
is a Pres-byterian college — Allahabad."

Mr. Dee picked up his cup. "Indeed?" he said, with a vague,
reflexive politeness perhaps engendered by the cup. "Mrs. Dee
and I are of course communicants of the Dutch Reformed."

"Of course," said the doctor, with an equal flexion. At a

signal of his hand, the two women departed, followed by the nephew. "Very interesting," said the doctor, turning back to Mr. Dee. His eyelid lifted suddenly. "Reformed — from what?"

Mr. Dee set down his cup, at which he had but sniffed. "It refers to the Dutch settlers, sir. This is an early settlement. Very early."

"Ah, ah," said Bhatta. "And I come to it so late."

Mr. Dee lifted his chin above his collar. Under his parochial gaze the doctor's little pleasantry vanished, incense into ozone. "You understand, therefore, the board's concern over your plans?"

"Plans?" The doctor's shoulders vibrated to his smile. "They sprout around me like roses — these plans. But I myself — "

From under Mr. Dee's carnelian seal, the newspaper clip was withdrawn, and laid on the Moorish table. "Yours, sir?" he said. He sat back. A thin pink elated his starved cheek. He coughed once, and then again, and the cough had a dry, pre-served tang to it, an old flute long laid away in the musty con-fabulations of lost authority.

"T-t-t," said the doctor, studying the clipping. "Always in such a hurry, those terrible ladies." He chuckled. "A man's castle is not his house, har?" He leaned forward to place the paper back on Mr. Dee's side of the table, studying him. "You would like yourself to build a guest-house here, Misser Dee?"

"Garner — " said Mr. Dee. It was a measure of his feelings that he did not append "Mr.," and of his arteries perhaps, that they held.

"Dr. Bhatta — " said Garner. "Perhaps you're not yet . . . aware of the road's laws on this." He hesitated, then, squirm-ing like a boy under the tutorial glare of Mr. Dee, he repeated them: no commercial enterprise, no subdivided renting, no double dwellings. "And no additions to existent buildings," he concluded. "Except of course for members of the same family.

It's a — " He stopped. "Well — it's a hopeful attempt to keep things as they are."

"It is a real phil-osophy, this zoning," said Bhatta. "How lucky for me that Indian families are so large."

"Not large enough, sir, I think, to include all the readers of the *Times*," said Mr. Dee.

"What a peaceable world that would be," said the doctor. He sighed. "Then, perhaps the *Tribune*. But certainly, first the *Times*." He cast a sudden glance at Garner; it was the practiced side glance of the dead-pan joker, that mere facial cracking by which he chooses to honor a chosen auditor. "But you need not worry, Misser Dee. Miss Leeby is very talented — you should see the new bathroom. But she is not yet capable of a gar-den apartment."

Mr. Dee stood up. He bowed, and his bow too had a stored flavor, like the cough. "As Mr. Garner would have to tell you legally, it's the principle of the thing."

"Prin-ciples," said the doctor. He studied his hands, as if he had a number of such concealed there. He sighed, looking up at Garner. "The distance from *a priori* to *a posteriori*, that is the history of the world, har, Misser Garner? That is what I keep telling the ladies. Love is infinite; therefore its services should be. Then they come running from the kitchen to tell me the curry is finite." He stood up, turning to Dee. "It is a Christian dilemma also. You have had experience of this, per-haps . . . in the Dutch Reform?"

"Do I understand sir . . . ?" Mr. Dee's voice dropped to the whisper reserved for indecency. "That you *charge* for meals at these celebrations?"

"No, no, Misser Dee. It is like the party some people ask us here at New Year's. The ladies to bring casseroles. The men to bring bottles. It is the same with us. Only without bottles." He paused. "Perhaps you will stay today. A special occasion. No casserole required." He too bowed, with a plastic gesture toward the rear of the house, and Garner became aware that the noise from that region had been replaced by a powerful, spice-scented breath of cookery.

Mr. Dee flushed, and moved stiffly toward the door. In the nacreous light from its one high pane, his nostrils quivered once, membrane-pink, and were pinched still. "I thank you, sir. But Mrs. Dee has something very specially prepared."

As the doctor opened the door for them, Garner spoke. "Matter of fact, Dr. Bhatta . . . my wife and I did want to ask you. It's, er . . . it's about the lady who seems to be living in the summerhouse. Because of the children, we were — naturally a bit concerned."

"Ah, Miss Prager. Yars." The air coming through the door was balmy, but the doctor's face seemed to Garner for a moment as it had seemed on their winter encounters in front of the stores — as if it denied any imputation that it could suffer cold. "Tell your wife there is no cause to be concerned," he said. "Miss Prager will not touch anybody." His voice lingered on the word "touch," and with this his glance returned to Garner, its customary air of inner amusement regained.

"Summerhouse!" Mr. Dee pecked past both men and angled his head outside the door. Turning from what he saw, he confronted Garner. His chin sank into his collar. "So you already knew, sir, that we had a case in point there!"

An elderly limousine rolled slowly up to the doctor's gate. It stopped, motor running. Its klaxon sounded once — not with the tut-tut of present-day horns, but with an "Ay — ooyah" Garner had not heard for years.

"Ah, how kind of them!" Mr. Dee waved a gay, an intimate acceptance toward the car. He nodded stiffly at the doctor. "If you don't mind, Garner, perhaps you'll walk me to the car?"

Going down the path, his military gait made it clear that it was not assistance he required. At the car, the chauffeur, stooping, held open the rear door. He and Mr. Dee seemed of an age.

Mr. Dee paused. "From the board's point of view, I find this unaccountable of you, Mr. Garner. Personally, I can see that man's engaged your sympathy." He put a hand on Garner's arm. "Let me give you a warning my father gave me: Beware of the man who won't admit he likes money — he'll end up with yours." He turned to get in the car, then paused again. "Darjeeling!" he whispered angrily. "If that was anything but plain pekoe, I should be very much surprised!"

Garner watched the car disappear up the road, half amused, half impatient over the way he had wasted the haven of his Sunday morning like a schoolboy dangling beneath the concerns of his elders. He had been interrupted in his soothing routine of those repetitive acts of repair for which his house, blessed incubus, had an endless appetite. Out of habit, he looked at the river, pouring along south as private and intent as the blue skeins one remembered to notice now and then in one's wrists. How far up it did one have to go, these days, before one came to the real places, short-summered and Appalachian-cool, where a broken window was vital to life, a lantern was a lantern, and the ground woke every morning to its own importance? Too far for him, staked to the city like a dog on a string. This was as far as he could go.

Turning to go, he faced the doctor, who had followed him down the steps.

"He has much mo-ney, this Misser Dee?"

"No. Actually . . . almost none. The car was a friend's."

"It is not his own property he defends then, this little dragon?"

"Well — no."

Bhatta burst into laughter. Silent chuckles shook his belly, tinted his jowl. "Excuse me, Misser Garner. Really I am laughing at myself — for not yet being assimilated." He mopped at his eyes with a large ocher silk handkerchief. "So — he is only a proxy dragon, har?" He swung around for his usual appraisal of his own house. His eyes flicked past the summerhouse, and he bent to probe a heavy finger into a rose. "Well . . . every man has to tell himself some little tale in the dark, har? So as not to really see himself in the mirror the next morning." The rose sprang back, released. "Even in this clear air. Even an early set-tler."

Over at the far edge of his own property, Garner saw Amelia turning their car into their driveway. Children tumbled out of the car — his own, and several of the neighbors' — and ran into the house. He waved, but Amelia followed them in without seeing him. And perhaps because she had innocently not seen him malingering here, and because, although he rarely saw his children romantically, he had for a moment caught them aure-oled against the silent witch-point of the summerhouse, he spoke in sudden anger. "It's Miss Prager's story I'd like to have. And if you please — the facts. I'm not much for metaphor."

"Really?" The doctor squinted. "I would have said other-wise. But, as you say. Do not blame me if the facts are odd." He motioned to a bench, on which they seated themselves. Bhatta buttoned the top button of his shirt, shot a cuff, making, as it were, professional corrections to his appearance, and began to speak, with astonishing briskness. "Last year, a patient is very grateful; he gives me a house. Before he sails for Europe, he says to me, 'Bhatta, between us mo-ney would be an indeli-cacy. Take from me this house, which I have bought unseen for taxes, near the beautiful section of Brooklyn Heights.'"

Bhatta paused, shook his head mournfully, and went quickly on. "But when the ladies and I go there, I think probably he is not so grateful after all. Not a rescuable house. Even Miss Leeby shakes her head. We are sadly locking the door, so the wind will not blow it into the harbor, when Miss Leeby goes down cellar to look once more at the pipes. And there, in a room

at the back, is Miss Prager. Fainted, we think. No — it is cata-
tonic, and malnutrition. We talk with the neighbors; only one
old lady is there who remembers. And what she tells us — "

The doctor spread his hands. His voice had become measur-
ably softer. "Imagine, Misser Garner. A family has been mil-
dewing in that house for twenty years. Years ago, there were
three people, the father, the mother, the daughter. Lutherans,
very strict, very distant. The father absconds from his bank —
he was president — taking with him much mo-ney. Later on,
gossip says that he comes secretly back, but no one is ever
sure. Only the old woman we speak to remembers — the neighborhood is no longer Lutheran. Only Miss Prager, the daughter,
is seen, night and morning for years now, coming from the
bank, where she has always been cashier. The neighbors know
of an invalid upstairs in the house, but not whether it is a man
or a woman. There is never a doctor. At night, one light upstairs, one down. Then, some months before we come — a fire
in the house next door. Prager's is only smoked out, but the
firemen remove for safety an old person from the top floor.
Hugely fat, this person, too fat to move, long hair, and a dreadful sore on the leg. From the description — maybe diabetic
ulcer. Even in the smoke, the neighbors say, they can remember the smell from the leg. After that — nothing. They do not
remember when Miss Prager stops going to the bank. They do
not know her. The house is closed. They do not remember when
they no longer see her at all. It is a busy neighborhood, Brooklyn."

Garner shivered in spite of himself, and shook himself to
cover it, to shake himself free of the doctor's persuasion, which,
even in briskness, had a soft insistence, as if on some central
metaphor to which his listener must be privy too. The wind
had become more positive than the sun — and Amelia would
be wanting him in. But he had been a boy in neighborhoods
not too far from such as the doctor had described, and he was

remembering, with the self-induced chill of childhood, crabbed parlor recluses candled fitfully between curtain slits, dim basement monks whose legend, leaking from the areaways at dusk, scattered the children from the stoops. "Was it . . . it was the father then?" he said.

Bhatta's broad lips curved in a sudden Eastern symmetry. "A fact we do not check, Misser Garner. When we bring her home with us she is . . ." He shrugged. "She carries her cage with her, and we cannot persuade her out of it. To humor her fears, the ladies fix her the little place there." He pointed up the hill. "But I find the bank, Misser Garner. Natur-ally," he drawled, "if she has resources, we must find them for her. And what they tell me there, although they do not realize they are telling me it . . ." Bhatta paused, hands outspread. "Picture it, the same bank, but so modern, so airy now. At each desk, young ladies with hair like brass bowls. It is hard to imagine Miss Prager there. And the manager, in his cage that everyone can see is real — such a new young man, in a suit the color of chicken skin, and a bump in his throat that moves like a bobbin. He knows nothing of Miss Prager's father. Such a man does not deal by memory. Such a place cannot afford a memory. But 'Miss Prager,' he says — 'until a year or so ago? — quite so. There is the Social Security index, the personnel file — and on the card there, yes, a little record of something that was not — quite so.' Two or three telephone calls, two or three moves of the bobbin, and there on the manager's desk — although of course he does not see her — lies Miss Prager and her twenty years."

Bhatta paused again. There was no defense against his pauses, Garner thought with violence — one pushed against them in vain, as one resisted a concert conductor who inexorably took his music slow.

"Banks are so jolly in your country," said Bhatta. "Like the one in the village here — a little white cottage with window boxes. And when your ladies take the children inside, the children do not hang on their mothers' skirts. They slide on the floor, and sometimes the manager gives them a little plastic penny bank — the way the baker gives them a cookie. Banks should be like the English bank in India, when I was a boy. A stern place, full of dark whispers, where the teller scoops up the mo-ney with a black trowel, and weighs it on a swinging chain-scale from Manchester. Then, at least, a child can be warned."

"You mean Miss Prager had embezzled?" said Garner.

Bhatta whisked out his handkerchief again, flirting it as if it concealed something maneuverable behind. "I forget you are a lawyer, Misser Garner. And so direct — like all Americans. Your honest men and your crooks — all so direct. It is a pity. You lose much." He touched the handkerchief to his lips. "No, I do not mean. Miss Prager was true to the bank. She herself owed them nothing. And alas, they owed her nothing. She had embezzled — only herself."

Across from them, the back door of Garner's house flew open, and eight or ten children rushed pell-mell from it and ran up Garner's hillside. Behind the high rhododendron and barberry, their creamy voices scuttled excitedly, belled by the loud, authoritative birthday voice of Sukey.

"I must go," said Garner, getting up. "My kids are having a party. They're up there now, having a treasure hunt. You see — our hill's kind of their playground. Even if you gave me your assurance that Miss Prager is not . . . dangerous . . . I'd hate to think she might frighten them in any way."

"She will not go near them, Misser Garner. She will not touch them." The doctor rose too, placing a hand on Garner's arm. "You see — *literally* she will not touch anything. She is afraid of her own hands. That is what the bank tells me. One morning they find her at the cashier's window, in a daze. Her hands will not touch the mo-ney, she says. She is resting her hands now, she tells them. Naturally, what can they do? A cashier who will not touch mo-ney! That must be why she is starving when we find her. She tells us too that she is resting her hands. But actually she is afraid of them. She does not like to touch herself with them." Bhatta smiled, releasing Garner's arm. "Pitiful, har? Actually, rather a common form . . . but developed to the extreme. We have done pretty well with her. Now she feeds herself, and she will work at clearing the brush. But you have seen how sometimes she forgets, and holds her arms?" The doctor cocked his head, listening to the children's voices. They were chattering excitedly, and syrupy wails came from the younger ones.

"Charming," said Bhatta. "What is this game they are playing?"

Garner explained.

"But how charming! And what is in the little bags?"

"There's my wife, coming after me I guess," said Garner, and indeed Amelia was advancing toward them. Through the opening in the hedge, the children trooped after her and surrounded her. "Daddy! Daddy!" shrieked Sukey.

Amelia quieted her with a gesture. She nodded briefly to the doctor, and knitted her brows meaningfully at Garner. Her face was pink with reproach. "John! The bags are gone from the hill. Every one of them. There's not one!"

"Somebody stole them! Somebody stole them!" Sukey danced up and down with excitement.

The other children took up the refrain and the dance. Garner looked at his youngest, Bobbie, who was aping the others with improvisatory glee. "You don't suppose that he — ?"

"John, he's not capable of it. They've disappeared. Besides, the children have been with me every minute. We only put the bags out last night. You know what I think?" She took a step toward Bhatta, her mild face dilated. Taking their mood from her, the children clustered round her, staring at the doctor. There was no brood-hen room for them in her narrow tweed skirt, but she pressed them against her with her prematurely knuckled, detergent-worn hands. "I think it's that person you — you have up there!"

"Thought I saw someone moving around up there this morning," said Garner. "Before it was light. Forgot all about it."

"Pos-sible," said the doctor. "If so, remarkably interesting. Why do we not go and see?" He bent benevolently toward Sukey. "You are really having your hunt, har? Let us go and see."

"Indeed not!" said Amelia. "You children come back to the house with me." But led by Sukey, the children had already escaped her, and were running up to the hut. It was clear that the presence there was no news to them. Garner and the others reached them just as they drew back at the railing of the pavilion, their little ferreting noses arrested in uneasy obedience.

The doctor knocked gently at the center shutter, to which a knob of wood had been crudely affixed. Behind his bulbous, stooped form, the blind pavilion, little more than man-high, and puzzled together from old splinters of the past, had the queer coyness of a dollhouse in which something, always on the run from the giant thumb, might be living after all.

"Miss Prager?" said the doctor softly. "Miss Prager?"

There was no answer from within, nor did the doctor seem to expect one. He pushed inward the unlocked shutter, and stepped inside. For a moment they could see nothing except the small, swelling flame of a hurricane lamp. Then he opened a shutter at the back and daylight filtered in, neutering the lamp, winking it into place on a chain hung from the roof-point. Half the rough wood hexagonal table that had once filled the place, paralleling the sides, had been cut away, leaving room for a small pallet. Behind it, on part of the window seat that encircled the room, there was a pile of underclothes, a mackinaw, a pitcher, besides some cracker boxes still in their bright paper. Next to these, a pair of black house slippers with

curled silk pompoms glistened unworn, as if presented by hopeful nieces to an intractable aunt. Behind the other side of the
table sat Miss Prager. In the current of air between the two
shutters, compounded of the hot funk of the oil lamp and the
tobaccony damp of wood-mold, she sat motionless, upright,
arms spread-eagled on the table, in front of all the little gutted
bags.

Sukey cried out sharply, "There it — !" and hushed. But they
had all seen the dime-store money, neatly rectangled in piles,
the toy snakes and babies tumbled to one side.

At Sukey's cry, Miss Prager wilted into consciousness. Her
elbows contracted to her sides. She was working in a narrow
space, the elbows said. Her hands moved forward, picked up a
packet of the money and shuffled it expertly, counting it out.
One two three four, thump. One two three four, thump, the
hands went, moving of themselves. The middle right finger
flicked the bills like the spoke of a wheel. At each fifth thump,
the spatulate thumb came down. Miss Prager stared fixedly at
the lamp, but all the while her hands moved so lucidly that
one almost saw the red rubber casing on the middle finger,
the morning business sun, glinting on withdrawals and deposits,
behind the freshly wiped bronze bars. Beneath her fixed gaze,
her hands went on transacting without her, and came to no
conclusion.

This was what they saw before the doctor closed the door,
and stood with his back to it. He looked over the children and
picked out Sukey, who was standing well forward, one arm
pressing her small brother to her stubby skirt, in angular imitation of her mother. The doctor beckoned to her, as to the
natural leader of the children. And she was, she would always
be, thought Garner, seeing his daughter in that quickened out-
line which drama penciled around the familiar. Here was no
city febrile, here was none of that pavement wistfulness of
tenure such as Amelia and he, even middle-class as they had

been, had known as children. She was more intrepid, more secure, because they had grounded her here.

"She's got our bags," said Sukey.

"So she has," said the doctor, smiling. "She has been ill, and did not know they were yours. I tell you what — suppose you all come back after lunch, har? Meanwhile, the ladies will put all the things back in the bags, and hide them on our side of the hill. That will be exciting, har, to hunt in a new place? And in each bag, for each child — there will be a prize from India!"

And so it was arranged. Garner, following behind Amelia to herd the children inside, saw Miss Leeby enter the summer-house, and shut the door behind her. Later, after lunch, as he carried the debris of cake and ice cream into the kitchen, while the front of the house rang with the shrieks of blindman's buff, he saw two figures through the kitchen window, which had a view of Kuyper's hill as well as of his own.

It was the nephew and Miss Daria, stooping here and there on their part of the hillside, to hide the bags. He barely knew them, that ill-assorted pair, and it could be assumed that they scarcely knew each other, but he found himself looking at the two figures, rounded over in the blameless posture of sowing, with the enmity of a proprietor watching his boundary lines, his preserves. It was not, surely, that he resented the foreigner, the alien. He and Amelia were of the college-disciplined gener-ation that had made a zeal of tolerance. But for the first time, watching these two figures from a ménage that had suddenly bloomed next door to him like an overnight morel, he felt a shameful, a peasant creeping of resentment, almost an ab-dominal stiffening against persons that different — and that near. Let them keep their difference, but at a distance, he thought. At closer range, a foreign way of life, wrong or right, posed too many questions at one's own. Questions that he was not up to answering as yet, that he was not interested in having answered. Bhatta no doubt made a career of posing questions at the uncertain, holding out the bait of answers to be rendered at a stiff fee. "Way of life" was a flabby phrase perhaps, thought Garner, but since he and Amelia were conducting themselves as thousands of well-meaning couples all over the country were, he presumed that they had one, although its outlines might be obscure. If their affiliations — he thought of Mr. Dee — were still too vague to bear perspective, he supposed that time would sculp them clearer, doing for the contemporary what it had done for all others. Perhaps his own affiliation to his way of living was not old enough, not deep enough, for self-scrutiny. "It doesn't do to get too thick," he muttered to himself. "It won't do."

So, when Miss Daria came to the door, with the message that "the Doctor would receive them now" — there was no doubt that the doctor's ladies thought him the personage to others that he must be to them — Garner relayed the message to Amelia. She came into the kitchen, shunting the children before her, herding them with an abstracted tongue-lash here, a pat on the buttocks there, showing her own physical sense of herself as still their nursing center. All the neighborhood mothers of younger children had this; it was in the tugged hang of their daily clothes, in the tired but satiate burr of their voices, it was no doubt what grounded them.

"You're coming too, aren't you?" she asked.

"Thought I'd like to get that drain dug." He heard his own tone, the plaintive bleat of the weekend householder.

"John — it's Sukey's birthday." She went out the door without saying anything more, but he knew from her voice, her face, what she was thinking, was silently saying to him. "More contact with the children," she was saying. Fathers must have more contact with their children. All the mothers prated this to one another, and to the husbands, bravely arranging weekend excursions in which fathers had the starring role, taking the briefcases from their deadened arms at nightfall and hand-ing them the babies sleeked from the bath, sidling the older children nearer for advices, ukases from the giant combat world of downtown. "Touch them, put your arms around them more," Amelia had once said to him. "Get down on your knees and play with them more," all the conniving mothers said, trying to give substance to these vague father figures that flitted from home at something after seven and returned at something before. And the mothers had other fears, Garner thought, fears that they shared, squirming self-consciously in the naked antiseptic light shed upon them by the magazines they all read, the books by female anthropologists who warned them of momism, of silver cords, of sons turned feminine and daughters wailing in a Sapphic wilderness.

Now that he thought of it, the remarkable thing was that in this modern world — supposedly of such complexity, such bewilderment that one could only catch ideas, precepts, on the run, and hold on to them no longer than the draining of a cocktail — people like Amelia and himself and their friends here, people who would be referred to as the educated classes in any country less self-conscious than America, were actually all the time imprisoned in a vast sameness of ideas. It's a loose theology we're in, he thought, a jelly-ooze littered with leaflets, with warnings and totems, but it holds us, in its invertebrate way, as firmly as any codex thundered from those nineteenth-century pulpits from which we have long since decamped. Even the phrase "nineteenth-century," which he had used without looking at it, as one spent a coin — was it anything more than a part of this, an old examination marker, a paper flag stuck in a bog?

Certainly his father, the lawyer, and Amelia's, the professor in a minor college, both born in roughly the late eighties, had been holdovers from that century, and he remembered, with fair accuracy, that they had been, if anything, more remote from their children than he, Garner, was from his. He could hear their voices, his father's, self-sufficient and nasal, spewing authority, and the professor's, taciturn and weighty, but with the same mantle of importance. That is what these men had had, he thought, a sense of their own importance, a sense of their own identity, solidity, in a world where the enterprise rested with them. When they had entered the dining room, heavily, of an evening, they had brought with them an illusion of a larger, a giant world of combat, but — and this was the point — it had not been an illusion either for them or their wives. And this, thought Garner, this was really what Amelia and the other mothers were after. They were trying to recast the fathers of their children in the image of *their* fathers. They wanted this authority for their husbands, they wanted them to exude this importance to the children. Poor Amelia, Garner thought, biting his lip, but laughing inwardly, for it was funny, and what could one do, when afflicted with thoughts like these, except get into perspective, or out of it, and laugh? She didn't want to let the children see, she didn't want to see for herself that father thought of himself as only a dog on a string.

He slipped out the back door. In a few minutes he'd go up the hill, where he could hear the children, already hard at their hunting. He'd roughhouse with them, get down on the ground with them, anything Amelia prescribed. Through the leaves he could see her watching the play, preserving a certain distance from the doctor's ladies, who were also watching, and the nephew, who was running and cavorting with the children — he could not be more than eighteen or twenty.

Above them, in its small clearing, the pavilion was quiet, as usual; there was no telling whether or not the doctor had removed his charge to the main house. How incredible it was, in hindsight, the calm way they all had acted, after that one fell glimpse into the private pit of that poor thing in there! For that is what it had seemed like — the tiny black core of the place, the one flame lighting the objects displayed there (he remembered the slippers — like the amphorae set beside graves), and outside it, above it somehow, the white, saved faces of the children, peering over the crater at the clockbound movements of the damned. Then the doctor had closed the door, and immediately they, the conniving adults, had all acted so very naturally — the doctor, of course, with that composure of his which was more than professional, almost artistic, and he and Amelia, acting at once in concert, on another tenet of their theology, the leaflet that said "Never show fears before children. Never communicate anxiety to the young." In time of atom, in time of death and possible transfiguration, act secure, and they will take security from you. He sighed, and without meaning to, walked around to the front of the house, the river side. The leaflets never told you what to communicate, what to show.

The river was in a quiet mood today, scarcely breathing, one of those days when its translucence gave a double depth to the air and moved like a philosophy behind the trees. He often thought of it as it must have been four hundred years before, when its shores, not yet massed with lives like pinheads on a map, had been hunting grounds for other Indians. Any gardener who went deep enough along here turned up their flints, their oyster shells. It must have moved along much as now, in the aboriginal silence, beneath an occasional arc of bird, the warning plumes of human smoke still countable above the pines. For almost two hundred of those years now, it had passed to the sea only through the piling cumulus of the city, that Babel of diversity so much feared by Mr. Dee. And now the people were returning north along its current — the diaspora of the pins — sailing northward on the frail skiffs of mortgages, wanting to take strength from the touch of the ground, from the original silence. For diversity had at last scared them, scared us, Garner thought, who were born to it. It is a busy neighborhood now, Brooklyn and all the other places, where birth and death are only a flicker of newsprint, and a life can embezzle itself, without a neighbor around to know. So we radiate, but only twenty miles or more at best — for there is still father's string. But we're all up here looking for identity, he thought, for a snatch at primeval sameness, and if we haven't got it yet, if so far we have nothing but the looseleaf, newsprint theology that we brought with us, who's to say what an emigration, what a man's century can bring? He took a deep breath, and it seemed to him that the breath contained a moral effluence from the river, a clean draught of the natural beauty and goodness of the world.

So armed, he walked up his neighbor's hill. Up at the crest, the hunt was over apparently; most of the children in view were squatted here and there, chattering and swapping over their loot. Some of them were waving the tiny silk flags and brilliant kerchiefs that must be the doctor's prizes. They had certainly started something with their innocent hunt, their bread-and-milk birthday game. Wherever there were children, of course, it was always difficult to avoid interchange, keep one's distance, but he imagined that Amelia, who managed their social life up here so efficiently, would find some firm way of maintaining the distance. Certainly she, like himself, would want to fend these people off, this extraordinary household whose difference, exhaled like the incense floating in its parlor, had invaded their calm, routine-drugged Sunday and made of it this lurid, uneasy day.

And that there was a fraudulence, too, about these people — he would bet on it, on his sense of something beyond the mere fact that incense always had a certain fraudulence to Western nostrils. If he, Garner, for instance, had seen part of his army service in India, instead of sweltering in the rum-and-Coke familiarities of Fort Bragg, he might at least have been able to judge better whether Bhatta's rope-trick style of utterance came merely from that other way of life over there, in which Bhatta himself quite naturally believed. But even if Bhatta's manner was actually only the stock-in-trade of those yogas who coined temples from California pensioners, or conned elderly occult-seekers in Fifty-seventh Street lecture halls, then, according to the storekeepers down in the village, Bhatta must be an unsuccessful specimen of that breed. "Beware of the man who won't admit he likes money!" old Dee had said, having the advantage of *his* theology there. It was no trouble to place people, if you had long since been placed yourself, and Mr. Dee was like a clean old piece of litmus paper preserved from that simple experimental era when answers were either pink or blue. Bhatta, an intelligent man, whatever else he was, had tipped to this at once about old Dee, had immediately bypassed him in favor of more impressionable material like Garner himself perhaps, member of a generation that had been schooled so tonelessly free of prejudices that it had nothing left with which to anneal its convictions.

Gaining the crest of the hill, Garner saw the doctor talking to Amelia, who was listening politely, soothed enough, evidently, to have dropped for a moment her eternal watchtower count of the children. He was just in time, too, to see the doctor dismiss the two ladies and the nephew with a lordly sweep of the hand. They came down the path toward him, the nephew skipping ahead. He had one of the little flags in his hand, and he nodded and grinned like a jack-in-the-box as he skipped by, gurgling something in what Garner supposed to be Bengali, or Hindustani, or whatever the boy's native language was — until the syllables separated themselves in his ear, and he realized that the boy had said, "Jollee good fun. Jollee good." The doctor's two secretaries followed behind. Their smallness, their washed out once-blondness suggested, if village rumors about their real status were true, that the doctor might have a certain predilection for type, but beyond this Garner noted again what scant similarity there was between them. Miss Daria's short, surprisingly heavy legs stumped down the rocky path on high heels, her hair was sleazily girlish on her shoulders, and her dirty satins had the dead-beetle-wing shine of party clothes descended to daytime use. Beside her Miss Leeby, although earth-stained, looked cleaner; she had the inaudible gentility of a librarian whom some climacteric had turned gnome of the garden, and her hands were full of plant cuttings. Both women smiled vaguely on Garner as they passed, and he fancied then that there was a similarity — of smile. These were nun-smiles that they had rendered him, tokens floated down from a shared grace, and shed upon the unsaved. It was clear that the doctor's ladies, at least, had found their messiah. What was less clear was whether the messiah believed in himself. There were these suddenly contracting glances of his, these graceful circumlocutions about money — certainly he couldn't keep away from the word, if only to decry it — these heavy sighs over the gap between practice and principle. Were they the honest man's ennui with the world — or intended to suggest such? Or if Bhatta was a swindler, was there some little subcutaneous grain of honesty that weighted him down? For at times there was certainly a suggestion that, although the doctor might climb his rope-ladder, even pull it up after him in full view of the spectators, at the last moment he could not quite make himself disappear.

"Oh there you are," said Amelia. "Dr. Bhatta has been telling me about Miss Prager." Garner picked up Bobbie, who was squatted over some private game in the middle of the path, and set him on his shoulders. Bobbie tightened his knees around Garner's neck, hooting, then squirmed to be let down. Under Amelia's quizzical look, Garner set him back on the path.

"Dr. Bhatta has given us a prize, too," said Amelia. Glancing at it, he saw that it was one of the books that he had seen at the doctor's house. He nodded his thanks to Bhatta, and slipped the book in a pocket.

"A few prin-ciples," said Bhatta. "They would interest the little man, har? This Misser Dee?"

"He was more interested in your restaurant," said Garner. "The menu on the wall."

"Restaurant?" said Amelia.

"We had, at one time," said Bhatta. "On Twenty-sixth Street. The ladies' enterprise." He smiled at Amelia, with a touch of the manner he had used to cozen Sukey. "All you American ladies have the desire to open a shop, har? The hat shop, the tea shop. You are remarkable ladies."

"I gather you served both hats and tea," said Garner.

"Har?"

"I mean, uh . . . 'Curry with Turban.' "

Bhatta chuckled. "My friend who gives me the house in Brooklyn, you remember. He is such a very smart businessman. A middleman, you call it. He tells them, 'Package it. That's what sells. The package.' So they package it. Forty-two turbans in linen and silk, forty-two glass Kohinoors from Dennison's. Special trays for the turbans. A special boy to carry, and to wind them on the customer."

"What a clever idea!" said Amelia.

Clever enough to feint her away from dark thoughts of Miss Prager and the children, Garner thought, and for a moment he too smiled down on her, though fondly, with a touch of Bhatta's condescension.

"Yars," said the doctor. "But for our own friends, who have not the tourist mon-ey — I think that we must do something for them too. So we fix for them a nonprofit item."

"Oh . . . 'The Mahatma Ghandi Curry,' " said Garner.

The doctor nodded, swaying happily in an undercurrent of the private merriment that seemed to dash him constantly between the joke on others and the joke on himself. "They are very enthusiastic. So, at the end — " He spread his hands. "We have all this Ghandi trade — and no Maharajahs!"

Garner and Amelia smiled, as they were plainly meant to do. It was really impossible not to be warmed, won, Garner thought, by the doctor's disarming habit of making game of himself.

"Curry — with Loincloth?" said Garner.

The doctor threw back his head in a gust of laughter that set him jiggling from belly to cheek, with a violence almost alarming in a man of his weight. He laughed until his eyes watered; a tear overflowed and ran, mud-tinted, down his dark face. How seldom one sees that happen these days, thought Garner, meanwhile grinning with the sheepishness of the man whose quip has received more than its due.

Bhatta poked him in the ribs. "Now you are making the metaphors, har?" He mopped at the tear, loosened his belt a notch, easing his mirth as a woman might ease her girdle, and bent toward Garner and Amelia, meanwhile gazing absently out over the river, which was spotted with a flotilla of small boats, the larger craft of the professional shad-men who came every year under some immemorial right, and here and there a solitary fisherman, one of the householders from shore, sinking his long-handled net for the first early crab of the season. "You understand, of course," said Bhatta, lowering his voice with mock secretiveness, "underneath the names and the trimmings — it was all the same curry!"

This time it was the Garners who, after an instant's gap, exploded into laughter, while the doctor's lips only curved in the slightest of smiles, his head nodding and nodding, his veiled eyes presiding above their laughter as if he had known all along that he would be able to nudge them toward friendliness. And this was the man's talent, Garner thought, whatever lay beneath it — this talent for flipping the absurd and the serious over and over like a coin, a shell-game perhaps, at which the onlooker was dazzled, confused, but so warmed and joined that here were the three of them standing together, in a circle together under the gently dropping evening light — three friends who have kindled, sighed, and lapsed into end-of-day quiet, each looking inward for a moment at the same tender picture, at the *faiblesse* of man, poor homunculus, with his absurd nets and boathooks, grappling for fish and for flashing non-fish in the salt wave-shadows of living.

It was Amelia who recovered first. "Where do you suppose Bobbie's gone off to?" she murmured, indicting herself for this moment's indulgence, in which she had forgotten to keep tabs. For as Garner knew, as she had often confessed, her servantless immersion in the children's days, her almost never being apart from them, had somehow resulted in her being unable to enjoy without guilt those personal pauses which were every human's need; it was as if she felt that her constant, tensed awareness of the children was the placenta through which they were nourished still, and at the second she truly forgot them, they would as surely die. "Doctor Bhatta — " she said. "Do you plan to . . . will you have other people like Miss Prager up here? To live?"

The doctor was looking up in the air. "Such a day!" he said. "Like a magnifying glass!" He pointed to one of the hemlocks, one of the great trees which always seemed to Garner to lift this region bodily out of the suburb into the misty realm of the uncorrupted, the undiscovered. "High as a church, har, that tree? Yet one sees the three twigs at the top." He turned to Amelia. "Other people?"

"Well, I — I mean . . ."

He knows what you mean, thought Garner. And now the evasions will come twinkling down again, from the trees, from the air, from anything handy — a rain of silver, of silver-*paper*, on us, who are so regrettably direct.

"I mean — disturbed people," said Amelia, bringing out the phrase with an unhappy flush.

"Disturbed?" said Bhatta. "Miss Prager has the importance to be mad — in an age that does not take its mad people seriously. A man splits in two? Shhh — he is only upset. He must learn better how to swallow his century. If not — a very sad case of hic-coughs." He turned to look at the summerhouse. "And all the time," he said softly, "there are these sealed-off lives, these pieces of crystal — " He turned back to the Garners. "You have seen her. You would say she is — how old?"

Garner thought of the leathered skin, the dead hair hanging like a ledge from the over-articulated skull. "Perhaps — fifty?"

"And you, Missis Garner?"

"Well . . . yes . . . about that."

"She has worked in the bank, they say, about twenty years. And according to the employment records, the Social Security, there would be almost another thirty before the retirement. She is thirty-six." He nodded at their stricken faces. "Think of it. She would be about sixteen, when placed in the bank. Maybe a couple of years older when the father absconds. The bank lets her stay on; she is innocent, she has the mother to support. An ordinary story." Bhatta clapped his hands together. "But from then on . . . imagine. The father sneaks back; the two women hide him. Sometime later, perhaps, the mother dies. Miss Prager goes back and forth to the bank, night and morning. And all those years, while she is working to keep the secret, the city is taking her secret away. The neighborhood changes; the old neighbors are blown away. Even in a bank, the city blows things away. Who is to notice, to remember, if an old man were to come out of his door, to come out on his stoop, among a hundred other stoops, and sit in the sun?"

The Garners were silent. Then Garner spoke. "You're convinced it was the father, then?"

"A lawyer could perhaps check better," said Bhatta. "But as for me, I am innerly convinced." He looked down his hillside, wider and steeper than Garner's, but as wild, although here and there old terraces had been brought into view. On the road at the bottom one of the long, red motorcoaches from the city came to a wheezing stop. "Such a pure case," he said. "Such a classic of money-injury. All for a reason that no longer exists."

"You'll . . . keep her indefinitely?" said Amelia.

The doctor shrugged, threw up his hands. "Someone must. In any case, do not worry, Missis Garner. The ladies will soon build some places on the far side of the hill. Then we will put her there."

"There's a very fine state hospital. Quite near by." At the doctor's look, Amelia paused, again with a flush.

"And you say she has no resources?" asked Garner.

"None. I am sure." Bhatta's tone was almost one of pride.

"Quite the responsibility!" said Garner, and immediately regretted his own dry tone, its edge of disbelief, which the doctor was too subtle not to have caught. Ashamed, he told himself that it was a low envy which made one disparage in others the charity one had not got oneself. For after all, what did he have on the doctor, other than the mutterings of a few shopkeepers and his own carping intuition, both of which might be vulgar sides of the same thing, that fear of the stranger which was worse than vulgar, which college and International House and all that had taught him was the curse of the world? And which was against the very *laissez faire* of this place, which he had so boasted about in town.

Down at the bottom of the road, the bus moved off, with the familiar air-brake groan that was the only city noise along here, discharging a flood of exhaust gas on the passengers it had left at the stop. There were fifteen or twenty of these, and from the direction of their slow assault on the hill, it was apparent that they were the doctor's guests. Even at a distance they seemed a strangely assorted group — a periphery of nervous colors moving with brio around a more portly center of navies and browns. As they climbed nearer, Garner thought that they indeed resembled the lecture crowds he remembered from the days when he had had to squire his mother through her spiritualism period after the death of his father. In the center, there were a number of women very like his mother, vigorous elderly matrons, seemly in corsets and Footsaver shoes, wearing the flowered toques he had heard Amelia call "New Jersey hats." A few sallow young women were with them, and several elderly men. Among these latter, one wore pince-nez attached to a heavy black ribbon, and there were two or three shocks of melodramatic white hair. The color that framed the group was Asian; it came from a melange of brown skins, orange and yellow scarves, vanilla pongee suits topped here and there with a creamy turban, and the gauzy saris of three interchangeably lovely girls.

The doctor raised an arm, and saluted the people below.

"We must go, John," said Amelia. "And Dr. Bhatta — I don't want you to think that we . . . It's certainly a very fine thing of you to do."

"Har?"

"I mean, about Miss Prager."

The doctor's glance was on his guests, who had lingered below to admire the garden behind the main house. "You think?" he said, turning, and his face, softened by a question, was for once, almost open. Then it closed. "After all," he said, looking down the hill, "I receive so much. Possibly for me also — it is therapy to give." He made them both a little bow, but his smile was pointed at Garner, and one eyelid drooped again, as if he had just offered him something very special, very risible indeed.

"Yes, we must go," said Garner. "But I do want to . . . it's only fair for me to tip you off — " He was careful to make his voice friendly, surprised at how much he wanted it so. "If you do build without consulting the board . . . I'm afraid you're in for a spot of trouble."

"Ah, in that case — " Bhatta's voice was gay. He put a comforting hand on Garner's shoulder. "In that case it will be good to have a friend at court." He released Garner, waved again to the crowd below, and started off down the hill, carefully shuffling his carpet slippers along the narrow path. The grades were not easy to negotiate and the doctor's slippers must have made it harder, but with each turn that brought him nearer his guests his carriage heightened, his demeanor expanded. A ridge of shrubbery obscured the moment when he met the group, then he emerged, borne along in its chattering center, his tonsure inclining, his arms stretched in greetings papal and serene. At a point just below the little summerhouse, the doctor turned suddenly, waved up at Amelia and Garner, and then went on. The three Indian girls, who were nearest him, stood arrested too, looking inquisitively upwards — three fays, peacock, citron and lapis, fox-printed in gold. One of them said something, giggling, and the strange words, rebutted by the air and the river, traveled upward to the couple on the hill. Two answering chirps came from the girl's companions, then the three of them turned their backs, and a jingle of laughter wove between them as they ran after the doctor, who was just disappearing around the corner of the main house, his bald head shining well above the clustered others, a dark stamen in the declining sun.

It was late that night, long after the slow evening which daylight-saving time had prolonged, when Garner, drowsing over the Sunday paper, raised his head, realizing that he had been asleep and had been startled awake. What he had heard must have been the wheeze of the last bus to the city, the voices and farewells of the doctor's departing guests. Amelia had gone to bed early, as she so often did these days. "Never can understand why you insist on sitting up," she had said, kissing him good night, "just to fall asleep in a chair." He could not have said why himself, unless it was perhaps that by so doing, by this small intransigence against the wise routine for a man who had to get up at six, he was prolonging an illusion, a weak midnight illusion that time, undictated, was his own.

He got up, kneading his eyes, and went to the window. Down the way, near Petty's, the one faint roadlamp made a crooked pearl in the glass. Apparently there was a moon, from the look of the shadows on the road, but it must be high over the house already, and not large. It was the winter moons up here that were enormous, riding so close and intimate in the black air that the cornea felt itself naked against them. He remembered the first one of these they had seen their first winter up here — the great disc rising heavily from the water, as if unseen hands were having trouble pushing it upward, then the white path-shine on the water, and Amelia standing at the window, saying, "Look John . . . look! It's coming in the window . . . If I opened my mouth . . . it would float right in."

Well, they'd come a long way since then, ten years, and his moments of such lyrism were not many. Before him, in the light of the single reading lamp under which he had fallen asleep, the house stretched, doubled in the gloom, but still such a large house — the sitting room where he stood now, the parlor, the dining room, all furnished with relics of both their families, and looking almost regal in shadows that obscured the raffiish touches of the children, the farm-size kitchen where they all really lived, the study off the hall. In the half-light, with the little Victorian effects with which Amelia had placated it here and there, it was true that its ancient purpose sometimes revealed itself too starkly, and it stood declared for what it was, a home that belonged with those feudal servants, that stipulated, at the very least, one of those vanished households of accessory spinsters and aunts. At these times, it was true, sometimes at the very moments when he and Amelia and their friends were congratulating each other on their living in a place where one did not have to keep up with the Joneses in the usual way, he had a sense of unease, as if the grain of their lives had too suddenly appeared, revealing them all in another silhouette — keeping up with the shadowier Joneses of the past.

Late voices came again through the night — the remaining guests of his provocative neighbor, no doubt — he could hear one of the women calling the dog. "Lili . . . Lili . . . come on in, Lili . . ." the voice said. The air of America is so clear, Bhatta had said that morning — so very, very clear. Certainly the man had a passion for clarity, or else an irony for it — it ran through his conversation like a motif. One wondered what he was like at home, when not playing to the gallery. Perhaps he was a man who could never be at home — a strain on anybody, that. Hindu, Brahmin, whatever he was, with his hybrid education there would still be a kind of Eurasian sense of values — no harm to that, perhaps good. But if so, Bhatta would be sure to make capital of it. Yes, that would be his pitch, was his pitch. "We are none of us at home in the universe, lads — lords and ladies. I can show you how to handle that better than most. Meanwhile, let us share our amusement at our dilemma. And let us also share — " No honorarium to be required, of course. But, the universe being what it was, it was probable that the secretaries would pass the plate.

Garner left the window, hesitated with his hand on the switch of the lamp, sat down again in the chair. Yes, that could be how the cult might be formed, the coterie. He found himself thinking of such, not this one, but some other suited to oneself — some warm little member-world, banded together in a decameron of talk.

Stretching in his chair, he felt the small book in his pocket, the one Bhatta had given Amelia. He took it out, idly thumbing through it. This was for the gallery for sure, the power of print for the flowered toques. It was not in these fluent pages that one would find out where, in the happy slang phrase, Bhatta "lived." He read on. *Stone in the grass, I must examine you very carefully. You may be a piece of the North Star, cast upon the grass.* No, not here. He snapped the book shut. A folded paper fell out of it, the same he had replaced in the book at the doctor's this morning; Bhatta must have taken the same copy from the top of the pile. He hesitated; in general, though fallible, he'd managed a normal decency about such things. But probably it was only a grocery list, or perhaps the recipe for that inimitable curry. And in Bhatta's case — case was a word that might well be used; the man himself went out of his way to present himself as a brief full of tantalizing pros and cons, teasing one to make of it what one could.

Unfolding the paper, he saw that it was a letter addressed to Bhatta. *Dear Dr. Bhatta,* the letter said, *I beg of you not to say that I must stop wearing my glasses at meetings or else pay the $700 fine. What I paid last time exhausted my funds until next quarter, and the family will not consider it. They will not realize what the meetings mean to me. I know that you do not agree about the glasses, but the truth is I cannot get about without them. I ask you please to reconsider. If you will ask Miss Daria to write and say I can come to the next meeting, it will make me very happy indeed.* The letter, typed, was signed tremulously, almost indecipherably, in ink. Then there was a typed postscript: *At the very next quarter I will pay what I can.*

So, thought Garner, so. So that's where Bhatta lives. The old son-of-a-bitch. Underneath all that diversionary laughing gas, or tear gas — or rather, some formula that managed a sparkling precipitation of both — there had been only something as bare as this. If the letter had said "my crutches" for instance — well, one had heard of neurotic symbols which a doctor might reasonably be pressuring a patient to discard. One had heard also of the psychiatrists' disarming emphasis on the importance — to the client, of course — of the latter's psychic need to make payment. But eyeglasses! The letter postulated some sad fool, an old fool perhaps, with the aching, grave-humble naiveté of the old. Or one of those sclerotic old business eggs, who addle without warning. It would be a rich simpleton, or one at least with access to some money. No one knew better than Garner, a lawyer, how wistfully ingenuous the sudden simplicities of the rich could be. The worst of it was that Bhatta had at no time, in no sense given any of this the lie; if confronted he was quite capable of roguishly pointing this out. One taught the therapy of giving, quite naturally, Misser Garner, to those who could.

Garner looked at the letter again — it was a definitively good address, midtown Park, engraved, and on thick bond. The signature, three-named, was shaky — William Something Bertram, or Benthan; added to the letter, the humility of the postscript, it did suggest some old gaffer hanging to the fringe of his family, of the world, some poor old mottled pear that would not fall. A person sick with nothing more than loneliness, perhaps even persistently healthy (if Bhatta had found nothing better than the glasses to fix on) and driving his family crazy, as such people often did. Wanting nothing more than still to be involved, to be one of the member-world.

Garner stood up and pushed the book well back on a high shelf, the letter inside it. He'd been right about the fraudulence then — from the first. It was ugly to find oneself so handily corroborated. And to have been one of the simpletons, too. He had never examined the term "confidence man" for what it said, for what it shouted plain. He had merely lightly appraised Bhatta in the humorous terms of the sellers of gold bricks, of shares in the Brooklyn Bridge. Not as trafficking on the frozen-out, on people who only wanted to come in by some fire, to belong. No, this is too real, he thought. It sins somewhere, he thought, bending his head to an obscure inner heat, surprised at his own use of a word from which the leaflets had long since emancipated him.

He turned out the light, and in the darkness the moment of

the three of them by the river suddenly formed again, as if he had turned on another lamp that shed the triple-enclosed, mauve light of dusk. He saw the three of them again, he, Bhatta and Amelia, in that pause so warmly joined, laughing there by the river. Wasn't that to be weighed in the scale for Bhatta? Or was it to be taken out of context as one of the good mysteries — exempted from its origin as was the true-love poem of the poet who frequented whores? "Ah, the hell with it," he said aloud. To hell with it, whatever it was — living in the country, the long Sunday — whatever had made him feel the way he did. As he went up the stairs he still tasted it — acid, greensick — the feeling of the man who had been proven right.

In bed, he could not sleep. It was that over-alert, hypertensive hour of the night when the tireless free-associational sheep ran on and on, one idea carrying another's tail in its mouth, and still another part of the mind hallooed behind, catching, concluding, with a fake brilliance from which nothing ever could be salvaged the next day. The sheets were cool; he could be grateful for that, for in another few weeks, although the thick-ledged downstairs areas of these old houses would still be damply chill, the dormered top stories filled slowly with a summer-long hot must, through which one moved weakly, cramped for breath, regretting the flesh on one's bones. Someday, when he had the cash, he would insulate. Yet, even as he lay here, flinching before the anticipated river-valley heat that would arrive, sometimes in June, inexorably in July, he felt a submerged pleasure at knowing how the summer nights would be here — the hot pall under the eaves, the languid spiders woven suddenly out of nowhere — each year. It was a satisfaction to a man not brought up to houses or the firm groove of the seasons, to be able to say, sighing with the heat, that it was this way every year. His hand was in his grandfather's; his grandfather was saying, "Tomorrow's the twenty-eighth of August. Tomorrow the locusts will be here." It corroborated something. It —

He got up, swearing under his breath, and hunted for a cigarette. If his mind hadn't circled him back to that word he could have been asleep by now, and he had, he had to get up at six. Noiselessly, he crossed past Amelia's bed and opened the window from the bottom, so that the drifting smoke would not wake her. No moon just now. One sound, the faint tweaking of the river, heard only if one knew it was there. Nobody plying the hill tonight. He crept back to bed and sat listening, smoking. No sound from Miss Prager, the small and sealed.

Curious that he did not believe that the doctor had lied about her, even in the light of the letter downstairs. He was a man who would not bother to lie. Rather, he was a man who had grasped the mordant advantages of telling the truth as he saw it — aware that he told it well, and that a peculiar vision was a prize for which people would pay. Tapping his paradoxes like a set of metaphysical tumblers, he would make a coaxing music that set his audience agape, and their pockets too. And always careful to remind them of the great paradox that was money, such a man, coming upon Miss Prager, that "classic of money-injury," might carelessly keep her to remind himself.

Creaking, the river moved against the land. Is all the evidence in, in? There was something that Bhatta had said — Ah, you think it devious, perhaps . . . from *a priori* to *a posteriori* — the history of the world . . . how wise of you, Misser Garner, not to admit the connection between money and the work one loves . . . banks should not be so jolly . . . Miss Prager has the importance to be mad.

Garner put out his cigarette and lay back, tightly closing his eyes. No, there was something else — but with a man like that, the evidence would never all be in. Lucky for himself, no doubt, that he had found that letter — not having Mr. Dee's prescience about tea. For Bhatta's tunes were catchy indeed. His phrase for Dee, for instance. "The proxy dragon," he had said, smiling — and there, for all time, was little Dee, fixing his small, gorgon face against the future, advancing like a lone stockholder waving a proxy from the past. And every now and then, in an aside as Elizabethan as the doctor's handkerchief, there was the deliberate trail of a phrase pointing the listener to Bhatta himself.

Garner sat up, straining forward. The doctor had been above him, on the steps. Behind him, the river lay like a thick darning needle; in front of him the wind had been making its shot-taffeta changes on the lawn. Once more the yellow kerchief whisked; the heavy finger probed the rose. "Well . . ." said the doctor's voice, "every man has some little tale he tells himself in the dark, har? So as not to really see himself in the mirror the next morning." Or had it been — so as to be able to *look* at himself in the mirror the next morning.

No matter, thought Garner, leaning back on the pillow; it was Hobson's choice. For, once you saw how much the man might want to be caught, you saw much indeed. "Perhaps for me also it is therapy to give." How delicately, satirically he could have been showing them the irritating little wound of honesty that held him up by the heel! For then the storekeepers would be right, in a way — as, no doubt, storekeepers, until the last trump, always would be; Bhatta was not a successful swindler. Devious man that he was, it might be that life had withheld from him only the power to be consistently so. It would be no wonder then if he talked so much of clarity — this hoist illusionist who could not quite make himself disappear. And Miss Prager could be the tale by which he hung. Suppose that, a swindler, he still set a secret table for one of the swindled, for Miss Prager, hoaxed by someone greater than he? Suppose that he kept Miss Prager, for whom no funds would come next quarter, and this was the tale that he told to himself in the dark?

Now certainly I should be able to sleep, thought Garner. But time passed and he did not. Lying there, he listened to the river moving against the land. I'm just past forty, he thought, and my own evidence is already more or less in. What would it be like for him and Amelia if they lasted to eighty, for people like them who, leaning against the leaflets, might find that they leaned against wind? Or did age always come, stripping the critical function with gentle narcosis, making of any past, because it was the past, a good backbone? He turned on the pillow. Lucky Bhatta, lucky Dee. Who each has his tale for the mirror, and therefore no doubt sleeps well. Less lucky Garner, who has so many tales to tell himself for the daytime — of Amelia, the house, the children — but for the six o'clock mirror has none.

After a while he looked over at Amelia, a dark shape of comfort sleeping, but it was the hour past love, the courtroom hour of the night, when the soul, defending, shrank to the size of a pea. So, after a while, when he had reached that black level below pride, where one need no longer pretend that one was not pretending, he began cautiously to tell himself a tale he might once have had.

He was walking along the river, according to the tale, and he was very near the place where he belonged, the real place — in fact he had only been away from it a day. It was just before dawn, and along the opposite shore there was a narrow stencil of light. He was up before it, because it was natural to be so when one worked the land, and he was wearing a thick sweater, because this was a short-summered region and the mornings were Appalachian-cool. Before him, as he walked, there was a whiteness along the grass that was sometimes hoar, sometimes the wind at the underside of the blades, but whatever the season, he always thought of it as the waking power of the ground. It ran ahead of him, leading him to the real place, and when he got there he stood for a moment, as he always did, standing on the land. This was the moment of safety, of a wholeness something like the moment after love. For although he was up a trifle earlier than the other people, he knew that they were somewhere nearby, and that they would soon be up and about with him in the simple member-world. All day long he and they would be working, in a nearness past need for arranging, and the land and the river worked with them, weaving them all the good backbone.

This was where the tale always ended, whether it failed him or brought him through until morning. But tonight, just before he came to the end, there was a sound that brought him suddenly back to the real world outside. It was the sound of something soft brush-brushing across the grass, and at first, thudding with night-terror, he thought it was the whisp of a scythe. Then he heard, blended with it, the light scampering of an animal, and breathing, he took it to be the sound of someone walking a dog — the dog scratching here and there on the gravel, and behind it, the shush-shush, soft and irresolute, of carpet slippers on the grass.

He stole to the window again, but nothing could be seen on the hill. Telling himself that the night made special fools, he crept downstairs and stepped outside his door.

The doctor was standing still, his back to the stone urn in the center of his moonlit lawn, looking up at his house. His dog stood behind him, its eyes glinting like glass, waiting as it often waited during the doctor's morning inspections — although it was always the women who walked the dog. Whining now, it tugged with its muzzle at the hem of the doctor's coat. The doctor put a hand back of him to quiet it. "Eh Lili . . . shhh Lili . . ." he said. He had moved to face the hill, and was looking up at the summerhouse. Still the dog whined, bracing its hind legs in the direction of the gate, and at last the doctor turned. "Poor Lili . . . you want to take me for a walk, har?" he whispered, and the river brought his words to Garner's ear. "Better take me, har. Better take your old man for a walk."

At the word "walk" the dog bounded, ran a few paces toward

the gate, then stopped to look over its shoulder to be sure that the doctor followed, and in this way, with the dog alternately trotting and checking, the two of them came to the gate. The moonlight brought out the ungainly lines of the old bitch and the fallen-in silhouette of her master, his head prolapsed on his chest above the downcast belly, the long coat dribbling behind him like a nightshirt, making of him that poor show which any man might be at this hour, alone. I ought to get a dog again, thought Garner, hankering suddenly for the old mongrel, dead of age, whom they had not replaced last year. Nights like this, when a man can't sleep, he can walk his dog. Or the dog can walk the man.

Outside the hedge, the dog trotted north, along the road toward Garner's house. Garner leaned into the shadows of his doorway, but the dog, head to the ground, nosed him out, snuffed familiarity and dismissed him, and intent on some trail now, trotted on. The doctor raised his head, and in the thin light of the roadlamp the two men looked at one another. By day, it was always the doctor who spoke first, and Garner, taken at a loss in his shadows, awaited the florid greeting. But Bhatta said nothing. Gravely he nodded, and again, and the nod was like a touch. Then, doffing a hand against his temple in mute salute, he bent his head and moved on.

Garner listened to the sound of his shuffling, soft and hesitant and human, until it melted into the dark. It is the sound that ends the nightmare, he thought. Not the sound, necessarily, of mother or nurse or brother. Just the sound of *other*, of someone awake too, and dealing with the dark. A warmth crept up his throat. That the old man had not said anything, he thought — that was the thing. That such a man, so wedded to talk, should have signaled only, as between two who shared the freemasonry of mirrors, and have said not a lingering word.

Sleep hit him then, a dead salt-wave, and only habit brought him back up the stairs, to his bed. Sinking down, he doffed two fingers against his temple, in the general direction of north. Let the night make its fools, their gestures, that daytime might well rescind. It was a good thing. Let it. It was a good thing — to have a friend at court.

In the red-black landscape behind his lids, he sank down, down, watching the retinal images — tiny black dots circled with red — that swarmed ceaselessly upward only if he did not quite look at them, of whose origin he had wondered about since a child. They swarmed on; they were pinheads, they were people bent over the hillsides in the attitude of sowing; they were pulling salvation like turnips from the soil. Among them was a man, not Garner, somebody else, poor homunculus, and he was bent over too, hugging his image, his foolish tale. As he bent, his string dragged behind him, but he did not see it, for his chimera was strong. He was building a world, a little antique world of allegiance, where he would be hailed by name on the main street, neighbored in sickness and until death, and there were roots for the commuter's child. The people around him pretended not to see the string, for they had them too. Even as the fences went up, same on same, and houses burst upward like sown teeth, same on same, he and the people pretended, for they were building themselves into an antique perfection, into that necklace of fires upon the brotherly dark where once life burned steadily from farm to farm to farm.

Watching them, Garner slept. His knees curled to his chin, like a child who had world without end before school, and in his dreams he smiled too, a child snailed in sleep. All around him were the unguided missiles of sleep, of dream, but he flew between them, above them, with his story. Across his still face the night moved at bay, harmless against this impermanent marble, so intact and warm. Whatever there was in the mirror, he would not have to look at it until morning, not until morning, world without end away. Until morning.